PRAISE FOR *THE QUIET PEOPLE*

'You may think you know where it's going, but you couldn't be more wrong. A true page-turner filled with dread, rage, doubt and more twists than the Remutaka Pass' Linwood Barclay

'Paul Cleave is an automatic must-read for me, and *The Quiet People* shows why – it grabbed me by the throat, shook me around and left me breathing hard. Fantastic, and highly recommended' Lee Child

'The sense of dread builds unstoppably in this gripping page-turner about a missing child, the son of two crime writers who make their living plotting murder. Paul Cleave's pin sharp prose, astute characterisation, edge-of-your-seat, shocking set pieces and gut-wrenching twists create an intense, chilling read elevated by touches of humour and a tender portrayal of family relationships' Gilly Macmillan

'Another blisteringly good read from Paul Cleave ... Gripping from the first page and full of deliciously dark twists and turns. You can't be a true fan of crime fiction if you're not reading Cleave's books' Tom Wood

'What. A. Book. I don't think I breathed from about halfway through to the end. A masterpiece from a crime genius' Susi Holliday

'Cleave conjures a wrenching tale that moves swiftly and hits hard, like a middleweight boxer who has poise, power and style. Cameron's life spirals into some awful places, yet the crackle in Cleave's sentences and a dark seam of humour prevent things from getting too bleak. A superb novel from a champion storyteller' Craig Sisterson

'What starts out as a slow burn, quickly ratchets up the tension and the twists, sending you spiralling down a hill of depravity and desperation' Kirsten McKenzie

'Fast paced and entirely gripping ... a rollercoaster ride of thrills, shocks and emotion' Jen Med's Book Reviews

'With mind-bending twists and hold-your-breath chapters, *The Quiet People* is a flawless, genius example of a gripping, twisted thriller' The Reading Closet

'A masterclass in storytelling ... The tension is ramped up until it's barely bearable' From Belgium with Booklove

'Every single page grasps your attention ... shocking, heart-wrenching and suspenseful' Live & Deadly

'Always on the edge of your seat with Paul Cleave ... five stars' Mystic PT

'This book comes at you with unrelenting pace and by the end every emotion had been wrung from my body' Grab This Book

'Really good twists and turns. And that ending. Perfect' Mrs Loves To Read

'Perfectly captured the grief and conflict between Cameron and Lisa Murdoch. Tension mounts as mistrust and guilt grows ... a gripping read' The Book Review Café

'A really frantic and exciting ride, *The Quiet People* truly is a class act' Swirl and Thread

PRAISE FOR PAUL CLEAVE

'Uses words as lethal weapons' *New York Times*

'A cinematic, raging, rollercoaster of a plot with a wry humour ... *The Quiet People* is wildly entertaining and will keep you guessing right to the end' *New Zealand Herald*

'Cleave's whirligig plot mesmerises' *People*

'This thriller is one to remember' *New York Journal of Books*

'On almost every page, this outstanding psychological thriller forces the reader to reconsider what is real' *Publishers Weekly*

'Compelling, dark, and perfectly paced, New Zealand writer Cleave's psychological thriller explores the evil lurking in us all, working relentless magic until the very last page' *Booklist*

'A superb novel from a champion storyteller' *Crime Watch*

'Cleave writes the kind of dark, intense thrillers that I never want to end. Do yourself a favour and check him out' Simon Kernick

'Tense, thrilling, touching. Paul Cleave is very good indeed' John Connolly

'Relentlessly gripping, deliciously twisted and shot through with a vein of humour that's as dark as hell' Mark Billingham

'An intense adrenaline rush from start to finish' S J Watson

'A riveting and all too realistic thriller' Tess Gerritsen

'A gripping thriller ... I couldn't put it down' Meg Gardiner

'This very clever novel did my head in time and again' Michael Robotham

ABOUT THE AUTHOR

Paul is an award-winning author who divides his time between his home city of Christchurch, New Zealand, where most of his novels are set, and Europe. He's won the New Zealand Ngaio Marsh Award three times, the Saint-Maur book festival's crime novel of the year award in France, and has been shortlisted for the Edgar and the Barry in the US, and the Ned Kelly in Australia. His books have been translated into more than twenty languages. He's thrown his Frisbee in over forty countries, plays tennis badly, golf even worse, and has two cats – which is often two too many. Follow Paul on Twitter @PaulCleave, on Instagram @paul.cleave, on Facebook: www.facebook.com/PaulCleave/ and his website: paulcleave.com.

Orenda Books
16 Carson Road
West Dulwich
London SE21 8HU
www.orendabooks.co.uk

First published in New Zealand by Upstart Books in 2021
This edition first published in the United Kingdom by Orenda Books in 2021
Copyright © Paul Cleave 2021

ISBN 978-1-913193-94-2
eISBN 978-1-913193-95-9

Typeset in Garamond by typesetter.org.uk

Printed and bound by CPI Group (UK) Ltd, Croydon CR0 4YY

For sales and distribution, please contact *info@orendabooks.co.uk* or visit
www.orendabooks.co.uk.

The Quiet People

PAUL CLEAVE

**ORENDA
BOOKS**

To my neighbours – who, I have learned, for years have heard me singing when I'm in the shower.

I am truly sorry.

Prologue

Lucas Pittman has to hurry.

They have already been here asking their questions, the two detectives, the woman with the muscly arms and the man who wore a nice suit that, if Lucas worked and saved for the next ten years, he still wouldn't be able to afford. Of course, that math is based on prison wages, where it used to take him a day of cleaning blood and shit off bathroom floors to scrape together only a dollar.

He won't go back to jail.

He can't.

And he doesn't have to, if he's quick.

The room under the house is marginally bigger than a prison cell. It has four cinderblock walls and a concrete floor, and a single well-hidden door. The police searched his house and never found it, and isn't that the point of a hidden room? To stay hidden? His dad sure as hell thought so, and if it weren't for the fact his father would sometimes chain him to the bed down there, along with others, even Lucas would never have known it existed.

Even so, if the police are coming, and they do manage to find the room, finding it empty is a hell of a lot different from finding it with a couple of drugged children inside. He doesn't want this to end, but what choice does he have? Somebody knows. That couldn't be any more obvious – but what isn't obvious is who.

He opens the closet door in the hallway. Jackets hang on hooks and shoes litter the floor. He scoops the shoes out, then lifts away the carpet and removes the baseboards. It always takes a little time, and in the past Lucas never minded. After all, he's done real time, and he knows the difference between having to spend two minutes gaining access to a room, and spending ten years being confined in one. But now it's different, because now there is Zach Murdoch, and having Zach Murdoch in his secret room has changed everything.

He hurries with his work. Slotting the baseboards out reveals the holes he can slide his fingers into to pull the square piece of floor up. He lifts it and leans it against the wall. He climbs quickly down the ladder.

There is no time to hesitate.

The boy is still drugged. He's wearing a yellow T-shirt with a picture of a bus on it. Lucas used to wear a similar one when he was that age. He can remember his mum giving it to him for Christmas one year, and his dad tearing it off him the next. He's going to miss this boy. He's going to miss seeing him in the clothes that remind Lucas of his childhood. He's going to miss giving him a better life than he had growing up.

Limp, the boy is so light there's no difficulty carrying him up the ladder. He puts the floor back into place, and the baseboards, and the carpet, and then the shoes. It's all taking too much time.

He carries the boy quickly to the car in the garage. He squeezes him into the trunk. If there were room for both boys, this would go twice as fast, but there's not, and he never anticipated having to move two children at the same time. He can't exactly prop one up in the front seat, and if he tried, he knows his neighbour would be the first to see – the neighbour who listens when he shouldn't be listening, and pries when he shouldn't be prying. When did a man's business become everybody else's?

He adds the short-handled spade. He can hear his dad's voice rattling around in the back of his head, telling him there's no need to dig two separate graves, that one larger one will get the job done.

He gets the garage door open. He reverses the car down the driveway. He glances at his neighbour's house, and his neighbour is looking out of the window at him. He's on the phone. He's probably calling the police.

He should have killed him months ago.

He ought to kill him when this is over.

He gets onto the street. He leaves his house behind. He takes lefts and rights, working his way north, to the edge of Christchurch to go beyond it, out to where his dad showed him how to bury a body all those years ago, back before diabetes took his dad's leg, then his sight, then his life. Every part of his body wants him to go faster, to put as much distance between himself and his house and get this over with, but he fights the urge, keeping the needle hovering on the speed limit. Last thing he needs is to be pulled over. He swears at every red light and thanks God at every green. His car is making a weird ticking sound. It's been doing that for the last few weeks and he's been meaning to get it looked at, and what if this is the trip where it gives up? He should have taken it to a mechanic as soon as the noise started. He breathes in deep, and breathes out slow, and tries not to make any noises in case that's what puts the car over the edge.

There are no sirens. No police cars. But then there are. Coming up fast behind him. They've found him. He was hoping for more time. He puts his foot down. He breaks those speed limits he was a moment ago conscious of not breaking. The ticking gets louder, and faster, and higher pitched, but the car still feels the same. His heart is racing. He has to dry his palms on his shirt, one at a time. The patrol car is fifty metres behind him, and now forty, and now thirty. A second car swerves out from traffic and closes in on him too. A siren appears in the mirror. An unmarked patrol car. How many are there?

He can't go back to jail.

Anything but that.

He puts his foot down and pulls away. The patrol car matches his speed. He drives faster – if you drive fast enough in New Zealand, and dangerously enough, the police are required by law to call off the chase. Which Lucas sees as a rewards-based system. He swerves in and out of traffic. The patrol car stays with him, but then slows up and hangs back. Up ahead, traffic is getting thick. He needs to turn off. There is a gap in the flow of traffic coming towards him. He can squeeze behind a white van and in front of a large truck. The gap will line up with a cross-street, or at least close enough that he can make it happen. It will be tight, but he can make it.

He eases his foot off the accelerator and turns behind the van, narrowly avoiding the bumper, then puts his foot back down. For a moment he thinks the car is going to choose that instant to die on him, that the ticking will become screaming as belts pull away from pulleys and cogs strip away teeth, but it holds on, and the engine surges, and the car surges, and even though the gap is tighter than he thought, it's okay, the car makes it through, he's going to—

The truck hits the car, compacting it before sending it flipping through the air. Metal twists and glass shatters and the gas tank ruptures. The first time the roof hits the ground, it's lowered by half, hitting Lucas Pittman in the head. When it hits the second time, he gets his wish of never having to go back to jail. The car comes to a stop, the young boy in the yellow T-shirt and red shorts bouncing around in the trunk. A moment later the fire begins.

SUNDAY

Chapter One

The park is trampled grass pathways and pitched tents. There are stalls, and queues of people, and rides, and bright lights and music everywhere. Balloons slip from small hands and head for the sun. There are scraped knees and grass-stained elbows and hotdog-induced sore stomachs. There is laughing, and crying, and yelling, and heat, and dust, and carnies are yelling to come on over, to step right up, to test your skill. Summer has officially arrived, and it smells like popcorn and candyfloss.

The carousel is made up of kiwis; two-legged flightless birds instead of four-legged flightless horses. Each has a long beak that slopes into the ground behind the legs of the one in front. Zach laughs as the carousel operator hoists him onto the last free one. We've been queueing for the last ten minutes. The carousel is colourful, with bright patches of paint slapped over spots of rust on the edges, all lit up by a thousand flashing bulbs. The kiwis start circling, and Zach disappears and reappears, each time pulling a different face for me to photograph, his dark, floppy hair covering his glasses the first time, then his fingers in his ears, or his nose, or tugging down at the bottom of his eyes, smiling, frowning, tongue out, big grin, small grin, no grin. Then the music slows, and the kiwis slow, and the carousel has barely stopped before Zach jumps off. He hits the ground running.

'Bouncy castle,' he yells, and takes off for the castle that's bending and bobbing in the distance.

It's the opening day of the fair, which will last through the rest of December and into the middle of January. There are thousands of people here, kids on rides, kids in queues, kids struggling to eat ice cream before it melts, parents following them around. The air tastes sweet and feels charged with excitement. It makes me long to be a child again, to be the one running through the crowd exploring it, rather than running through it chasing my seven-year-old son, whose blood became rocket fuel the moment we got out of the car. There's no queue for the castle, and only half a dozen kids on it. The guy operating it has more gaps in his mouth than teeth. He's armed with a leather bag on his waist for making change, and a bucket and mop for cleaning up the messes that come with bouncy castles. The castle is big enough to hold twenty kids. There's a ramp to climb up on the inside and a slide to go back down on the outside. I hand a ticket over, and the operator tells Zach to take his sandals off, which Zach does, kicking them in different directions once he's handed me his glasses. He looks like he's about to dive head-first into the castle, but then slows and climbs on tentatively. The other kids pause to watch for a few seconds. I've seen this before. Zach is one of those kids that other kids watch to figure out, sensing he's a little different, and every time I see it, it hurts. I pick up his sandals and stand off to the side of the operator. Mostly the operator spends his time flicking through an auto magazine, looking up on occasion to make sure the bouncy castle is still bouncing.

Zach climbs in. One of the children talks to him for a moment, then leaves him alone. Zach stands by himself, bouncing softly, seemingly unsure of what to do. I snap more photographs of him and send them, along with the earlier photos, through to Lisa. She's at home working on the edits for next year's novel. I watch the photographs as they send, then watch the dots as Lisa forms her reply, and then read the results: *Looks like fun!* I text her back and tell her I wish she were here, and then the dots, and then, *So do I.*

I tuck the phone into my pocket. Zach has disappeared deeper into the castle. The entire structure is swaying back and forth as kids trample across it, the group now joined by a pair of twin sisters dressed in identical outfits, their mum taking photos of them as they play.

I move a little closer so I can find an angle to see Zach. I need to make sure none of the kids are giving him a hard time. Only I still can't see him. He must be up the top of the ramp in a blind spot, waiting to slide down the other side. Or he's hiding from me. Breaking into impromptu games of hide-and-seek without telling us is one of his things. Only I don't think he would be hiding here – we've had *the conversation* plenty of times as we laid out the ground rules for the fair. No running away. No hiding. He's to stay in sight at all times.

There are no kids coming down the slide. No queue up the top. Is someone up there blocking him? It wouldn't be the first time. I walk a loop of the castle, looking up and looking down. No Zach. The small voice in my head – the parenting one that always goes *what if* – reminds me this is the environment I've seen in countless movies where one moment your child is there, and the next moment they're in the back of a stranger's van. I stop at the front, looking in. The twin girls are jumping on the edge of the castle. One of them stops to look at me, and the other one bounces into her, and they both tumble out. They land by my feet. I reach down to help them back up, one taking my hand, the other one getting up by herself, looking at me suspiciously as she does. They jump back in.

'Zach?'

Zach doesn't answer, but Mr What If does. Mr What If is the voice of my imagination who comes out to play when I'm working. It's the voice that sends my characters down paths I'm not expecting, who can take any everyday situation and turn it on its head. What if that guy has a knife? What if the door is locked? What if they don't call the police? Only now Mr What If isn't playing around when he says, *He's gone. Somebody has him. Somebody is smuggling him through the crowd.*

'Zach?'

You need to hurry.

I climb into the castle. The floor sinks under my weight, and the kids all struggle to stay balanced. I clamber up the ramp to the top. There's nobody up here. I clamber back down. All the kids have stopped playing. They're staring at me.

'There was a boy in here, this high,' I say, putting my hand to my chest. 'He's wearing a Superman T-shirt. Anybody see him?'

None of them answers.

The floor sinks and sways as I walk across it, and a small boy loses his balance and falls into me. I try to help him stay upright, but he falls over, and then I trip over him, and in the process end up knocking one of the twin girls back out of the castle. She hits the ground hard, and starts crying, then gets up and limps off to her mother, who is still looking down at her phone.

Zach isn't here.

Mr What If was right.

My son has gone.

Chapter Two

Only my son can't be gone. Not really. That's something that happens to other people, like car accidents, and cancer, and houses burning down.

Do something.

I'm still carrying Zach's sandals. I'm still keeping my shit together. Of course I am. Kids don't go missing. Not really. Except for when they do. Which this isn't. Can't be. Because this is a good area. This is a good city, and these are good people.

I help the boy who ended up under my feet back to his. He's

the kid I saw talking to Zach. I kneel so I can face him. 'Have you seen—'

'Don't hurt me,' he says.

'I'm not going to hurt you,' I say, and I reach into my pocket for my phone. He turns to go, and I grab his arm. 'Please, wait,' I tell him. 'Let me show you a photograph.'

'Get away from him,' a man yells, storming towards me. He's bald, maybe thirty, angry-looking.

He isn't the only one coming towards me. So is the mother of the twins. Also thirty, also angry-looking, with long dark hair tied back. The twin that ran to her is crying, and the one that is still in the castle is staring at me. I suddenly see it all from their perspectives. I've jumped in here and tossed their kids around like bowling pins. I get to my feet and climb out of the castle.

'I'm sorry,' I say, putting my hands up, still holding the sandals. 'I didn't mean to—'

That's as far as I get. The man who yelled at me shoves me hard in the chest. I fall back against the castle.

'Wait. I—'

'What did you do to my daughter?' the woman asks, her voice high-pitched, her finger pointing at me. She is standing next to the man who shoved me. I push myself off from the castle to get back to my feet.

'I—'

'What are you? Some kind of child molester?' she asks.

'No. Of course not. I—'

'He had his hand on my son,' the man says.

'I saw,' the woman says. 'He's probably touched all the kids in here.'

'I was just trying to—'

'He hurt me,' the boy says.

I put my hands back into the air. 'Wait, please, I—'

The man pivots on his feet and punches me hard in the

stomach. I fall back into the castle, squashing the base of it, making the other twin spill out. Instead of getting back to my feet, I roll off the side and sit on the ground, winded. The man scoops up his son and walks away with him, but not before pointing down at me and telling me that if I ever hurt his son again he will kill me.

The woman reaches for her other daughter, who is crying loudly, while her first daughter is crying a few metres behind her. 'You should be ashamed of yourself,' she says, then uses her phone to snap a photograph of me.

I don't answer her. I look back into the castle, in the hope that somehow Zach has reappeared. He hasn't.

He's gone, Mr What If says, his voice louder as my fear fuels him. *Gone, and you're never getting him back.*

'I'm calling the police,' the woman adds.

'I didn't mean to hurt them,' I say.

'Tell it to your lawyer, creep,' she says, and she walks away, her children following.

The operator comes over and helps me up. 'You okay?'

'I can't find my son.'

'He climbed off a minute ago,' he says, bending down to pick up my phone while I bend down to pick up Zach's sandals. He hands me the phone. 'It was when you were looking at this.'

'Why didn't you tell me?'

'Why weren't you watching your kid?'

I hate him for being right. The woman with the twins is on her phone, staring at me, no doubt giving my description to the police. The girl who bounced out of the castle a minute ago is still crying, but the first one seems okay.

'Did he go with somebody?'

'I don't know. Maybe.' He points into the crowd. 'He went that way.'

'What's in that direction?'

'All the things that aren't behind me.'

I go into the crowd. I need to find somebody in authority. A security guard or a cop. There must be an administration area, somewhere kids and parents go when they get separated or hurt. All I can see are thousands of people having too good a time to care about anybody else. All these people could be helping me, and now Zach is missing, and...

And there he is, up ahead, in the line for The Aztec Hall of Mirrors. He's talking to a girl the same age as him. She has candy-floss stuck to her fingers and is trying to wipe them on her dress. She's staring at Zach and listening, but not saying anything. I hold back, wanting to go in there and hug him, and equally wanting to ask him what he was thinking; but that's the problem – he wasn't thinking. He's seven years old. He's doing what seven-year-old kids do. This world that shifted off its axis a minute ago now shifts back. It settles into its rightful place.

I go over and take his hand and tell him it's time to leave. He asks if something is wrong, and I tell him no, that everything is okay. He doesn't seem so sure, and he looks like he's going to cry, which is his fallback position when things aren't going his way. I pre-empt it by telling him we can grab ice cream on the way home.

'Can I have any flavour?'

'You can choose from whatever flavours are there,' I say, because I have to be specific with Zach. If I tell him he can have any flavour, and that flavour turns out to not be available, the world will end. 'Do you remember what we've told you about walking off?'

'Never to do it,' he says.

'So why did you?'

'When?'

'You left the bouncy castle without telling me.'

He thinks about it. He plays back the last few minutes in his mind, and then he says, 'One of the boys in the castle called me weird. I didn't want to stay. I'm not weird, am I?'

'Of course not.'

'I waved at you, but you weren't looking.'

'Then you should have waited.'

'Why would that boy say that to me?'

'People always say things they don't mean.'

He thinks on it for a few moments, then says, 'Like when you and Mummy tell me I have to wash my hands before dinner? You don't mean that?'

'Of course we mean that.'

'I'm confused,' he says. 'I might need two ice creams instead of one.'

I laugh at that before realising he's not joking. We've got through the grounds and have entered the stream of people slowly leaving. The roads are full of parked cars and drivers looking for spaces. We're parked in a lot a few minutes away with a hundred other vehicles. I get the back door open and Zach climbs into the car seat. A few rows away I can see the guy who punched me. He's loading his kid into a dark-red sedan. The kid is still crying. I consider going over there and apologising to them, but that considering comes to an end when the guy looks up and sees me. He gives me a look that tells me I wouldn't get within five metres before he puts me down. I think about what the characters in my books would do. Some of them would march over and beat the hell out of him. Others would drop him in a hole never to be found again. I have the urge to tell him that I kill people like him for a living. That if anybody here could get away with murder, it'd be me.

Instead of doing any of that, I get into the car and we drive away.

Chapter Three

There's a fruit-and-vegetable store halfway between the fair and home, an old barn converted into a shop, signs out front with smiling raspberries and strawberries doing jazz hands, all of them fading in the sun. The store is open-air, with one long wall entirely removed. Seeing the crates of fruit makes me hungry. This place always does a roaring trade in the summer, and today is no different. There's a counter where ice creams are scooped from a glass-topped freezer into cones or bowls by a freckly girl wearing a Santa hat. There's a line full of people all in shorts and tank tops and jandals, the jandals making flipflop sounds as they slap against floor and feet. We have to wait for ten minutes, but it's worth it, the ice cream a balm to my frayed nerves. We sit hunched over one of the picnic tables, both of us with mixed-berry ice cream dripping down our hands as we race to eat them in the heat. The world might be back to normal, but my body hasn't calmed all the way down. The Bad that populates my books just whispered my name and stroked a finger down my neck. A train of ants marches up the leg of our table empty-handed then marches back down full of goodies. Behind us, pohutukawa trees with their fluffy, hedgehog-like flowers offer us some shade.

'Am I in trouble?' Zach asks. He's been eating his ice cream the way all seven-year-olds eat them – messily, and in a hurry, as if some other kid is going to take it from him. His glasses are back in the car. When I took them out of my pocket earlier to give them to him, I found one arm had been broken off when I was knocked down.

'You're not in trouble,' I say, 'but we'll talk about it when we get home, okay? How's your ice cream?'

'So I am in trouble,' he says. He's stopped eating. Ice cream is dripping off his fingers onto the bench.

'No, of course not. Come on, how about you finish your ice

cream and we'll head home, huh? We can put up the Christmas tree, if you like?'

He starts back on his ice cream and thinks about it for a few moments, then he asks, 'Will I be in trouble when I get home?'

'No.'

'I don't believe you.'

I didn't want to discuss it here, but he's determined to. 'The thing is, Zach, your mum and me, we both love you so much. We always want to know that you're safe. When you disappear like that it frightens us. You know you shouldn't have walked off like that, right? What if you had got lost?'

'But I wasn't lost,' he says, using his seven-year-old logic. 'I knew where I was and I knew where you were. You were by the bouncy castle.'

'Because I thought you were still inside the bouncy castle, and when I realised you weren't, I went looking for you. What if I had gone looking in a different direction and not seen you?'

'But you did see me.'

'We'll talk about it when we get home.'

'It's not my fault you didn't see me,' he says.

He's right about that. 'What would you have done if you had come out of the hall of mirrors to find I had left?'

The question blows his mind. He stares at the ice cream and starts spinning the cone in his hands. 'Why would you be gone?'

'Because I had gone looking for you. Maybe I thought you had started walking home. What then?'

'I don't know.'

'Just ... in the future, make sure we know where you are. Otherwise anything can happen.'

'Like what?'

Like what? The list is too long, but every example starts the same – it starts with a stranger. It starts with the *what if*, and barrels down a highway full of dark rooms and duct tape.

'Like you could have gotten lost.'

He stares at his ice cream, saying nothing, then turns it over and smashes it onto the bench. It's what I was hoping to avoid.

'It's okay, Zach, it really is. You're not in trouble. I promise you.'

He picks the cone up and slams it down again.

'It's going to be okay.'

He starts screaming. Loudly. A high-pitched scream that makes everybody turn towards us. I can feel myself becoming red.

'Please, Zach, can you stop doing that?'

He picks up the squashed cone and throws it at me. It hits me in the shirt and falls onto my shorts. People on the same bench as us get up and leave. One of them says, 'Learn to control your kid, mate,' on his way past.

I reach across the table and take Zach's hands. 'It's okay,' I tell him. 'It's okay.'

He stops screaming. He stares at me. His face has gone red, and there are tears in his eyes. It's been months since he's done something like this in public, but over the years we've figured out the best way to deal with it, and that's leave the situation.

I get up. He starts screaming again when I go to pick him up, and he tries batting me away, but I scoop him up and hold him under my arms with his feet kicking out the back and his arms swinging out the front. He screams and cries as people stare at us, shaking their heads. I hear somebody say, 'This is why some people shouldn't have kids,' and I lower my head and keep walking, feeling two dozen sets of eyes burning into my back.

I get out to the car and get Zach into his car seat. He keeps swinging his arms as I get his seatbelt into place. I get into the front and put Zach's favourite CD into the stereo, but he screams over it the entire drive home.

Chapter Four

'I would have freaked,' Lisa says, after I've told her how the afternoon played out. It's seven in the evening, and Zach calmed down when we got home, though he wouldn't talk to us during dinner and for the last thirty minutes has been unwinding in his bedroom before bedtime. I'm sitting with Lisa on the back deck, both of us side by side on the outdoor couch. We have our feet up on the coffee table, each of us with a glass of wine. The sun is still up over the neighbour's roof, and won't sink beneath it for another hour.

Lisa waves her hand at a bee that passes us by. There's a lavender plant next to the deck that attracts them that I keep meaning to get rid of, only Lisa won't let me. Lisa is a little shorter than me but in much better shape, due to the fact she goes to the gym for spin classes three, sometimes four, times a week. She has the same dark hair as Zach, only longer, cut shoulder length, and at the moment tied up into a bun. She has the same green eyes as Zach too.

I'm not so sure she would have freaked if it had been her with Zach instead of me. Lisa is the calmer of the two of us. If we were ever in an accident, she'd be the one to get us through it while I flopped around on the floor, an emotional wreck. Maybe that's why we work together so well. She's a planner – she'll plot out in advance what it is she wants to write, whereas I start with a blank page and go for it, feeling my way as the characters and situation grows.

'I can't believe that guy hit you,' she says.

'I know.'

'And that woman, wow. They couldn't see you were looking for Zach?'

'I didn't get the chance to explain.'

'Do you think she called the police?'

'Probably. She took my photo too.'

'Maybe they're out there looking for you right now,' she says. 'Maybe we should turn on the TV and see if your description is on the news.'

When I don't answer her, she starts laughing. 'I'm kidding,' she says. 'You know, I bet she hassled the bouncy castle guy into getting her money back, and he would have told her what happened.'

'Yeah. Makes sense.'

She finishes her drink. 'We do need to talk to Zach again to try and make him understand what he did was wrong.'

'You think the one thousandth time is the charm?'

'Yes,' she says, and she smiles. 'Come on, let's go.'

'I'll go,' I say.

'By yourself? You think you can defuse a CZM by yourself?'

CZM is short for Crazy Zach Mood. We like the way it sounds like a dangerous element that could be used in a dirty bomb.

'I don't know, but it was my fault what happened today.'

'It wasn't your fault,' she says. 'It was … you know … one of those things.'

'Either way, this one is on me.'

'Okay. Good luck. I'll make you a gin and tonic while you're gone.'

We head inside. Our house is single-storey, with an open-plan kitchen and dining room, which we painted last summer, corners and skirting boards since then knocked and chipped by toys and shoes and elbows. The same goes for the hallway and the four bedrooms down there, two of which are offices, one Lisa's, and the other mine, the places where we tell our friends we like to make bad things happen. Zach has the room at the end of the hallway, with north-facing windows that get the sun and overlook the street. His walls are covered in posters of various cartoon characters that, I imagine, over time will become posters of musicians and movies. There's a map on the wall with coloured pins showing the places he's been. He has what looks like a bunk bed, but is actually an elevated bed on top of what Zach calls his 'secret hideout'. There's a bookcase, the books arranged by colour, whereas last month he had arranged them by height. There are stars stuck to the ceiling that absorb light during the day and glow at night.

Zach is on the floor, talking to a superhero he has tried jamming into a car that wasn't designed for superheroes, in the hope he can run it into one of the dinosaurs that is considerably larger. His choice of protagonist isn't keen on fitting, which is evident from the fact three of his four limbs have been popped from his joints. He doesn't look at me when I crouch next to him.

'Who's winning?' I ask.

'Nobody.'

'We need to...' I say, then let it trail off. Talk about today? Talk about his behaviour? I don't have the strength for it, and even if I did, it wouldn't change a thing. 'We need to get you into bed. Would you like a bedtime story?'

'No.' When the superhero still won't fit into the car, he picks him up and pulls off the remaining arm, and then the head.

'You sure? We can carry on with the Harry Potter one.'

'No,' he says. He tosses the car and the pieces of his superhero into a toybox Lisa bought to replace the one that had become too small. He climbs the small ladder up into his bed and digs himself under the covers the wrong way around so I can only see his feet.

'I'm going to run away,' he says, his words muffled beneath the blanket. 'I'll run away, and you won't even miss me.'

'That's not true.'

'Then you can go back to being happy because you never have to tell me off anymore.'

'Zach...'

'I hate you.'

'No you don't.'

'Yes I do.'

Suddenly I feel incredibly tired. I want this day to end. 'Okay. Okay, Zach, well, if you're going to run away you're going to need to pack enough clothes and enough food to get you through to your first pay cheque.'

'What?'

'You're also going to need to get a job, because you're going to need to be able to pay for things. You'll need to rent a house, and pay taxes, and make your own meals. It's going to be a lot of work.'

He doesn't say anything.

'Or you don't run away, and you stay with us, and you don't have to worry about any of those things. We still haven't put up the Christmas tree. How about if you don't run away, we take care of it tomorrow? Would you like that?'

'No.'

'You don't want a Christmas tree this year?'

'No.'

'Do you at least want Christmas?'

'No.'

'If you change your mind, let me know. I love you, Zach.'

'No you don't.'

I turn on his nightlight and close the bedroom door.

MONDAY

Chapter Five

I wake up needing coffee. Which is how I wake most mornings, which is twice as true this morning because of the small hangover from the gin and tonics Lisa made last night. As I get older, it takes fewer of them to make me feel this way.

I can hear Lisa in the office. She's more of a morning person, eager to clear away any emails that have come in overnight. I drink my coffee and go online and read the news and wish I hadn't, story after story confirming how far apart all of us are on everything. Climate change exists and no it doesn't. We need fewer guns, or is it more? We're all paying too much in taxes, except for rich people, who aren't paying anything. Politicians are angels or demons, depending on who you vote for. I don't know why I bother reading any of it. Weather report says we could get thirty-degrees. We're already at twenty. Thank god for air-conditioning.

When I go to make toast, I find we're out of bread. I pour a bowl of cereal for Zach and then head down to his room. He's not in his bed. He's not under it either. I head into Lisa's office. She's tapping at the keyboard. She doesn't need coffee to wake up. 'You've seen Zach?'

She shakes her head, and doesn't look up as she types. Her hair is sticking out on several angles and a seam from her pillow has carved a line into her face. 'You check the secret hideout?'

I tell her that I did. Then I carry on searching. I check inside closets. I check the lounge, looking behind couches and curtains. I check the pantry in the kitchen, and then the cupboards. I try the bathroom, and the laundry, and the garage. I look in the car.

I go outside and walk around the yard. Then I go back to his room. I check the secret hideout under his bed again. The closet. I stand in the middle of his room and turn in a circle. The window is open. I hadn't noticed that earlier. We always keep it closed at night. The window is too high for Zach to have reached and opened, but his tipped-over toybox is in front of it.

Then it comes to me, what Zach said last night about running away.

I lean out the window. The plants below are trampled.

There's a twitch at the back of my brain. Mr What If is waking up.

I check Zach's closet. His schoolbag is gone. I rush into the kitchen. I told him he'd need to pack enough food to get him through to his first pay cheque. Gone are cookies, and soft drinks, and the bread I couldn't find earlier, and a jar of peanut butter and jelly.

I race into Lisa's office. 'He's gone.'

She keeps typing, and because she's heard 'he's gone', and not 'HE'S GONE', she says, 'What do you mean?'

'He's run away. His bedroom window was open.'

'But he can't reach—'

'He's tipped his toybox over so he could.'

Now she hears it. She spins in her chair and gets to her feet and rushes into Zach's bedroom. She does what I did. She calls for him, and she looks under the bed, and then in the closet, and then she looks out the window. 'The plants are trampled down there,' she says.

'I saw.'

I tell her about our conversation last night, about him threatening to run away. About his missing schoolbag, and how he's raided the pantry.

She shakes her head, and her jaw tightens, and she says, 'He told you he was going to run away and you didn't stop him?'

'It was classic CZM. I didn't think he meant it. Why would I? It's not like he hasn't threatened it before,' I say, which is true. He says it every month. In fact, if he stopped saying it I would be worried.

'Did you check in on him before we went to bed last night?' she asks.

'No.'

'Damn it, Cameron, why wouldn't you check on him when he told you he was going to run away?'

'CZM,' I say.

'Is that going to be your answer for everything?'

'I didn't think he meant anything by it.'

'Then you thought wrong. For all we know, he's been gone twelve hours. Call the police. I'm going to look for him outside.'

Lisa slips on a pair of shoes and goes outside in her pyjamas. Mr What If is stomping around insisting on being heard. *What if Zach is gone forever? What if he's at the bottom of a storm drain?*

I call the police. A dispatch officer answers. I tell her who I am and where I live and that our son, Zach, has run away.

'When was the last time you saw him?'

'Last night, when we put him to bed.'

There's a slight pause on her end as she registers that Zach hasn't been seen in twelve hours, and that twelve hours is a lifetime. 'Have you contacted neighbours and family members and friends?'

What if he's at the bottom of a hole?

'We're doing that right now. My wife is outside knocking on doors,' I say, and how far can a seven-year-old kid go in twelve hours? Then I realise it's not twelve, but thirteen. I can see Lisa through the window, moving up and down the street calling Zach's name.

'I have a patrol car en route to your house,' she says.

What if he's at the bottom of a grave?

What if...

'Shut up.'

'Excuse me?'

'Sorry, that wasn't meant for you.'

'Who was it meant for? Your wife?'

'I wasn't talking to anybody.'

The dispatch officer asks what Zach's state of mind was. Had we fought? Has he run away before? How well does he know his neighbours? 'Are there any parks in your neighbourhood? Somewhere Zach likes to play?'

'What?'

'Parks. Somewhere he might possibly—'

'I should have thought of that. There are two.' Of course he's going to be at one of them. 'I'll go and check.'

'The patrol car is only a few minutes out. I suggest you wait until—'

'Wait? No chance.'

I hang up. I go outside and call out to Lisa. She appears on the footpath a few houses down. She races towards me.

'The police are on their way. They suggested he may have gone to a park.'

She nods quickly, convincing herself this is likely. 'Of course. Of course that's where he is.'

'I'm going there now.'

'He might have gone to the school too. Or even your mum's place.'

The truth is he could have gone anywhere.

'Have you called her?' she asks.

'I'll do it now, and I'll check the parks, and the school.'

'I'll keep knocking on doors until the police arrive. Make sure you take your phone with you.'

I go inside and grab my car keys. I don't bother getting changed out of my pyjamas, but I pull on a pair of sneakers. I push the button in the garage to get the door rumbling open. I back out the driveway too quickly, clipping the letterbox and knocking it over. I get the car into gear, and then the wheels are spinning as I fishtail down the street.

Chapter Six

Detective Inspector Rebecca Kent lines the tyre iron up with the lug nut then steps down on the end of the handle. Like celebrity deaths, flat tyres come in threes for her, meaning it's good money there'll be two more before the year is out – hopefully not when she's at high speed chasing down some psychopath. She gradually applies more bodyweight until the nut shifts. She has lost count of how many times in movies she's seen people on their knees struggling to muscle a tyre iron to change a wheel, only to have some serial killer show up. Why they never think to stand on the end and use their bodyweight, she doesn't know.

She tries to remember the last time she had a flat, then groans and rolls her eyes when she realises the last time she had a flat tyre she had four all at once. That is if she wants to get technical about it. Four tyres, all popping the same way the entire car popped. She had barely climbed out of it before it exploded into a wreck of flying metal and glass. Despite the summer heat, the memory sends a chill through her body. Even though the person who planted those explosives can no longer hurt her, whenever Kent climbs into a car and turns the key her body tightens with the anticipation that there will be a loud click, a deafening explosion, and then nothing. She still dreams about it. Still carries the scars, both inside and out. There are days when even walking past parked cars makes her nervous, and in a world full of cars, that means she's often on edge.

She jumps when her mobile rings, then gives a small laugh. It's going to be one of those days.

She takes the call. It's her partner, Detective Inspector Ben Thompson. They've been working together for the last three weeks, and so far it's been successful – certainly more successful than her previous two partnerships, one partner having died, and the other having quit the force. She wonders if that's also one of those things that happens in threes, and what the time frame needs to be for it to count.

'Hey,' she says.

'Where are you?'

'In my driveway. I got a flat,' she says, lining the tyre iron up with the second of the lug nuts.

'Damn. The first of three, huh?'

'It is.'

'You want a hand with it?'

'I'll manage.'

'Listen, we got a missing seven-year-old boy, name is Zach Murdoch. His parents are Cameron and Lisa Murdoch.'

'Why do they sound familiar?'

'They're crime writers,' he says, and she remembers them now. She met them briefly five years ago at a writers' festival up in Auckland. A colleague of hers was interviewing two non-fiction crime writers one evening, and while she was with him backstage as he was getting ready, she ran into the Murdochs as they were getting ready to leave. They were mid-thirties, good-looking, a lot of chemistry. She remembers Cameron making jokes about his greying hair, saying it started changing colour the same time as the reviews started coming in. He was trim and rough-shaven, and funny. Lisa was even trimmer and dressed to show it off. She looked like if she fell over she'd land in a yoga position. She was funny too. She remembers when they left they were holding hands.

She pushes down on the tyre iron with her foot. 'I met them a few years ago. They seemed nice. When was the boy last seen?'

'Last night, around seven o'clock. They went to get him this morning and he's gone. Wife is asking neighbours if they've seen the boy, and the husband is out driving, looking around. Officers are on the way to the house. Hopefully the kid is holed up in their backyard, or maybe hiding in the neighbour's garage. But...' he says, then trails off.

'But?'

'But the dispatch officer says the husband was odd on the phone. He told her to shut up after she told him officers would be on the way, and when she asked him about it, he said he wasn't talking to her.'

'He was talking to his wife?'

'I don't know. He said his wife was outside speaking to the neighbours.'

'So who was he talking to?'

'I don't know. Dispatch officer did say he sounded panicked, though. Look, probably the kid is hiding half a block away, and I hope he is, but...' he says, and then he trails off again.

Kent moves onto the third nut. 'But?'

'It's probably nothing. But these guys are crime writers.'

'Meaning?'

'Don't writers always say "write what you know"?'

'I don't know any writers, and I figure my two minutes with the Murdochs five years ago doesn't count.'

'Well, it's something they say.'

'What are you getting at, Ben?'

'I'm thinking, what if this is the other side of the coin? Instead of writing about all the things they know, what if this is the time they're acting upon it?'

Chapter Seven

The closest park to our house is Haydon Park. It's three acres of grass bordered by trees, then fences, then houses, with a small section in the middle for a fort, and monkey bars, and a merry-go-round, and no Zach. I call Mum on the way. She doesn't answer.

I drive to the next park – this one another five minutes in the same direction. Antberry is four times the size of Haydon, with all the same kinds of features but on a bigger scale – a bigger fort, bigger playground, bigger trees, longer fences, bigger houses bordering them. The empty playground looks like one of those playgrounds about to be thrown sideways – along with cars and mannequins and buildings – in the atomic-blast testing videos of old. There's a woman in tight activewear almost as bright as the sun jogging the perimeter at a decent clip. I jog in her direction, hoping to cut her off. She sees me, and I wave at her. She quickens her pace and skirts around me by fifty metres and back out to the street. I do a circuit of the park. No Zach. Nothing to suggest he came this way – nothing to suggest he didn't.

I get back to the car as a patrol car pulls in behind. A man gets out from behind the steering wheel, and a woman gets out from the passenger seat. The woman is early thirties. Tall. Long dark hair tied back and cold blue eyes. She looks like a high jumper. 'What are you doing here, sir?' she asks.

'I'm looking for my son.'

'You match the description a jogger called in a few minutes ago, right down to the pyjamas, of a man who tried to accost her. You want to tell us what you're really doing here?'

'Exactly what I said. I'm looking for my son, Zach. He's run away. I was trying to ask that woman if she had seen him. That's all.'

'Uh-huh,' her partner says. He's shorter, stockier, and older by ten years. He looks like a wrestler. He has a thick neck and ears some professional rugby players get where the insides are bigger than the outsides. 'Why didn't you call the police?'

'I did.'

Both their expressions shift, not much, but enough to see it.

I carry on. 'Fifteen minutes ago. There are police on the way to my house now. They're probably already there talking to Elsie. I was checking the parks, and now I'm heading to the school.'

'What's your name?' Wrestler asks, less sceptical now.

'Cameron Murdoch.'

'And Elsie is your wife?'

'Yes. I mean, no. I mean, my wife's name is Lisa.'

'So who is Elsie?' he asks.

'Elsie is a nickname for Lisa,' I say.

'A nickname?' Wrestler asks.

'It's her initials. L and C for Lisa Cross.'

'And where do you live, Mr Murdoch?' he asks.

I give them my address. The wrestler asks the high jumper to check on it, and she ducks back into the car to do just that.

'How old is Zach?' Wrestler asks.

'Seven.'

'And when did you last see him?'

'Last night at bedtime. We only noticed this morning he was gone.'

'So your son has potentially been missing for...' He glances at his watch, but before he can do the addition I answer for him.

'Thirteen and a half hours.'

High Jumper gets out of the car, and there's a second shift in tone when she says, 'We're going to escort you back home where two officers are currently waiting for you.'

'I need to go to Greenbark Primary. That's his school. He might be there.'

'We'll take care of that,' she says.

'But—'

She cuts me off. 'Please, Mr Murdoch, the sooner you help us, the sooner we can help you.'

I could argue it, and waste more time, only the result would be the same. I get into my car, and they follow me home.

Chapter Eight

I try calling Mum again, and this time she answers.

'Is Zach there?'

'Why would he be here?'

'He's run away. We haven't seen him since last night. Can you—'

'He's what?'

'He's run away. Can you check around your house and yard? It's possible he's gone there.'

'Of course. Of course. I'll do that right now,' she says, and she sounds panicked.

There's a clunk as she puts the phone down on the kitchen bench. She calls out for Zach, and I can hear her opening and closing doors. Her voice fades, and after a minute it gets louder again. She picks up the phone. 'He's not here,' she says, almost out of breath. 'Have you called the police?'

I look in my mirror where the patrol car is right behind me, making sure I don't zigzag off into other directions. 'They're looking for him.'

'I'll get dressed and come right over.'

'Don't do that. Stay at home and keep an eye out for him.'

'Have you tried the parks?'

'Yes.'

'And his school?'

'The police are looking there now.'

'Listen, Cameron, he's going to be okay. I know it. Don't let your overactive imagination tell you otherwise,' she says, even though I can tell she's trying to rein hers in.

'I have to go.'

'Ring me as soon as you can.'

'I will.'

'I mean it. As soon as you can. I'll be praying for all of you.'

I arrive home. There's a patrol car out front. I turn into the driveway, avoiding the fallen letterbox. The garage door is still open but I park in front of it. The patrol car that followed me turns around and drives away, probably to the school. I go inside. Voices are coming from the lounge.

Lisa is sitting on one couch, and two officers are on the one opposite. Two men. One of them big and bald – another wrestler, and the other one thin and wiry – another high jumper. Maybe it's Big and Tall day at the station. The big guy is taking notes. Everybody looks at me as I come in, Lisa with hope on her face, a hope that disappears because Zach isn't with me. She stands and comes over. She's been crying. Her eyes are swollen. The two officers stand up. They introduce themselves. The wrestler is Michael Woodley and the jumper is Matthew Waverly; names only a parent could tell apart.

We don't shake hands, and I sit down.

'We have units looking for your son,' Woodley says. He has a deep voice and a kind face, and keeps looking back and forth between Lisa and me, like he's watching a tennis match. He tells me Zach's favourite clothes – a Superman T-shirt, a blue jacket with a hood, and a pair of brown shorts – are gone. It's the same outfit he wore yesterday, meaning he pulled most of it out of the hamper.

'I have a picture of him in those clothes from yesterday,' I say, and I pull out my phone, 'other than the jacket.'

'Your wife showed us earlier,' Waverly says, and he has a matching voice, and also a warm look on his face, but spends most of his time watching me. These guys are the first responders, trying to keep us calm. If there is a storm coming, they will be gone before it hits.

'I showed them the photos you sent from the fair,' Lisa says. 'I also gave them the one we took a few weeks ago in your mum's backyard. It's a better photo.'

I remember the photo, Zach posing with his hands on his hips and his foot resting on a football as he flashes his big, toothy smile for the camera.

'Lisa was just saying that Zach's bike is still here,' Wrestler says, and why hadn't I thought to check earlier? 'But what about a skateboard, or a scooter, or rollerblades – anything that could make him travel faster, and further?'

'Nothing like that,' Lisa says.

'Does he get pocket money?' Woodley asks.

'No,' I say.

'You've called his friends?'

'Not yet,' Lisa says.

'Okay. Why don't both of you call them, and family, and anybody else you can think of. We have some detectives on the way to help out. I'd also like your permission for us to look around the house. It may be hard to believe, but we've responded to many missing children in the past only to find them hiding somewhere, upset because their parents wouldn't let them watch TV or play Nintendo.'

'Look anywhere you want,' Lisa says.

It's now nine o'clock. It's been an hour since I discovered Zach was gone. Fourteen hours since I last saw him. Christchurch is four hundred thousand people. Small enough that you always run into people you know whenever you go anywhere. Which means there's a chance I could get in my car and pick a direction and spot Zach walking along the footpath.

'I'm going to head back out and look around. You might have a hundred people looking for Zach, but a hundred and one would be better.'

'We need you here,' Waverley says. 'Like we said, we have a couple of detectives on their way. The best thing you can do for your son is to stay here and make some calls while you let us do our jobs.'

He's right. Of course he is.

As Waverly and Woodley make their way through the house, Lisa and myself get to work phoning everybody. We have similar conversations – 'Hi, it's Cameron/Hi, it's Lisa, Zach has run away, have you seen him? Please let us know if you do. No, I'm sure he's fine. No, I'm sure it's just kids being kids. Yes, we'll let you know once he's back.' We do this, and the police officers look into the nooks and crannies of our house, all the places a small child could hide, and I suspect also all the places a small child could be hidden – I'm not oblivious to the fact that when children go missing, it's the parents the police first suspect. The patrol car that escorted me earlier is now parked opposite the house. Original High Jumper and Original Wrestler are talking to the neighbours, all of whom are easy to find since they're outside watching what's going on. Another car pulls up and a man in a suit gets out, probably one of the detectives. He crosses the road and steps onto the yard, moving along the house and out of sight from the window.

We keep making calls. To family. To teachers. To parents. To neighbours. I pace the lounge. I tap out phone numbers and try to sound calm. My body is a mess. Some organs are tightening and some organs are loosening and my brain is on fire. Lisa won't look at me. I'm the one who should have checked on Zach last night. I'm the one who should have known he was going to run away. I'm the one who made light of it when he said that he would.

That makes me responsible for all of this.

And you're the one responsible if he never gets found.

I tell Mr What If to shut up, and he does.

At least for now.

I carry on making calls.

Chapter Nine

There are still smudges of exhaust and road dirt on Kent's fingers from dealing with the wheel. She pops open the glove box and goes through a handful of tissues wiping it away before climbing out of the car. The street is full of single-storey houses twenty years old. She can remember when this whole area used to be farmland, back when she was a kid. Her dad always used to say one day Christchurch was going to need more houses than it did cows, and then that day came.

The Murdoch house is red brick, the bricks uniform in size and shape but not in colour, as though parts were dipped into a coal mine. Three bedrooms, maybe four, a dark concrete-tile roof with moss growing on the edges. At the moment there are a few neighbours hanging about, some of them the Murdochs will have spoken to already, news of the missing boy slowly making its way through the neighbourhood.

Thompson is already here. He's late thirties, lean, tall and good-looking, blue eyes and a square jaw, and finger-length dark hair neatly parted to the side. He's wearing a shirt that's half a size too small for him so it can show off his gym curves. He's standing next to a broken letterbox to the side of the driveway. The damage looks fresh, probably knocked over by Cameron speeding out to look for his son. Or to hide him? She can thank Thompson for that thought. She doesn't say anything, but she's annoyed at him for suggesting this could be a case of crime writers putting into action what they write. He has a folder in his hand.

'You been inside yet?' she asks.

'Was waiting for you.'

'Anything out here?'

'Something,' he says.

He leads her across the front yard. Through the lounge window, she can see Cameron Murdoch pacing back and forth, talking on the phone. Thompson points out which room is which as they pass them, stopping at the last room of the house, which is Zach Murdoch's. The window is open.

'What am I looking at?'

'The garden,' Thompson says.

The garden along the front of the house is full of green lilies, spaced a metre apart, tall enough to be falling over each other. They've been flattened outside the window, presumably where Zach landed. Thompson pulls aside one of the fronds. There is a footprint in the dirt facing the window. Fresh-looking, and too big to be a child's.

'Shit.'

'Yeah. One of the officers found it earlier. Somebody stepped there, broke the fronds, then when they stepped away the fronds covered it. Probably didn't see it. The parents certainly didn't.'

'Anything else?'

'That's it, for the moment. Right now, the Murdochs are calling everybody they can think of. You want point on this?'

Thompson offering means she doesn't have to remind him he took point last time – a boy who went missing but was found two hours later, hiding in a neighbour's garage. 'Yes. Cameron Murdoch say anything to anybody about who he was telling to shut up?'

'No, and nobody has asked.'

'Okay. Okay,' she says, thinking about how she's going to start this. 'That footprint. I don't like it.'

'Nor do I.' He hands her the folder. Inside is a form she needs the parents to sign, and a photograph of Zach. He has his foot resting on a football and is offering a big, goofy smile to the camera. He's wearing a pair of glasses, with the left lens patched.

'Anything else?'

'Yeah. Dogs are going to be useless. If this kid has been gone since last night, there's no tracing him, and even if he's been gone for only a few hours we've contaminated the scene so much the dogs won't know what they're doing.'

He's right. Police dogs are good at tracking an offender in the moment and no good at tracking down a kid who disappeared half a day earlier.

'You want me to call Burke?' he asks.

Aside from being one of the dog handlers, John Burke also has a pet bloodhound. He once told her his bloodhound, Archie, was like a Terminator – that if you gave him a scent, he would track it down until he found it, or until the trail stopped. The boy who went missing two weeks ago and was located in a garage was found by Archie – a job that took the dog all of two minutes. They can track a scent that is almost two weeks old, and they can track it a long way – a hundred kilometres if need be, even longer. Archie has helped find others in the past too. She's always thought it was a shame there aren't bloodhounds on the force, but, as Burke told her, they're not cost-effective.

'Call him. Let me know when he's here. I'll head in and talk to the parents.'

'I'll get things up and running out here.'

She walks across the yard and goes inside.

Chapter Ten

We're back in the lounge, Lisa, myself, and the two patrol officers, when the second of the two detectives shows up. The first one from earlier hasn't come inside yet, but I've glimpsed him a few times through the window. The second one I recognise from the news. Detective Inspector Rebecca Kent. She's serious, her face and jaw tight, brow furrowed. Her expression is one of somebody trying to set fire to the room with their mind. She looks trim, and tough. Her shirt and pants have smears of grease on them. She has dark hair tied back into a ponytail that goes to her shoulders and bright-blue eyes that look hard, that look like they've seen a lot of bad shit – confirmed by a finger-width scar running between her jaw and her right ear. It's shiny and catches the light different.

She introduces herself. We don't shake hands. 'May I?' she asks, and points towards the couch Waverly and Woodley have just vacated.

'Please,' I say.

She sits opposite us. Woodley and Waverly go outside to join the search.

'First thing I'm going to ask you to do is sign this,' she says, and she opens a folder she's carrying with her. Inside are two pages clipped together. 'It's an authority to allow us to circulate photographs of Zach in the media.'

I look at the forms. I don't read them, because to read them would take a couple of minutes, and that's a couple more minutes that allow Zach to get even more lost.

'Got a pen?' I ask.

'You should at least go through it,' Kent says.

'Is it what you said it is?' I ask.

'Nothing more.'

She hands me a pen. I sign the form. Lisa signs it too. Kent slips the form back into the folder and sits it square to the edge of the coffee table between us. Then she pulls a pad from her pocket, flips it open and makes a small note.

'Reports of Zach running away will be on the radio at eleven o'clock,' she says, and I look at my watch. That's forty minutes away. 'We'll then run his picture on the TV news at twelve. His photograph will be widely circulated, including bus stations and hospitals. Has Zach ever run away before?'

We both shake our heads. Then, Lisa says, 'He's spoken about it. A few times. Well, more than a few. The thing is, Zach can be ... difficult.'

She writes something down. 'Difficult?'

Lisa carries on. 'He can be quick to anger,' she says. 'And, I hate to say it, but he ticks a little differently sometimes too. Teachers have suggested he may be autistic, so we had him tested two years ago. The doctors agreed he wasn't on the spectrum, but ... well, like I said, he can be difficult.'

'Not *that* difficult,' I say, because right now we're looking like parents who might have reached their breaking point. 'I'd say he's more challenging than he is difficult.'

'Challenging rather than difficult,' Kent says.

'He's a good kid,' I say. 'We just want him back.'

'We all want that,' Kent says. 'Is he on any medication? Anything we need to be aware of?'

'Nothing,' I say.

'Does he have any allergies? Food, hay fever, does he have asthma?'

'Nothing,' I say again.

'I saw Zach had a patch on his glasses. Does he have amblyopia?'

Amblyopia, where one optic nerve doesn't fully develop because the other one dominates it. Kids have the good eye patched in the hope the weaker nerve can strengthen. If things haven't gotten better after the age of seven, they're not going to – so we've been told. 'He does. We have an appointment next month with his ophthalmologist to discuss if there have been any improvements and how long we should continue with the patching.'

'It's a battle with him to keep his glasses on,' Lisa adds.

Kent writes something down. 'Was he upset about anything?'

'He was,' Lisa says. 'Because of what happened at the fair yesterday.'

'Tell me.'

I lay it out for her, taking Zach to the fair, and how I lost him when he left the bouncy castle without me seeing because I was on my phone. Kent doesn't say anything. She's probably heard it a thousand times and doesn't judge anymore. Or maybe she does, but keeps it to herself. It's how kids disappear or fall off playground equipment or end up on the bottom of swimming pools – parents checking the online world while their kids have accidents in the real one. I tell her about the confrontation with the man who hit me and the woman with the twins. She writes it all down.

'I took him for ice cream after. We spoke about what happened, and he had a meltdown. He started screaming, which is nothing new. When that happens we usually pick him up and leave. He was still upset when he went to bed. He said he was going to run away, but I didn't think he meant it. Of course I didn't think he meant it.'

'Does Zach have a mobile?'

'He's only seven,' Lisa says.

'Please just answer the question,' Kent says.

'No. He doesn't have a mobile,' Lisa says.

'Does he have a device of any kind?'

'He has a tablet for his cartoons,' Lisa says. 'It's still here.'

'Does Zach have any social-media accounts?'

'No,' I say.

'We're going to need to check anyway. We often see children of Zach's age, sometimes even younger, owning tablets and using them for—'

'Zach can barely read,' Lisa says, 'let alone type a message.'

'Okay,' Kent says, and she makes a note. 'Has he taken any other clothes with him?'

'I haven't checked,' Lisa says. 'As soon as I saw his favourite clothes gone I stopped looking. Should I go and look?'

'Soon,' Kent says. 'Tell me more about last night.'

I lay it out again. We had dinner. Lisa bathed Zach, then he played in his room. The conversation I had with Zach about him running away, about how he would need clothes and food, and have to support himself. 'If I had thought for one moment he was really going to run away, I'd have tied him to the bed.'

'You've tied him up before?' Kent asks.

'No. Of course not. I only mean if I thought he was going to run away I'd never have said the stuff I said, and we'd have kept an eye on him. But he says things all the time he doesn't mean. Every time he gets upset he tells us that he hates us, that he wants to go and live with his grandparents. Zach ... sometimes his emotions come in bursts. He can be frantic one moment and a dial tone the next.'

Kent writes it all down. 'What's he like with strangers? Let's say he's walking by himself, and a stranger approaches him. Is he going to talk to them? Is he going to hide? Will he turn and run?'

'Is that what you think happened?' Lisa asks. 'You think a stranger picked him up?'

'I don't think anything at this stage,' Kent says. 'But I need you to answer the question.'

'He'd be polite,' Lisa says. 'Talkative. He likes people and trusts them, and always thinks they're going to like him back.'

'So if somebody offered to help him, he'd say yes?'

'Yes,' Lisa says. 'He wouldn't know if they had ... well ... other intentions. He's learned all about "stranger danger", but he's gullible. If somebody told him we had asked them to pick him up, he'd probably believe them.'

'So you do think that's what's happened,' I say.

'As I said, I'm not thinking anything at this stage.'

Yes she is. She's thinking a lot of things and none of them good.

Kent carries on. 'Have you done any gardening recently?'

'What?'

'Any gardening. Have you spent time in your garden over the last few days?'

'No. Why?'

'There's a footprint outside your son's bedroom window.'

'It must be Zach's. The plants are trampled from where he landed.'

'The print was under the fronds, and it's not Zach's,' Kent says. 'It's an adult print. What size are—?'

'Wait, back up a moment here,' I say. 'What are you saying?'

'I'm saying there's a footprint in the garden outside your son's room. Could it be yours?'

Everything changes. A moment ago we were dealing with Zach running away. He'd run away and gotten lost, or was hiding somewhere. Now Kent is telling us things Mr What If has been voicing throughout the morning. *See? And you didn't want to listen. What was it you thought yesterday? Wasn't it that kids disappearing is something that happens to other people, like car accidents, and cancer and houses burning down? If you'd taken a moment to think about it, you'd have realised that you're other people too.*

I look at Lisa. Her hands are balled so tight her nails must be cutting into her palms. She's staring at me. Her eyes are brimming with tears.

I shake my head. 'The print isn't mine,' I say, and I get to my feet. There's a sharp pain, like indigestion, ripping across the side of my abdomen. Something in there is on fire. Cracks are spreading inside my head. Walls are coming down, tearing at the wiring as they crumble. I move around the room, because moving is an action, moving is making something happen, whereas sitting is letting the chips fall where they may. 'You're saying somebody has been watching our son through his window.'

'No. What I'm saying is we found a footprint in the garden that we're going to need to identify.'

This is no longer a CZM. Zach has been sweet-talked out of his room.

'You think somebody took him,' Lisa says, her voice not much louder than a whisper.

Kent taps the top of her pen against her notebook a couple of times, then says, 'Look, Mr and Mrs Murdoch, your jobs give you a better insight than most when it comes to what's going on here. You know we need to consider all possibilities, and rule as many out as quickly as we can. The faster we can do this, the faster we can narrow down what happened. I'm not suggesting any scenario here. All I'm doing is collecting every piece of information I can. Now, how about you sit back down, Mr Murdoch, and we can continue.'

'How the hell can I continue when you're telling us somebody took our son?'

'Your son is why I need you to sit back down and answer my questions.'

I sit back down. I don't like it, but I do it. Then again, I haven't liked anything about today. Not one bit. It's obvious now that Kent, and the other police officers, they're all thinking that Zach didn't run away at all, but that somebody has come along and taken him.

Chapter Eleven

Both parents are barely holding on. Kent knew coming in that things were going to change quickly once she mentioned the footprint. Right now, they can't think anything other than a stranger came to their window. The temperature in the room has gone up. She can feel the heat coming in waves from both the Murdochs.

'I want to come back to this incident at the fair yesterday. This man who hit you, did he say anything to suggest he recognised you?'

'Nothing, and I doubt that he did. Being a writer is an anonymous job. I bet there are probably only two or three authors in the world you could identify. The idea this guy could have recognised me is incredibly unlikely.'

'I recognised you,' she says. 'We met backstage five years ago at a festival in Auckland.'

'We did?'

'For a few minutes. I met both of you.'

He shakes his head and looks at his wife, who is also slowly shaking her head. 'I don't remember.'

'You do have a profile, Mr Murdoch. If he's read one of your books, or seen you in an article, then it's possible he recognised you.'

'You think that man came here?' Lisa asks.

'You think he followed me home?' Cameron asks. 'That he came here, tapped on the window and convinced Zach to leave with him?'

'I need to cover all the possibilities,' Kent says. 'You said earlier Zach could be convinced to go with a stranger.'

'Yes, from the street, but not climb out through his window and go with one. Zach ran away. He said he was going to, and he did, and the footprint in the garden is something else. Maybe somebody was going to try and rob our house. Have you checked if there have been any burglaries in the neighbourhood?'

'It's being looked into. You took photographs of Zach in the bouncy castle?'

'I did.'

'Is it possible you got one of the man who assaulted you?'

Cameron checks his phone. He swipes through half a dozen photographs, then shakes his head. 'Nothing.'

'Okay. We'll work on tracking him down. I also need a list of all of Zach's friends. It's possible he made plans before leaving school on Friday. Maybe a few of them were all thinking it'd be fun to catch up, and all the others thought better. I've seen it happen. Zach might have thought ten of his friends were all—'

'None of his friends have adult-sized shoes,' Cameron says.

'I can get you a list,' Lisa says.

'I'll also need a list of places he's gone to with his friends, hangouts or playgrounds where other parents have taken them. We'll check the parks again, and we still have officers searching the school.'

'Okay,' Cameron says, and despite the temperature rising, he looks pale, on the verge of passing out.

'Mr Murdoch, when you called this morning to report Zach missing, who were you telling to shut up?'

'Excuse me?'

'You were telling somebody to shut up. Who?'

Cameron looks to his wife, who is staring back at him, her mouth tight as she frowns.

'It was nothing,' he says.

'Then you have no reason not to tell me.'

'I was telling myself to shut up.'

'Yourself?'

'I know it sounds crazy, but when I write, I have this voice inside, like ... like this voice I try to use on the page.' He stares at her, and when she doesn't say anything, he carries on. 'That voice, the moment I figured out Zach was missing, it started throwing all these possibilities at me.'

'Like?'

'Like the kind we write about.'

'You were telling a voice to shut up.'

'I wouldn't put it like that, but yes.'

'You hear other voices?'

'Again, I wouldn't put it like that, but no. I don't hear voices.'

'Except for the one you were telling to shut up.'

He sighs, and he says, 'I've told you what you asked, it's up to you if you want to accept that.'

That's good, she thinks. A good answer, and she does believe him – after all, she has a voice just like it, doesn't she? The one that, every time she starts a car, says, *Maybe this time.* And hasn't she told that voice to shut up on more than one occasion?

Thompson comes into the lounge. She introduces him to the Murdochs, and he nods in their direction, then he says to her, 'Burke is here.'

Kent stands up. 'We're going to need some of Zach's clothes.'

'There's a hamper in his bedroom,' Lisa says.

'I'm on it,' Thompson says.

'Okay,' Kent says. 'Let's head outside.'

Chapter Twelve

We follow Kent outside. Cordons have been put up twenty metres either side of the house, where people are gathering. Opposite, watching us from the other side of her rose garden, is our eighty-year-old neighbour, Mrs Mulvaney. Every Christmas she brings over freshly baked muffins, and on Zach's birthday she makes him cookies. She's always lovely. Always. Only now she's staring at us like the police have uncovered a dozen bodies in the yard.

Reporters are gathering at the barricades. Cameras are focusing on us. Soon they will interview neighbours. They will call us 'The Quiet People'. It's a name we coined from neighbours who talk to reporters and say things like, 'We can't believe he killed his boss. He was always so quiet, always keeping himself to himself.' Or, 'We can't believe she drowned her children. She was always so quiet, we hardly ever saw her.'

Thompson comes outside carrying a T-shirt. 'Can you confirm

this belongs to Zach?' he asks, holding it up, as if we're laundering T-shirts for other seven-year-old boys.

'Yes,' Lisa says.

He hands the plastic bag to a guy wearing police coveralls. He has a bloodhound on a leash. The bloodhound has a droopy face and floppy ears, and a look on its face like it's about to complain about the heat.

'When was the last time you walked with Zach to his grand-mother's house?' Kent asks.

'A while,' I say. 'Months. Maybe longer.'

'And his school?'

'We've been driving him.'

'The parks?'

'We hardly ever walk to Antberry. Last time we did was last summer. As for Haydon, we walked there last weekend.'

'Has Zach been out and about over the last few days?'

'Not really,' Lisa says. 'I mean, he plays in the backyard, but never out the front. He had the fair yesterday, and on Saturday we took him to my parents.'

'When was the last time you remember him walking around out here?' Kent asks.

'I...' I say, but I don't have an answer. 'I'm not sure. Usually if we're out here we're going somewhere, and mostly we drive. There was Haydon Park last weekend, but that might be it.'

She walks over to the dog handler, and I can hear her telling him everything we told her. Then the dog gets a whiff of the clothes then walks with its nose to the ground, following an invisible path out to the street. Kent and Thompson walk to the side of the yard, out of earshot, to update each other, then Kent comes back.

'How long have you lived here?' she asks.

'Nine years next month,' Lisa says.

'So Zach has lived here his entire life,' Kent says. 'He must be familiar with the area?'

'Most of it,' Lisa says. 'Especially the route to the parks and to his school, and to his grandmother's house.'

'Kids who run away will usually stick with the streets they know,' Kent says. 'I'll get a map in here soon and get you to show me the streets he's familiar with. It will be like ripples in a pond, all expanding outwards from the house. We'll focus on the streets closest to begin with, but it's possible there will be bigger streets that will act like a barrier for Zach, streets he knows that once he crosses he'll be in unfamiliar territory. Kids of Zach's age who run away won't usually try crossing wide, busy roads, especially when they don't know what's on the other side.'

We head back inside. We take up the same places as earlier. Almost. The difference being that Lisa puts a little distance between herself and me. Before, we were pressed up against each other, now there's enough room for another person.

'We've collected all the shoes from your house,' Kent says, 'except for the pair you're wearing. If you don't mind?'

I take my shoes off, and Thompson comes forward and holds open a plastic bag. I drop them inside, and he carries them out.

We discuss Zach's school. Kent wants to know if there are any new students or teachers, or if any of the original ones have been taking any unusual interest in Zach. My right leg keeps jiggling. The headache is getting stronger. The distance on the couch between my wife and myself has grown without me seeing it happen. It's one o'clock now. Zach has been missing anywhere up to eighteen hours. Kent asks for the details of Zach's doctor. Lisa finds the information, and the sooner Kent calls him and gets rid of the notion that Zach was walking into doors on a regular basis, the better.

An officer brings a map in. Kent spreads it out over the coffee table, and we point out the streets that Zach is familiar with. More people come into our house. Kent explains what is going on with every new person. Somebody takes a comb from the bathroom with Zach's hair on it. It's for DNA, they tell us, which has an ominous feel about it. DNA is what you use to identify somebody who can't identify themselves. Zach's tablet is bagged and taken away for a computer forensic expert to examine.

We're fingerprinted, for what Kent calls 'elimination purposes'. If they find prints around the window, they want to know if they're ours or belong to somebody else. Thompson comes back and signals to Kent that he has something, and they talk for a minute in the hallway before they both head outside. I get up and walk over to the window and watch them.

Chapter Thirteen

Kent follows Thompson back out to the trodden lilies. There are more police here now, more reporters, more neighbours gathering beyond the barriers.

'There is nothing on the bedroom window,' Thompson says. 'It hasn't been pried open, there are no fingerprints outside it, but there are none inside either.'

'None on the windowsill?'

'Nothing.'

'Doesn't make sense.'

'I agree. A kid climbing out his window is going to leave them everywhere.'

'You don't think he climbed out his window?'

'I don't know,' he says. 'I just know he wouldn't have wiped it down on his way out. There's more too. I followed up on what you were saying about their trip to the Hagley Fair. A woman called the police, said a guy abused both her girls. She took a photograph of him.' Thompson hands her his phone. 'It's blurry, but it's Murdoch. Call came in at two fifty-five. She says he threw her girls out of the castle then ran away. One of them has a broken collarbone.'

'Poor kid,' she says, 'but has to be an accident, right? You ever go into a bouncy castle as an adult? I went into one with my niece last year – it's like walking on a waterbed. Murdoch probably fell over.'

'Not according to her, but sure, I don't see a guy with the profile that Cameron Murdoch has storming into a bouncy castle and tossing kids out of it. Either way, she's made the accusation.'

'Go talk to her. See if you can diffuse this thing before it gets in the way of everything else. Make sure she doesn't post that photo online. See if she can tell us anything about this guy who assaulted Cameron.'

'You think this other guy took Zach?'

'I don't know. I mean, people have done worse with less provocation. He might have come here, found Zach had opened the window, helped him outside, then wiped everything down. That's why there are no prints. If the woman from the fair took a photo of Murdoch, it's possible she got one of the guy that hit him. Also, there must have been somebody operating the bouncy castle, let's see if we can track them down too.'

'On it.'

'Burke checked in yet?'

'He has. He said the dog couldn't find a scent to the grandmother's house. It must have been some time ago, like the parents said. He made a loop of the block, and the only scent the dog found was one heading to Haydon Park. He's following it. Said he'll keep us updated.'

'Cameron's shoes?'

'Nothing in the house matches what we found in the garden. You think we put the parents on TV?'

A press conference with the parents would do two things: if Zach was out there somewhere, then it couldn't hurt to appeal to who had taken him. It would also give the public the opportunity to look at the parents, and think back on if they've seen them doing anything suspicious of late. 'I've been considering it. What do you think?'

'Can't hurt,' he says.

'Yeah. That's what I'm thinking too.'

'What are you going to do? Bring the Murdochs in? Or keep interviewing them here?'

'Not finding any fingerprints on the window or the windowsill is concerning,' she says. 'Let's bring them in and separate them.'

She hands him back his phone then heads inside.

Chapter Fourteen

The day keeps heating up. Sweat rolls down the sides of my body. There are more people in the house. Some are wearing white nylon suits as they go about searching the nitty-gritty. I watch Kent walk back across the lawn to the front door. When she comes inside, she looks different somehow, tighter, as if every muscle in her body is being squeezed.

'What's happened?' I ask.

'Take a seat,' she says.

'Just tell us.'

'I will, when you take a seat.'

If every muscle in Kent's body is being tightened, every one in my body is being loosened. It's a struggle making it back to the couch.

'What time were you at the bouncy castle yesterday?'

'I don't know. Three o'clock maybe?'

'You took photos on your phone. Can you check?'

I check. 'Two fifty-three.'

'The woman you were telling me about, she called the police.'

'She say what happened? About the guy who sucker-punched me?'

'No. Did you touch her daughters at all?'

'No, of course ... Wait, I did. They fell over. It was when I was approaching the castle. They bumped into each other and fell out, and I helped one of them up.'

'She's saying you abused them. That you went into the castle and threw them out.'

'No. That's wrong,' I say. 'I mean, yeah, I went into the castle, and I think one of them might have fallen out when that happened. Actually, when the guy hit me, I fell back in and I think the other girl fell out too. But they were accidents.'

'One of those girls broke her collarbone.'

I run my hands through my hair and lean back. 'I ... I'm sorry. I didn't mean for that to happen. For any of it. I was trying to find Zach. Tell her I'm sorry, and of course if there are any medical bills I'll cover them.'

'She says you were trying to molest another boy.'

The headache is immediate. It's right behind the eyes, a dull warm ache from which a bolt of lightning emerges. 'That's not true. I put my hand on a boy's arm. I had seen him talking to Zach a few minutes earlier. I was trying to show him my phone. I was going to show him a photograph of Zach. That's when his dad came over and everything went bad.'

Lisa has her knees curled up to her chin. I feel like I'm having an out-of-body experience, one where my soul has drifted off and been plucked out of the air by Rod Serling. *Meet Cameron and Lisa Murdoch, a husband and wife who write crime fiction, whose stories grow arms and legs and take on life in* ... The Twilight Zone.

'It's an accusation we have to follow up.'

My brain is being pinched, the sensation making the lounge walls sway and bulge as the furniture shrinks and shudders. It could be an embolism, maybe shock, maybe a touch of everything that ails. I get back to my feet. Movement is momentum. I get to the window. My ears are ringing.

'Mr Murdoch?'

'No,' I say.

'No?'

'No, I didn't touch that boy, not in the way they're making it sound, but if that man thinks I did, if he came here for Zach, how could he have known Zach was going to run away? And we still don't know he didn't just run away. The shoeprint in our garden, did it match any of my shoes?'

'No,' she says.

It's not the answer I wanted. I was holding out hope I had stood there and forgotten. 'Has the dog found anything?'

'Nothing yet.'

I know how good bloodhounds are. We've used them in books before. Their sense of smell is a thousand times better than a human being. They are so good that their ability to find – or not find – evidence can be used in court in other countries. The only place Zach has walked from our front door over the last week is to Haydon Park. There should be two trails – one to the park, and one to where Zach went last night. It shouldn't be taking this long. The only reason a bloodhound wouldn't find Zach would be if Zach isn't there to be found. It would mean Zach got into – or was placed into – a car.

The storm that has moved into the lounge has increased in pressure. The headache is no longer warm, but hot, and the lightning strikes inside my head have increased in frequency. The walls are still bulging, and the furniture is all fluid, it's all jelly.

I head into the kitchen, grabbing the walls, the furniture, and even an officer, to stay balanced. I pull painkillers out from the top shelf of the pantry and swallow them down with water. I hold on to the kitchen bench as the floor rocks and sways beneath my feet.

I look at Lisa, her own storm so cold it's frozen her into place. Then she looks at me, and in that look I can see everything I need to know. When we get Zach back, we may never move past this.

'Given the way things are taking shape,' Kent says, 'I think it's best we continue these questions at the station.'

Chapter Fifteen

I change out of my pyjamas into a T-shirt and shorts. All of my shoes have been taken into evidence, but I have been left with a pair of jandals that I put on. Lisa changes into jeans and a T-shirt. The pills are doing their job, and the lightning strikes aren't travelling as far, nor are they as frequent. We get into the back of a dark-blue sedan without the need for anybody to tell us to watch our heads. Kent gets into the passenger seat. Officer Waverly gets in behind the wheel.

I can't shake the feeling we're being arrested as we roll out of the street, barriers at the end pulled aside to let us pass, neighbours' heads turning to follow our progress. Local and national media vans have been joined by international ones. Nobody speaks. Waverly makes a series of lefts and rights, and Lisa won't look at me. I stare through the window at the city that has turned out to be as malevolent as we paint it in our books. We pass houses I've driven past thousands of times that today all look different, big shadows behind windows hiding all sorts of craziness – and, perhaps, hiding our son. Who really knows their neighbours? I don't – because one of them has been watching our family, and the rest of them are treating it as entertainment.

We reach town, going from tree-lined roads with stop signs and nice homes to parking-meter-lined streets with traffic lights and office buildings. We drive parallel to the Avon, a narrow river that snakes its way into the city then snakes its way back out, people sitting along the banks staring at the dark water as they eat late lunches or early dinners before throwing their fast-food wrappers into it. There are Christmas decorations everywhere, Santas up in

windows, tinsel hanging from lampposts, snow painted around
the edges of windows. New Zealand is a white-Christmas country
in spirit only – in reality we're on the wrong side of the planet for
snow in December. We're on the side that fires up the barbecue
for breakfast and spends the day in the sun.

The police station seems the only building in town without
Christmas decorations. Maybe they were stolen. A large iron gate
rumbles open, and we take a ramp down into a parking lot. My
jandals slap against my feet, and our footsteps echo across the
ground and bounce off the concrete walls as we walk to the elevator, making the four of us sound like eight. Kent pushes the
button, the doors open, and we step in, Waverly first, then Lisa,
then me, then Kent. The doors close, and the four of us sound like
four again.

We ride up to the fourth floor. There's no elevator music. No
talking. Just the hum of technology at work. The doors open, and
we step out in the opposite order from how we stepped in.
Straight ahead is an open-plan area with two dozen desks, many
of them backing onto each other, many of them unmanned as the
detectives are somewhere else looking for Zach. There are filing
cabinets and tables lining the walls, as well as posters promoting
the police force and some smaller posters with pictures of New
Zealand's most-wanted criminals; a photograph of Bilbo Baggins
has been pinned into the number-one position.

Kent leads us past a large conference room, windows lining the
wall, letting us see that it's been turned into a taskforce room.
Against the far wall is a long board with a photograph of Zach in
the centre, with other photos and notes around it, next to it all a
large map of the neighbourhood stabbed with pins. We end up in
a room the same size as my office back home. There's a square table
in the centre and a view out over the city. It doesn't look like an
interrogation room – but that's what it is. I sit with Lisa on one
side, and Kent asks us if we'd like anything to drink. I don't know

how to answer. What if I say yes, and a butterfly flaps its wings, and Zach dies? Or worse, what if I say no, and Zach still dies, but suffers more first?

'Mr Murdoch?'

'I ... I don't know.'

'I'll get you both some,' she says, which is good, because my throat is dry, and my mouth feels like I've been huffing on a bag of dust. Kent closes the door behind her on the way out.

It's the first I've been alone with Lisa since we were making phone calls this morning.

'We'll get him back,' I say. 'I promise.'

My words are hollow, and she knows it, and she proves this by saying, 'You can't promise that. You know how this goes. You know where this could be leading.'

She won't look at me. I put my hand on her shoulder, and she pulls away. I feel like crying again. She's staring at the table, her body hunched forward, her arms folded.

'Why, Cameron? Why would you tell Zach it was okay to run away? Why would you say something so stupid?'

'I thought...' I say, but don't finish. It doesn't matter that I thought it was another CZM. What matters is the butterfly flapped its wings, and Zach disappeared. 'I'm sorry,' I say. 'I'm so, so sorry.'

She slaps me. The sound echoes around the room. It stings. Her face is red and tight. Her hands are shaking. This isn't Lisa. She might look like Lisa, but this isn't her. This is somebody I haven't seen before. 'It's *your* fault!'

I don't know what to say, and before I can figure it out, her face softens, and she raises her hand to her mouth. 'I'm ... I shouldn't have said that, and I shouldn't have hit you. Oh my God, I can't believe I did that.'

'It's okay,' I say.

'I don't blame you. Of course I don't.'

The door opens. Kent comes in carrying two bottles of water. She hands one to Lisa, and Lisa doesn't take it, so Kent sits it on the table. A woman leans in the doorway. She's wearing a dark top that is tight against her body. She looks like she could bench press a car. Behind her is a detective dressed in a suit that looks out of my price range. 'Lisa,' Kent says. 'Would you mind going with Detectives Vega and Travers?'

Lisa doesn't say anything, but she nods and sniffs, wipes her hand across her face, then leaves her water behind and walks to the door. Kent closes it and sits down opposite me. I was expecting them to separate us so they can compare our stories, but even so, it hurts.

'Should I call my lawyer?'

'Do you want one?'

'Isn't this where you tell me that only guilty people need them?'

'Is that what you are, Cameron? Guilty?'

She's using my first name now. It means she's going to play Good Cop. She's going to become my friend. 'Of course not, and the longer you keep me here, the longer we do this, the worse that is for Zach. We should be out there looking for him, not sitting here playing games.'

She tightens her mouth, her chin jutting outwards, tightening her scar and making it shine. 'I assure you, Cameron, none of us are playing games.'

I flatten my hands on the table. I breathe out slowly. 'Look, I'm sorry. It was a poor choice of words. I know nobody is playing any games. I'm frustrated. And scared. I want Zach back. I want to be out there looking for him.'

'Of course you're scared. I would be too,' she says, relaxing now as she becomes my friend. 'I know you know I have questions I need to ask, questions that may ultimately have no point, but I need to ask them anyway.'

'Ask them.'

'How are things between you and Lisa?'

'She blames me for letting Zach run away, and why wouldn't she?'

'What about before today? How are things between you?'

'Fine. Everything is fine between us.'

'What's it like working together?'

'How does this help Zach?'

'Please just answer the questions, Cameron.'

'It's great. Everything is great.'

'See, if it were me, and I had to work and live with the same person day after day, I think I'd struggle. Especially with what you guys do. Each of you with creative ideas jostling for position. I'd have thought the stress of work life would bleed easily into home life when two people are working and living together. It must be tough.'

'It's not tough at all. We work well together, and we live well together, and if you're trying to suggest anything different, then you—'

'I'm not suggesting anything.'

'Okay. Okay, good. Because things are great.'

'Do you argue much?'

'I just said—'

'All couples argue, Cameron. Are you telling me you're different?'

'Well, no, of course not. I mean we argue, but we don't fight.'

'What sort of things do you argue about?'

'Jesus, I don't know. Small stuff. Unimportant stuff.'

'In front of Zach?'

'Never.'

'How are sales?'

'Excuse me?'

'Book sales. Are they good? Bad? You going broke?'

'I still don't see what—'

'Humour me.'

'Sales are fine. We're comfortable. We don't have a mortgage, and we have money in the bank.'

'How much money?'

'Why?'

'Because if somebody calls, asking for a ransom,' she says, 'we may learn a lot from the amount that they ask.'

I hadn't thought of that.

'This is why all the questions, Cameron. You'd be helping all of us out, especially Zach, if you got rid of any preconceptions of what you think is going on here and just answered what I ask.'

'You're right. I'm sorry. We have around a hundred thousand in the bank.'

'Do your friends or family know how much you earn? Do you talk about it in interviews?'

'No,' I say. 'I mean, some of my friends might have some idea. So if somebody calls in asking for a hundred-thousand-dollar ransom, you think it will be somebody we've spoken to?'

'Or somebody your friends have spoken to,' she says. 'It could be somebody in publishing. Your publishers must have an idea of what you earn. Agents, editors, these are all possibilities. Maybe an accountant, or somebody who works at the bank. When does the new book come out?'

'In six months.'

'Who does most of the writing?'

'It varies from book to book, but it balances out around fifty-fifty.'

'You ever overrule Lisa? Or she overrule you? Must be difficult with two separate egos creating one piece of fiction.'

'It's a job,' I say. 'That's how we see it.'

'A united front,' Kent says.

'Exactly.'

'So nobody getting jealous if fans or reviewers like your stuff more or her stuff more.'

'What's good for one of us is good for both of us. Look, I know where you're going with this, and I'd get it if Lisa were the one that was missing, but she's not, so this all feels pointless.'

She leans back in her chair and cups one hand around the back of her neck. She rolls her shoulders and flattens her other hand against the table. 'Listen, Cameron, I'm going to be perfectly blunt with you, is that okay?'

'Go for it.'

'I know you're having the worst day of your life, but I'm here to help you. You need to let go of this notion that we're looking at you as if you're the bad guy, and start looking at it from our point of view. We need to rule each thing out as it comes along and as quickly as we can. The more open and honest you are with us, the more we can help Zach. Five minutes ago you'd not even thought that somebody close to you – somebody who has knowledge of your finances – could be behind this. You're a smart guy. But right now you're on the inside, and on the inside your view is muddled. Which is why I'm here. It's my job to ask questions you haven't thought about. I know you think because you write crime novels you're smarter than us, but—'

'I don't think that at all.'

'Good. Because we're on the same side here. We all want Zach back.'

Having put me in my place, she leans forward.

I feel ashamed. My face feels hot. I take a drink of water.

'You're right,' I say. 'You're absolutely right. About everything. I ... You know, I imagine what it's like to be in this situation all the time. I put people in this situation. I put myself into their shoes and I figure out a ... a *real* way for them to be, but this is different. I don't know what to do. My son is out there, and I don't know what to do.'

'You have two choices: you either help us, or you fight with us. Only one of those things will help us get Zach back.'

'I know. I'm sorry ... I just ... I can't think straight. Jesus, I feel ... One moment I feel numb, the next I feel like I want to burst into tears, and a moment later I want to scream. I want him back. I want him back safe and sound. I want to wake up and have had none of this happen.'

'I can't wave a wand and turn back time, but what I can do is promise you we're going to do everything we can to find him.'

'Tell me what you want to know. I'll tell you anything.'

'Good, then let's start with the basics,' she says, and we do, we talk about my marriage, and we talk about the fair yesterday, and we keep talking, and three o'clock becomes four o'clock becomes five o'clock, the same questions asked differently, the same answers told differently, Zach still as lost as he was in the beginning, each passing hour filling me with a deeper and darker dread that I'm never going to see him again.

Chapter Sixteen

It's late in the afternoon when Kent steps out of the interview room. She's doing her best to stay open-minded about the Murdochs. Their shock and fear seem genuine, but what is also genuine is the statistic that when children go missing, in most cases one or both parents are responsible.

Also genuine are Zach's glasses.

She hasn't mentioned the glasses to the Murdochs, but it's a detail that's been nagging her after she learned earlier his spare pair haven't been found. His primary pair were broken at the fair yesterday when Cameron Murdoch took a punch, and they were found on the kitchen table with one arm snapped off. However, the backup pair are not in the house, and, according to what Cameron said earlier, Zach's glasses are kept on the boy's bedside table.

A search of the house over the last few hours has failed to find them. Why would Zach take the one thing with him he was the most resistant to wearing? He wouldn't. And if somebody took the boy, wouldn't the glasses also be the last thing they would take too?

It's bugging the hell out of her.

She goes into the breakroom, where Thompson is making coffee. The room is big enough to fit a small table, a bench and some small appliances, but not much else.

'Want some?'

'Sure,' she says, and leans against the doorframe, watching him pour it. 'How'd you get on?'

'I started with the bouncy-castle guy. Tony Palmer. He saw it all unfold, and it's pretty much like how we guessed. Murdoch went into the castle, and kids fell over. The girl who broke her collarbone fell out after Murdoch was punched and fell backward. The woman from the fair is Gwendolyn Munro. I spoke to her second. She stuck to her story, but relented when I explained I had spoken to the bouncy castle operator first, along with the circumstances of why Murdoch was inside the castle. She agreed it was possible the girls fell out, but even so, she says Murdoch should never have gone in. I asked her if she would have gone in if she lost one of her kids, and she admitted that she would have, but it was different for her because she was "a woman". He says the last part using air quotations.

'She have any photographs of the guy who punched him?'

'Nothing. There's no surveillance at the fair either. She assures me she hasn't posted the photograph anywhere online, and I told her it would be in her best interests if she didn't. I spoke to Vega and Travers. They interviewed Lisa. Says her story hasn't shifted from what we've been learning all day. I'm thinking, if the parents are involved, it's not a one-parent thing. If one of them did it, both of them did it.' Thompson hands her the coffee. 'Talking to teachers and neighbours, they're all saying Zach was hard work. I mean, really hard work. One of Zach's teachers said, "I don't know how they survive him." If they did do something, it's possible the trip to the fair yesterday might have been a last good day for Zach. They wanted to give him something nice before giving him a final goodbye.'

'That's bleak,' she says. 'Heard from Burke?'

'He's sticking with it, but says it's a dead end. He says if Zach had walked himself somewhere, his dog would have found him. He said he'd bet his house on the fact Zach Murdoch got into a vehicle.'

'I keep thinking about what you said on the phone this morning, about writers writing what they know, and this being the flipside to that. I mean, this is what they do, right? They tell stories. They plan things through. Is the footprint in the garden genuine, or one they placed to shift suspicion away from them? Same with the glasses,' she says, then explains her concern about them, and he agrees, saying it doesn't make sense.

'You believe that story about Zach saying he was going to run away?' she asks.

'I don't know. I'm sure kids say stuff like that all the time. I know I did.'

'I did too,' she says.

She sips her drink. It's hot and doesn't have a lot of taste, but she wasn't expecting it to. People don't come here for the coffee.

'The husband seems defensive,' Thompson says.

'He is.'

'Overly so?'

'I'm not sure. I think being a writer makes him look at things different. I think the moment he called the police he knew he was going to be a suspect. It makes him hard to read.'

'Where are we at with the TV thing? We doing it?'

She looks at her watch. It's a little after five o'clock.

'If we're going to,' he says, 'we need to decide now.'

He's right. First, they're going to need to prepare the Murdochs. Something like this isn't easy, and it takes time, but she thinks they can get it done. She pours the rest of her coffee down the sink.

'Let's do it.'

Chapter Seventeen

Kent comes back into the room, bringing Lisa with her. The fluorescent lights have burned a whiteness into Lisa's skin and finished it off with a tinge of blue. She sits without looking at me. Kent doesn't sit down. She stands opposite us, and she says, 'If you're okay with it, we'd like to put you on TV.'

I don't know why, but I didn't see this coming. I should have. After all, I've seen it plenty of times. Parents going on TV, begging for their child back, begging for information. They're painful enough to watch, and must be infinitely worse to experience. The parents always look like they've just walked off a long-haul flight. Both Lisa and myself have been on TV before, but on morning shows on comfortable couches, where presenters with big smiles tell us they've loved our most recent book, and can we please tell them where our latest idea came from?

'Do these things ever work?'

'We need to get your story out there,' Kent says. 'We need to appeal to the public. Somebody knows where Zach is, and if they're watching, you'll have a chance to tell them how much you miss your boy, and to ask for his return.'

'But does it work?'

'You don't want to do it?'

'Of course we'll do it,' I say.

'Lisa? We really want a united front,' Kent says, echoing what she said earlier.

'Huh?'

'I asked if you'll do it.'

'Does it ever work?' Lisa asks, repeating my question, and I realise Lisa is slipping away.

'It can,' Kent says, which is a very different thing from 'it does'.

'Okay. Okay, let's do it,' Lisa says.

'Good,' Kent says. 'We're going to get somebody in here to talk over what's going to happen. Given the timing, the press conference is going to be live. Which means we have to get it right. I know you're both in shock, and scared, and we'll prepare you as best we can. I wouldn't be asking you to do this if I didn't feel it was important. We're going to write you a script that we'll want you to follow very carefully.'

'Why can't we talk from the heart?' Lisa asks.

'Because if you get up there and freeze, it won't be of any use to us. A script gives you something to focus on.'

'Okay,' Lisa says.

'Okay,' I say.

'I'm going to send Detective Inspector Camilla Russell in to get you fully prepared. Is there anything you need first?'

'Is the dog still looking?'

She hesitates for a moment, and then says, 'Yes, but so far with no luck.'

'You think Zach got into a car, don't you?'

'It's becoming more likely.'

Kent closes the door on the way out, leaving us with the knowledge that Zach no longer wandered down a rabbit hole and got lost, but rather somebody, or something, clawed their way out and pulled him in. The world is ending. The storm that came into our house earlier has followed us into the police station. Lisa folds her arms and buries her head into them. It's almost five-thirty. My headache is coming back. Kent has all but confirmed Zach left our house with somebody. I finish off my bottle of water then start on Lisa's untouched one.

'I'm worried the police are losing time by thinking we did this,' I say. 'We should get a lawyer. As soon as this TV thing is over I'll call one.'

She looks up at me and shakes her head.

'You don't want a lawyer?'

'I want my own lawyer,' she says.

That hurts even more than when she slapped me earlier. 'You think I did this. You think I hurt Zach.'

'Of course not,' she says, 'but I think it's in each of our best interests to have somebody looking out for each of our best interests.'

The united front is breaking down.

I don't know what to say. I don't even know where to begin.

The door opens. A woman in her late fifties comes in. Her hair is a mixture of blonde and grey, and her glasses are red and large, the frames as thick as fingers. She introduces herself as Camilla Russell. She has a warm smile, and she nods slowly, as if agreeing how awful the situation is.

She tells us what to expect, then coaches us on what to say. Then she says they can give us fresh clothes to wear, and the chance to clean up a little, which we do, each of us spending ten minutes in separate bathrooms to freshen up. I come out wearing dark pants, and a shirt and tie. I'm loaned a pair of shoes. Lisa wears a grey blouse and black pants. When we get back into the interrogation room, Camilla tells us the public is going to judge us. That it's inevitable. She stresses we need to stick to the script and to stay calm, and honest, and open. We read the script and it's not complicated. I tell her that I'm ready. Lisa does the same.

Kent comes back in. She smells like coffee, and there are crumbs in the creases of her top. She brushes them away, but misses the grease stains that have been there all day. Camilla points it out to her, and Kent shrugs it off and says it'll be fine, which I like, because it means she isn't interested in how she looks on TV, that all she cares about is finding Zach.

We follow them out to a different elevator from the one we took before. We take it down to the ground floor, none of us saying anything. The doors open onto a corridor with pictures of plants on the walls, but no actual plants. We stop at a door at the end. People are talking and moving about on the other side. A lot of people.

'Just remember, stay calm,' Kent says.

'Okay,' Lisa says.

'Okay,' I say.

Kent opens the door and we follow her through.

Chapter Eighteen

The noise level in the room goes up. The room is long and rectangular, with a low stage stretching across the front and a row of doors along the back. It's at capacity, a hundred people in chairs, plus more standing around the edges. Everybody is watching us. We follow Kent up two steps onto the stage. We take our seats behind a long table littered with microphones and recorders. Journalists take photos, a thousand clicks from a hundred cameras, all of them searching for the best angle to show the parents' desperation.

This crowd of reporters has seen it all before. This isn't their first missing child. It's not their first set of grieving parents. The flashes from the cameras are blinding. One gets caught in my eyes, floating across my field of vision no matter which direction I look. Kent taps her finger against a microphone, and it pulses sharply through the speakers.

The noise level drops. I picture people on news desks saying they're about to cut live to a developing situation in Christchurch, that of a seven-year-old boy who has gone missing in suspicious circumstances.

Kent introduces herself. There are no other sounds. No voices. No clicking cameras. She says Zach Murdoch hasn't been seen since he went to bed at seven o'clock last night. She says the police have grave concerns for him. They believe Zach set about running away from home and has been picked up by a passer-by, or possibly even coaxed out of his bedroom. I can already imagine people reacting to that. What kind of parents let their kids run away? Easy. Parents who don't care about their children. What kind of parents let their child get abducted? Easy. The kind of parents who are doing the abducting.

Kent lists off a litany of numbers:

Zach is seven years old.

He wasn't discovered missing until eight o'clock this morning.

The person who abducted him has a thirteen-hour head start.

Zach has now been missing twenty-three hours.

She describes the clothes he ran away in. She asks anybody with information to please come forward. She says it's possible Zach has been in communication with somebody and thought he was sneaking out to meet a friend. She asks people to be on the lookout for friends or family acting differently. There is a small digital clock at the end of the table. I could swear we've been out here no more than sixty seconds, but I can see Kent has been talking for five minutes.

Everybody in the room turns to face us, and I realise we've been introduced. I look at the script, but when I go to talk, I find my voice has gone. There's dead air. I cough into my hand, and the noise echoes from the speakers, making people in the room flinch. I reach for the glass of water and knock it over, and say, 'Fuck.' and that echoes through the speakers too, and I say 'Fuck' again in reaction. The water soaks into one of the recorders, and the display goes blank. I try to say sorry, but the word gets stuck in my throat.

Lisa quickly takes over, reading my part of the script. 'Zach ran away last night and,' she says, then pauses to get her breath. Her hand is shaking. 'He ran away, and we're scared for him. He's just a little boy,' she says, and even though she's crying, and words are getting stuck in her throat too, she finds the strength to carry on. 'A little boy who misses his parents and wants to come home.' Then she moves on to her part of the script. 'We know that somebody out there is helping him, but for some reason hasn't yet come forward. Please come forward now. If for some reason you're too afraid to call the police, you can talk to somebody you trust, or take Zach to a hospital.'

The script is meant to humanise Zach, us, even the person who took him. It's giving his abductor an out. It's telling them that we think they're a Good Samaritan who has found Zach and hasn't reported it because life has gotten in the way. But like we asked Kent earlier, do these things ever really work?

Lisa slides the script over to me. I take a sip of her water, cough a little, then drink some more to fight the dry mouth. I look at the words, but the headache is blurring my vision. I put the script down.

'We just want our son back.'

Kent can see we're done, and she takes over. 'Again, if anybody has any information, please call the number along the bottom of your screen.'

That turns out to be a cue for everybody in the room to talk at once. Hands go up and questions are shouted and cameras click, the flashes scraping at my headache. None of the words can be heard as they blend into one, but then somehow the journalists decide who gets to ask that first question. I can't tell who asks it.

'Mr Murdoch, there have been reports that you hurt a young girl at the fair yesterday, that you broke her arm. Can you comment on that?'

Before I can figure out how to answer, Kent leans into the microphone, and says, 'Mr Murdoch was involved in an altercation at the Hagley Fair yesterday, where a young girl fell, breaking her collarbone. This doesn't relate in any way to Zach's disappearance, and the matter has been resolved.'

Overlapping voices, out of tune for a moment, then, like before, a single question emerges, only this time I can see where that question is voiced from – a man in a bow-tie in the front row, and really, who wears a bow-tie to this kind of thing?

'Mr Murdoch,' he says, and I recognise him. Dallas Lockwood. I spotted him the moment we came in and wish I hadn't. Lockwood is the kind of guy who, after shaking hands with him, you would check to make sure you still had your watch. He used to be on TV but got fired. He used to have a column in the newspaper but got fired from that too. I'm not sure if he got fired for being an asshole one too many times, or if that one extra time was particularly bad. Ten years ago he pitched a crime novel idea to us. We never read people's unpublished novels or use their ideas, and we said that to him. The problem we faced was the idea he pitched was similar to the book we had recently finished writing. When our book came out he publicly accused us of stealing it from him. We were lucky our novel had gone through editing, so we were able to prove we had written it well before he contacted us, but even so the whole episode was horrible. We still sometimes get asked in interviews if there was any truth to Lockwood's accusations. He never did become a novelist, and these days he has a web show where he spouts conspiracy theories. Whatever it is he's going to ask, it's going to be bad.

'The girl wasn't the only person you hurt yesterday at the fair. Half an hour ago I got a call from a man who caught you filming and molesting his child. Has this matter also been resolved?'

The room goes quiet. Nobody was expecting this question. Lockwood is baiting me, and I know I need to keep my mouth shut, but it's been a long day. The worst day of my life. The fear and anxiety has been building up, and there's been no release valve for it. Kent is starting to answer, but I cut her off. 'That's bullshit,'

I say, a bit too firm, a bit too loud, the valve cracking open enough to ease some of the pressure, but there's still a lot left.

Lockwood carries on. 'Is this the first time you've been caught molesting a child?'

He emphasises the word 'molesting'. Or at least it sounds like he does. The word hangs in the air, surrounded by bells and whistles and neon.

'We're done here,' Kent says.

The room explodes with questions.

'Of course not,' I shout, needing to make my innocence loud enough to drown out the M-word, because if people believe that, then they'll believe anything. The valve is opening again, but the pressure is still building. I realise what I've just said, and feel stupid for falling into the trap.

Before I can correct myself, he says, 'So you have been caught before.'

'That's not what I mean,' I shout. 'I was talking to his son! I was asking him if he had seen Zach. I was showing him a photo of Zach on my phone. He went missing at the fair. So what? We're not supposed to ask other kids for help if our children wander off?'

'Zach went missing yesterday?' Lockwood asks, and why isn't anybody shutting this guy up? Or me, for that matter.

'No. Well, yes, but not like that.'

'Then like what?'

Kent picks up a microphone. 'Zach wandered off at the Hagley Fair yesterday, and Mr Murdoch was simply questioning others nearby if they had seen him. There was a misunderstanding, which led to one child falling over and being injured. Zach was found a minute or two later, waiting in line at another ride. At this stage we have no further comment on what happened yesterday, other than to say it's unrelated to Zach's disappearance.'

Lockwood has the floor as everybody else sits back, aware that what he has is potentially more interesting than what any of them have. He says, 'So your son disappears while you're being accused of molesting a child. Tell me, what were you doing last night when he went missing again?'

I bang my hand on the table. The release valve pops like a cork. Two of the recorders fall off the edge. 'Stop saying that!' I say.

Stop. Shut up. Turn around and walk away.

I can't. The fear, the anger, the idea of Zach suffering because I told him it was okay to run away. It's the Red Mist, and the Red Mist is something you can't back away from. How many of my characters have suffered from it? The Red Mist is self-sabotage. It's reaching the point of enough being enough. It started as a headache that made sharp lines curve, it made walls throb and the floor sway, it was lightning behind my eyes, and now it's a bomb going off. Everybody here, all of us, are going to get hit by the shrapnel.

I stand up, put my knuckles on the table and lean forward. 'I know what you're all thinking. I know what the statistics are. But I didn't hurt my son. Yes, a girl fell over yesterday at the fair. I fell into her after I was punched, and I'm sorry she got hurt, I really am. The man who hit me, he was an asshole, an asshole who punched me when he should have been helping me. I didn't get aggressive when he came over, he came over already aggressive, and I never touched the guy, and I didn't hurt his son, and if you call me a child molester one more time I'm going to...' I stop talking.

Everybody is staring at me.

Of course they are.

I warned you.

Lockwood smiles at me. 'You're going to what, Mr Murdoch? Kill me? Is that what you do when people upset you? Did your son upset you?'

I take my hands off the table. My arms hang loosely by my sides. The Red Mist evaporates, leaving me in tatters.

I want to take all of it back.

'Obviously Mr Murdoch is upset,' Kent says, which is a fair summation of the day. 'It's an extremely emotional time for the Murdoch family, and I'd ask you all to take that into consideration. Their son is missing. Cameron Murdoch is afraid and concerned, and I'd like to think that anybody here willing to put themselves into his shoes could see themselves acting the same way.'

She turns towards me. 'This way,' she says, in a much lower voice, and she puts her hand on my shoulder and gently pushes me towards the door.

My legs are heavy, and I trip on the stairs and stumble forward, grabbing the wall to stop myself from going down. We get into the corridor, and it's swaying. I slide to the floor and put my forearms on my knees. I resist the urge to hang my head in my hands. Kent gets the door closed and turns towards me, and now it's going to be her turn to snap. She's going to ask me what the hell I was thinking, and I'm going to sit here and take it.

Only she doesn't yell. Instead, and calmly, she says, 'He baited you.'

'I know. I'm sorry.'

'You made this about you, when it should have been about Zach,' Lisa says, her voice cold.

'I'm sorry.'

'Your house is a crime scene,' Kent says. 'You're not going to be able to return there tonight.'

'When, then?' Lisa asks.

'In the morning. Do you have somewhere you can go?'

'Yes,' Lisa says. 'To my parents.'

Her parents. My parents. Our friends. No doubt my phone is filling up with missed calls and text messages with offers of help, offers of best wishes, optimistic quips about how everything is going to be fine.

Camilla joins us in the corridor. She's slowly shaking her head, disappointed that I didn't stick to the script, that I didn't stay calm – two things she repeated several times for us to do. 'That didn't go to plan,' she says, and like Kent earlier, her words are a fair summation.

'Things would have gone better if we'd known the media knew about yesterday,' I say, the whine obvious in my voice. I hate hearing it.

Instead of answering, Kent says, 'We think it's best you go back to your parents' and rest. We'll have somebody escort you there. Stay there tonight and don't go out. We'll be in touch with more questions, and of course any updates throughout the evening.'

We go back up to the fourth floor. We go into the bathrooms so we can change back into our clothes. Losing my temper so quickly in front of the cameras has been damaging. It has shown the police, and the world, that I'm the kind of guy who, if angry, is capable of anything.

Chapter Nineteen

I meet Kent back in the interview room. 'Are you going to talk to Dallas Lockwood about the man from the fair? See who he is?'

'Yes. So you know Lockwood?'

I tell her about his accusations that we stole his idea.

'So he has a grudge,' she says.

'Every time a new book comes out, he writes us the worst reviews possible. Look, can we do another press conference?'

'There are no do-overs.'

'I can put things right.'

'By standing up and losing your temper?'

'I didn't mean for that to happen. How bad is it?'

'It wasn't good,' she says.

'Put me back in front of the camera. I'll do or say anything you need me to say.'

'What we needed was for you to do that ten minutes ago. I'm sorry, Cameron, but we can't put you back out there.'

'What about Lisa? Can you put her back out there?'

'Not today.'

'Tomorrow?'

'Maybe.'

'Maybe,' I say. 'Great. Any other maybes I should know about?'

'Go to your parents'. Get some rest. We'll be in touch.'

'Where is Lisa?'

'Gone.'

'Gone?'

'She got changed and left. An officer is giving her a ride to her parents'.'

I try to put her words into an order that makes sense, but she's given me a bunch of square pegs to push into round holes. I pound at them, but nothing works.

Kent carries on. 'She said she wanted to be alone. A couple of officers are going to give you a lift. Like I said earlier, you can't go back home until tomorrow morning. Would you prefer to go to a hotel or a friend's house rather than your mother's?'

What I'd prefer is to go and be with Lisa. Only I'm not wanted there. I may never be wanted there again.

'I'll go to my parents' house.' At forty years old, it seems like I still need my mum.

Kent leads me back to the elevator. I'm back in my jandals again. She hands me off to a pair of constables – Constable Veich, a guy with large biceps that stretch at his shirt, and Constable Green, a woman young enough to look like she's the daughter part of Bring Your Daughter to Work Day. Veich has a shaved head and a permanent furrow above his eyes, making him look like a man determined to let everything in the world bother him. Green has finger-length hair swept to the side and a couple of nasty-looking pimples on her chin she's tried covering up. She's thin and tanned, and doesn't look like she's seen enough to hate the world like her partner. The elevator arrives, and Veich and Green step in, and I follow. The doors are starting to shut when Kent puts her hand on them, opening them back up.

'One more thing,' she says. 'You said Zach was resistant to wearing his glasses.'

'What?'

'Earlier. This morning. When we were talking about his eye condition. You said he was resistant to wearing them.'

'That's right.'

'Do his teachers monitor him at school?'

'All the time. If he takes them off, they make him put them back on. They know he hates it, but it's necessary.'

'And in the mornings, does he put them on? Or do you make him?'

'We make him,' I say. 'Where are you going with this?'

'You said earlier he has two pairs, and his main pair were broken at the fair, and that he had to use his second pair once you got home. We can't find them.'

'Okay. So what are you telling me here?'

'With everything you're saying, why would Zach choose to take his glasses with him?'

'Because,' I say, and then can't add to it. Why would he? It's not like he's going to put them on to walk the streets. In fact, every time Zach leaves the house, we have to remind him to go and get them.

'It's a curious fact, wouldn't you agree?' Kent asks, and she lets the elevator doors close.

Chapter Twenty

Kent goes into the bullpen, where Thompson is sitting at his desk going through photographs on his computer.

'Was that you?' she asks.

'Was that me what?' Thompson answers, not looking up.

'Who fed that information about the girl from the fair to the press?'

Thompson twists in his chair to face her. 'Why would I do that?'

'To see if Murdoch would react onstage.'

He frowns, takes a few seconds then says, 'Honestly, I thought about it, but if the Murdochs are innocent, then it would be one hell of a dick move, so no, I didn't do it. And if I were to leak something it wouldn't have been that. But fuck you very much, Rebecca, and thanks for the vote of confidence.'

She sighs heavily, and her body sags. 'Shit, I'm sorry.'

'As for the guy who assaulted him, he must have called Lockwood directly. He's not telling us who that is, but we're looking into it. Or did I leak that information too?'

'Like I said, I'm sorry.'

'You can make it up to me.'

'Yeah?'

'Yeah,' he says, looking back at the computer, where there's a photograph of Zach at the beach. 'You can take over for me here while I get us some dinner, and you're paying.'

'These photos are from the phones?' Earlier, the Murdochs unlocked and gave them access to their phones. Other detectives have been trawling through emails and contacts and social-media accounts.

'They are. There are three thousand split across both phones.'

'Seems like a lot of photos for people who don't own a cat.'

'They've travelled a lot, so there are lots of pictures of different cities and book festivals, but mostly they're of Zach. It seems like the Murdochs never met a photograph they could delete.'

'How far through are you?'

'Barely scratched the surface,' he says, staring back at the computer as he continues scanning through them. 'I'm going through them backward. Could be something here. Might not be. It's not like there's going to be a photograph of rope, duct tape and a shovel.'

'Okay,' she says, and she reaches into her pocket and hands him some cash. 'Bring me back a chicken salad.'

They swap places.

'Murdoch's reaction during the press conference, what do you make of it?' he asks.

'I know I didn't like it, but I don't know if it means anything. If some asshole was publicly calling you a child molester on live TV, would you sit there and take it?'

'Probably not. And after the kind of day Murdoch has been having, I guess definitely not. How'd he take the news his wife left without him?'

'Disappointed,' she says. 'His world is falling apart.'

'Yeah. Of course. I'll be back soon.'

Thompson disappears towards the elevators, and Kent flicks the arrow button on the keyboard, moving from one image to the next. Everything will need to be looked at closer – especially the more recent ones – and not by her, otherwise she'll be here for days. But she's happy to go through them while she thinks about the day, and while she waits for her dinner to arrive.

Thompson comes back from the elevator a minute later. 'I just got an email about the shoes.'

'They've been found?'

'No, but we know what brand and model they are, and the fact they were in production eight years ago,' he says, and he shows her a photograph of them. 'You know, if Murdoch did plant that print outside the bedroom window, it makes sense he'd use an old pair he had lying around rather than go and buy a new pair, so if that is the case—'

'Then he might be wearing them in an older photo.'

'Exactly.'

He forwards her the email so she can have a picture of the shoes for a reference, then she goes back to the beginning where Thompson started.

Chapter Twenty-One

Constable Green tells me how sorry she is about Zach having disappeared, and her partner gives her a glance suggesting she should keep her sympathy to herself. I rest my head back and listen to the traffic. The patrol car smells like bleach. If the person who took Zach saw the press conference, how will they react?

We reach the suburbs, which are as grim and dirty as town. Plastic bottles and fast-food wrappers have been cast to the sides of the roads. There are dirty-looking homes, dirty-looking yards, dirty-looking fences. My parents' house isn't faring any better. Weatherboards with rot that need cutting out. Lichen on the roof and moss on the downpipes. Small things that look bigger today. Things that have gotten worse since Dad died. There are no media vans outside.

Veich pulls the patrol car over and Green gets out and opens my door for me. None of us say goodbye. Earlier, the police searched Mum's house and yard to make sure Zach wasn't hiding there – her house being a logical place for Zach to go. He knows the way. It's a walk we've made on summer evenings, first with either Lisa or myself pushing a pram, then with Zach riding on my shoulders, then with him walking it.

I ring the bell. The patrol car waits against the kerb with the engine running. I stare at the marigolds along the front of the house while I wait. They look exhausted from a day in the sun. Mum opens the door. She is seventy – doesn't look any older, doesn't look any younger. She has grey hair that stops short of her shoulders – she uses it to cover her ears, one of which has the top part missing after her older brother bit it off when they were kids. A pair of glasses hangs around her neck and rattles against a small silver crucifix when she moves. She looks like she should be cataloguing artefacts at a museum. She's been crying. She steps forward and puts her arms around me and holds on tight. The patrol car pulls away.

'I'm sure he's okay,' she says. 'He's just wandered off and gotten lost, but somebody will find him. You know what he's like.'

'The police think somebody took him.'

She lets go. 'Why? Why would anybody take such a sweet, sweet boy?'

I could give her a dozen answers. Two dozen. None of them good.

She looks out at the porch and the pathway and the footpath. 'Where's Lisa?'

'At her parents'. She wanted to be with them.'

'We should go there too,' she says. 'We should all be together.'

'Not tonight.'

'I don't ... What is it you're not telling me?'

'There's nothing.'

'There's obviously something.'

'We'll go there tomorrow.'

She doesn't push it. I follow her inside. The hallway is full of photographs of our family. Mum and Dad. Lisa and Zach. Me. Grandparents who were around when I was a kid and grandparents who were gone before I was born. There are photographs of family cats over the years, each cat irreplaceable until another one came along. I can smell furniture polish. Everything is spotless. Mum has put her worry into cleaning.

If my parents' house – I still see it as my parents' house even though Dad has been dead four years – fell into a sinkhole and was uncovered in a thousand years, historians would know what 1979 looked like. We go into the dining room. Her well-worn Bible is on the table. She puts on the kettle because that's what mums do when things are bad. She did the same thing when they took Dad's body away. He was killed in a freak accident. He was mowing the front lawn and stepped onto the road so he could turn to go back in the opposite direction, and was hit by a car he never heard coming. He didn't hear it because Mum had bought him noise-cancelling headphones for his birthday a month earlier. He couldn't hear a thing with those headphones, which thrilled him no end. He used to joke that he really needed them so he wouldn't hear Mum snoring at night.

She pulls two cups from the cupboard. 'I've been praying for you all day,' she says.

'Thank you,' I say, because it would only upset her if I said prayer had the same success rate in finding missing children as going on TV and asking their abductors to hand them over. My parents weren't overly religious, but the closer my mum gets to meeting God, the more she believes in Him. The shock of learning I wasn't marrying Lisa in a church brought that meeting with God ten years closer.

'Is there anything else I can do?' she asks.

There is nothing anybody can do, and nothing I can do. Even sitting at the dining table is a betrayal of Zach. How can I drink tea when Zach is lost? How can I eat, or sleep, or shower or function in any other way? I should be out there looking for him. 'Not really.'

'Would you like to pray with me?'

No. 'Yes.'

She sits next to me and holds my hand with her left and the Bible with her right, and she tightens her grip and she prays, and I look around the kitchen trying to piece together how my life has reached this point, wondering if there are ripcords hidden here that I can pull to escape this nightmare. She asks God to watch over Zach and to keep him safe, and to bring him home, and I figure if God was going to help out He would have done it the moment Zach reached for the window.

When we're done, Mum makes our drinks. She brings mine over for me. 'What do the police know?'

The tea tastes like ash. I let it sit on the table going cold as I stare at it, telling Mum everything that has happened. She tells me she saw the news. She tells me she's never seen so much pain in people's faces before and that her heart broke, and tells me again she's been praying all afternoon. She says the journalist with those horrible questions was a nasty piece of work. She asks what the detective lady is like, and I tell her that she's good, that she's sharp, and that we're in capable hands, but I don't tell her the detective has a growing suspicion I had something to do with all of this. She asks how Lisa is doing, and I tell her that she's a mess. Then I tell her about yesterday, about what I said to Zach last night.

She drinks her tea as she takes it all in. She slowly nods. She asks, 'Is that why Lisa isn't here?'

'She blames me.'

'Well, that's silly,' she says, because she's my mum, and mums need to be on our sides, don't they? 'You can't blame yourself. We all know what Zach is like. If we had a dollar for every time he threatened to run away, we'd all be living like royalty. If you want my opinion, I think it doesn't matter what you said to him last night. If he wanted to run away, he was going to run away. When he's back, and when we've all calmed down, Lisa will see that. Everything will return to normal. I know it.'

'I hope so, Mum, I really do.'

'When was the last time you ate?'

It takes me a moment to realise it was last night. 'I'm not hungry. I'm going to take a shower,' I say, and I push myself away from the table.

'I'll get your room ready.'

My bedroom is a time capsule from when I was a teenager. A single bed against the wall, a chest of drawers opposite with a lava lamp on top, next to a clock radio with a crack in the front. There are posters of Pink Floyd albums I used to listen to with my best friend. We'd crank up the volume and smoke weed when my parents were out. I laughed about that with Lisa when I first brought her here to meet my parents. I still had some of that weed stashed under a floorboard in the closet, and we sat out in the backyard and smoked it while my parents sat in the lounge watching their shows.

I'm halfway out of my T-shirt when the doorbell rings. I tell Mum I'll get it. I pull my T-shirt back into place on the way to the front door. I open it. Detective Kent is there. I hold on to the door for balance and wait to see if she's here to answer Mum's prayers, or my worst nightmares.

Chapter Twenty-Two

Cameron Murdoch has the look on his face she's seen on others who have answered their doors to her after the sun has gone down. When people see a police officer standing on their step in the dark, they assume the worst.

'Can I come in?'

'You found Zach?'

'Not yet,' she says.

The panic leaves his face. He leads her through to the lounge and introduces her to Evelyn, his mother.

'Is there any news on Zach?' Evelyn asks.

'Nothing yet.'

'How can there be nothing? You've been looking all day.'

'We're working as hard as we can, Mrs Murdoch.'

'Then you need to work harder, and faster. He's out there some-where, and he's scared, and—'

'It's okay, Mum,' Cameron says.

'It's not okay. None of this is.'

'Can you let me talk to the detective for a bit?'

'Of course,' Evelyn says. 'Can I get you anything, Detective? Coffee? Tea?'

Kent doesn't want anything, but it will be a good opportunity to get Evelyn out of the room. 'Coffee, if you have it. No sugar, and milk.'

Cameron takes the couch, and Kent takes one of the two matching chairs, a coffee table between them. The lounge suite has floral patterns on the sides not facing the windows, and is faded bare by the sun on the sides that do. There are family photographs on the wall. Cameron and Lisa and Zach are up there in the mix.

'I need to ask you about this,' she says. She takes the photograph she printed earlier from the folder she's carrying. It's of Cameron, sitting on the deck behind their house, his legs bent so he can rest his elbows on his knees as he drinks a beer. He's looking at the camera. He looks exhausted. He's wearing what could be garden-ing clothes. The photograph was taken two months ago.

'What am I looking at here?'

'Your shoes,' she says.

She watches his eyes as they move down to the shoes. No doubt he knows why she's showing him this, but even so, he asks, 'What about them?'

'Where are they now?'

He thinks on it and then says, 'With you, I imagine. Didn't you take all my shoes?'

'Not these ones. So, again, where are they?'

He frowns. He slowly shakes his head. He looks genuinely con-fused. 'All I can tell you is where they usually are.'

'Which is?'

'They're gardening shoes. They're usually so dirty I kick them off at the back door and leave them outside.'

'They're not there now.'

'Then where are they?'

'That's what I would like to know, Cameron, because the shoes in this photograph match the print found in the garden. You want to think again if you've had any reason to stand in your garden outside Zach's bedroom in the last few days?'

'I haven't,' he says. 'Maybe Lisa threw them out. She was always threatening to, because they're old and falling apart.'

'My partner asked Lisa already. She also has no idea where they are.'

'If they're not outside my back door, then whoever took Zach took them as well. It's the only thing that makes sense.'

'And why would they do that?'

'To make you think the very thing you're thinking.'

'Which is?'

'That I stood in the garden with those shoes to make it look like somebody else was there, then threw them out, but I didn't. I didn't make that print. I promise you.'

'Okay,' she says. She leaves the photograph on the coffee table, grabs the folder, then gets to her feet.

'That's it?'

'That's it.'

Cameron stands up too. 'Earlier you were saying we were on the same side, but it sure as hell doesn't feel that way now.'

'I'm on Zach's side,' she says.

'The shoes are a coincidence. I bought them years ago. There have to be thousands of pairs like them in Christchurch.'

'We know,' she says. 'I'll see myself out.'

He stays where he is standing and watches her go.

Chapter Twenty-Three

I pick the photograph back up. I look at my jogging shoes that became gardening shoes on their way to becoming trash. The photograph was taken the first day we gardened after the winter. Our yard always gets away from us before then because it's too cold and too wet to do much about it. I can remember the day well. I got a thorn from a rose bush jammed under my fingernail so deep Lisa struggled to hook it out.

There can be no doubt now that somebody took Zach, and that same person is making me look responsible for it.

Do something.

Mum comes into the lounge. She's carrying a tray with three coffees on it, along with a plate of Anzac biscuits. Even under these circumstances she still has to be polite. She asks where Kent is, and I tell her she had to rush away.

'Without her coffee?'

'Without her coffee. I'm going to take a shower.'

I head for the bathroom.

You're the crime writer, so do something. Figure out what one of your characters would do, then do it.

'Shut up.'

Make me.

Fine. I will.

I detour into the kitchen. I open the cupboard where Dad stored the whisky we'd buy for him when we travelled. He was afraid of flying and never left the country, so this was his way of experiencing the world. There are still plenty of unopened ones, as well as several mostly full bottles. I grab the closest one. In the bedroom I crack the seal and take a swig, and a second and a third. Getting drunk isn't going to help Zach, but staying sober means staying raw, and raw leads to thinking that Mr What If's ideas aren't half bad. I also drink to blur the images of the things being done to Zach, because that's where my mind goes, of course it does, the mind of a crime writer always looking for and finding the worst in everything. I strip down and wear a towel to the bathroom, taking the whisky with me. I take another swig.

I turn the shower on and let the room fill with steam. I sit on the floor with my back against the wall and the water pouring over me. I wrap my arms around my knees. I can't make any sense of the day. I can't figure out what to do next. I feel so incredibly lost. So useless. What kind of man am I? What kind of father? What kind of husband? The answer is the same for all three – one who's not worth a damn. One who let this happen to his family. One who should be able to figure out how to find his son.

You really should. After all, the folks in your books don't sit in the shower feeling sorry for themselves. They take action.

Mr What If is right. They take action.

I get out of the shower and work away at the whisky. Mum has scooped my clothes off the bedroom floor, and I can hear the washing machine going. I find an old pair of pants and a flannel shirt that belonged to my dad. My mum never got rid of his clothes. She says she likes having them here.

'How about you help me out here, Dad?' I ask, talking to a wardrobe full of his old clothes. 'How about you tell me where Zach is?'

Dad doesn't answer. Maybe he can't because he's dead, and ghosts don't exist. Or maybe they do exist, and he can't hear me because he was run over wearing noise-cancelling headphones and, like ghosts in movies, he is forever to haunt the world in the outfit in which he died.

I head back into my room. The bottle of whisky has dropped by a quarter. I call Lisa, and she doesn't answer, so I call her parents, and they don't answer either. I leave the bottle behind and head to the lounge. The house is swaying, and I sway with it to keep balanced. My mum is sitting in front of the news. She has had her coffee and eaten all the biscuits. If she can tell I've had a few drinks, she doesn't say anything. On the TV is footage of me losing my shit at the press conference.

I slump at the opposite end of the couch and watch. I try to remember what was going through my head at that moment but can only recall a little. The Red Mist was running the show. Watching it now is like watching a stranger who looks like me but doesn't think like me. I'm watching Cameron Murdoch getting controlled like a puppet. I feel equal parts shame and anger. Lockwood played me for a fool.

The anchorman reminds me of Detective Thompson, with perfect hair and an expensive suit, the kind of guy who looks good delivering bad news. He says since the broadcast earlier this evening, Zach has been spotted at parks, at restaurants, at the beach and once riding a toy rocket outside a supermarket. He's been spotted in Christchurch, Dunedin, Nelson, Wellington, Auckland and even as far away as Sydney. Each instance has been followed up by the police, costing valuable time and manpower. Then the anchorman shifts position, and he says there is breaking news, and I feel my body go cold. With a new bout of energy, he says that the new All Blacks squad had just been named for a rugby test match overseas against England. I turn the TV off.

I go back to my bedroom and sit on my bed and stare out the window. I watch the last of the light drain from the sky, which it does, and then I watch the insects smash into the streetlights, which they do. There's a van parked opposite the house. I can see the glow of a cigarette from behind the window. A camera operator or a reporter waiting for the next stage in the story. It's only a matter of time before one van becomes two, then two become four, then four become a hundred. I close the curtains. The alcohol is numbing the raw, like I had hoped, but is failing to quieten the idea that I can go out into the city and find Zach.

Come on, you need to do something.

But what?

Mum knocks on my bedroom door. It's ten-thirty. She tells me she's going to go to bed, but asks if I need anything before she does. She looks at the now half-empty bottle of whisky on my nightstand, then says, 'I wish there was something I could do.'

She's been crying. All evening Mum has been strong for me, and in my grief I have forgotten to be there for her. I hug her goodnight, and now I'm the one telling her that everything will be okay. She becomes heavy in my arms, and I have to brace myself to hold on.

Mum heads off to her room. I pace mine. *The police are suspecting you more and more by the minute. If you don't do something now to find Zach, soon you won't have the chance.*

The whisky hasn't dulled Mr What If's ideas, but maybe the weed will. I open up the closet and pry up the floorboard. The jar I put under there twenty years ago is holding on to one final joint. I open it, thinking it will either be mouldy or dry, and it's the latter. The joint won't be as potent, but I haven't smoked since that night I introduced Lisa to my parents, so hopefully things will balance out.

I take my bottle of whisky, grab a box of matches from the kitchen, and I head out the back door into the yard. I take a drink, and I light my joint, and I sit in a deckchair. My hands shake, and my eyes water. I get the smoke in deep and hold it. It burns my lungs. I exhale and repeat, over and over, sticking with it, alternating with the whisky. It's still warm outside. Cicadas are singing from the bushes as they try to woo other cicadas, though it sounds more like one string being stroked to death on a violin than singing.

I stare up at the stars. Can Zach see them? Is he looking out a window at the same view? I get that children can disappear and not leave a physical sign behind, like a dropped schoolbag or a fallen shoe, but how can there not be anything spiritual? Not a ghost – of course not, because Zach is fine – but a vibe, or a feeling, some sense of whether their presence came this way or went that way? There must be a tear in the fabric of reality. Not a neon sign, but something, maybe something only a parent could see.

You would see it.

I would. A trail of light, maybe pinpricks, like diamonds, or long swirls of colour, like ribbons, floating on the air like the scent of a steak in an old cartoon.

You can find it, and you can follow it, and it will lead you to Zach.

'Where do I start?'

Your house, of course. But you can't go out the front. People will see you.

'Now we're talking.'

I hoist myself out of the deckchair. Everything is ... heavy. I walk to the fence, covering the ground slowly and not understanding why until I look at my feet and see that I'm taking baby footsteps. Zach's football, the one that he's stepping on in the photo, is in the middle of the yard. I try to kick it into the bushes, and end up falling over instead, hanging onto the bottle to save it. I get up and reach the back fence. I put my hand against it, pushing it, seeing how solid it is after all these years.

Then I go about scaling that fence on my way to finding Zach.

Chapter Twenty-Four

The evening has gotten away from her. She's the last person on the fourth floor, Thompson being the second to last, and he left thirty minutes ago. For the last few hours she's been going through reports that have come in through the day, all while picking through a chicken salad that has gotten warm. The list of sex offenders in the city is a long one, and detectives have been making their way through it. Thankfully the list of paedophiles, along with those caught with child pornography on their computers, is smaller, and today two dozen of them have been interviewed and crossed off the list.

Her eyes are heavy, her back is sore from sitting at her desk, and her mind feels numb. Looking through interviews of men who have been convicted of the darkest things imaginable is giving her a headache. Some of these men she knows. Some she even arrested. None have given the interviewing detectives any reason to suspect they could be involved. Detectives have been able to look through houses. A few people had rooms set up as children's bedrooms, with posters on the walls and toys on the floors. A few had sex dolls, child-sized, some dressed as girls, some as boys, dolls that weigh the same as children, solidly made, the idea of that making her stomach turn. Like always when she sees or hears about those dolls, it sparks an internal debate. Are paedophiles better off having access to them so they can play out their fantasies? Does it quench a desire, or fuel it?

There are interviews from neighbours of the Murdochs, from friends, from colleagues. The Murdochs' bank accounts have been gone through, receipts examined – they've looked for references to hardware stores where tools for restraining and hiding bodies are often found, but there's nothing there, and if they had bought anything like that she's sure they would have used cash.

Zach's tablet has been examined. There were no social-media accounts on it, and no evidence Zach has been in contact with anybody. Children from Zach's school have been questioned, none of them saying they had plans to meet up on Sunday night or Monday morning. Zach's family doctor has been interviewed. Zach was a healthy seven-year-old boy who had never shown any signs of abuse.

There have been false sightings of Zach all day long. There have been ransom demands from people pretending to have him. There have been death threats coming in through Cameron and Lisa's website. She doesn't know if the Murdochs have been online since all this began, but if they haven't, they're going to be in for one hell of a surprise. Already there are hundreds of comments on their social-media pages calling them child killers. The abuse isn't contained to those sites either, but on other sites where books are sold and reviewed. Dozens of one-star ratings have been posted since the disastrous press conference.

On her desk is a cardboard box with every book the Murdochs have written. Shops all across the city were sold out, and they had to contact the publisher for copies, boxes of them couriered down earlier. She looks through hers, reading the back covers, looking for any that deal with missing children, of which there are two. She will take them home with her.

She is in the elevator when her phone beeps. A message from Thompson.

Watch this.

He has included a link.

She clicks on it. It's a news website. There's a video. She presses play.

Zach Murdoch is sitting at a picnic table, visibly upset. Sitting opposite is Cameron. Cameron's face is bright red, and she can't hear what he's saying, because Zach is screaming. Zach throws what's left of his ice cream. It hits Cameron in the chest and leaves a mark. He reaches across the table and grabs his son's hands as people sitting nearby stand up and leave.

Zach stops screaming, but starts up again when Cameron gets to his feet. He scoops up the boy, legs kicking out the back and arms flailing out the front, and carries him off like a suitcase tucked under his arm.

Chapter Twenty-Five

I used to climb this fence as a boy, back then climbing to retrieve a cricket ball or football that had sailed over. I can scale this fence with my eyes closed, all from muscle memory. At least that's what I thought, because then the fence creaks, and my limbs creak, and my legs are longer and don't line up with the original footholds. I'm heavier too, so the fence wobbles because it's aged twenty-five years since I last did this, and I wobble too, for the same reason. It isn't until I get to the top that I realise much of the problem is I'm still carrying the whisky bottle, and since I've made the effort to bring it this far, I continue on with it as I climb down the other side.

The house belongs to Mr and Mrs Garratt, who bought the place within months of my parents buying theirs. I've known them so long they're almost like backup versions of my mum and dad. We'd have barbecues at their house, and they'd have barbecues at ours. Mr Garratt was an avid reader of crime novels, and when I was a teenager he'd lend them to me. I often think if I had grown up in a different street I wouldn't have become a writer.

The night is warm. And quiet. And calm. It's almost a full moon. The backyard is bathed in a dull, bluish light. The grass is short, and brown and crispy. I don't know if I've had too much to drink or not enough. Walking is slow, and thinking is sluggish, and the joint is almost gone.

I reach the side gate. The bolt keeping it closed is rusty and tight. I pour a shot of whisky over it, then work it up and down quietly until it slides to the left. I get out onto the street.

I look at every house as I walk. Some have dark windows, some have lights behind them, each one has the potential to be hiding Zach. Outside them all are wheelie bins that have been rolled out for tomorrow's collection, yellow-topped ones with recycling in them and green-topped ones with lawn clippings and food scraps. Each one of those could be hiding Zach too.

I carry the whisky, but I don't drink from it. I've had enough.

If that were true, you'd have left it back at your mum's house, or in the backyard, or by the gate, or left it sitting on the Garratts' letterbox, or at the neighbour's house, or in the front yard, or—

'I get the point.'

I look at every house, thinking that if the police had put any real value on my son, they would have searched all of them. They would have tossed furniture onto front yards all over the city to search and explore every inch. I pass house after house, all of them different in one way, all of them the same in another, and I stare at windows and doors looking for

something

anything

because there can't be

'Nothing.'

I flick the butt of my joint into the gutter. I never litter, but fuck it. It's a day of firsts.

When I hold my hand in front of my face, it looks bigger than I remember. Colours dance in front of my eyes, but they're not the ribbons of light I'm looking for. I take a right at the next block and then a left so I can take the same route Zach would have taken to come here. There are no cars, no pedestrians, just me and my half-empty bottle of whisky that, if I knew Zach was safe and sound, would be half full. There are no signs of Zach. No fallen shoes, or schoolbags. No rifts in time, or space, or ribbons of light.

The police barriers come into view two blocks from my house. They're being dismantled and stacked into the back of a station wagon, while other officers stand around watching. I keep walking. There are media vans on this side of the departing barriers, but everybody is calm, which must mean there is no more story to be wrung from the day. The other folks who came for the show have all gone. The station wagon with the barriers in the back does a U-turn, then comes towards me. I duck into a neighbouring property and hide behind a row of lavender. My heart is pounding. I stay down until the station wagon passes, then I pop my head up to make sure the coast is clear. It isn't. Across the street a man in dark clothing steps out from behind an oak tree. He doesn't look in my direction, because he's staring down the road towards my house. If he were a reporter, he'd be up there with the rest of them. So who is he?

It could be the man who took Zach. You do know bad people often return to the scene of the crime.

I don't know whether Mr What If is right about who I'm looking at, but I know he's right about criminals returning to the scene, so when the man across the road moves, I move with him. He turns right at the end of the block, and I stay twenty metres behind him, ducking behind trees and parked cars when I can. He walks at an even pace and he never looks back. When we get to the end of the block he turns left. I keep my distance.

He steps onto the property that backs onto mine. I stay with him. I get to the backyard in time to see him disappearing over the fence. I step carefully through the vegetable garden to the fence and stand on the bottom rail so I can peer over the top.

The man is pulling himself up and through the bathroom window.

He's not here to take anything from my house – he's taken everything there is to take; he's here to leave something behind, to plant something to cement my guilt with the police. He goes through the window head-first, and when his feet disappear I lower myself over the fence, a trespasser in my own backyard, and prepare to climb through the window to the bathroom, a trespasser in my own house.

Chapter Twenty-Six

I can't climb into the house. I need to call the police, only I can't, because the police still have my phone. I'm going to have to go out there and tell them. I either go back the way I came and approach them from the street, or I move around the house and hope the man inside doesn't see me.

You can't. You go out there and the cops are going to shove you against a car, turn you around, cuff you, talk over you and yell at you before you get the chance to explain yourself. Nobody has believed anything you've said so far; why would they start now? You'll open your mouth to explain the situation, and the police will tell you to shut it. The man in black will hear the commotion and flee.

Mr What If makes an excellent point.

Excellent Point are my middle names.

The climbing is difficult – again in no small part because I'm holding the bottle of whisky – however, the bottle itself is no longer a bottle but a hammer; the contents of that hammer have spilled out into the garden. I reach the bottle through and sit it on the ledge, then follow it. I go slow, and I rest my hands on the edge of the tub while my feet slide over the windowsill. When I'm in, I retrieve the bottle and move to the hallway door. I hold my breath and listen. All I can hear is my heart as it beats loudly, the blood pumping in my ears, all made louder by the whisky and weed flooding my system – a system that might be misfiring. Did I even see a man in black, or was I so desperate to see him that the chemicals I've absorbed conjured one out of thin air?

I concentrate, and I focus, and then I don't need to do either of those things because I can hear footsteps coming from Zach's room to my left, and I know this man is real.

I move slowly down the hallway. I step into the bedroom, where I can see a dark shape near the window. There's a gasp of surprise from him and one from me, and then we're charging at each other.

I swing the bottle, and it hits something hard and metallic. A moment later I'm punched in the face, setting off flares and colours that float through my vision. The joint I smoked makes everything happen in slow motion, which wouldn't be such a bad thing except my reactions are in slow motion too. He punches me again, this time in the stomach. I'm still holding the bottle, so I swing blindly with it, and there's a grunt as it makes impact, along with a dull thud as it hits the guy, maybe in the arm or in the shoulder. I swing again, higher this time, and there's another thud, this one more solid, deeper, a crunch going with it. There's a heavy thump as he hits the ground.

Then.

Nothing.

I keep hold of the bottle, ready to swing it at the next sign of movement.

Only there is no movement.

I crouch down next to him, my knee hitting something, and I pick it up. It's a phone. I tap the home button and the screen glows softly. It's cracked. I point it at the man on the floor. He's unconscious, or dead, or somewhere in between. It's Dallas Lockwood. Of the 'you stole my book' Lockwoods. I check him for a pulse. He has one. The world might be better off if he didn't, but I wouldn't be. Lockwood didn't take Zach. He's here for a story, or to make my story even worse.

I sit down and lean against the wall. My head hurts from the blow, and I'm puffing hard, and it's not like getting hit made me sober. The fight only lasted ten seconds, yet I feel like I've scaled Everest. I get my breathing under control, then head to the front door to get the police. I have my hand on the handle when Mr What If starts talking.

What if the police don't believe you?

What if Dallas Lockwood lies to them and says he followed you here?

What if they think that, not long after losing your temper on live TV, you assaulted the reporter who made you lose it?

And then the big one. *What if going out there makes things worse?*

I let go of the handle. I feel flat. And tired. And angry. Moments ago I was about to confront the man who took Zach. Instead of the nightmare ending, it's still going. I head back to the bedroom. Lockwood is starting to groan. He's going to wake with one hell of a headache.

I reverse my earlier journey, taking the bottle and his phone with me. Out through the window, across the backyard, the fence, the neighbour's backyard, the street. Lockwood will be a few minutes behind me. He won't risk hanging around.

I try out my new phone. It asks for a pin number, so I put it on the ground and stomp on it until it stops asking. I put the empty bottle in a recycling bin a block away from my mother's house. Then I cross the Garratts' front yard and move the rusty bolt back into place and climb the fence – easier this time.

I go inside, clean up in the bathroom and take some painkillers, my mum sleeping through all the sounds I'm making.

In bed I stare at the ceiling even though I can't see it. I wait for the headache to fade. It doesn't.

Zach has been missing a day and a half.

I close my eyes, thinking there's no chance of falling asleep.

I'm right.

TUESDAY

Chapter Twenty-Seven

I fight the urge to phone Kent at five a.m., and again at six, but give in at seven. She doesn't answer. I leave a message to call me back, along with Mum's landline number. I call Lisa. She doesn't answer. I call her parents. They don't answer. My head hurts and my mouth tastes like carpet, and I promise myself never to drink alcohol again – a promise I can see myself breaking before the day is out. At least there's no more weed left.

My clothes are in the dryer, so I put on more of Dad's – a pair of shorts that are a little tight, and a T-shirt with a print on the front that's so faded there's no telling what it used to be. His shoes, which I wore last night, fit okay, a pair of sneakers with a strap of Velcro that goes across the top, which people used in the eighties when shoelaces all became too complicated.

My mum is an early riser, and today is no different. She's making us breakfast. The last time I ate was Sunday night, before putting Zach to bed. I'm starving, and Zach might be starving too, but even so I have to eat – I have to keep my strength up so we can find him.

'Is that a bruise on the side of your face?' Mum asks.

I rub the spot where Lockwood hit me. 'I walked into the door last night on my way to the bathroom.'

'You need to be more careful,' she says, then asks how I slept. I tell her I slept fine.

'You don't look it,' she says. 'Shall we pray again?'

'Maybe later?'

She turns back to the pan. I can tell she's upset with me, but I don't feel like correcting that. Mum dishes up bacon and eggs. We sit at the table the way we've sat at this table thousands of times over the years, sometimes with my dad, then sometimes without him. I shift food around with my fork before taking a bite, and then I devour all of it, each mouthful a guilty mouthful. We don't make any conversation. I wish I'd said yes to the power of prayer. A rubbish truck drives past the window, picking up the bins outside.

Kent calls me at seven-thirty. I ask her if there are any updates, and she says there's nothing significant, but she would like me to come to the station this morning. I ask her if I can go there now, and she says no, she isn't there yet, and we settle on nine-thirty. I wonder if the insignificant thing is what happened at my house last night. She tells me my house has been cleared and I can return there.

I update Mum. She has forgiven me for not wanting to pray. I rinse the plates and load up the dishwasher before asking if I can borrow her car and her mobile. Her phone is large and heavy, and her car is small and old. The driver's seat sags, and the engine struggles to turn over. A spider climbs out of the air vent, then climbs back in when the engine catches. I hit the remote, and the garage door squeaks and squeals and opens; I back out of the garage, and I hit the remote again, and the door squeals and squeaks and closes. Across the front, slapped on thick with red paint, are the words *Child Killer*.

I tighten my hands on the wheel and stare at the two words. Drips have run down from them, making it look like blood. *Child. Killer*. Two words. They didn't write 'Child Abductor'. Or 'Parents Let Child Wander'. But *Child Killer*. Because they think I murdered Zach. Because they believe this is the first morning in seven years we've all woken up and Zach is no longer in it. Which would mean tomorrow would be the second day. And the day after the third. And so on, days rolling into one another, an endless amount of them when Zach is never going to come home from school, never going to laugh at the dinner table or cry when we won't let him watch TV, when he won't skin his knees or get wiggly teeth or drip ice cream all over his hands. It's not just this version of Zach they think is dead, but the future versions. The ones who go to high school, who learn to drive, who get a girlfriend, who don't come home until two in the morning. There will be no Zach that gets a job and leaves home and gets married and makes little Zachs. No Zach to roll his eyes at his hopeless parents. No Zach to put us into a retirement home.

The Red Mist returns. I want to knock on doors and find who did this, then drag them back and forth across those two words like a rag to wash them off. It's an irrational thought, but right in this moment irrational thoughts are all I have. The person in the van parked outside the house last night, is that who did this? If I hadn't snuck away, I could have heard it happening and stopped it.

I call Kent and tell her what's happened. She says she'll send somebody around to look into it.

I open the door so the words face the ceiling. I go inside and tell Mum, and she cries, and she tells me everything is going to be okay.

'Because you prayed, Mum? Is that why?' I regret the words as soon as I've said them. 'I'm sorry. I shouldn't have said that.'

'It's okay,' she says, but I can tell it isn't.

'I have to go,' I tell her. 'I love you, Mum. I know I never say it, but I do.'

This gets her crying even more. I leave her in the lounge to her tears and tissues and head back outside.

Chapter Twenty-Eight

Kent gets off the phone from Cameron Murdoch. She knew about the vandalism to the garage door. An unmarked patrol car had been parked down the street, keeping an eye on the house. There was another one parked outside the farm where Lisa's parents live. She wanted to know if either of the Murdochs were going to leave their houses last night, and if so, where they were going. When the officers called in that they were witnessing people from a nearby van painting on the garage, they were instructed to do nothing. She didn't want there to be a confrontation. She didn't want the Murdochs to know they were being followed. As it was, the Murdochs didn't leave their houses until this morning.

'Sorry about that,' she says, sliding her phone back into her pocket. She's tired – last night she read the first fifty pages of one of the books she took home before falling asleep. It was about a family who went for a picnic, the two children running into the woods to play and only one of them coming back. It's nothing like what's going on with the Murdochs now, but then again, she didn't think it would be. If this was unfolding like one of their books, it would only serve to make them look guilty. Then again, they'd probably say they'd have to have been insane to plot a crime based on one they wrote. 'You were saying?'

The woman carries on. Her name is Deborah Hubbard, and since Kent has been here, it's occurred to her that even if the world could stop climate change, Hubbard could single-handedly keep the skies polluted with the amount of cigarettes she's going through. They are standing outside Deborah Hubbard's house, where her wheelie bin has been tipped over, all the recycling inside it dumped into the gutter. Hers isn't the only one. Every bin in the street is lying on its side, plastic bottles and cardboard and garden waste scattered across the road and footpath. Other neighbours are cleaning theirs away, but most haven't noticed yet or haven't had time. They are only a minute away from Antberry Park, where Cameron Murdoch drove yesterday morning, looking for his son.

'I was saying it happens every month or so. Doesn't matter what bins are out, they don't care. Neighbourhood kids, no doubt. I know we're not the only ones who have called the police in the past, but I guess there's nothing you can do, right? Otherwise you would have. Tipped-over rubbish bins isn't exactly a priority, is it. Hopefully the kids will grow out of it, or shift away, or get hit by a truck,' she says. Then she grimaces, and she adds, 'I don't really mean that last one.'

'It must be frustrating,' Kent says.

'We've been living here for forty years, and for the first thirty-eight of those everything was fine. Only now it ain't. We pay our taxes, and governments and councils take and take from us, and when we need something back, nobody cares.'

Kent doesn't want to get off-topic. 'Tell me exactly where you found the clothes.'

'Well, they stood out, because everything else is recycling, right? Or garden waste. I don't know what bin they came out of, because everything was mixed up when they got tipped over, but, people being people, they always throw shit into bins that ain't theirs, and the kinds of people who don't care about that probably don't care much about the environment either, but I care, and the recycling and garden bin ain't no place for clothes, so I scooped them up and tossed them into the waste bin.'

This week it's the yellow and green bins that get picked up in this neighbourhood. Next week it'll be the red and green bins – the red being for general waste. The green bins are picked up every week, and the red and yellow ones alternate. This part of the city, they're collected on Tuesday mornings, most people putting them out the night before.

'Sammy, my husband, he'd have thrown them into either of

those bins and be done with it. He thinks recycling ends up in the same place as everything else. I'd rather him throw recycling into the trash than trash into the recycling, if you know what I mean.'

'I do. So you were saying you picked up the clothes and threw them out?'

'Right in there,' she says, and then points towards the corner of the house where the fence meets the garage. There's an alcove next to the back door where the bins are stored. The red-topped bin is there with the lid open. 'I used a stick, on account of the blood on them, because I didn't want to touch that. Then I went inside, and I was reading the news, and I saw that report about the missing boy, and there was a picture of the clothes he went missing in, and I thought, hey now, those were the clothes I just picked up. So I took me a look, and sure enough I was right, so I took them inside and called you.'

'We're grateful you did,' Kent says.

'The shoes I wasn't so sure of. The picture in the news is of new ones, but the ones I found look like they got mauled by a lion.'

'And your bins are always left outside?'

'You can thank Sammy for that. I always think it'd be easier leaving them in the garage where we can have at them, but he says they stink and they get in the way. So we leave them out the back door.'

'They're there all the time?' Kent asks.

'Pretty much.'

'So anybody has access to them.'

'I guess so. I told Sammy we should leave them on the other side of the house, and he always asks what the point is. He says it's not like anybody is going to steal them.'

Zach's clothes, and Cameron's gardening shoes, are on their way to the lab to be examined. The recycling bin too. The blood on the T-shirt is concerning, but there isn't enough to jump to any conclusions – she's been told there's maybe a tablespoon's worth, and she knows that on clothes a tablespoon of blood can look like a quarter of a cup. If it is Zach's blood, it's likely from a minor wound.

'Doesn't make sense, though,' Deborah Hubbard says.

At the moment Kent is thinking about how she can use this discovery to her advantage. The press don't know. If one of the Murdochs did throw these clothes into the bin, then there may be a way to trick them into coming back. 'What doesn't?'

'If those clothes belong to that kid, why separate him from them? I'm always watching reruns of *CSI*, so I know how these things work. Makes no sense to me that if they killed their boy and buried him, why not bury him with his clothes too?'

It's a good question, and one that Kent has been asking herself from the moment she got here.

'Aren't these people meant to be crime writers?'

'Meaning?'

'Meaning they can probably plan the perfect crime, but the one thing they can't plan for is bad luck. And that's what this is, right? Bad luck for whoever left these clothes here. The Murdochs, I've read all their books. I'm a big fan. An older book of theirs, one of the main characters is a crime writer. It was my favourite of theirs. I remember something the character said. I looked it up when I was waiting for you to arrive, so I could get the line right. The guy, he says, 'Maybe that's the thing about crime writers – you just can't trust them.''

Chapter Twenty-Nine

The hangover affects the way I see the world. It's making the morning brighter and slower. It's making the car louder and the roads busier – though I suspect that last one may not be because of the hangover. It takes me twenty-five minutes to drive to Lisa's parents' farm with an engine that runs well but a chassis that puts every bolt and rivet to the test. The spider from earlier climbs out of the vent and onto the dash and watches the view that starts out with people driving to work, and ends with people driving tractors. Pine trees hedge the boundaries between farms, and ditches create boundaries between the farms and the road. The landscape is littered with slowly pivoting irrigation systems that look like jungle gyms where the manufacturers didn't have any paint. Beyond here, the farms get bigger, stretching out across the Canterbury Plains – the plains a part of Canterbury Province, which is as flat as a chessboard and from above would look like it too, if a chessboard had a thousand green squares and none of them straight. At one point I have to sit in my car and wait while sheep spill onto the road as they are moved from one paddock to another by farmers on quadbikes. Zach loves it when this happens, his face glued to the window as he waves at the sheepdogs as they zigzag back and forth, yapping away.

Andre and Rita Cross own a small farm along the edge of the city bridging the gap between suburbia and big-farm country. It's two hundred acres of mostly hay, which every December or January we help bale up and stack to the detriment of our muscles. There are a few sheep, half a dozen cows, some chickens, and no media. There's a chest-high gate spanning the width of the gravel driveway that I have to swing open before I can drive through, then have to swing closed so the dog doesn't escape. Not that I can see the dog. The farmhouse is ten years old, white-brick walls and a dark-steel roof designed to look like overlapping tiles. The entire building is ringed by a well-oiled brown deck that Zach calls 'the moat'.

I get out of the car, and the dirt from the gravel driveway slowly settles behind me. It's hot out here. It's a big sky and at the moment there's nothing in it except the sun. The view is one I would love to have when writing – mountains on the horizon, paddocks rolling into the distance, long boundaries lined with trees hiding the neighbours, none of whom are within shouting distance.

I step onto the deck, but don't make it to the door before it opens. Andre comes out. He's in his late sixties, six foot tall and wiry, with veins that pop out of his deeply tanned arms that would make bodybuilders and heroin users jealous. There are white circles around his eyes because he always wears sunglasses when he's outdoors. He has buzz-cut grey hair that's a holdover from his days in the army, and a trimmed moustache to match. The only time he's ever mentioned his days in the army was when I started dating Lisa. He told me he saw some bad shit when he was overseas, and if I hurt his daughter he'd be forced to see some more. Now he's giving me a look that suggests that time has come. He crosses his arms, making the muscles bulge and the veins stick up. Behind him, Kahn, their ten-year-old golden retriever, comes out and sits on the deck, watching me.

'Elsie isn't here,' he says. He's always called Lisa 'Elsie' to the point if I asked him where Lisa was, he might respond by asking who I was talking about. His voice is gruff. His words are clipped. 'Even if she were, I wouldn't let you in.'

I don't say anything.

'You're not welcome here,' he says.

'Come on, Andre. You know I'd never hurt Zach or Elsie.'

'The man I saw on TV last night sure looked capable.'

'I guess we don't all have the luxury of army training to keep us calm when being accused on live TV of being a paedophile.'

His jaw tightens. His eyes narrow. He looks like he wants to hit me.

'I want to see Elsie.'

'I want you to leave.'

'This is bullshit.'

'You heard me. I want you to leave.'

'Please don't do this. I don't mean to sound angry, or upset anybody, but I'm scared. That's all.'

He keeps staring at me.

'You always think you know what you'd do in a situation like this, but you don't. You can't even think. All you can do is react, and I reacted badly. I'm sorry.'

His jaw loosens and tightens, making the side of his face flex.

'Jesus Christ,' I say. 'What do you want me to say?'

'Elsie told me what you said to Zach. Way I see it, there are two possibilities. Zach, he's a tough kid to look after. I know you struggle with him. I saw the video of him freaking out when you were having ice cream. I—'

'What video?'

'I know you must have moments where it's all too much for you, and yesterday was one of those moments. Personally, I think you told him it was a good idea to run away, because you wanted him to. Whether you wanted him gone for a few hours, a few days, or for good, I don't know, but when he said to you he was going to leave, you encouraged it.'

'Fuck you, Andre.'

He pokes a finger into my chest. I don't back up. Kahn gets up off his haunches and growls at me. There was a time when Kahn loved me, but that time ended when Lisa, his favourite person in the world, got pregnant. Lisa has always thought it was cute that Kahn was jealous. I don't know if that's what it is – or even if that's a thing – but what I do know is ever since then Kahn has hated me.

Andre carries on. 'Elsie ... when she came here last night, she wasn't Elsie. She was a ghost. A shell of the person she used to be. I've never seen her like that. Never knew that sort of thing could be inside her. *You* did that to her.' He pokes me again. 'That's what something like this does, Cameron; it reveals who we really are. I used to see it in the army all the time. Men and women trying to behave one way, behaving another when the shit hit the fan, and you get a real measure of their worth in that moment. Me, I'm getting a measure of yours, and you're an angry guy struggling to keep his mask from slipping, but I see you. I see you for who you really are.' He pokes me again for good measure. 'If Zach doesn't come home, she won't survive it. We'll do everything we can for her, but I know she won't survive it. And if you've had anything to do with him disappearing, you won't survive it either. If you hurt that little boy, I will kill you. I'm not kidding, Cameron. This isn't hyperbole. If you hurt that boy, I will take your life.'

'Like I said, fuck you, Andre.'

He jabs me again, harder this time, forcing me off the moat and back onto solid ground. He keeps pointing at me. 'You're not welcome here anymore. No matter how this thing pans out, and I pray to God we get Zach back, I don't want to see you again, you got it?'

'Andre.'

He turns around. Rita is standing in the foyer. Rita is an older version of Lisa. Same dark hair, but greyer; same eyes, but eyes that have seen more; same face, one that is usually only a little more worn than Lisa's, but today looks like it's been spun through the dryer. This is Lisa in a hundred years, not thirty.

'Enough of that,' she says to Andre.

'He needs to know,' Andre says.

'And he knows. There's no need to keep telling him.'

He turns back towards me to say something else, but by now Rita has come outside. She puts a hand on his shoulder, and he turns back towards her.

'You've said your piece, now go back inside so I can say mine.'

He points at me again. 'Remember what I said.'

He disappears inside, but I imagine him waiting beside the doorway within earshot. Kahn stays sitting on the deck, watching.

'I'm sorry about what's happening to you all,' Rita says, and she puts her hand on my arm but doesn't go in for the hug. 'For what it's worth, Andre's grief has got his thinking all messed up. I don't think you had anything to do with what happened, despite what people are thinking.'

'Is that what people are thinking?'

'I take it you haven't seen the news?'

I shake my head. 'Andre said there's a video from when Zach flipped out at the berry farm?'

'Yes,' she says. 'There's more too.'

'Do I want to know?'

'No. I can't imagine that you do. Listen to me, Cameron. I've always thought of you as a good person. What we saw last night, I know that's not you. Not really. But what we saw was something that's inside of you, and it frightens me that it's something Zach or Elsie might see if things aren't going your way.'

'I would never do anything to hurt them.'

'I know that,' she says. 'Of course I know that. You would never. Until something happens to change that. I'm scared for Zach, for Elsie, I'm scared for you. When Zach comes back we're going to need some time. All of us,' she says. 'Andre shouldn't have said what he said about you not being welcome here anymore. But things won't be like they were. I don't know how they'll be, only that they'll be different.'

'I understand,' I say, but I don't. We should be the united front Kent talked about. We should be rallying around each other, not divided like this.

'Where is Elsie?'

'She left half an hour ago. Andre offered to drive her, but she wouldn't have it. She took my car. She thought about calling you, she really did, but as to why she didn't, you'll need to ask her.'

'Was she going home?'

'That's what she said. She said she's meeting Detective Kent later this morning. What happened to your face? You get into a fight?'

'I fell over,' I say. 'We're going to find Zach.'

I wait for her to say *I know*, or, *of course*, and when she says nothing, I turn around and walk away. For years every time we came here Rita and Andre would stand outside waving as we left, watching until we got to the gate. Now they're back inside with the door closed before I even reach my car.

I leave the gate open when I leave. If the dog runs away, then so be it.

Chapter Thirty

I have an hour before meeting Kent, so I return home, a trip that takes longer than it should because I get stuck behind a guy towing a jetboat who is probably heading out to the Waimakariri River, which starts in the heart of the South Island before winding its way through a hundred and fifty kilometres of landscape before spilling out into the Pacific Ocean a little north of Christchurch. On a still day we can hear the engines of the jetboats from our house seven or eight kilometres away, and Zach will pretend they are dragons, and he'll race outside and look for them in the sky.

The road outside my house is so thick with reporters and on-lookers that I have to park two blocks away, where Lisa has parked Rita's car. Reporters swarm me with questions, and the onlookers swarm me with requests for selfies. People are holding up signs, some say *Justice for Zach*, others say *Justice for Ivy*. I have no idea who Ivy is.

I keep my head down and forge forward. There are two patrol cars parked directly outside my house, but there should be twenty. Four officers block the crowd from following me onto my yard. I get to the front door and realise I don't have a key, but it turns out it's not an issue because the front door is unlocked. I step inside and close the door against the noise of all the questions still being yelled.

The house is different. It takes a few moments to recognise it, but the atmosphere has changed, Zach's loss palpable, the tragedy of it having formed a monster that hides in the shadows – but physically the house is different too, having taken on different layers of tidiness. The upper layer, where Zach can't reach, is all parallel lines and even distances. Prints on walls, photographs spaced evenly across flat surfaces, souvenirs from countries all laid out just so. Then there's the middle layer, where couches and chairs and tables are all squared up or at ninety degrees, nice angles pleasing to the eye, a holdover from Lisa's Feng Shui phase years ago. There's often a mixture of Zach's things on top of them – books he's flicking through, cars he's playing with, action figures off to war, a result of Zach's current messy phase. That phase gets messier around the bottom layer, where Zach's toys are shoved up against walls or under couches, the typical mess seven-year-old children make when making a house a home. All of that is here, but different, every layer shifted by a few degrees, furniture nudged, everything picked up and put back, but not exact.

I call out for Lisa. She doesn't answer.

I pass our offices, where the shift isn't as subtle; drawers tipped upside down, and folders and documents dumped into cardboard boxes. My computer is gone. My laptop and tablet are gone. Lisa's office hasn't fared any better. In our bedroom the bed has been moved and the mattress turned over, and all the clothes from our drawers have been stacked on it. We have a spare mobile kept in the top drawer, along with our spare credit card, some foreign cash, a pair of international SIM cards and our passports, all of it gone.

Lisa is in Zach's bedroom, lying on his bed, hugging one of his jerseys. She has changed into some old clothes of hers she left at her parents' years ago. Her knees are tucked up to her chest, and her head rests on a balled-up jacket of Zach's. The room has been treated with respect. The things that haven't been taken away have been put back into place.

Lisa's eyes are the only things that move as I step into the room. I put a hand on her hand, and she doesn't flinch. She stares at me without any expression. Her eyes move to the bruise on the side of my face, but she doesn't say anything.

'How are you feeling?' I ask, knowing how she feels, hating the question, but I don't know what else to say.

She doesn't answer. She looks like I feel, like she hasn't slept and is being torn apart from the inside. I sit on the floor against the wall where I sat last night. I stare at the spot where I left Lockwood. There's no sign he was ever here. When Zach comes back we're going to sell the house and look for a corner of the world where these things don't happen.

Good luck.

We sit in silence. After a while I get to my feet. Lisa isn't watching me anymore. 'We have to go. Detective Kent is expecting us.'

She doesn't answer.

'Is there anything I can do? Anything I can say?'

'You can take it back,' she says. 'The last two days. Take it all back and make it so it never happened.'

'I wish I could.'

'But you can't.'

'You know I can't.'

'Then stop asking me if you can do anything.'

'Are you coming to the police station with me?'

'No.'

She doesn't add anything else.

'I love you, Elsie.'

'Stop calling me that. My name is Lisa.'

'Okay. I'm sorry.'

I walk out of the room, turning back when she asks, 'Have you seen the news today?'

'Not yet.'

'Mum's tablet is in the lounge. Why don't you take a look? Why don't you look at everything?'

I go out to the lounge. The tablet – a gift we bought for Rita last year – is on the coffee table. I haven't been online since all this started. There is a moment of hesitation – unless human nature has changed overnight, this is going to be bad. And I know it's going to be bad because Rita warned me earlier.

Even so, I go online.

I was wrong about this going badly.

It's far worse than that.

Chapter Thirty-One

We're the first news story that comes up. Of course we are. The headline is 'A Very Murdoch Mystery'. There's an accompanying photo from the press conference last night. I'm standing behind the table, leaning forward on my fists, my face red and the veins in my neck ropey. My mouth is open as I'm in the middle of saying something. This photograph is evidence that Andre was right when he said I am a man whose mask has slipped.

The article covers the basics. Zach disappeared. The police believe somebody has been watching him, and Zach's attempt to run away led to his abduction. The police have grave fears for his safety. Then the article focuses on us. A crime-writing duo who have knocked out eleven bestsellers over the last eleven years, some of those books dealing with children who have gone missing. The article doesn't say we reap what we sow, but it does mention the irony, that we have made a career out of everyday things that hurt everyday people, only to have those same everyday things come back and hurt us. The article mentions the police are looking for a pair of shoes, and goes ahead and describes them, and there's a picture too, but there's no mention that I own an identical pair. It goes on to say the girl who fell out of the bouncy castle is Ivy Munro, and that her mother has refused to comment on the case. There is a link to a video somebody shot yesterday of Zach screaming and throwing his ice cream at me. I pick him up and tuck him under my arm, the way we always do. I've never seen myself do it, but it looks like child abuse. Was it? No, because Lisa picks him up the same way – you just have to sometimes. The article finishes off by saying that in cases like these, the parents are often the first suspects.

Other articles are similar, and I scan through them hoping I can learn something new, which I do: I learn our Facebook page has been bombarded with comments, so I go there to check it out, thinking that maybe somebody who has seen something useful will say something useful. There's an icon to tell me there are two direct messages. I click it. There aren't just two messages, but two hundred – all of them have been read, most likely by the police, the latest two only having come in a minute ago. I read the newest message.

Rot in hell you child rapist.

I read the second message.

You deserve a bullet. #JusticeForZach. #JusticeForIvy.

The older messages are similar, as are the comments posted publicly, of which there have to be at least a thousand, most of them including the hashtags *#JusticeForZach* or *#PrayForZach*. People telling me what they're going to do if they ever see me alone, from shooting me in the back of the head to skinning me alive and putting me on display. A minority of fans say we are in their prayers, that they know we're not capable of what the other lunatics are saying. Anything they can do for us, just ask. Zach will be okay, and how can they get a signed copy of our latest book?

There are memes. Photos from the press conference have been posted. The worst one is an angle where it looks like I'm pointing back at myself. There's a bold caption saying, 'This guy gets what it's like to kill your son'.

I don't know who I hate more. The whackos who want to kill us, or the whackos who find humour in all of this pain.

I log into my email, aware I'm running late to meet Kent. There are two accounts. One is the joint account for our writing, where readers can contact us through our website, and one is my personal email account. I start with my personal one, knowing our fan email account will look like our Facebook page. All the new emails that have come in over the last day have been read by the police. Mostly they're from friends and family, all concerned and asking how they can help. There are work emails from publishers and editors dealing with the new book. There are insurance bills and newsletters, and the general stuff that builds up in your inbox whether your child has been kidnapped or not. There's an email from Jonas Jones, a self-proclaimed psychic – though I guess they're all self-proclaimed – who has written books on communicating with the dead, and who now has his own TV show about solving cold cases. We met Jonas years ago, as we have the same New Zealand publisher. Lisa had coffee with him back then because we were basing a character on him – not that he knew that. Though, thinking about it, he should have. She said he came across as a genuinely nice guy. I read his email. He tells me he can help, and to give him a call. I hover my finger over the delete button, then, for the first time ever, I wonder, what if it's not all bullshit? I email him back to ask what he needs.

I switch email accounts. All the fan mail that has come in over the last day has been read by the police. I was right to think it was going to be the same as our Facebook page. Die this way, die that way, suffer this way, suffer that way. People pray for us. Others pray to hurt us.

I look out the window, where the journalists and onlookers are waiting. It's a scene from *Dawn of the Dead*, where the zombies are milling about, calm and contented, until something whets their appetite.

That whetting happens a moment later when I step outside. The police help me to my car, the first block full of people, the second block free. I swing the car around and drive away. Nobody follows. It takes me fifteen minutes to get to the police station, and another five to find a parking space. I'm forty-five minutes late. I head through the front door and talk to an officer behind a desk, who tells me to take a seat. On the walls are posters recruiting new officers, with slogans like 'Make a Difference' and 'Be Somebody'.

The elevator dings and the doors opposite open. Kent steps out and signals me over.

Chapter Thirty-Two

Cameron Murdoch looks tired and dishevelled, and there's a bruise on the side of his face. They reach the fourth floor. She takes him into the same room they were in yesterday, and they take the same seats.

'We've spoken to over three hundred people so far,' she says, 'so far most of them neighbours. We're in the process of cross-referencing all of their statements so we can get a picture of who was where on Sunday.'

His hair is pointing in all directions, and he runs a hand through it, but it doesn't help. 'Did you look into other disturbances in the area? Other burglaries?' he asks.

'We did,' she says, 'and there was nothing.'

'What about this guy from the fair who hit me? You know who he is?'

'Not yet.'

'Not yet? Somebody must know, since Lockwood knows.'

'Lockwood isn't giving up his source, but we're working on it.'

'I'm thinking, you know, he might have followed me, right? He was mad enough to punch me, so maybe he's mad enough to punish me by taking Zach.'

'It's a lead we're working on,' she says. 'You were saying yesterday

Dallas Lockwood accused you of stealing his idea. Have there been similar accusations?'

'Never. Is this all you have?'

'We're still speaking to people who live near Zach's regular haunts. We're talking to teachers, and students and parents. We're talking to everybody.'

'It's not enough.'

'We've got people searching wheelie bins too.'

'What?'

'It's possible other evidence used to get Zach out from his house was dumped.'

'In a wheelie bin?'

'Yes,' she says, watching him closely. 'Bin day is today, but many were accessible on Sunday night. We've got the collection trucks holding off until we've gone through them.'

'All of them?'

'If we can, yes. It will take days,' she says, wanting him to think he has time to retrieve the clothes if he's the one who put them there. The bin will be returned and placed under surveillance. 'Criminals dump things in those bins all the time, thinking they won't be searched, but if there's anything to find we'll find it.'

'Like what?'

'Zach's schoolbag maybe. Or his glasses.'

'Or even Zach. You think he's dead, don't you?'

'No.'

'Good, because he isn't. If he were, I'd know it. I'd feel it, somehow, and if I thought he was, if I really thought for one moment he was dead, then I wouldn't be here right now. I'd be at home eating a bullet.'

'You have a gun, Mr Murdoch?'

'No, I don't, but I wouldn't need one. All I'd have to do is offer myself to the people writing all that shit online about us. Have you seen the crowd growing outside my house?'

'Your story has captured the public's attention in a way I haven't seen in a long time,' she says. 'A lot of bad things have happened in this city, and a lot of bad people have gotten away with it. The pressure builds, and every now and then a case will come along and that pressure explodes. Zach's disappearance is that case. I've seen the emails and the online anger, and I know you had to be helped to your car earlier. We've assigned more police to your house for your protection.'

'Criminals often return to the scene of the crime. Whoever took Zach could be standing in that crowd outside my house right now. Are you watching them? Are you interviewing them?'

'We are. We're filming everybody who shows up. Anybody suspicious will be spoken to. We're monitoring all your messages, both the public and private ones. Anybody who threatens you will be warned and possibly charged. There's something else you should know. People are capitalising on what's happened and are asking for a ransom.'

'I don't understand.'

'Something like this brings people out of the woodwork. You had three emails yesterday from people saying they had Zach, asking for money. We followed through with every one, and each was fake.'

'I didn't see them.'

'We deleted them so you wouldn't panic. But I'm going to give you back your phone before you leave here, which will give you access to new emails as they come in. We will continue to monitor your account, and if we see them we will take care of them. It's important if you do see one, that you don't respond or delete it.'

'What if one is real?'

'Then we will discuss that with you and deal with it.'

'People really do this? They pretend to have taken a missing child so they can ask for money?'

'It's not uncommon.'

'And you arrest them?'

'We do.'

'It's sick. Doing something like this, when parents are scared and willing to do anything, it's—'

'I agree,' she says, and she'd put each and every one of them in jail if she could. 'Now, I want to come back to something we spoke about yesterday, about your career.' The shift in subject throws him. She carries on. 'I asked you how your sales were going, and you said they were good. That's not entirely true, is it?'

He shrugs. 'Look, I wasn't trying to hide anything from you, but a whiff of failure can end a career. If you're failing in one country, it may just be a matter of time before you're failing in another. It doesn't take long for the rot to lead to erosion. When people ask how things are going, we say they're going great. It's a survival instinct. Things have been tough for everybody.'

'You mean for other authors?'

'Yeah. Plenty of writers are losing contracts. People spend more time binge-watching TV these days than they do reading, and there are plenty of folks who find ways to pirate books for free. So yeah, it's true we're not doing as well as we used to be doing, but having the mortgage paid off gives us room to breathe.'

'You're spending more than you're earning, mostly with travel.'

'We have no choice. It's all about shaking hands and meeting people. If we don't travel to promote the books or meet our publishers, then our careers dry up.'

'Our forensic accountant says at the rate you're going you'll have to remortgage your house within the next three to four years.'

'It's not like that. We've got a new book coming out in six months.'

'That's the book that was supposed to come out this month? Before Christmas?'

'It got delayed.'

'We spoke to your agent. He said you've struggled on the last few books, and this one has required more work than previous ones, and that the delays were on your end. He said your publishers are becoming increasingly annoyed about it.'

'Sometimes life gets in the way, you know? And every time we're out there promoting a book is less time we're at home writing one.'

'Your advances are getting smaller, as are your royalty cheques.'

'Publishing is tough at the moment.'

'Can you explain to me what a mid-list author is?'

'Excuse me?'

'Your agent, he said you and Lisa are suffering from the mid-list curse.'

'Then I'm sure he also explained what that is.'

'He did. He said it's when publishers will spend money to promote authors who are incredibly successful, and they'll spend it on debut authors, but not so much on those in between. He said it can be close to impossible to get off it,' she says.

'It sums it up.'

'It must be frustrating seeing things happen for other authors and wishing it could happen for you. Must make you think that no matter what you try, you're never going to get the success you want. Mid-authors, sometimes they just disappear, and nobody bats an eye.'

'What has this got to do with Zach?'

'You take Zach with you when you travel, right?'

'Not every time. It depends on school, but yes, we often take him, probably more times than not.'

'Must be expensive.'

It takes him a few seconds to answer. No doubt he can see where she's going with all of this. 'We manage.'

'And his behaviour and mood swings, I imagine it's hard working from home when he's there, especially during the school holidays. I saw the video from yesterday at the berry farm. I can imagine if that happened on one of those long-haul flights, or on a train somewhere or at a festival, it would be tough.'

'Like I said, we manage.'

'Do you take him to meetings with you? When you're onstage with Lisa, do you have somebody babysitting him?'

'I know what you're getting at. You're trying to establish a motive where there isn't one. That video you saw, sure, Zach can be like that, but it's rare.'

'How rare?'

'Once every month or two. Things build up for him, then he vents.'

She bites her tongue, and doesn't say, *Like you?* Instead, she asks, 'Did he vent on Sunday night?'

'No. I mean, a little, because he said he was going to run away, but it wasn't like it was in the video. We love having Zach with us when we travel, and like I said, we have a new book coming out soon that will turn things around.'

'Your agent told us how frustrating the market has become, and that things are on a downward trend for you. But you're right, it's not just you, but plenty of other writers too. You have a job you love, but one you can't know is sustainable.'

'You're barking up the wrong tree,' he says.

'And what tree is that?'

'You think we saw Zach as getting in the way of our lives, but you're wrong. Our lives are better off for him being in it. We would give everything up for him, everything.'

'Okay,' she says. She leans back. 'That's it for now.'

'That's it?'

'Let me get your phone for you.'

She leaves him in the interview room and goes into the task-force room. Cameron's phone is in an evidence bag. Earlier, after discovering Zach's clothes and Cameron's shoes, and matching the blood type on the T-shirt to Zach's, they were able to obtain a warrant that allowed them to install tracking software on the phone. She grabs a second bag too, this one with his wallet inside. She goes back into the room and has him sign a form so she can hand them over.

'What about my car?'

'Forensics will have it cleared later today. The bruise on the side of your face,' she says, as she walks him to the elevator. 'You want to tell me what happened?'

He reaches up and touches it. 'I walked into the bathroom door during the night.'

Maybe it's true. What's the alternative? That his mother punched him?

'What happens now?'

'There are a lot of things going on behind the scenes. There are a lot of man hours going into this. We're doing everything we can.'

'You have anything other than platitudes?'

'Go home and be with your wife. Wait there until we have some news.'

'That's it?'

'That's it,' she says, and she takes the elevator down with him, and she stays standing in it and watches him go out onto the street.

Chapter Thirty-Three

I stop a few metres from the police station and stare down the street at nothing in particular, just cars and pavement and rubbish bins and people and, thankfully, no media. I feel like one of those guys who's been thrown back in time and has to ask a bystander what today's date is. A car races by. Somebody leans out the passenger window and screams 'homo' at me. I can't tell whether it's because he thinks I'm gay, or if this is how he identifies himself to strangers. This is one of those Christchurch things. It's the price you pay to live here. New Zealand is like that. Clean and green. Stunning beaches and mountains that will make your jaw drop, rivers and lakes so beautiful it can make you believe in a higher power. Friendly, innovative, good-natured people who will do anything to help. But we're also a nation where more babies and children are beaten to death per capita than any other country. We're a nation where wives are assaulted by husbands and girlfriends assaulted by boyfriends for not having dinner ready on time, for looking at somebody wrong, for the national sport team losing. We're a nation that has ads on TV to remind us to not drink and drive, not to shake our baby to death when it's crying, to call for help rather than killing ourselves when things become too much.

The guy leaning out the window calls the next guy a retard before disappearing around the corner.

I walk to the car. I keep my head down, and nobody else talks to me or screams abuse. I check my phone. It still has some charge. There are missed calls and messages from people I don't know, probably reporters, that I will listen to later. Jonas Jones has emailed me back saying he can come to the house this afternoon. I tell him that would be good.

There is a larger police presence when I get home, but there are more people too. There are distinct groups of people. There's the media, comprised of folks with cameras and microphones. There's the looky-loos, folks curious whether a real-life show is much different from a TV one. Then there's the third and largest group – folks who brought the show with them. They're carrying placards with photos of Zach on them, some with the old chestnut *Child Killer*, others with photographs of me with a bull's-eye over my face, lots of *Justice for Ivy* and *Justice for Zach*.

There are now patrol cars parked at the start of the block using a barrier to allow or deny traffic, but they're not stopping people from walking. I reach the barrier. 'Don't run anybody over,' the officer tells me, before moving it aside.

I roll forward, not running anybody over like the officer asked. I can hear the crowd chanting something, but can't tell what it is. I pull into my driveway but don't have the garage door opener because I'm driving Mum's car. I get out, and the chanting becomes clear: 'Ex-e-cute. Ex-e-cute.' I know some of these people. There are neighbours, there are parents from school, there are people from restaurants and cafés that we visit. Media folks get past the police and push microphones and cameras in my face. I try to back away, clipping the wing mirror. When I reach out to stop myself from losing balance, I knock somebody's microphone to the ground. The police tell everybody to back up and tell me to get inside, which I do, locking the door and leaning against it. I listen to the shouting, then go into my lounge and listen to it from there instead. I peek out the window at all the people filling the street. On the other side of that madness Zach is still out there.

Chapter Thirty-Four

Lisa isn't home. I call Kent, and she tells me Lisa was driven to the station half an hour ago. We must have been there at the same time.

'Do you know if she'll be coming back home?'

'I don't know what her plans are, but I'll tell her you called.'

I go back online. I go to the missing-persons website run by the police. Zach's profile is the top one. Height, weight, blood type, all the data is there. I scroll down the page. There are so many missing people it should be added to the list of things New Zealanders are good at. Mostly these are adults who have decided to live off the grid, but not all of them. There are cases where foul play has been suspected, wallets and phones and cars left behind. There are other missing children. A father who took his son overseas when it was his weekend to have him, and now can't be contacted. Another father who took his son camping two summers ago on the West Coast, neither of them to be seen again. Down south an eight-year-old boy disappeared a year ago after a fight at a park with his parents. He refused to leave, and his parents drove away to prove a point, only to return two minutes later to find their son gone. There is a small girl, Zach's age, who went missing two weeks ago after she fell off the back of a boat and disappeared into the water.

I switch off the tablet and turn on the TV. Like I knew it would be, the lead-in for the midday news is Zach's disappearance. They are crossing to the scene for a live update. Our house, other media, the crowd of people, all of it appears on the screen. Seeing the world outside my window being broadcast back inside is surreal. The reporter has his sleeves rolled up and the top of his shirt open, a real working man slogging it out in the summer heat to give us all the important updates. He's mid-twenties, with hair slicked to the side and square-framed glasses. I've seen him on the news before, and in the past he always seemed like a decent-enough guy, but not today.

Rolled Sleeves confirms there have been no significant updates, though police are following a number of inquiries. He says a very tired Cameron Murdoch has returned home to an angry chant of protesters, then one of those protesters gets their ten seconds of fame when he says, 'If Murdoch is happy to beat up girls who get in his way on a bouncy castle, imagine what he's willing to do to his own son.'

'Cameron Murdoch,' Rolled Sleeves says, 'put on another display of emotion earlier when, rather than answering one of the many questions put forward to him by the media, he grabbed and threw a reporter's microphone to the ground.'

There's footage of the moment where I reached out to stay balanced, knocking down the microphone. It makes me look bad, but I'm looking bad anyway, looking anaemic and dishevelled, and wearing clothes that no longer fit.

The screen cuts back to Rolled Sleeves. He says I'm currently holed up inside, his terminology making it sound like I've taken hostages. He says Lisa was taken away earlier and driven to the station for more questioning, that separating the parents in any investigation is common.

Then Rolled Sleeves moves on to the activity on social media. He says police are talking to and will prosecute people who are making threats. He says over the last twenty-four hours our books have accrued hundreds of reviews across multiple websites, most of them – but not all – one star. A screenshot comes up with two of them.

'One Star! I would give this book less if I could. I don't need to read it to know it's garbage. These people are murderers! Don't buy their book!'

'Five Stars! I particularly liked the bit where they killed their son in real life!'

He says it's more publicity than we've ever had, which makes me want to put the old adage of all publicity is good publicity to the test by going outside and strangling him.

The crowd outside gets louder, and people on TV all turn in one direction as they follow somebody walking towards the house. The camera shifts away from Rolled Sleeves and focuses on Jonas Jones as he steps onto our driveway.

Chapter Thirty-Five

Jonas Jones, in his suit and tie, looks more like an insurance assessor who enjoys telling sick people they're not being covered than he does a psychic. His hair is slicked back and his tan is over the top, his teeth so glaringly bright I'm worried the windows are going to melt. He has a leather satchel slung over his shoulder. I had forgotten he was coming over.

One of the police officers comes to the front door. He asks if I'm expecting Mr Jones, and he manages to ask this with a straight face, and I manage to tell him that I am, also with a straight face. He signals Jonas to come through. Cameras follow Jonas as he strolls casually to the front door, basking in the attention on the way. That's when I realise he isn't here to help us; he's here to help himself. Something that should have been plainly obvious I failed to recognise through my hope and grief. When the questions come – and of course they were always going to – he takes a few moments to give a statement, saying he's here at the request of the Murdoch family. He says what we need to focus on is getting Zach back safely, in whatever way possible. He says thank you, as if the media have done him a service by listening to him, and I figure they have.

He steps through the door, and I close it behind him.

'Hell of a crowd out there,' he says. He puts his hand out. 'It's nice to see you again, Cam, though I wish it were under better circumstances.'

I shake his hand. It's cold and clammy, maybe as a result of Hell having frozen over. It must have for me to have let him in.

'Is Lisa here too?'

'She's at the police station.'

'Have there been any updates?'

'Nothing yet.'

'Okay then. I suggest we get started.'

'What do you need from me?'

'Coffee, if you've got it.'

I lead him through to the kitchen. He tells me how sorry he is to hear about what is happening. He tells me that Zach looks like a really neat kid, before going on to say he can see the effort the police and media are going to in order to paint me in a bad light. 'I want to let you know I don't believe any of this garbage they're saying about you. I don't need to be psychic to see that.'

It's the nicest thing anybody other than my mum has said to me since Zach disappeared. I resist the urge to hug him. Have I gotten this guy wrong all these years?

'I know why I'm really here,' he says. 'I know you don't believe in psychics, but I also know that you know a good psychic can read a room. Only reason you really let me come here is because you think I might see something the police have missed. Am I right?'

He is right. Speaking to the dead isn't what makes a good psychic psychic – it's being able to see things in plain sight that others would miss. 'I'm willing to do anything, try anything, to get Zach back.'

He slings his satchel over the back of a kitchen chair and leans against the table. He asks me about Zach, about what kind of boy he is, what his favourite things are, movies, toys, cartoons. When the coffee is ready we sit at the table. He stares at me as I talk to him. There is something engaging in that look, like he's examining the very inside of my soul, and for the first time I can see why people believe in him. Then again, people believed in Charles Manson too. Jonas Jones can't talk to the dead – no psychic can – I know this for an absolute fact, and today I'm willing to be wrong.

'How about we start in Zach's room,' he says, when he's finished his coffee.

We start in Zach's room. I stand in the doorway while he touches clothes, and toys, and books.

'Does he have a favourite toy?'

'A plushy ghost.' We bought the ghost for Zach when he turned three. They'd sleep together, and watch TV together, and play together, until last summer when it was demoted to the toybox. I go through the toys that have been tipped out, but can't see it. I look around the room. 'He's about this big,' I say, and spread my hands thirty centimetres apart, looking like a fisherman describing the one that got away, if the one that got away was a plushy ghost, because it isn't here. It's not under the bed, or in the closet or in the drawers. Zach must have taken it with him.

'He has this,' I say, picking up a stuffed squirrel that Zach named Mr Squirrel when we gave it to him years ago. 'He loves the squirrel almost as much as the ghost,' I say, which isn't true, but true enough.

He holds the squirrel for a few moments, then tucks it under his arm so he can turn his palms up to the sky, catching all the vibes and feelings and thoughts that are raining down that no mere human being can see. He closes his eyes and tilts his head as if he's listening for a far-off voice. He nods, and he smiles and says, 'I can feel Zach's presence. It's so strong. So vibrant. Zach ... Zach's a special kid. Different from others. Am I right?'

'He's strong-willed.'

'He is. I can feel it. I can also feel another presence.'

'What kind of presence?'

'A good one. There's somebody close to you, somebody keeping an eye on Zach. It's ... it's hard to tell, exactly. An older person. Somebody who died not recently, and not a long time ago, some-body who ... wait,' he says, and I wait, and he crushes his eyes closed and tilts his head. 'His name ... David, it's David. No, not David. Damien,' he says, then shakes his head and tilts it a little further, tuning in that voice from the other side and making it clearer. 'That's not right. Something like that. Dennis maybe?'

'My dad's name is Dennis,' I say, well aware the voice telling him that didn't come from the other side, but from Google.

'Yes, yes, of course. Dennis is your father,' he says, slowly moving his head from side to side. 'I can see that now. He wants you to know that Zach is okay.'

I'm angry at Jonas. He's a fraud and a charlatan, and my dead dad would tell him that if he were really here, but instead of asking him to leave, I ask, 'Does he know where Zach is?'

More of the tilting head. 'Your father doesn't know, only that he's okay, and that ... and that ... Wait, I don't understand,' he says.

'Don't understand what?'

He scrunches his face tighter. 'Your dad is saying there's somebody else with Zach, only ... it's not somebody ... it's ... I can't make it out. Do you know somebody named ... William?'

'William?'

'No, not William. Will. Will ... Willy? Do you know a Willy? Your dad is saying that Willy is okay too.'

I feel a shiver run down my spine. 'Willy is the ghost.'

'No, he's not a ghost ... he's ... I'm not sure.'

'No, I mean Willy is Zach's toy ghost. The one I can't find.'

'Oh,' Jonas says. 'Okay, that makes sense. Zach is safe, and he's finding comfort with Willy, that's what your father is telling me.'

A search online would have given him my father's name, but not Willy's. We've never mentioned him onstage or in any interviews.

'Can I look through the rest of the house?'

'Of course.'

I show him around, Jonas carrying Mr Squirrel with him. It reminds me of the day a real-estate agent first showed us the place. Our first book was doing well, and royalty cheques were coming in, and we wanted a bigger house, a nicer house, somewhere we could have children. Then Zach came along, and Jonas Jones is right – Zach is different, he is a special kid, and it's that specialness that made us take our time about having another child; a prospect we stopped discussing a few years ago.

'Well?' I ask, when we're back in the dining room. 'Do you know where Zach is?'

'It's not that simple.'

No. I didn't think it would be.

'He's alive, I know that. He's not near. Not far away. Water. I think he's being kept in a house near water.'

'The beach?'

'Or a river.'

Which doesn't help, because everywhere in New Zealand is near the beach or near a river. It is, after all, a country made up of two large islands and a bunch of smaller ones, with hundreds of rivers in hundreds of directions. Saying Zach is near water is like saying the sun is near space.

'I'm sorry I can't give you any more. I have a better feel for Zach now, and your dad, so I will continue to try. I promise.'

I feel like a fool for ever letting this man into my house. 'How did you know about Willy?'

'Your father told me.'

'You came here already knowing,' I say.

He nods slowly. 'I came here to help you, not argue with you. It's up to you whether you want to believe. Being psychic doesn't give me the ability to tell you what to think.' He picks up his satchel. 'Can I take the squirrel with me?'

'Sure, but Zach is going to want him back when we find him.'

'Of course.'

We shake hands at the door, and then there's an explosion of shouting and questions as he steps outside. A police officer walks with him as he enters the fray of cameras. He stops to answer questions, allowing himself to become part of the biggest news story going around.

After all, that's why he came here, isn't it?

I go into the kitchen and pour a good-sized gin and tonic. I lean against the bench with my drink in my hand and my back to the window. That's when I see it. On the fridge. Zach's drawing of our family. Mum. Dad. Zach. We're standing outside a wonky house with a wonky roof and a wonky door. There's a single window in the middle, and a yard that has so many angles it would be impossible to mow. But the small boy – Zach – is holding hands with his friend. His friend is half Zach's height, and has a drooping sheet over him, with eyes and a mouth. We're all labelled with messy handwriting. Mum. Dad. Zach. Willy the gost – no 'h'. Jonas would have seen the picture when he was looking around the house. He'd have figured out who Willy was when I started telling him about the soft toy. When we couldn't find Willy, he gambled that Zach must have taken the toy with him. It's what psychics do. It's who they are. Not people who talk to the dead, but people who excel at watching the living.

If he was lying about the ghost, then he was lying about knowing Zach was still alive.

I toss my drink into the sink and call Detective Kent.

Chapter Thirty-Six

They're in the taskforce room, four of them, Kent, Thompson, Vega and Travers. They're bouncing around what they've learned from the books and what they've learned from watching media interviews the Murdochs have given over the years. The table in the taskforce room has Zach's clothes and Cameron Murdoch's shoes on it, as well as a dozen empty coffee cups and plates full of crumbs, Travers and Vega both having just devoured mince pies. So far none of them have come up with a plausible theory as to why Zach's clothes would have been dumped separately from wherever Zach is being held.

The interviews the Murdochs have given and the panels they have been on during their careers are, at least from a prosecution point of view, gold. However, Kent is keeping in mind something her colleague said, the one who chaired that panel years ago where she met the Murdochs the first time. Her colleague showed a side of himself that she never knew was there, and later, when she mentioned it, he said it was like he put on the mask he thought the audience would want to see. Like her colleague, the Lisa and Cameron Murdoch in these interviews aren't the real Cameron and Lisa, but a version of themselves they show to the public. Even so, some of the things they say are damaging; lines like, 'We kill people for a living', and, 'if anybody can get away with murder, it's a crime writer'.

There is a panel called Getting Away With Murder, where Cameron says, 'I hope Lisa never falls down a flight of stairs. The more the evidence suggested she fell, the more the police would figure I'd know how to make it look like an accident.' Lisa says, 'Cameron always has to be nice to me, because I know how to make him disappear.' Then later, on the same panel, she says, 'I have no doubt we could plot the perfect crime if we had to. It's what crime writers do every day. It's all about selling the misdirection.'

The interviews are in front of audiences, and it's obvious they say these things to go for the joke. However, if Lisa did fall down a flight of stairs, Kent suspects Cameron Murdoch's assessment may be true – the more evidence suggesting he was innocent, the more they might start to suspect him. After all, isn't that what is happening now?

Her phone rings. She recognises the number. 'It's Cameron Murdoch,' she says, and people pause the videos they're watching and stop clicking at keyboards and turn towards her. A few minutes earlier they saw on TV Jonas Jones leaving the Murdoch house. She's dealt with Jones before. He's a psychic who used to be a car dealer, and she isn't sure in which capacity he would have lied more. She also isn't sure why the Murdochs had him over – one theme they've discovered in the books is a constant disrespect for all things psychic.

She takes the call.

'Zach has a favourite toy,' Murdoch says. 'It's a plushy ghost, around thirty centimetres, give or take. It's not here. Did you take it?'

She doesn't remember seeing anything like that. If it was taken, it would be with the rest of the evidence from the house. She has a list on the table in front of her, as well as access to photographs of every item on her laptop. 'Text me through a photograph, and I'll call you back.'

'Is there any news?' he asks.

'Not yet.'

'Is Lisa still with you?'

'She was earlier, but I believe she's now on her way back to your house.'

'Jonas Jones was here,' he says.

'I know.'

'He thinks Zach is still alive. He thinks he's near water, and that he's okay.'

She rolls her eyes. It's such an automatic reaction she's thankful she's on the phone to Cameron and not standing in front of him. 'We'll keep that in mind.'

'I get it,' he says. 'He's full of shit. But he's not wrong about Zach being okay.'

'Text me through that photograph.'

'I'll do it now.'

They hang up. The toy disappearing could mean a few things. Best case is it helps in keeping Zach calm. Worst case is he's been buried with it. When parents kill their children and try to hide the crime, they often bury them in a favourite blanket, clutching their favourite toy. Murdoch must know that, and that it looks bad for him, yet he's called anyway. More misdirection?

A photograph of a plushy ghost comes through to her phone, along with a message that says, *The toy's name is Willy*. In the photograph Willy is at the beach, propped up by a bucket of sand, next to Zach, who has been working at building a sandcastle.

She sends back a text to acknowledge she has the photograph, then shows it to the others. 'Anybody recognise this?'

None of them do. She doesn't see any reason the ghost would have been taken into evidence, and she confirms this by going through the list.

Thompson's phone goes off. He nods and listens, then says, 'You're kidding. Uh-huh. And we can't stop him? Uh-huh. Okay. Thanks.' He hangs up and turns towards her. 'You remember that journalist last night who wound Murdoch up?'

'Dallas Lockwood.'

'That's the one. He's getting interviewed on TV tonight. Apparently he's also pieced together all of this,' he says, spreading his arms out to indicate the books, the interviews, the articles.

'We knew it was only a matter of time before the media went down this path,' she says.

'Yeah, but in the hands of Lockwood, that path is going to be a bloody one. We're going to need to put more officers outside the Murdoch house, because after this evening those crowds are going to get bigger.'

Chapter Thirty-Seven

The crowd outside gets loud, and a moment later Lisa comes through the front door. She's been crying. Her hands are shaking. She looks like she's lost five kilos. I step forward and she steps forward and we wrap our arms around each other, and it feels good, it feels amazing. We're finally the united front.

'I'm sorry about this morning,' she says, 'and sorry about my dad.'

'It's okay.'

'I'm sorry about everything. I don't blame you, I really don't, but it's hard, and I don't know what to do, I don't know what to think, or what to say. I can't imagine a life without him. I can't.'

'We'll find him.'

'Do you think so?' she asks, almost pleading it. 'Do you really?'

'I'm sure of it.'

She smiles. The saddest smile I've ever seen. 'I think so too. I heard you had Jonas Jones here. A psychic, Cam? Really?'

'He thought he could help. I didn't see the harm.'

'I...' she says, and then she stares at our intertwined fingers. 'I guess I'd have done the same thing. I'd have thought this is bull-shit, but what if it's not?'

We move into the lounge. I tell her what Jonas said. About Zach being safe. Near water. That Willy is with him. 'I rang Kent. She said they didn't have Willy, which means Zach took him.'

'How did Jonas know Willy was with him, and not with the police?'

I have given this some more thought. 'He guessed. He saw all the other toys here, and figured if the police hadn't taken them, they wouldn't have taken Willy. And if they did have Willy, then Willy would only have been with Zach in spirit.'

I put my arms around her. I tell her about the photo I sent Kent. Zach was making a castle at the beach, and Willy sat watching. A few minutes after the photo was taken, a wave came in and took Willy back out with it. Zach screamed and cried, and I had to go out after the ghost, which looked like it was going to be easy because Willy started out floating, but then became difficult when Willy became waterlogged and sank.

'I thought we were going to be in big trouble, but then a minute later that wave came in and returned Willy to shore.'

She smiles. 'Remember when we got home? We put Willy in the washing machine on a gentle cycle, praying he wasn't going to fall apart.'

It's a good photo. A good memory.

That evening we were able to pull Zach back from the threshold of a CZM when Willy came out of the dryer in one piece too, and Zach was able to take him to bed.

'Willy ended up being okay, the same way that Zach is going to be okay.'

She cries harder then, her body shuddering as I hold on tight.

Chapter Thirty-Eight

Kent calls me a few minutes before six. 'We've been given a heads-up there is something you're going to want to see on the news.'

'What kind of something?'

'A Dallas Lockwood kind of something, and what exactly that is I don't know. I wanted to ask you if there's anything we should be worried about.'

'Like what?'

'Maybe something that goes back to when he accused you of stealing his idea? Maybe something to do with Zach?'

'I don't know what he has. Can't you ask him? Or get the station to ask him?'

'No.'

'So he could be going on TV and spouting all kinds of bullshit. Is that what you're telling me?'

'I'm telling you we don't know what he'll say, but given the way the public is perceiving this case, and Lockwood's brand of journalism, we're going to post more officers outside your house.'

'Are we safe here?'

'Yes.'

'Are you sure?'

'Our people know what they're doing,' she says. 'I'll call you if I learn anything else.'

She hangs up.

I find Lisa standing in the middle of Zach's bedroom, staring at a poster with a bunch of superheroes on it saving the world. It doesn't have any contact numbers for us to call them. I tell her what Kent said.

'Maybe it's a good thing,' she says. 'Maybe this guy has figured out something that can help us.'

'If he wanted to help us, he would have told the police what he had.'

I consider telling Lisa about what happened here last night, but decide against it. She will insist that we tell the police, but we can't. Telling Kent I came back here when I wasn't allowed to would only serve to make me look guilty. On top of that, I don't know if Lockwood figured out I was the one he fought with.

We go to the lounge to watch the news. I peek out the window at the crowd. There are more people. More signs. *Justice for Zach. Justice for Ivy.*

I turn on the TV as they cross over to Rolled Sleeves. He's standing outside our house. He says the same things he said earlier today, then adds to it, saying the story has gone international, especially in the countries where our books sell. He talks about the crowds outside our house, the online hate, the many book reviews that have been posted over the last twenty-four hours. He talks about two radio DJs who have been suspended after they played a song on air this morning that they wrote overnight. It's a folk song from our perspective, played with a fiddle, and sung by both DJs. They play a section from the chorus.

> *Killing our son was a whole lot of fun*
> *We swear we didn't fiddle him for long*
> *If you want to have us fiddle your children*
> *We can include them in our fiddling song.*

Lisa shakes from hearing it. The fiddling solo starts, then the TV cuts back to Rolled Sleeves. The DJs getting suspended tells me there is still hope in the world, but it's short-lived, because Rolled Sleeves says the song has gone viral, and that others are recording their own versions to share. Already an online petition to reinstate the DJs has collected more than ten thousand signatures.

Rolled Sleeves wraps up by saying they'll be taking a more indepth look on tonight's episode of *Seven Now*, which is a current-events show that focuses on one or two stories of the day. He says they'll be talking to Dallas Lockwood for more information.

The feed goes back to the station. The story changes. It moves on to the boy-racer crisis in Christchurch. Teenagers and twenty-something-year-olds trying to replicate what they've seen drivers do in movies, their efforts seeing them added to the road toll. And yet, with nothing else to do, we carry on watching stories about politicians who shit over every idea unless it's their own and insist that two plus two doesn't equal four if the other side says it. There's a story about whales beaching themselves up north, farmers down south complaining about not enough rain – after complaining for the last month there's been too much, then there's sport and weather, like any of it really matters.

Outside, people are launching into the fiddling song.

The news folks fade out, and a different set of news folks fade in. There's a guy in a sharp suit with an even sharper haircut. Marcus Shaw. He's a good-looking guy – but aren't they always? He looks serious – but don't they always? Serious eyes and a serious smile all set in a square face with a square jaw. He wishes us a good evening. Then he says that tonight they're going to take a closer look at Cameron and Lisa Murdoch and the disappearance of their son, and with him in the studio is Dallas Lockwood, a journalist whose online blog garners tens of thousands of views every day within New Zealand alone.

Lockwood is wearing enough makeup to cover whatever damage I did to him last night. He smiles at Shaw then smiles into the camera, and then he says it's a pleasure to be there, and I don't doubt that it is.

I grind my teeth and ball my hands into fists.

This can't be good.

Of course it can't be.

Chapter Thirty-Nine

Lockwood has done his research. He's studied our interviews. He's gone through newspapers, and magazines and TV appearances. He's watched clips of Lisa and myself onstage at writers' festivals, some here, some overseas – of which there are many. In interviews we often field the same questions: Where do you get your ideas? Why did you both want to become writers? What's it like writing as a duo, how did that begin, how does it work? I'll say something one year and say the opposite the next. My views change. Not on big things, but on little things. We evolve. The books evolve. Our styles evolve. Sometimes we go for a laugh onstage, other times we'll keep it low key – all depends on the audience. Dallas Lockwood has cherry-picked sections from these interviews, including clips from a panel where I say if anybody could get away with murder, it would be me, and that I hope Lisa never falls down a flight of stairs because I would look guilty. Lisa says she knows how to make me disappear. We were joking, and the audience was laughing, only the laughter is cut from the footage. We say we could plot the perfect crime.

Lockwood talks about magazine articles where we've said similar things, those articles being shown, the sections highlighted. One after the other after the other, hammering the point home.

By now I'm leaning forward on the couch, my legs shaking. It's not just interviews and media that Lockwood has studied, but our books too. He talks about an older book where the main character, a crime writer, tells the police that he's smarter than them. He talks about another book, in which a seven-year-old girl goes missing at a family picnic, then reads a passage from the opening chapter, from the kidnapper's point of view.

'"Kidnapping is all about becoming a magician. You get the police to look here instead of there. It's misdirection, and an easy one, because the police will always look for the obvious. The key to making people disappear from this world is to show the police a different kind of obvious."'

Lockwood puts the book down and looks into the camera. 'What we have here isn't a different kind of obvious, but parents who believe they can get away with murder. But don't take my word for it, take theirs.'

There's another panel. I'm onstage with Lisa. I say, 'Never trust a crime writer. We're always figuring out how to pin everything on you.'

Shaw says, 'Wouldn't somebody who has said all these things publicly be a fool to try and put any of it into practice? Isn't it inviting suspicion?'

'Back then they couldn't have envisioned a day where they might want to disappear their son. And whether they did or didn't, it doesn't matter, because it's a double bluff. They can say, "How stupid do you think we are that we'd try the very thing we say we could do?" Look at this afternoon for example.'

'This afternoon?'

'With Jonas Jones.'

'I don't follow,' Shaw says.

Lockwood smiles. 'The Murdochs set all their books in Christchurch. There are plenty of characters that overlap, mostly small ones. There's a psychic in four of them, just a small background character, but they don't paint a pretty picture of him. In fact, the psychic in their books is often the butt of their jokes.'

'Okay,' Shaw says, and it's obvious he doesn't follow. Nor do I.

'The Murdochs have said several times in interviews they don't believe in psychics, and yet today we see a psychic show up at their house. Why?'

Shaw still looks confused. I'm confused. Lisa looks confused.

Lockwood carries on. 'It's about putting on a show. About making people believe they are doing everything they can. Cameron Murdoch knows his every move is being watched. He didn't ask a psychic for help because suddenly he believes; he asked for help because he likes the optics. He wants people to think he's doing everything he can. Cameron and Lisa Murdoch know how to paint a scene. However, today's discovery will now let people see the truth.'

'Today's discovery?'

'We know the police were looking for a pair of shoes that were used to create a footprint in the garden outside Zach Murdoch's bedroom. Today those shoes were found, and I can confirm they belong to Cameron Murdoch. What does that suggest? It suggests Cameron planted a footprint to make it look like somebody had taken his son. I can also confirm that Zach Murdoch's blood-soaked clothes were found alongside Cameron Murdoch's shoes.'

My heart stops.

'Cameron Murdoch, perhaps both of the Murdochs, are as guilty as hell.'

'We can't know that.'

'Perhaps, but what we can know with absolute certainty is that we're dealing with people who for years have been saying this is exactly the kind of crime they could get away with.'

Chapter Forty

Kent gets off the phone from Cameron Murdoch, a call in which she told him it's true Zach's clothes have been found, but they weren't blood-soaked like Dallas Lockwood said – that there was about as much blood as you'd expect from a cut finger. He sounded genuinely distraught, and angry that she hadn't told him earlier. Was it an act? Lockwood, along with a growing percentage of the public, sure as hell thinks so.

She thinks how Sunday might have gone. Cameron, already on edge from being punched at the fair. Zach, becoming hysterical while they were having ice cream. Cameron lugging him out to the car. Did Cameron try to get his son to stop crying, and he shook him too hard, maybe bounced his head into something solid? Or was there an accident? The kid is running around at home, and trips and falls, or perhaps he rolls out of his bunk and breaks his neck. Accidents aren't always ruled accidents – and maybe the Murdochs are thinking they'll get a detective who's had a bad day and has a point to prove. So they roll the dice and stage a kidnapping. They use an old pair of shoes to leave prints in the garden and they open the window, and they pack Zach's bag full of food, and they get rid of him, along with his toy.

Makes sense.

And Zach's glasses?

Easy. They're scooping everything together the same way they would every morning before he goes to school, and the spare glasses get scooped up too out of some kind of muscle memory.

And the clothes being dumped, along with the shoes?

Not so easy.

Why pack Zach's bag with food so it looks like he ran away and then leave footprints in the garden to suggest he was abducted? And, if they were pushing the abduction angle, why not jam a screwdriver into the window so it looks like it was prised open? Why dump the clothes and shoes separately from the schoolbag? Why not keep everything – including Zach – in the same place?

She pushes herself away from her computer. Around the fourth floor, other detectives have been watching the same broadcast, and she wonders which of them leaked the information about the shoes and clothes being found. It's possible Deborah Hubbard, the woman who found them, couldn't keep her mouth closed between tossing cigarettes into it, but she suspects that's not the case, that the same person who leaked information about what happened at the fair with Gwendolyn Munro is the same person who leaked information about the shoes to Lockwood.

Either way, Lockwood's interview has been damaging for the Murdochs. She's going to need more officers guarding the house, because she thinks the crowd in the street is going to grow.

WEDNESDAY

Chapter Forty-One

Kent is stuck in traffic on the way to work when her phone goes. Up ahead, a truck delivering bread to a supermarket has run up on the kerb and taken out a lamppost, the lamppost falling into traffic and blocking the road. She takes the call. It's Mason Clark. Clark is one of the forensic technicians working through the evidence taken from the house.

'I saw the news last night,' he says. 'I guess Lockwood just killed your surveillance on the bins. I'm guessing you're annoyed.'

'I am,' she says. If Cameron did dump the clothes, there's no reason for him to go back. She's annoyed about it alright.

'Well, I might have something. We've been working all night on something. There being no fingerprints around the window or windowsill in the boy's bedroom doesn't add up, right? Well, I can now tell you he didn't climb out the window at all. He couldn't have.'

'Tell me why.'

He tells her why. When he's done, he tells her again.

'You're sure?'

'A hundred per cent.'

'I'll be there soon.'

They hang up, and she calls Thompson. Up ahead cars are getting jammed up as they try to do U-turns. She's going to have to do the same. Thompson answers. She spells it out for him. They haven't been working together long enough to know each other well, but she can tell he's excited.

'He's sure?' he asks.

'He seems to be. You really think we're on the right track here?'

'You don't?'

'I don't know.'

'What's not to know? You saw the way he treated his kid in that video, and we know he has a temper. If somebody was setting him up, his shoes would have been left at the house, or easily found with Zach's clothes a block away. We know Zach's window wasn't prised open, and we know if he had climbed out he would have left fingerprints and scuff marks there, and what Clark just said clinches it for me. We also know Zach was a difficult kid and a financial drain who was a drag on their career.'

'They said Zach spoke about running away. Why not stick to that story? Why make it look like he had been abducted?'

'We'll find out when we bring them in. One of them will break.'

'Okay,' she says, and a car toots at her when she starts a U-turn. She ignores it. 'I'm on my way to the station. Let's get a warrant and go pick them up.'

Chapter Forty-Two

The sense of loss is so crushing, so crippling, that when I try to get out of bed I can't move. The headache is back. I went to bed thinking that I wouldn't sleep, but I have, on and off, over the last eight hours. Lisa isn't in bed next to me. Her side hasn't been slept on. I find her in Zach's room, on his bed, still asleep, or pretending to be. There is a melody stuck in my head, and it takes me a few moments to realise it's the solo from the fiddling song.

It's Day Three, and the media and the folks online are eager to remind everybody that Day Three is when the investigation moves into the recovery mode. Today is the official start of the police no longer looking for a boy, but for a body, and maybe that's been the case since they found blood on Zach's T-shirt. I go out to the lounge and peek outside. I don't know if it's the fact it's Day Three, or Lockwood's report from last night, but something has brought far greater numbers into the orbit of our house. There are bigger signs and angrier messages, but at the moment everybody is calm, eating breakfast, and drinking coffee and chatting among themselves, most of the signs not even being held up. A young guy who lives diagonally across from us has staked a sign into his front lawn, saying people can use his bathroom for two dollars a visit. There's already a queue to his door. He also has a barbecue set up and is selling hotdogs, and there's a queue there too. The media vans have doubled in number, and the newer ones have doubled in size. There is a group of young men dressed up as priests and nuns. They're all drinking. I ring Kent. She doesn't answer. I leave a message.

Lisa comes out of Zach's bedroom. She's wearing her clothes from yesterday, having slept in them. I'm still in mine too, having done the same. I make coffee and neither of us says a word. The morning is made up of slow movements. The kettle boiling, stirring the coffee, carrying the cups to the table, all of it arthritic. Even walking across the kitchen floor is slow, the air syrupy and dragging over us, the floor boggy. We sit at the table and sip our coffees, possibly the worst I've ever tasted, even though I've made them no different from any other. At eight o'clock the crowd outside grows lively, and a few moments later the doorbell rings.

I let Kent in. She is followed by Thompson. We sit in the lounge like we did on Day One, only this time Lisa is next to me, and we hold hands. Kent puts a folder on the table. It's closed. She has a thing for folders.

'We have some more questions for you,' she says. Her tone is flat and unpleasant.

'All that stuff Lockwood said on TV is bullshit,' I say.

'There's no denying he pointed out some serious coincidences,' she says.

'No, he didn't,' I say. 'You can't judge writers by what they write. The books – that's a different universe for us. Just because we can write about serial killers doesn't mean we are those people. Otherwise every crime writer in the world would be in jail.'

Thompson leans forward. He's resting his elbows on his knees. 'That being said, it must take a seriously sick mind to come up with the things you write about.'

'I can say the same thing about you,' I say. 'About both of you. After all, it must take a certain kind of personality to surround yourself with people's pain and misery and death. I mean, at least ours is only fiction, but you have a job where every day you see the worst. What does that say about your mind? That you get off on it?'

The answer isn't spontaneous, but something our crime-writer character said to police in a book years ago. Thompson looks like he's about to stand up when Kent puts her hand on his knee. 'We take your point,' she says.

'Do you?'

'Yes,' she says. 'But tell me, do you believe what you've been saying at these festivals? Do you really think you can get away with murder?'

'No,' I say, but truthfully, I don't know. I think I could. Or at the very least I think I'd have a much better chance than most.

'It doesn't sound that way,' Thompson says. 'I mean, how difficult could it be? After all, the police are stupid and narrow-minded, and unable to look beyond the obvious.'

'Come on,' I say, 'that's just something one of my characters said.'

'But you thought of it.'

'I thought of it because there are always stories of people being freed from jail after DNA has cleared them. Every other occupation in the world, if you make a mistake you're held accountable. If a doctor amputates the wrong limb they'll never be a doctor again. Crash a plane and you'll lose your licence. Cost a client thousands of dollars at an accounting firm and you'll get fired. But what happens to cops who arrest the wrong person? Nothing. And yet we're meant to trust people who have proven themselves to have made wrong decisions in a way we would never trust that doctor, or pilot or accountant.'

'You have an extremely low opinion of police officers,' Thompson says.

'Only the ones who make mistakes.'

Kent cuts in. 'Tell us about Jonas Jones. Why would people who look down on psychics invite a psychic into their house for help?'

'Lockwood was wrong about that. It wasn't for show. Jonas is harmless enough. We've met a few times, but no, I don't believe he talks with the dead. I don't believe in any of that stuff.'

'And yet you still had him come here,' Thompson says.

'I was hopeful.'

'Hopeful in something you don't believe in,' Kent says.

'Why not? Why not try everything to bring Zach home, whether I believe in it or not?'

'Okay,' Kent says.

'Good,' I say.

'But Jonas Jones isn't the reason we're here,' she says.

'And nor is Dallas Lockwood,' Thompson says.

Kent picks up the folder. 'I have something I want to show you.'

Chapter Forty-Three

They form a semicircle in Zach's bedroom with their backs to the door and a view of the window opposite. Outside, a beach ball is being batted around in the crowd. Dallas Lockwood's piece on TV and his subsequent blogposts since then have brought more people into the street. She was right to have arranged more officers to protect the scene, but now she's thinking there may not be enough.

'You said Zach's window was closed on Sunday night,' she says.

'It's always closed,' Cameron says.

'You don't open it on hot nights?'

'No. If it gets too hot we'll put a fan in his room and leave his bedroom door open, but we always keep his window closed.'

'Let's put your author imagination to the test,' Kent says.

'This isn't a game,' Cameron says.

'And I'm not kidding around. This is important, Mr Murdoch. I want you to tell me how you think Zach climbed out his window.'

'Okay. Okay, sure,' he says, and he looks around the room. 'Well, there was a toybox,' he says, and he points to the corner where there is a pile of toys. 'He emptied all that out of it, turned it over, carried it to the window and climbed on it. Is this where you tell me there's no box? Because there sure as hell was one two days ago.'

Kent opens the folder. 'This box,' she says, and the photograph of the box has been taken while it was still in front of the window. It's a wide shot of the room. She holds it so the perspective is the same. 'Makes sense what you say,' she says. 'It's the same way we pieced it together. Zach isn't tall enough to jump up and drag himself over the windowsill without climbing on something, and if he had tried it, we'd see scuff marks all down the front from his shoes. So Zach empties the box, tips it upside down, and steps onto it. Kids love to climb. Is Zach a climber?'

'He is,' Cameron says.

'The first time he started climbing one of the trees in the backyard, I almost had a heart attack,' Lisa says. 'He'll climb anything. We're in constant fear that a broken arm or a broken leg is just around the corner.'

'Has he done it before? Climbed out the window?'

The two parents look at each other, then Cameron says, 'Not that I know of.'

Lisa shakes her head. 'I've never seen it.'

The window has two latches, one at the top, one at the bottom. You flick them out, and the window swings sideways on two pivot points. Easy for an adult. Not so easy for a kid. 'How does he get the window open?' Kent asks.

'Easy,' Cameron says.

'How does he reach the top latch?'

'He...' Cameron says, then stops. He's seeing the problem. Even standing on top of the plastic box, Zach wouldn't be able to reach it. 'Maybe he reached up with another toy and banged at the handle until it opened. Then he tossed whatever toy he used back into the heap.'

'Tidying up after himself,' Kent says.

'Exactly.'

Kent nods. It makes sense. And it's what they first thought too. Only it didn't happen. 'This box,' she says, and she taps the box in the photograph, 'we took that box with us. And then we went out and bought a dozen identical boxes,' she says, but it wasn't 'we', it was Mason Clark who figured this out. 'See, our forensic guys are looking at the toybox and they're thinking it doesn't really look that strong. The plastic is thin, but it's designed for holding bits and pieces, not for supporting the weight of a seven-year-old boy.'

Lisa lets go of Cameron's hand and lets her arms fall to her sides.

Kent carries on. 'So our guys, they see Zach's last trip to the doctor three months ago has him weighing in at twenty-five kilograms. They start placing twenty-five-kilogram weights in the centre of the box where a young boy might stand, and the weight breaks through and leaves jagged edges of plastic in its wake. So they figure somebody as young as seven would know the box is stronger on its edges, so they choose another box and shift the weight, and though the plastic doesn't cave in, it cracks. They have ten more boxes, and they take ten more shots at it, and no matter how they place the weight the box breaks or cracks.'

Cameron shakes his head. 'Twelve isn't many boxes.'

'You're right. That's what I said. And I'm going to tell you what they said to me. They said they went out and got hold of another dozen, and what they got was another dozen breakages. See, the plastic isn't strong at all. Doesn't need to be. Which means Zach didn't tip it upside down and use it to climb out his window. We know he didn't climb out, because we'd have found his fingerprints along the windowsill.'

Lisa is crying. Cameron reaches out for her and she takes a step away.

'The scene was staged so it looks like Zach climbed out his window, and right into the wrong place at the wrong time as somebody walked by. Now, I believe in coincidences and will never rule them out, but this one … this one bothered me.'

'We didn't do this.'

'It was impossible for Zach to get out that window by himself.'

'What did you do?' Thompson asks. 'Carry him out the front door, or drive him out through the garage?'

Cameron takes a step back. He looks like a trapped animal. She can hear his breathing quicken. He looks like he's struggling to stay balanced. 'We didn't do this,' he says, and his words are so weak she has to strain to hear him, especially over the noise from the crowd outside. 'I know how it looks, but we didn't … we didn't do this. Somebody is doing this to us.'

Thompson steps forward. A set of zip-tie cuffs have appeared in his hand.

'No,' Cameron says. 'Don't do this. Please don't do this.'

But they're doing it.

They place Cameron and Lisa Murdoch under arrest.

Chapter Forty-Four

Thompson tells me to turn around and put my hands behind my back. Instead I turn to Kent, and I say, 'You lied. You said you weren't narrow-minded. You said we were a united front.'

'Is this where you tell us how useless the police are?' Thompson asks.

'You've got this all wrong.' I put my hands out in front of me, trying to ward off what's coming. Kent has no emotion on her face. To her I'm not the first child killer she's locked up, and I won't be the last. Thompson looks like he wants to speed the process along by shooting me. I can't let him put the cuffs on me. If he does, it's all over. If he does, then they can never be convinced they're wrong.

Lisa is shaking her head. She has a hand covering her mouth to hold on to a scream. She has backed into the wall.

Thompson turns me around. He wrenches my hands behind my back and secures them, the notches on the zip-tie cuffs clicking loudly. Then he turns me around, and I get to watch Kent doing the same thing to Lisa.

We're escorted out of the room, Kent with her hand on Lisa's elbow, and Thompson with his hand on my shoulder. Lisa looks unsteady on her feet, and I feel the same way. We reach the front door. Kent opens it. There are more officers out there than yesterday, but the crowd has grown too since Kent and Thompson showed up. There are four, maybe five hundred people out there. There's a patrol car in the driveway parked on the other side of Mum's car. I don't fancy our chances of getting there in one piece.

Kent comes to the same conclusion, because she closes the door, turns back towards us, and says, 'I'll bring the patrol car into the garage. We can load them into it in there, then wait for an escort.'

'No,' Thompson says. 'Let's take them straight out.'

'The crowd wants to kill us,' I say.

'You're suddenly shy of the media?' Thompson asks.

'You've seen the death threats.'

'We have it under control,' he says.

'Let's—' Kent says.

'It'll be fine,' Thompson says.

'It won't be,' I say. 'Come on, they're—'

'Shut up,' he says. He opens the door then shoves me through it. The crowd starts booing. Signs are raised. Chanting quickly spreads.

'They will, they will, molest you.
'They will, they will, molest you.'

There's a small step down from the porch to the path. I almost trip on it. Last thing I see before stepping down to ground level is the group of priests and nuns. They've formed a human pyramid, four on the base, three on them, then two, then one. They're chanting loudly. Maybe that's where it started.

Thompson says something to me, but I can't hear what. Reporters are yelling questions at us, but I can't make them out. 'They will, they will, molest you' drowns out the rest of the world. We have to go back, but Thompson keeps pushing me forward.

The media moves to intercept us. The officers try to hold them back, but they're outnumbered. Cameras and microphones are in our faces. Many of the reporters are from the conference on Monday night, but they look different, their faces have taken on a manic desperation for a story. I see Rolled Sleeves. His feet get tangled, and he goes down, one knee crashing into the ground, an elbow from another reporter catching him in the face before he can get back up, his glasses hanging from one ear. We reach Mum's car and have to go around it.

Seeing the media move forward convinces the crowd to do the same. The chanting breaks down, replaced by yelling. An egg explodes into my shoulder. I don't see where it comes from until the second one is launched – Mrs Hathaway, Zach's primary school teacher, only it's not her, but a facsimile of her, same face, same clothes, but hate-filled eyes I've never seen before. Her voice when she screams at me to 'Die, motherfucker, die!' sounds like her too. For some reason I remember the report card she wrote: 'Zach is a well-liked student who is a pleasure to have in class, even though he does tend to disrupt it.' Mr Knowles, the principal, who always wears bow-ties and suspenders, is next to her, shouting, 'Justice for Zach, Justice for Zach!' Another egg comes from Zach's teacher, this one hitting Thompson. She fires off two more that sail by. Alarms are going off up and down the street as people clamber on top of cars to get a better view. Rolled Sleeves has fallen again, and this time the crowd swallows him before he can get to his feet. Somebody screams from the direction of the priest/nun pyramid, and somebody shouts for help.

'We have to go back,' Kent yells.

'Keep going,' Thompson says. We're halfway to the car. An officer is getting the back door open while the others are telling the crowd to back off. A *Justice for Ivy* placard sails through the air and bounces off the back of Mum's car. An officer points a Taser into the crowd and yells for people to 'Get back, get back, get the fuck back!'

They don't.

When somebody goes to launch another placard, he fires his Taser, only he gets knocked at the same time, the two thin lines fly through the air and into the groin of a cameraman, who doubles over so fast he slams the camera into the pavement, plastic and glass smashing. The officer points the now-fired Taser back into the crowd, warning again for people to get back, only they don't, because they know as well as he does he's had his one shot.

We're two-thirds of the way to the car.

'We have to go back,' Kent shouts again.

She's right. We're not going to make it to the car. A brick comes hurtling through the air. Thompson ducks, and I duck, and Lisa and Kent duck, and it sails over us and crashes through the lounge window. An officer – the wrestler with the inside-out ears – wrestles the brick-thrower to the ground. Somebody with a placard swings it against the wrestler, who turns around and grabs it on the second swing, then pulls that person down, the placard seesawing between them. A man with tattoos all over his arms and neck bends down and picks up our broken letterbox. Thompson turns me back towards the house.

It's too late. Several of the reporters have already circled behind us, blocking our retreat. In the centre of them is Dallas Lockwood. He has a sneer on his face, and he's holding his camera ahead of his body, going for a closeup. There's the sound of breaking glass behind us. Warm bodies prod against me from all directions. We turn back towards the car. I can no longer see it. I have a vision of the crowd falling away, and all that's left is the chassis; the wheels and windows and seats and electrics all stripped away. Part of the crowd tries to get the chant up and running again, but it doesn't catch. A guy carrying a baseball bat comes at us. He yells that God's plan for Zach didn't include me killing him, and he swings it, but at the same time somebody falls in front of him, knocking him off balance, the bat hitting somebody else. A figure makes his way forward, and I recognise him: it's the guy from the fair on Sunday who punched me.

'You molested my son!' he screams.

'Get back,' Thompson says, and he shoves the guy in the chest. The guy steps back, then trips on a fallen placard, and ends up on his ass. 'Stay the—' Thompson says, his sentence cut off when an egg hits him in the face, Mrs Hathaway having reloaded and re-launched.

The man from the fair gets to his feet. He comes at me. Thompson doesn't stop him, because Thompson has let me go so he can wipe egg from his eyes.

'Don't,' I say, but the man does. He takes a swing. I turn to my side, because turning is all I can do with my hands cuffed behind me. His fist catches me in the face, glancing off the same spot Lockwood punched me two nights ago.

The crowd goes wild.

People throw their hands into the air and cheer. The man gets in a second swing. He aims for the same place, and gets it. This time there is no glancing. His fist drives through me. A flare goes off inside my head as I'm rocked back. I can't put my hands out to grab anything to fight for balance. I bounce off Thompson's shoulder before crashing into Lisa, who also has her hands cuffed behind her, meaning she can't balance either, and Kent can't help her, because she is fighting back a man in a T-shirt with a picture of an electric chair on it.

Lisa falls.

Hard.

There's a sickening crack as her head hits the pathway.

The chanting stops.

The crowd goes quiet.

Chapter Forty-Five

The street comes to a standstill. Everybody here has become a part of something, a part of a moment they created. The thud of Lisa's head against concrete has a definitive sound, a finality, the sound of something forever changed that can't be changed back. Arms fall to sides and faces go pale as most question why they came here. They sent us death threats and held up signs about justice. They wanted this, and now they have to live with it. Placards are lowered. Some are dropped.

In the distance, sirens.

People move back. The man who hit me trips over. He puts his hands behind him and crabs away. I want to scream at him, at everybody, to ask them if they're happy now, to ask, isn't this what you wanted? Only I don't. I don't have time for them. Later, definitely, but not now.

'Help her,' I say, to Thompson, to Kent, to anybody. Lisa is motionless. The anger, the fear, has disappeared from her face, and nothing has replaced it. 'Please help her.'

The main crowd, swept in on the tide, is sweeping back out. Officers move forward and form a circle around Lisa. We can see the car again. Thompson puts his hand on my shoulder and pushes me towards it. The crowd recovers enough from the shock for people to point their phones at us.

'I have to help Lisa,' I say.

'It's under control,' he says.

'Get off me,' I say.

'Get in the car.'

'Get off me!'

'I said—'

I knee him in the groin. It's cheap and dirty, and works. He cups both hands over his balls and leans forward. I move around him. I reach the group of officers. Kent has her fingers on the side of Lisa's neck, looking for a pulse. Blood is spreading from beneath her head. I don't see any movement. An officer is on the radio, calling for an ambulance.

Kent looks up at me. 'Get him out of here,' she says, to anybody who can listen, and that happens to be Thompson, because he's recovered. He grabs my shoulder and I tell him to leave me alone, to take my cuffs off, that I have to help.

Kent has gone red. Her scar ripples as the muscles in her face and neck tighten. She's in panic mode. Everybody is. 'I said get him out of here.'

'I'm not going anywhere.'

I'm wrong about that. Thompson drags me towards the car. He

shoves me into the back and gets the door closed. The driver's side window has been shattered, and the letterbox is sticking out of it. He moves around the car and pulls it out. I roll onto my back and I pound my feet at the window, first in the hope it will break, then out of a sense of protest once it becomes apparent it's not going to. The passenger door opens, and an officer climbs in. It's the wrestler with the inside-out ears. He's got a bloody nose and a swollen lip.

'Sit up,' he says.

I stop pounding. 'Let me out.'

'I can't do that.'

'I have to be with Lisa.'

'You know I can't let you out.'

'Is she okay? Is she going to be okay?'

'I don't know.'

'Can you at least sound like you care?'

Before he answers, the driver's door opens. Thompson uses his jacket to sweep glass off the seat then gets in behind the wheel. 'It's a goddamn shit show,' he says, getting the car started, and he's right, it is a shit show, but it's also a shit show of his own making.

'Is Lisa okay?'

He doesn't answer. He backs down the driveway quick enough and pissed-off enough to show that if anybody doesn't get out of his way it's going to be their fault. He gets the car into drive and we roll forward, running over abandoned placards.

'Is Lisa okay?'

'An ambulance is on the way.'

'You don't have to uncuff me, but at least let me stay. I have to be with her. She needs me.'

He doesn't answer. Just keeps on driving.

'What would you be doing if that was your wife back there, huh? You'd be doing anything you could to help her.'

Still nothing.

'What in the hell is wrong with you people?'

Nobody answers.

I'm still on my back. I slide around until I sit myself up. I'm not wearing a seatbelt. 'I'm sorry,' I say. 'I'm sorry I lost my cool, and I'm sorry I kneed you in the groin, and that I tried kicking out the window, but please, please, we have to go back. I need to be with her.'

Nothing.

'Come on, you owe me. Lisa wouldn't be hurt if it hadn't been for you. I warned you, and so did Kent, but you didn't listen because you wanted to put us on display.'

'You're wrong,' Thompson says, slowing for a corner then glancing back at me. 'I didn't want this, and you're wrong about this being my fault. You put this into motion when you killed your boy.'

I lie back down and continue kicking at the window. Wrestler tells me to stop, and I don't, and then Thompson tells me to stop, and I don't. Thompson pulls over. They get out, and climb into the back and restrain my legs with more zip-ties. They get me sitting up and they get the seatbelt around me. I keep swearing at them the entire time. Thompson tells me that he'll gag me if I make one more sound, and then he goes back into the front seat, and Wrestler stays in the back with me.

We're not going back. That's obvious. So I give up on swearing at them and go silent instead. When we get to the station, I don't put up any kind of fight. They cut the zip-ties around my legs then escort me to an interrogation room upstairs.

'Am I going to need to keep you cuffed?' Thompson asks.

'No.'

He takes them off, and I take a swing at him, but he's ready for it. He blocks it, turns me around and pins me against the wall.

'Are you done?' he asks.

'If Lisa dies, I will kill you.'

'You done?'

'No. But you are.'

He bounces my head into the wall. 'We'll see about that,' he says, and he lets me go, walks out, and locks the door behind him.

Chapter Forty-Six

Most of the crowd has drifted away, the way they do at the conclusion of a sporting match, only the hardcore fans hanging about for the after-show. Kent watches the second ambulance pull away; the first one contained a crowd member injured earlier.

She's angry at herself. She should have waited for more officers the moment she saw how big the crowd had gotten. What was she thinking? That a Christchurch crowd would be civilised? And Thompson – goddamn Thompson, pushing through the front door, insisting that everything was going to be okay, and she went along with it, went along when every fibre in her body was telling her it was a mistake. She doesn't know who to blame more; Thompson, or herself for letting him make that decision for her.

When she looks at her hands, they're shaking. They're covered in blood. She can feel some drying on her face too, but can't think how it got there.

Her phone rings. She wipes her hand on her shirt and answers. It's Thompson.

'I got Murdoch back to the station,' he says. 'How's the wife?'

'Not good.'

'Okay. Okay. Well, the guy who did this, he was arrested trying to leave the scene. Name is Spenser Barkley. He's at the station. Turns out he's the guy who Cameron had the altercation with at the fair on Sunday.'

She doesn't say anything, and a few seconds later he carries on. 'Look, Rebecca ... Jesus ... I ... I don't know what to say.'

'Uh-huh.'

'I'm sorry. I couldn't have known. I couldn't have.'

She thinks he could have. 'Uh-huh.'

'Look, this is on me, and I'll say that. I'll say I insisted. There's no reason both of us should go down for this. I don't want to lose my job,' he says. 'I didn't know. I didn't know it would be this bad. The crowd ... Jesus, Rebecca, they were rabid.'

'Did Murdoch give you any trouble?'

'No. I mean, yeah, he tried kicking out the windows of the car, but it was nothing we couldn't handle.'

She stares at the blood in the driveway. Next to it, Evelyn Murdoch's car has had both front and back windscreens smashed and the side mirrors torn off. 'You know this changes things, right? It changes how the investigation goes. He's going to lawyer up, and all the lawyer is going to want to talk about is how we messed up.'

'I know, but he did it. You know he did it. Either him, or both of them. You want me to come and get you?'

'I'll get somebody to drop me back.'

She hangs up. There are still several patrol cars in the street, and she asks an officer to drive her home. She stares out the window on the way, the officer taking a route that runs past market gardens that butt up against a McDonald's, which itself borders a bottle store. They turn off by a large lot where a retirement home is being built. The officer, trying to make small talk, gives up when he can't get anything back from her, though she is tempted to have him turn around and go back to the bottle store. Hell, he could drop her off at the retirement home too because she's not sure her career can survive this. She hates to think how this is playing out in the news right now.

When they get to her house, the officer waits in the car while she goes in. She was right about there being blood on her face. She cleans up, and changes clothes, then heads back out.

When they get to the station, she's told Lisa is in surgery. She's told the other person injured in the crowd has died. She's told Cameron Murdoch has been kept in an interrogation room without any contact for the last forty minutes.

She figures there's no reason to keep him waiting.

Chapter Forty-Seven

The room is square with four walls painted cream and no natural light. There are no mirrors. There are two cameras bolted to the ceiling in opposite corners. Scuff marks line the bottom of the walls, and the carpet has loops pulled up against one of the edges, as if there's a cat running around at night, picking at it. There's a metal table in the middle with scratches across the surface, some initials scored into it, various attempts to spell first names before running out of time: a Jac, and a Chri and a Raymo. It's not as nice a room as the one they first put us in when they were pretending we were all on the same page. I pace it. Movement is forward momentum, but maybe the only thing forward momentum has done over the last two days is bring pain to my family. I sit down.

I've lost track of time, so when Kent comes in, I don't know if it's been ten minutes or an hour. She comes in by herself. She's changed clothes. I guess she didn't like my wife's blood on her. Before she can sit down I tell her I want a lawyer.

'Okay,' she says, and she turns around, and before she can reach the door I tell her to wait. 'Well, which is it?'

'I want to see Lisa.'

'The doctors are working on her, and even when they've finished you can't go. Or have you forgotten you're under arrest?'

'Is she going to be okay?'

She sighs. Her shoulders slump. 'The doctors are doing everything they can.'

'I asked if she's going to be okay?'

'I ... I think you need to prepare yourself that the news may not be good.'

Which is another of those square peg, round hole situations.

'This is on you,' I say.

'No,' she says, 'this is on you. What you did to your son led to this.'

'Your partner said the same thing, and I think he believes that, but I don't think you do. I think you're better than him. I think you know what happened to Lisa has nothing to do with Zach, and everything to do with Thompson wanting to put on a show. Was it to shame us? Or was it so he could get his face all over TV? And you didn't stop him. You could have had more officers there. You could have pushed the media and protesters back to the end of the block. You could have insisted on the car being brought into the garage. But your partner wanted a big song and dance, and you went along with it, because you wanted us to look guilty because you want us to *be* guilty.'

'Are you done?'

'Your partner asked me that too, and you know what? No. I'm not done. I'm far from it. What did you think was going to happen?'

She doesn't answer.

I lean forward. I lower my voice. 'Please, I need to see her.'

'I already said you can't.'

'You can handcuff me to a wheelchair and park me outside her room under armed guard if that's what it takes.'

'I'm getting sick of repeating myself,' Kent says.

'Well I'm sorry if your attempt to get my wife killed is ruining your day.'

'You need to calm down.'

'I am fucking calm!' I say, the Red Mist taking hold. 'Can you at least tell me you got him?'

'Got who?'

'The guy who hit me. He's the one from the fair. He's the reason Lisa fell over, or are you going to tell me that's my fault too?'

'We have him in custody.'

'Will he be charged?'

'That's not my call.'

'No, the only calls you know how to make are bad ones. That's why Zach is still lost, and I'm in here, and Lisa is fighting for her life in hospital. I can promise you that if she dies, that son of a bitch dies too.'

She sighs heavily again, and then she says, 'I know you're emotional, Mr Murdoch, but here's a piece of advice. Don't make threats like that when you're around a police officer. It doesn't look good for you.'

I'm about to double down on it when I think better. She's right.

'I need you to be calm so I can discuss something with you,' she says.

'I want my lawyer.'

'And that's fine, but before they get here, I—'

'If I wanted to kidnap my son I sure as hell would have done a better job than this, and the fact that you can't see that tells me my characters have been right about you guys the entire time. You are stupid, and you're way too stupid to even see it.'

'You want to know what I see, Mr Murdoch?'

'No. I don't,' I say. 'What I want is for you to fuck off. I'm not saying another word until my lawyer gets here.'

Chapter Forty-Eight

Kent walks out, and the Red Mist returns to a simmer. She comes back a minute later and hands me a phone and a phonebook before disappearing. I look up my lawyer. The problem is that the law firm I use deals with property law, relationship law, squabbling neighbours, and divorces and taxes. They don't deal with innocent people being accused of kidnapping their children, or even with guilty people accused of the same. Even so, I have to start somewhere, so I call Robert Johnson, a guy whose nickname is Big Bob on account of him coming in close to seven feet tall.

'I already know why you're calling,' he says, after his receptionist puts me through, 'but this isn't in my wheelhouse. Leave it with me and I'll make some calls. I'll get you somebody.'

I leave it with him. Kent comes back and takes away the phone and the phonebook. The lawyer whose wheelhouse this is in steps into the interrogation room sometime later. She closes the door behind her. She introduces herself. Naomi Vaughn. She's no Big Bob, but she's close. She's six foot, lean, and serious-looking in her expensively tailored suit. She has silky black hair parted in the middle that comes down to her shoulders, and green eyes with flecks of brown that hardly blink while she looks at me. There's a small dot on the side of her nose where she either used to have a piercing or still has one after hours. We shake hands. Her grip is firm and dry. We sit opposite each other.

I point at the cameras in the ceiling. 'Will the police be watching us?'

'No. Can I call you Cameron?'

'Please do.'

'I'm sorry about your boy, Cameron, and I'm sorry about Lisa. And what the police are doing to you is a travesty. But I'm here now, and this is going to be tough, but I'm on your side. We're going to make them pay for all of this. We are now dealing with two separate things. First, we're dealing with Zach's disappearance and how the police have narrowed in on you without substantial evidence, and please don't think I'm cruel here, but also without a body.'

'He's not dead.'

She carries on as if I haven't said anything. 'I believe they've conflated what your characters say and do with what you say and do. The second thing we're dealing with is their wilful incompetence at your house. They purposely paraded you both out in front of the media and a hostile crowd to fulfil whatever agenda they had in mind. Either they knew there was a risk and ignored it, or couldn't see a risk when there clearly was. Either way, they messed up.'

'I don't know how Lisa is,' I say. 'They won't tell me.'

'Let me find out.' She stands and knocks on the door, and is let out. She's gone for a couple of minutes and then she comes back. She sits down and she says, 'The blow to Lisa's head is serious. She has a haematoma. Doctors are operating on her to stop the bleeding, with the plan to put her into an induced coma to reduce the swelling. At this stage they don't know what the short- or long-term effects are going to be.'

Round holes and square pegs.

'Did you hear what I said?'

'I did. Does that mean she's going to make it?'

'It's still too early to tell.'

'I want to see her.'

'I'm going to make that happen. But first we need to focus on why you were arrested. I know it's tough, but I need you to do this. You're no help to your family if we can't get you out of here.'

'Okay.'

'Good. The police want to question you. We have two options. I can force them to let us go to the hospital now. Given what has happened, we have leverage. With that in mind, Lisa is in surgery, so even if you were there you wouldn't be able to do anything except sit in the waiting room and wait. But right now the police aren't looking for anybody else, which means they're getting no closer to finding Zach. I know everything on the news last night was bullshit. I know Dallas Lockwood. Not well, but our paths have crossed, and he's a particularly unpleasant guy. If Lockwood screamed jump, I'd duck. The fact he thinks you're guilty tells me you're innocent. What he did last night was despicable, but it's done, and now the media and the public think for a crime writer to write dark and twisted material, you must be dark and twisted. And I hate to say it, but you haven't been doing yourself any favours. Any other situation I would be recommending that my client keeps their mouth shut, but this isn't a normal situation, so here's what I suggest. To get you to the hospital to see your wife, let's bring Kent and Thompson in here to—'

'Not Thompson,' I say. 'He caused this. Kent I can talk to, but not Thompson.'

'That's fine,' she says, 'and perfectly understandable. So let's get Kent in here, and we hash this out. At the very least we get to see what they have. Now, this comes with a caveat. We do this, but you have to stay calm. You look at me every time you answer a question, and you give me a chance to interject if I don't like where it's going. You understand what I'm saying?'

'I understand.'

'Let me explain it again, and this time really think about it. Kent is going to try and trip you up, so you stay calm, and you think through your answers, and you let me stop you.'

'I understand.'

'I'll tell Kent you've agreed to a thirty-minute interview, but then we're going to the hospital. She'll agree. They need to placate us, because right now they're afraid I'll be bringing a lawsuit against them for what happened to Lisa. And I will, but that's a different conversation. You ready?'

'Yes.'

She stands up and pushes her shoulders back and takes long strides to the door. She knocks, it opens, she disappears, and it closes, all like before. When she comes back a minute later, she comes back with Kent. Kent is carrying a digital video camera on a tripod that she sits to the side, pointing at me. She's also carrying more of her goddamn folders. Naomi sits next to me, and Kent sits opposite.

'Let's get this started,' Kent says, and she presses record on the camera.

Chapter Forty-Nine

Only they don't get started. Kent is laying out photographs of Zach's bedroom and the toybox when there's a soft knock at the door. A moment later it opens, and Thompson leans in. It must be important for him to interrupt. Perhaps Lisa Murdoch didn't make it. She flicks the recorder off and heads into the corridor.

'We have a situation,' Thompson says.

'Lisa?'

He shakes his head. 'A few minutes ago calls were made to the tip line, both concerning Lucas Pittman.'

Lucas Pittman. She recognises the name. He was one of the convicted paedophiles interviewed over the last few days, but was cleared from the investigation. He has convictions for robbery, for breaking and entering, and for assault. It's his conviction for drugging and sexually assaulting a minor that got him put away for ten years. 'I don't like where this is going,' she says.

'No. And you're not going to,' he says, and as he says it, they're walking into the taskforce room where other detectives have started to gather, some on phones, some tapping away furiously at laptops. 'Two callers, one saying he heard a child crying, the other one Pittman's neighbour who said he saw Pittman behaving erratically.'

'Why am I only learning about this right now?'

'Because I only learned about it one minute ago, and two minutes ago there was nothing to learn, only now officers are at Pittman's house. It's empty, so they went in.'

Which they can do without a warrant, because Pittman is a registered sex offender, and two witnesses have called to say they believe they've seen or heard evidence of a crime. 'Get to the part I'm not going to like,' she says, even though she hasn't liked any of this so far.

'They just found Zach Murdoch's missing bag hidden under a bed. It's definitely the kid's bag. Has his name written inside it, and that toy ghost Murdoch called about is in there too, and his glasses.'

Her stomach sinks. They've been wrong about everything. The only misdirection has been them looking to lay blame where it wasn't warranted, and now one person is in custody who shouldn't be, and another is fighting for their life.

'Neighbours say Pittman tore out of there in a hurry. We got patrol cars out looking.'

She feels sick. 'We need to get out there,' she says, and then grabs a chair and sits down to stop herself from falling. She needs a moment first.

'And go where? He could be anywhere.'

'We messed up,' she says.

'We don't know that. We don't know Pittman wasn't working with the Murdochs.'

'You don't really believe that, do you?'

'We can't know anything for sure.'

'He took their son, Ben. He took him, and he did everything he could to make the Murdochs look like they'd done it, and we ate it up. All of it.'

Before Thompson can respond, Detective Vega comes into the room. 'The neighbour who called it in says he was peeking over the fence because he heard Pittman stomping around his yard, like he was looking for something. Says he glimpsed him through the garage window and saw him loading something into the trunk of his car.'

'He thinks it was the boy?'

'He couldn't be sure, but says it was the right size.'

'We have to find that car,' Kent says, getting to her feet.

Thompson follows her. 'Where are you going?'

'I don't know. Being out there is a lot better than being in here,' she says. 'We can at least start with the house.'

They reach the elevator.

'What about Murdoch?' Thompson asks.

'We leave him where he is.'

'And tell him what?'

'Tell him nothing until we know what to tell him.'

The elevator arrives. She pushes the button six times to close the door once they're inside. They reach the parking lot and get into the car, her behind the wheel, Thompson next to her. Both of them are puffing. Her hands are shaking. Before she can get out of the parking lot the radio comes to life. An officer in an unmarked sedan has eyes on Pittman's red two-door sports car and gives the location. It's heading north, out to the edge of the city.

Thompson grabs the radio. 'Do not engage,' he says. 'Keep following until we have more units in place,' he orders, and he sounds tense. She knows he's thinking the same thing she's also been thinking – that their careers won't survive this. And maybe they shouldn't. Right now, she doesn't want to think about it. Right now, all she wants is for the boy to be alive and for them to find him.

Thompson carries on talking into the radio. 'It's possible the suspect is armed and dangerous, and that Zach Murdoch may be inside the trunk. I repeat, do not engage.'

More units are radioed to narrow in on the location. Kent gets the car out to the street. She heads north. Roadblocks will be put in place and the cordon tightened. Pittman can't get far. She puts on the sirens. Traffic pulls aside for her. They make it only two blocks when the radio comes back to life.

'Suspect is pulling away. I repeat, suspect is pulling away. I got an ambulance behind me reacting to something else. I think suspect is spooked.'

'Follow him,' Thompson says.

They make it two more blocks before the radio comes back to life. 'Be advised I'm abandoning the pursuit,' the officer says. 'Suspect is driving too fast and too ... oh shit,' he says. 'Suspect has collided with a truck,' he says, his voice higher than it was before. 'I repeat, suspect has collided with a truck. Send ambulances,' he says. Then, a moment later, he adds, 'The car is on fire. We can't get to it. If the boy is in the trunk, then God help him, because right now nobody else can.'

Chapter Fifty

'Is this some kind of tactic?'

'If it is,' Naomi says, 'it's not one I've seen.'

Kent doesn't come back after five minutes, and she doesn't come back after ten, and she doesn't come back after twenty. Naomi stands up and knocks on the door to be let out to find out what's happening, and then she doesn't come back after five minutes, and then she doesn't come back after ten.

Then Kent comes back by herself.

She closes the door behind her.

She sits down opposite.

The tight look of professionalism that's been on her features since I first met her on Monday morning has slipped. She goes to say something but can't form the words. Then her lips quiver, and her features shift, and her eyes look bigger. 'There's been,' she says, and she coughs into her hand to clear her throat, then tries again. 'There's been a development.'

'No,' I say.

'I'm afraid I have some difficult news,' she says.

I shake my head, small fast movements side to side. 'You killed her. You and your fucking partner killed her.'

'It's ... it's not about Lisa.'

Which means it's about Zach. The world sinks, and I sink with it. I stare at Kent, praying she'll throw me a life preserver, but she doesn't. Instead she throws me an anchor, because she says, 'Thirty minutes ago we found the man who took Zach, and ... and I'm sorry, Cameron, but I regret to inform you we also found the body of a young boy that we believe to be your son. I'm so sorry, Cameron. I'm so, so sorry.'

'Get out.'

'We need to—'

'Get out. Get. The fuck. Out.'

Kent walks out and closes the door behind her.

Chapter Fifty-One

I pick up the chair and jam it under the door handle. Then I pick up another chair and launch it at the wall. Two of the legs punch holes into the plasterboard before falling to the ground. I pick up the video camera and close the legs of the tripod and swing it like an axe. It explodes against the table.

There is banging at the door.

I flip the table. I pick the chair back up and throw it at the camera on the ceiling. It falls away, held on by wires. I do the same with the second camera.

I'm puffing. I kick at the half-written names scratched into the table, putting small dents into the Raymo and the Chri and the Jac, and then I move away so I can punch holes into the wall, fist shapes all over the room, knowing my fingers are going to break if I hit a beam and wanting them to, wanting the torn skin, and the blood, and the fractures, and the pain.

I scream with every jab and punch and kick and chair-swing. Blood flicks off my torn knuckles, drawing lines over the walls and splashing droplets onto the ceiling. More streaks down my wrists and forearms. This room, these things, this is just the start of it. I need more. I need to destroy, and need to expand the chaos, to make pain and hurt for others so that my pain can be shared. I need to smash every computer screen in the building, tip over every desk, hurl staplers through windows and bounce coffee cups off ceilings and … and…

And everything.

And nothing.

I collapse into the corner of the room. I wasn't there when Zach needed me. I was a bad dad, the worst dad, an awful dad, one who creates monsters on the page while not seeing the monsters around us. I rest my arms over my knees. I wonder if Lisa is the lucky one. In her coma, Zach is still alive.

I swing the back of my head into the wall. It hurts. I like it. So I swing it again. It doesn't make the same sound Lisa's head made on the pavement, and I want it to. All of a sudden it's the most important sound in the world, one I need to replicate

need to

have to

so I swing harder, and still it's not right, and maybe that's because it's only plasterboard and not concrete, but perhaps the metal table will suffice, so I get it onto its legs and before I can pound myself into it, the door bursts open.

It takes three officers to get me to the ground.

Chapter Fifty-Two

Time is different now.

An hour passes.

It's unlike any other hour I've experienced. It used to be that days ticked by. Life rolled forward. Zach got older, and I'd write another book with Lisa, and we'd pay bills, and Zach would go to pre-school, then school, and we'd go to the park, or the movies, or shopping, and we'd garden, and chat with neighbours, and that's what life was, each moment leading into the next.

Then Zach disappeared, and time changed. Every passing hour was an hour he was no longer home, that he was scared, that things might be happening to him. But also every passing hour was an hour closer to us finding him.

Soon Zach will have been dead two hours, then twelve, then a day, then a week. A new year will begin, and Zach won't see it. February and March will roll into April and May. He'll be dead all next year and the one that follows. In seven and a half years, he'll have been dead for the same amount of time he was alive. In eight years, he'll have been dead longer.

Square peg.

Round hole.

The police have propped me up in a chair in a different room. I've been shot in the arm with a mild sedative. I feel like I'm in a dream. A paramedic has cleaned my knuckles and bandaged up my right hand. Kent is sitting opposite me, and my lawyer is sitting next to me. Kent is telling me how it all played out. Sometimes I stare at her, sometimes at the wall behind her, sometimes at my hands. There's a view out over the city. In the books we used to pretend that Christchurch was Dante's Seventh Circle of Hell, but it turns out we weren't pretending at all. If I got up and ran at that window, would they get to me before I could open it and jump?

Kent tells me two calls were made to a tip line earlier, each concerning a man by the name of Lucas Pittman. Pittman had prior convictions that included sexual assault. Officers were immediately sent to the house. Nobody was home, and they went inside, and they found Zach's schoolbag, along with Willy. Moments later every police car in the city was tasked with finding Pittman, which one did, that officer told to keep his distance.

At the same time, a call came in from a farm to the north of the city. A teenager had flipped a quad bike and broken both his legs. The parents called for an ambulance, and the ambulance sped out to the farm. The officer who called in Pittman's location had no sooner made the call when the sirens of the ambulance wailed in the distance, coming closer.

Pittman, they suspect, thought the sirens and the lights were coming for him. He put his foot down. The patrol car abandoned the pursuit. That is another thing that people in New Zealand like to do – they like to try and outrun the police. There is an incentive to do so, because the fleeing driver knows the chase will be deemed too risky to pursue. And Pittman had more of an incentive than others. So the chase was abandoned, but Pittman kept speeding and took a sharp turn where he tried to beat a truck.

He failed.

The truck collided with the car. The car flipped and rolled and caught fire. They dragged Pittman out of it. He was bloody and broken. A truck did all the things I would have done to Pittman, but I didn't get the chance, because I was here and not out there. Pittman was probably killed on impact, and Zach ... Zach was in the trunk, Zach who, they tell me, surely died on impact too. They couldn't get to him. With everything they are saying, I have become a father who is praying his son was dead before the flames took hold of him.

So I sit still, and I listen as, over and over, the square pegs continue to be pounded.

Chapter Fifty-Three

Cameron Murdoch is flicking at the edges of the bandage around his hand. Kent's heart goes out to the guy. His world has collapsed, and she has played a major role in that. Lisa Murdoch is still in surgery, and if she doesn't pull through, she sees Cameron going home and eating that metaphorical bullet he spoke about yesterday.

'And Pittman? What do we know about him?' the lawyer asks.

The lawyer has dollar signs in her eyes, that's for sure. This case – and the way the police handled it – will dominate newspapers around the world for the next few days, the lawyer's photo there too as she advocates for justice.

She tells them what they know. Pittman was a catalogue photographer – shooting things like furniture, and cars, and tools and food, images that can be used as book covers or movie posters. But he used to be a wedding photographer. Fourteen years ago, he became obsessed with an eight-year-old boy he saw at a wedding he was shooting. The boy lived with his single mother. Pittman broke into their house while it was empty and hid in the roof cavity. After watching them for two days, he snuck down during the night and drugged them both before beginning his assault on the boy. With that in mind, they suspect Pittman may have done a similar thing with Zach Murdoch. What she doesn't tell them is that thirty years ago, when Pittman was still a teenager, his father had been a suspect in the disappearance of a teenage boy who had lived on the same street, and that it's looking like the apple didn't fall far from the tree.

'We're thinking it's possible Pittman gained entry to your house on Sunday when you and Zach were at the fair,' she says. 'We know Lisa stayed behind to work, but that she took a forty-minute break to jog through the neighbourhood. Pittman may have made his way inside then, possibly through a window accidentally left open, or even made his way inside while Lisa was still in there, choosing to hide somewhere before being able to gain access to the roof. We're searching the roof for any evidence of this,' she says.

'You didn't check the roof already?' the lawyer asks.

'We did.'

'And you saw no signs anybody had been up there?'

The question is a tricky one. On Monday police entered the ceiling, but they were up there looking for a body wrapped in plastic, not for scuff marks or evidence somebody had previously been hiding up there. She can't say that. Instead, she says, 'I don't have all the details on that right now.'

'You don't have the details.'

'That's right.'

'And now? Have they found anything up there?'

'They're still checking. But, if Pittman was up there, it explains a lot. He would have heard your conversation with Zach. It's how he knew to take Zach's bag to make it look like he ran away. We suspect he's been watching your family for some time. We think he saw your shoes and used them to plant evidence that would be found. We think it's possible that the discovery of Zach's clothes and your shoes was also planned. Two months ago a story ran in the newspaper about the bins being constantly tipped over in Westshire Street. We think he planted the evidence there, then tipped all the bins over, wanting them to be found, knowing local kids would be blamed for it. We think he organised everything in the bedroom to look like you had staged it. He may or may not have figured out the box wouldn't hold up to Zach's weight, but he certainly wiped down the window and windowsill, knowing an absence of fingerprints would have been suspicious.'

'And you fell for it,' the lawyer says.

Kent doesn't answer. She wishes the ground would open up and swallow her. Earlier, before she came in here, she was offered the chance to go home. Vega and Travers would cover for her.

Thompson was on his way to being suspended, and she would be too, if it weren't for the fact Thompson followed through on his promise of accepting full responsibility for marching the Murdochs out their front door. Even so, she wanted to stay. This was on her. She deserves whatever wrath comes her way. If Cameron leaps across the table and put his hands around her throat, she isn't sure she would fight back.

'How was Pittman caught last time?' the lawyer asks.

'Pittman miscalculated the dose of ketamine he gave the mother. She woke up. She beat Pittman with a bedside drawer. She broke his nose and jaw, and knocked him out.'

'I want to see Zach.'

It's the first thing Cameron has said since he was restrained earlier. 'You can't,' Kent says.

'You said earlier you *believed* the boy is Zach, but you don't know for sure, right? Don't you need me to identify him?'

'You can't see him, Cameron. Please, you need to trust me on this.'

'Trust you? After everything you've done? Now that is rich.'

'I know we've failed you, and Lisa and Zach, but please, Cameron, you can't see him. You can't. You don't want to see what the fire did as being your last memory of him.'

'Then how do you know it's Zach?'

'There will be an autopsy, and he will be formally identified with dental records, but we have no reason to suspect the boy is anybody other than Zach, and we know from evidence found at the scene that your son was there.'

'If he wants to see his son,' the lawyer says, 'then I suggest you let him.'

Kent sighs. She feels so damn tired. 'I'll make the arrangements.'

Chapter Fifty-Four

Kent drives me to the hospital. My lawyer doesn't come with us. She's promised she'll be in touch to discuss legal action against the department. She's eager to pursue it. It'll be good publicity for her. Career building, even. But coming to the morgue would be pointless. She doesn't need to see my dead son at $1000 per hour, or maybe it's $2000, but money doesn't really matter either, does it?

It's not like you can take it with you.

Kent asks three more times if I would consider changing my mind, and I tell her three more times that no, I want to see Zach. I also tell her I want Willy returned. She tells me she'll get him to me soon. I stare at the bandaging on my hand. Small spots of blood have blotted through it.

Things are different now. People are polite. Respectful. A mistake has been made, and all it cost was Zach's life, maybe Lisa's, and our reputations and careers. We're innocent, and it's been proven, and some of the public will accept that and some of them won't. Some will continue to write songs and make memes. Dallas Lockwood will sprout a conspiracy theory, and people will believe him, because people love to believe bad things. We learned on the way here that Lisa is out of surgery and has successfully been put into a coma.

We reach the hospital. It's a mishmash of different styles as wings have been added or renovated over the years, some three storeys tall, some twice as many, all of them with flat roofs scattered with antennas and air-conditioning vents. Out front, people in wheelchairs have IV drips plugged into one hand and cigarettes hanging out the other. Patients who look like they died thirty years ago are being helped through the doors. There are media folk already here, but not too many. They ask questions as we walk past. They're calm and respectful, the way they could have been from the beginning if they had chosen. They don't follow us inside. There are officers near the elevators and the stairs in case they try.

Kent uses a key on the control panel of the elevator to access the morgue below. We step back out into cinderblock territory, a long grey corridor with so many fluorescent lights the walls glow white. We go through a set of double doors where there are a couple of shapes beneath sheets. One of those shapes is smaller than the other. A woman in her mid-thirties with dark hair comes over. The coroner. She introduces herself, but I don't catch her name. She's lean and gaunt, and looks tired. We don't make small talk. We follow her to the gurney with the small shape, and I try not to look at the one with the big shape.

'Please,' the coroner says. 'You don't need to see this.'

'Yeah. I do.'

Kent doesn't say anything.

The coroner doesn't say anything.

We stare at the shape, gathering our thoughts, until the coroner says, 'Tell me when you're ready.'

Which seems like a weird thing to say. Because I came here ready to see something I could never be ready to see. Which is a paradox. Before she asked if I was ready, I was, and now on the other side of that question, I'm not so sure.

'I need a moment.'

'Can I get you something?' Kent asks. 'Some water?'

I look at her. The one thing I want she can no longer give me. I don't say it, but she looks away as if I have.

'I'm ready.'

The coroner puts her hand on the sheet, and the side closest to me slides up, revealing Zach's hand.

'Wait.'

She waits. I stare at the hand. It turns out I'm not ready because even now, even after the rage and anger and pain, after throwing furniture against walls and trying to recreate the sound of a skull breaking open, I was still holding on to the hope this wouldn't be Zach. The schoolbag that was found would belong to another Zach Murdoch, who happened to own the same kind of plushy ghost, because, after all, it's not like that bag and that ghost were the only ones ever made. The boy in the morgue would be the other Zach Murdoch. And, if by some cruel twist of fate this was my Zach, if it really were him, his skin wouldn't be black like this, it wouldn't look like a thin crust of molten lava that's cooled and set, then been broken. If this were my Zach, he would be covered in a dusting of soot that could be brushed off. His eyes would flicker open, and he'd look confused, and the coroner would say, 'It's a miracle, praise Jesus,' and they'd race him upstairs to the land of the living.

'I...'

The coroner covers Zach's hand back up. I can't manage the words, but she knows what it is I'm trying to say. *I can't.* I reach out and put my hand on top of his, the sheet between us. He still feels warm.

Kent and the coroner take a few steps back so I can talk to Zach. I tell him I'm sorry. That we love him. That he deserved better. That everything is going to be okay now. I tell him that he's a good boy. The best. That we're proud of him, that he has made our lives wonderful, he made them better, and we will miss him greatly. I tell him one day we will be a family again. I don't tell him he won't have long to wait. I want to tell him about all the things I won't get to show him, how to ride a bike, how to drive, how to shave, how to do up a tie, a lifetime of advice that doesn't count for anything when there isn't going to be a lifetime.

I tell him that I'm sorry I didn't protect him.

'When can we have him back?'

'Tomorrow,' the coroner says.

I walk back to the doors. Kent follows me. I stumble when I'm halfway there. I land on one knee and shrug Kent off when she goes to help me back up. I get to my feet and then collapse in the corridor. I sit down, and lean against the wall and sob into my hands. Kent doesn't know what to say or do, and I ask her if I can have that water now.

'Of course.'

She heads through the double doors, and a moment later I go in after her. I walk over to the other sheet covering the other shape. I pull the sheet away, and it's a man, a guy who could be thirty or forty or fifty, his age hidden by what death has done to him. Lucas Pittman. I know it's him, not because his head is distorted from the impact, or because of the holes in his body where bones are poking through, but because there's a toe-tag hanging off his foot. Lucas Pittman, written on there in black marker.

I tip Lucas Pittman onto the floor.

I get two good kicks into him before Kent and the coroner pull me away.

Chapter Fifty-Five

They get me to the elevator. There's no conversation. No small talk. The doors open. Kent pushes me inside gently and follows me, and the coroner stays on the outside looking in. Kent looks frustrated with me, but the coroner seems sympathetic. The doors close. The blood on my bandaged hand has spread, four separate spots across the knuckles almost touching. I stare at it while Kent doesn't tell me what I did was a mistake. She doesn't tell me I've contaminated evidence. It's not like Pittman is going to need his day in court.

What she does say is, 'I hope that made you feel better.'

'You know what? It did,' I say. 'It's not much, but all things considered, it's better than nothing.'

'Maybe we should wait on seeing your wife,' she says.

'I'll be fine.'

'You'll keep your temper in check?'

'Yes.'

She taps the button for the fourth floor. Like the police station, the fourth floor must be where all the action happens.

'Have any media made it up here?' I ask.

'No,' she says. 'And none of them have tried.'

'They're still at my house?'

'Some of them.'

'And the people protesting?'

'The public has been made aware of the situation,' she says.

'You mean the situation where you thought I'd murdered my son, but it turns out he was still alive, but then somebody killed him anyway?'

It's obvious she doesn't want to answer, but she does. 'They're aware of it.'

I realise then how tired Kent is. How hard this must be on her too. How strong she is to still be with me. Anybody else would have made me somebody else's responsibility. Kent is here because she messed up and she's atoning for it. She failed, and it must be eating her up. A child died on her watch. I can never forgive her, but I need to recognise this isn't what she wanted.

'So the assholes with the placards shouting death threats have gone?'

'Yes,' she says. 'We're tracking them all down. Every one of them will be spoken to and, if possible, all of them will be charged.'

'Thank you,' I say.

She nods. I notice her eyes are puffy. Today has broken her.

We get to the fourth floor. A doctor introduces herself to us. Doctor Lee. She's in her mid-forties, short, empathetic, softly spoken. She smiles sadly and tells me she's sorry for my loss, then without giving me a chance to respond, she tells me she's the surgeon who operated on Lisa. Kent tells me she'll return soon, then steps back onto the elevator. I walk and talk with Doctor Lee like they do in TV hospital dramas. We pass rooms where people are chatty, people are complaining, people are unconscious, where there are people with different amounts of limbs. The rooms are all muted colours, lots of plastic cups to drink from and plastic bottles to piss into, rooms with fake flowers, and real flowers and no flowers. We reach the last room, where six people in comas are hooked up to wires and tubes, looking like they've been assimilated into an old *Star Trek* episode. There are chairs for visitors to sit in, which at the moment are all empty. The room is warm and stuffy, and smells of disinfectant. Lisa is the closest to the door, which gives her less of a view than the folks by the window, but a better chance of escaping in a fire. The bandaging around her head is bulky. Her head has been shaved. Her face is puffy and bruised.

Doctor Lee explains the surgery, the bleeding, the swelling, the possibility that there may be permanent damage. 'It's important to have realistic expectations,' she says, and I wipe at my eyes and hold back the tears. I was a fool for thinking the doctors were going to say everything was going to be okay. I sit down and take Lisa's hand. In the moments leading up to her hitting the ground, she was afraid of me. She believed I had hurt our son. Is she living all of that in her coma?

'Will she remember what happened?'

'We don't know.'

'Will she know who I am? Who she is?'

'We don't know.'

'Can she hear us?' I ask.

'Yes,' Doctor Lee says.

'Can she understand us?'

'It's impossible to tell.'

'Does she ... know about Zach?'

'We haven't told her.'

'Can I have some time alone with her?'

'Of course,' Doctor Lee says, and she walks out of the room, and I'm left alone with my wife and five strangers, none of them knowing I'm here.

Chapter Fifty-Six

There are no spectators outside the Murdoch house, only media, and even then only a handful of those who were here this morning. One of them looks at Kent, sees the look on her face, and holds on to whatever question he was getting ready to ask. Maybe they're feeling as bad about the way things played out as she is.

There are cigarette butts and empty coffee cups scattered across the street, most of them in the gutter. There are broken pieces of plastic and glass, and even more glass in the driveway. Evelyn Murdoch's car has been towed away to be repaired. The front lawn has been scuffed up. Lisa's blood is still on the pathway. She had forgotten about the brick hurled through the lounge window. She'll make a call and get it fixed.

On the drive here she discovered why the crowd this morning was so large. Dallas Lockwood sent an email early this morning to his followers, saying Cameron and Lisa Murdoch's arrest was imminent and that an inside source suggested they were going to flee. He implored as many of his followers to stand guard outside the house to stop the Murdochs escaping before justice could be served. Lockwood, questioned about who that source was, is refusing to answer. If it were up to her, she'd put him in jail for a year and let him think about his career choices.

She goes inside. In the lounge she meets a woman wearing a white nylon suit. Vicky Curtis, with long dark hair tied into a bun and a bump in her nose from her time when she used to box. She has the hood of the suit pulled back and is drinking from a bottle of water. 'It was hot up there,' Curtis says.

'What have you got for me?'

'I got three of them,' Curtis says, and she holds up three separate plastic bags, each with a camera inside. The camera itself is a centimetre long and half as wide, a finger-length cable connecting it to a unit the size of a box of matches. The box provides power and transmits a signal. It records sound too. She's seen similar ones before. 'Easy to see why nobody found them on the first pass through,' she says. 'Kind of thing you'd have to be looking for.'

'Where'd you find them?'

'One above Zach's bedroom, one above the lounge, one above the master bedroom. The main unit was next to the recessed lights and covered by insulation, and the camera slid through a gap in the light housing and down the side of the bulb. The bulbs are LED, so there was no heat, which kept the camera safe. We've checked all the other rooms, but these are the only three.'

'Range?'

'Something like this, a hundred metres maybe. Probably transmitting to Pittman's phone while he was sitting out there in his car.'

Pittman's phone was destroyed in the crash.

'Battery life?'

'The units are motion-activated – it could last anywhere between a day and a few weeks, depending on how often they're triggered.'

'They're flat?'

'All were transmitting, up until I switched them off. I do know these cameras are fairly new, two months at the most. That's when these models came out. I'll call the manufacturers and see what else I can learn about them. Also, I couldn't see any obvious evidence that Pittman had been up there.'

'Except for the cameras?'

'Yeah, but those cameras could have been placed from below. You pull the recessed light down, thread the camera through, reach the box into the ceiling and put the light back. It'd be a safe way to do it – no risk of putting your foot through the ceiling.'

'So let's walk through this. Pittman wasn't hiding in the ceiling and watching, but had set cameras up there instead. Battery life means he's been here within the last two weeks. For all we know, he planted them two months ago and came back to charge them. Could be he swiped a key the first time he was here, so coming and going was easy. He's watching on Sunday night, hears Zach say he's going to run away, and decides to act. He can't exactly scramble around the house getting his cameras back without waking anybody up and figures they were safe up there anyway. He probably thought he could come back and get them once the Murdochs were in jail. You check them for fingerprints?'

'Not yet.'

'Okay. Get it done and let me know.'

She heads back outside. She walks down the side of the house and finds a garden hose. She turns it on, comes back and points it at the pathway. Half the blood washes into the garden, but the rest stays. She goes into the kitchen, fills up a bucket of soapy water, grabs a brush, and goes outside and finishes it off. People watch her and say nothing. She rinses everything down and returns everything where she found them.

She crosses the road to her car.

The back right tyre is flat.

Two down, one to go.

She kicks it, over and over, then stops when cameras start to point her way.

She signals a patrol officer over and asks him to get it sorted for her, then uses his car to drive to the station.

Chapter Fifty-Seven

I hold Lisa's hand and talk about the good times. How we met, how we fell in love, about the years that have followed. I go through a box of tissues. I keep seeing Zach's hand everywhere I look.

Her parents show up. They look like they're going to fall apart, physically. Limbs hang from joints, faces sagging close to the point of tearing. Lisa's mum's eyes are puffy from all the crying, and her dad's face is creased from all the frowning. Her dad starts out by apologising. Says the police have told them everything.

'I was wrong to have said the things I said yesterday. I can't help ... can't help but think if I had been more helpful, maybe things could have ended different.'

'You're right.'

'Sorry?'

'You're right to think that. Things could have ended differently, but now we'll never know.'

I can tell he isn't expecting to hear that, but he nods slowly and accepts it.

They sit in the room with us, but really I want them to leave. They ask over and over how something like this could have happened. They ask what kind of city we're living in. They ask what kind of person Lucas Pittman must be, what his parents must have been like, why he wasn't given life in jail for what he did to that young boy and his mum fourteen years ago. I don't answer them. I barely talk to them. I keep holding Lisa's hand, her mum telling me we'll get through this, her dad telling me we'll get through this. Rita offers to take care of Zach's funeral arrangements if I'd like her to, and I tell her that would be helpful.

Kent comes back. She's carrying a plastic evidence bag. Willy is inside. She hands it to me. I take it out of the bag and hold it to my face. I can smell my son.

'You should get your hand looked at again,' she says, noticing the blood on the bandaging.

I ignore her. Doctor Lee comes in and tells us that Lisa needs to rest, as if being here is disturbing her. I don't argue it. We head for the elevators. Lisa's parents get into one and hold the door for me.

'I'll get the next one.'

Rita looks like she's been slapped, and Andre looks down at his feet. The doors close, and I get the next one like I said, Kent shadowing me.

'Spenser Barkley is doubling down on his story about you trying to molest his son, but nobody is believing it.'

'That's his name? The guy from the fair?'

'Yes. Keep in mind he has to double down because he needs to show he wasn't in a right state of mind when he attacked you this morning. He has been charged with assault causing bodily harm, and he will appear in court tomorrow morning.'

'And then what?'

'Then he'll plead guilty or not guilty. If it's the latter, a trial date will be set.'

'Will he go to jail?'

'I don't know.'

'It's not fair,' I tell her.

'You're right, it's not. Nothing about this is. Where are you going now? Home? Or your mother's house?'

'Am I allowed to go home?'

'Yes. Let me give you a lift.'

'What about my car? Can I have it back?'

'I can have it dropped off to you tonight.'

'Okay.'

'My car is this way,' she says.

'I'll walk.'

'At least ... at least take a taxi. You've been in the news so much that—'

'Yeah. I get it. But I didn't exactly grab my wallet when you were arresting me this morning.'

'Let me pay for it.'

There is a taxi stand twenty metres away. Kent follows me to it and chats with the driver in the one closest. I climb into the back, figuring Kent must be thankful to get rid of me.

'Cameron,' she says, opening the door back up. 'You, well, I...' she says, and whatever it is she wants to say, she can't figure it out, and then the taxi driver says he doesn't have all day, so then Kent says, 'I'll drop your car off later.'

I close the door. The taxi pulls away. The driver talks about the weather. Talks about how hot it's going to be on Christmas Day. He asks if I have any plans, and I say yes, that my plan is to bury my son who was murdered this morning. The conversation ends.

Things have died down back home. There are two patrol cars outside my house, and a car parked opposite, jacked up, a police officer changing the wheel. The taxi driver pulls up my driveway and lets me out and doesn't hang around to see what happens. Mum's car has gone. There are a dozen reporters outside my house. A dozen cameras. I step forward and they all go quiet.

'My son is dead,' I tell them, and I don't raise my voice. The only other time they have been this quiet was right after Lisa hit her head. 'Zach was murdered while I was in custody. He was seven years old. He was my world. He was Lisa's world. A small innocent child who loved and was loved. On Sunday night a stranger came to our house, and he took our son away, and today that stranger killed him. Zach lived in the worst possible fear for the last few days, going through what I don't want to even imagine. While a man we didn't know kept Zach locked up in his house, while he prepared to violently murder him, while Lisa and myself broke with grief, the public made up songs, they made up images, they dressed up and paraded outside of our house, and they sent us death threats. You,' I say, and I point from one camera to another to another, 'you took the absolute worst thing in the world that could ever have happened to our family, and turned it into a parody. You enjoyed it. Our pain, our loss, it brought a sick sense of joy to all of you. Rather than helping, rather than helping find Zach, rather than trying to imagine what it must be like for us, you condemned us. Is this how the world is now? That we laugh at people's tragedies? Zach was a small boy. You didn't know him, but he was more than just a headline. He was real, we loved him, and through all of this you forgot that. Zach is dead, and earlier today my wife almost died right there,' I say, and I point at the pathway where she fell. The blood has been cleaned away. 'Many of you have blood on your hands, and yet nothing will change. Tonight you will eat dinner, you will watch TV, you will kiss your children goodnight, and you will wash the blood away, and tomorrow you will do this to somebody else. God forbid the next person it happens to is you. Shame on you. Shame on each and every one of you.'

The questions come. I walk inside and lock the door against them.

I walk through the house. It's different again. A shift in tone. In light. In feel. There are shards of glass on the carpet in the lounge from the busted window. The curtain is moving back and forth in the breeze, tearing itself on a broken piece of glass hanging in the frame. The brick has stopped short of one of the couches. I use the tablet to get an update on the news. There are stories from outside Lucas Pittman's house. A normal-looking house in a normal-looking street, neighbours saying he was always quiet, even if he was creepy. There's a story with Spenser Barkley being arrested, and it shows his house too, a different normal house in a different normal street, and Barkley was a quiet guy too, according to neighbours, only not creepy.

Quiet people. Both of them.

I use a phonebook and Google Maps to figure out where those normal houses are.

I change into dark clothes. I put on a baseball cap and tuck my wallet into my pocket. I charge my phone while emptying bottles of whisky and gin down the sink. I pack a bag and, before I can leave, there's knocking at my door. The police wouldn't let anybody past who wasn't meant to be here. I answer it.

'This isn't a good time, Andre.'

'It's not a good time for any of us, Cam. You going to invite me in?'

He steps past me, and I follow him through to the kitchen. He opens the fridge and grabs out a couple of beers and opens them both and hands me one. He leans against the kitchen bench, and I lean against the table, neither of us drinking.

'I know what you're thinking,' he says.

'No. You don't.'

'In the army, I lost people,' he says. 'Good people. In different corners of the world. One of them died in my arms. We were on patrol, and a buddy of mine – Rich Chesterfield – stood on a land-mine. One moment he was there, the next he was gone, bam, just disappeared into a puff of blood and smoke and sand. Then it all settled – and, well, now Rich wasn't gone at all, but still there, lying on the ground, screaming, both his legs gone. We told him to hang on, that he was going to be okay, but we knew he was done for, and so did he. The best we could do for him was hold his hands and not have him die alone. Every night I say a prayer for Rich. Until these last few days, I thought it was the worst day of my life.'

He's building up to a point. I'm in no rush so let him take his time. He swallows down half his beer and sits the bottle on the counter.

'The thing is, something like that, it changes you. I don't know what kind of man you would be if it didn't. We had all kinds of training to toughen us up, but that night, after we got rescued, I broke down. I thought I was done. I remember the dark thoughts as clear as a bell. Twisted thoughts. First, I wanted to hurt everybody who had a hand in Rich dying. I wanted to go out there, guns blazing, because my hurt was a shield, I was sure of it, a shield that made me invincible. In that moment I had no doubt I could walk through the rest of that minefield under heavy fire and I wouldn't get a scratch. My anger, my sorrow, it made me blind. None of that compares to how I feel today, and how I feel today can't compare to how you're feeling. But you need to know that your hurt isn't a shield. It's the opposite. The hurt puts ideas in your head that have every right to be there, but you can't listen to them. You can't. You still have Lisa. She's a fighter, but she's going to need you more than ever. Whatever notion you have,' he says, and he nods towards my bag sitting on the floor in the lounge, 'well, you'd be best to put that out of your mind.'

I don't say anything.

He nods, and he picks up his beer, then puts it back down. 'I should get going.'

We walk to the door. I open it. The media gets excited. Andre puts a hand on my shoulder, and I have the urge to shrug it off and remind him that yesterday he was poking me in the chest. 'Is there anything you need?'

'Nothing.'

'I can see you're fixing yourself to ignore everything I came here to say. Think of Lisa. That's all I ask. And if there's anything you need, you let me know.'

I watch him walk to his car. He doesn't answer any of the questions thrown his way. He pulls away as a van shows up. A window glazier. Two guys get out and approach the window from the outside.

I close the door. It's only a matter of time before the reporters get bored, or somebody else goes missing or dies and distracts them. This story has reached an end. Boy goes missing. Boy dies. Wife might die.

What's next?

That's my kind of question, Mr What If says. *And I have some answers for you.*

I'm way ahead of him.

I grab the bag and head out the back.

Chapter Fifty-Eight

I lower the bag over the back fence then follow it. I walk down the side of the yard and knock on my neighbour's back door. A moment later it swings open.

Simon Crawford is bald on top, with white hair around the sides and a chin sharp enough to cut glass. His flannel shirt and dark trousers are similar to what my dad used to wear, and what my mum would call an 'old-man uniform'.

'Jesus, Cameron,' he says. 'I'm sorry.' He offers me his hand. I shake it. 'I can't imagine what you're going through. If there's anything I—'

'Can I borrow your car?'

'Of course. It's yours for as long as you need it.'

I have the anger to walk a thousand miles, but even so, the car will make everything easier. I wait out front as he goes back inside, and a minute later his garage door rolls open. He backs out a twenty-year-old Toyota Corolla that looks brand new.

'Zach was too good for this world,' he says, when we swap places.

'He was.'

The car has a full tank of gas and no spiders climbing from the air vents. First thing I do is drive to my mum's house. Two of her neighbours are rolling paint over the garage door. *Child Killer* has bled through the undercoat, but is disappearing through the topcoat. I think they've underestimated how difficult the task is to make those words vanish completely. They nod at me to acknowledge they know I'm there, and they look sheepish, because this nice thing they're doing they should have done sooner, but maybe they agreed with the sentiment at the time.

Mum opens the door and hugs me on the front porch. She holds on tight and cries, but I can't, because when it comes to tears, I'm all spent. She holds on for a minute, and I hold her back, and there are some things in life your mum can't solve.

We head inside. We sit at the kitchen table, and she doesn't suggest we pray. Maybe she's done with it. She asks the same questions Lisa's parents asked – the 'what is wrong with this world?' questions – and I still don't have any answers. A parent should never have to bury a child, she says, and then doesn't know what to add to that, so adds nothing, and we end up sitting in silence. I was planning on staying here longer, but all of a sudden I can't stand it. I need to be alone. I tell her I have to go.

We hug on the doorstep, then I get back into Simon Crawford's car, and I drive from nice suburbs into less-nice suburbs into not-so-nice suburbs, and there I look for the shittiest motel I can find. The guy behind the counter is pouring tomato sauce over a plate full of sausage rolls. He doesn't recognise me from the news and tells me it's ninety dollars a night, which I figure is cheap for a nice motel but expensive for this one. I pay it. He hands me a chunky metal key attached to a chunky piece of plastic. I park Crawford's car outside my room and park myself inside a moment later.

I switch my phone off. I don't want Kent or anybody else calling me. Not even the hospital. I can't deal with any more bad news. There's an old digital clock radio on the nightstand. I set it to wake me up at midnight. I lie down and close my eyes. I won't sleep, but I'm hoping I can at least get some rest. I take Willy out of my bag and hold him against my chest.

I'd rather be at home. But at home I have the media outside, and family coming by, and the police with their updates, and knocking on the door, and questions from the street, and it's a production I don't want any part in. I need the peace and quiet of the motel room. I need to be away from everybody.

Because of what's to come.

I wait for it to get dark.

Chapter Fifty-Nine

The dozen or so reporters that were here earlier have doubled, having come back to shoot their end-of-day pieces. Moths are swarming and throwing themselves at the camera lights. Kent parks Cameron's car up the driveway. She wants to go home and sleep for the next two days. She feels so emotional that if one more bad thing happens today, she's going to quit her job and fly to the Caribbean and drink herself to death on a beach.

She doesn't knock on the door. She doesn't want to see again the look Cameron Murdoch has been giving her all afternoon. She hands the keys to an officer and tells her to give them to Cameron in the morning.

Her car has been fixed up. She gets into it. There's half a bottle of wine in her fridge at home, and some instant mac and cheese in the freezer. Now that she's thought about them, her stomach starts to rumble. But they're going to have to wait. She still has one more stop to make. Before she pulls away, a woman and her daughter place a bouquet of flowers at the front of the lawn, and a small teddy bear too. They put a candle next to them and light it. Others are walking towards the house carrying the same things.

She drives to Pittman's house. Like her previous stop, the street is empty of spectators, but there are a dozen or so reporters also doing the end-of-day wrap-up. There are patrol cars on the street, guarding the scene.

The house looks like it was built in the eighties, dark-green weatherboard walls and a gunmetal-grey A-frame roof. It's all clean and well-maintained, surrounded by a tidy yard. Inside is a mess, made that way from those who have searched it. There are bookcases in the lounge, dishes in the kitchen sink, jackets hanging over the backs of dining-room chairs. Nothing that stands out. Not until she gets to the children's bedroom, where the walls are painted blue and are covered in cartoon movie posters. She's seen plenty of those movies over the years with her niece. There's a bookshelf full of children's books and on top a line of teddy bears. There's a TV in the corner, one of the old tube ones that you only ever see these days lying in gutters when people are too lazy to drive them to the tip. It's on a cabinet, a DVD player beneath it, a bunch of movies lined up there too. There's a single bed with a duvet cover that has a large picture of a rocket ship on it. On a nightstand there's a lava lamp, an old Game Boy, a white-and-purple Furby, and an orange Tamagotchi. Everything in here feels like it came from a thrift store, except for the lifelike child-sized sex doll lying on the bed.

She has seen these dolls before in the homes of people like Pittman, and isn't surprised to see one here now. This particular doll is a boy, five foot tall, solid, forty kilograms of PVC and steel and silicon, human hair on top but none below, a special order. It has blue eyes and a dusting of freckles, and lips slightly parted and pointed upward at the end into a smile.

Creepy, yes.

Immoral, yes.

Illegal? No. And again the debate. Without the doll, would Lucas Pittman have hurt others too? Or did it fuel the fantasy?

She heads through a door in the laundry and out into the back-yard. There's a raised garden running the perimeter of the fence, almost knee-high, with a timber retaining wall. She makes her way over to a small shed that had the lock cut free earlier. She opens the door. There are shelves on the left full of gardening supplies;

in the middle is a lawnmower, and on the right tools hang from a wooden board. There's an empty hook with dried dirt on it. In the car crash, Zach Murdoch wasn't the only thing found in the trunk – the head of a spade was found in there too, the handle burned away. The spade suggests that even if Zach Murdoch was alive before the crash, he would not have been for much longer.

Her phone rings. She takes the call, and Vicky Curtis says, 'I have something for you.'

'You found prints on the cameras?'

'They were wiped clean, but I have something else. I contacted the manufacturer to get a precise release date for these models and to get better info on battery times. They said new firmware for the cameras was released on Monday. I checked the three we found – all three have the latest firmware installed, and that can't be done remotely. They have to be plugged into a computer for that.'

'They were updated on Monday.'

'Had to have been. Even if we had searched the ceiling more thoroughly on Monday, we wouldn't have found them – they couldn't have been there then.'

'So when did they go into the ceiling?'

'Sometime after we finished the search. Doesn't make sense that the Murdochs would put them in there. Why would they? To film themselves? Only time I can think the house was empty was Monday night. Maybe a reporter snuck in looking for an inside scoop? You know any reporters who would do something like that?'

She has somebody in mind.

'So where does that leave us with Pittman?' Kent asks.

'What do you mean?'

'First we thought that he had been hiding in the ceiling, but you saw no evidence he'd been up there. Then we find the cameras, only we know he didn't put them there. Is it a complete coincidence he chose the night Zach said he was going to run away to take him?'

'What else could it be?'

She doesn't know. But what she does know is that there are still things that don't add up.

THURSDAY

Chapter Sixty

I leave my phone in the motel room and head out. I drive from one neighbourhood into another, past sleeping houses and sun-baked yards. There's no media outside Spenser Barkley's place. A flag of the Silver Fern – New Zealand's official emblem – hangs limply from a flagpole next to the house, the Barkley patriotism on display. I park half a block away.

I pop the fuel cap on the car and jam a six-foot piece of garden hose I cut away earlier into it. The bandage on my hand makes everything tricky. I syphon petrol into the empty gin and whisky bottles. I also have a plastic fuel container for the lawnmower that can hold up to four litres. I put everything back into the bag, and it takes both arms to carry it, and even then I'm worried it's going to tear open under the weight.

I make it to Barkley's. I get the prybar out of my bag and ring the doorbell. This is where things can get tricky. Spenser Barkley is in custody, but there's every chance his wife, if he has one, is home, along with the child. Or maybe they're separated, and Barkley is a Disneyland Dad on the weekends and during the week he lives alone. Earlier in the day there were media here, so maybe the wife and kid have gone to stay with friends or family. I hope so. I don't want to hurt anybody, and I don't think I'll have to. The prybar will convince anybody to step aside and let me do what I came here to do. They can call the police from the front lawn later when the house is burning.

Nobody answers. I ring the bell again, and then again and again. I can hear it through the door. Then I try the door. It's locked.

The prybar is forty centimetres long. I jam one end between the door and the frame and pull. It slips out, taking a chunk of wood with it, leaving a bigger gap for me to try again. The prybar gets in deeper, and I yank on it and get my bodyweight into it. The frame bows, then splinters then cracks, and then the door busts open.

I step into the hallway and close the door behind me. The house is quiet. 'Hello?'

There's no answer. I turn on my small flashlight. I go into the lounge and put the bag on the couch and close the curtains. I turn on the lights. I do the same in the kitchen. I get everything lit up like a Christmas tree, except for the Christmas tree, which is in the corner of the lounge. I take Willy out of the bag. I sit him on the arm of the couch so he can watch. I take the lid off the plastic container and slosh petrol over the floor, the walls, the furniture, over family photographs of Spenser, his wife and their son.

I empty the bottles two at a time. I run petrol along the floor in the hallway and into the rooms. The first bedroom is the boy's room. He's not in it. Nobody is. It could be Zach's room. Similar bed, similar posters, similar toys.

Next room is an office. Could be Barkley is a budding novelist, or he holes up in here writing angry letters to newspapers and sharing his opinions online.

I go into the master bedroom. The bed hasn't been made, and has only been slept in on one side, the covers thrown back. I empty an entire bottle onto it.

I carry on into the next room.

I turn on the light.

Turns out the house isn't empty after all.

Chapter Sixty-One

The woman doesn't look anything like the woman in the photographs I've been pouring petrol over. That woman was tall, and strong and athletic. This woman looks like she was run through the photocopier, shrunk down forty per cent and had the colour removed. Her long blonde hair has been replaced by soft fuzz, and her big blue eyes are worn out, like they've seen a lot of bad things and know the time for seeing more is running out fast. An oxygen tube trails from under her nose to what looks like an air-conditioning unit plugged into the wall. Her arms are covered in bruised injection sites. Her face looks like it got peeled back, all the muscle and flesh beneath stripped away then glued back down. She's lying in a hospital bed in the centre of the room, currently angled up so she can face the door, or watch the TV – currently off – in the corner.

'You can,' she says, then slowly draws in a breath, and adds, 'put down the petrol. Unless you're here to put me out of my misery? You,' she says, and then takes a few more slow deep breaths, 'can if it will make you feel any better, but you should know if you stood there another day, two at the most, you'll get to see the same result anyway – though I guess it wouldn't be as messy.'

I don't say anything.

Nor does she, as she seems to recover from the effort it's taken her to say all of that. Her face tightens up, she inhales loudly then says, 'Unless messy is what you came here for?'

I still say nothing.

'Would you mind?' she asks, and she turns her head towards the table next to her, where there's a plastic pitcher of water and a plastic cup. I put the bottles down. I pour her a glass of water and hold it for her as she drinks through a straw. She closes her eyes as if it's the best water she's ever tasted.

'Thank you. Why don't you take a seat and chat with me a little, before you go ahead and do whatever it is you're itching to do,' she says, getting it all out on one breath.

I can smell the petrol. I can smell this woman dying. I close the door and open the window. It helps. I sit in the chair by the bed.

'I'm sorry about your son,' she says.

I picture Zach's black hand beneath the sheet at the morgue.

'It's a horrible thing what that man did to him,' she says, and then closes her eyes for a moment, focusing on breathing before she can carry on. 'I'm sorry about what happened to your wife. I'm sorry about what has happened to you.'

'You mean you're sorry about what *your husband* did to my wife.'

'Yes. I am.'

'What's your name?'

'Ellen.'

'Well, Ellen, I'm going to need to carry you outside.'

'I know you're angry,' she says, 'and you have every right to be. What Spenser did to your wife ... well, I don't have the right words for it. I know he's sorry. I know you have no reason to believe me, but he's a good man. What's happening to me is something he can't control, and he's frustrated, and he's wound tight, and he's taken that out on you. He can't lash out at me or the cancer, but he lashed out at you at the park on Sunday. He's nothing like the man I married. Nothing like the man he was even a month ago. Grief changes people. But I suspect the same is for you, that today you're not the man you were a week ago. But he's still in there, somewhere, and I bet the same goes for you too.'

She slumps deeper into the bed after the effort it's taken to say all of that. She coughs a little and smacks her hand at her chest, and I help her sip more water. She gets herself under control and carries on.

'The cancer eating my body is eating him too. I thought ... taking Brandon ... to the fair ... would do them both some good. I wanted

Brandon ... to have one good day because ... for a while there are ... only going to be sad ones, and you scared him, and I know ... you didn't mean to, but you did. I don't blame you, I don't, because I'd ... have done the same thing you did. But you need to know, Spenser ... at the time, he thought he was doing the right thing.'

'Did he think he was doing the right thing by coming to my house?'

She takes a moment. The effort she's going to here to talk to me could end up killing her. 'Of course not. He didn't ... mean it to go the way it did. I'm not ... making excuses for ... him. I'm just ... saying the way it is.'

'He made people think I molested your son. Lisa is fighting for her life because of him. You said a moment ago you would have done the same thing if your boy had gone missing at the fair. Imagine you had done that. Imagine people wrote songs about it, and joked about, and stood outside your house carrying placards and telling you they wished you were dead.'

'He made a mistake ... but he's still a good man. I know he is.'

'No. You just need to believe he is, because you're not going to be around much longer, and you need to convince yourself your son is in good hands.'

She looks at me as if I've slapped her.

'I'm sorry. That was cruel,' I say.

'Cruel, but true,' she says. 'If Spenser were ... here right now, I would drag myself out of this bed and kick his ass. But what ... happened to your wife was an accident, Mr Murdoch, and ... I'm hoping over time ... you can see that, and that you can forgive him. I need him ... to be shown ... kindness. I need him ... to go back to being ... the man I married so he ... can raise our son right.'

'I can't forgive him. And, if Lisa dies, he dies. I will make sure of it.'

She takes a few moments to think on that, then she says, 'I pray when your anger fades, you will see things different.'

'Praying doesn't work. I tried it.'

'None of this ... will bring your son back.'

'I know.'

'Burning down our house won't ... make you feel any better.'

'I'm willing to find out.'

She slowly nods, and she asks for more water, and I give her some. Then she says, 'In that case, help me outside. When the police come ... I will tell them that I did it. What are they going to do? Put me in jail?'

'Why would you do that?'

'Because ... your wife needs you ... by her side, and not in jail. Because I owe you ... for what my family did to yours. It was an accident, but you're right, if Spenser ... had never gone to your house, your wife would still be okay. I will do this, but only if you agree to one thing.'

'Which is?'

'That you ... think about ... what I've said. That you think about what you would have done ... if you had seen a grown man ... jump into that bouncy castle ... and put his hand on your son and upset him. I want you to ... think about those things, and I want you to ... promise me that you'll try and find your way back to the man you used to be.'

Chapter Sixty-Two

I help Ellen out of the bed, which is easy to do. She's all sharp angles, but there's no heft to them, no weight. I get her into her robe, and she tells me her son is with her parents, that her parents think a nurse is staying with her tonight, and that the nurse who has been helping thinks her parents are here.

'After what happened today, I wanted to be alone.'

It sounds like she is punishing herself. Years ago her orbit intersected with Spenser's orbit, they fell in love, they got married, she got cancer, and he got angry, and she's blaming herself for being the link in the chain that led to today.

Are you blaming her too?

I set her down on the front lawn. The street is still empty. No cops. No media. A van covered in bird shit and dust parked opposite that looks like it hasn't moved in years. A sleek convertible with sharp curves that are out of style behind it.

'Is there anything from inside that you want?'

'Nothing.'

'Choose a few things,' I say.

'Why?'

'Because people who set fire to their own homes take the things that are most important to them out first.'

'It's all important to me,' she says. 'You don't have to do this, you know.'

'I know.'

'You can't expect me to choose what to save and what to let burn.'

'In another day or two you won't even know.'

'That's mean,' she says. 'And I'll know now, and now is all I have.'

She's right. It is mean. 'Tell me where the wedding photos are. That's something people often save.'

She tells me, and then I remember what Pittman used to do for a living.

'How long ago did you get married?'

'Twelve years,' she says.

Pittman was in jail twelve years ago, which means there's no chance he shot their wedding. If he had, I'd let those photos burn. Instead I go back inside and grab them, along with some blankets.

'You know, I ... read one of your books years ago,' she says, when I hand the wedding album to her and drape blankets over her body. 'Your first one.'

'And?'

'And I didn't care for it much.'

I smile at that. I can't help it. Then I go back inside. I like Ellen. She's tough. In another life, we could have been friends. It's not her fault what happened. I pick up the bottles and the container and pack them into my bag.

'I know, this isn't what either of us signed up for,' I tell Willy, and Willy stares back at me. 'What do I do here?'

Willy doesn't answer, but Mr What If does.

You have two options. You punish somebody who doesn't deserve it, or you walk away.

When I come out, I hand Ellen her phone. 'I've changed my mind.'

'You're not going to torch it?'

'No.'

'If I could ... undo what Spenser did to your family, I would.'

'I know, but you can't. Nobody can.'

I turn and walk away from her petrol-sodden home. She calls out to me when I reach the footpath. Her voice is so soft that if the night weren't completely still I wouldn't have heard it. I turn back.

'I wish ... he had never gone to the fair,' she says. 'I wish ... he had never written ... to that reporter. It was that email ... that stupid email that made him do it.'

'What email?'

'From that reporter Spenser contacted. The one who spoke about you on TV.'

'Dallas Lockwood?'

'That's him.'

'Your husband knows Lockwood?'

'He follows him online. Over the last year ... Spenser has become ... well ... more susceptible to things. Lockwood tells people ... a certain kind of truth, and do you remember ... how we all used to ... laugh at the things people like Lockwood would say? Then one day ... we all woke up to discover ... half of the world wasn't in on the joke. That's what ... happened with Spenser. I thought he was ... in on the joke, only he wasn't, because guys like Dallas Lockwood ... and their brand of journalism ... made sense to him. I ask myself, was he always that way? Or is this what ... happens when you try to make sense of a world that's ... been broken by those who run it?'

'I wish I had an answer,' I say. 'Tell me about the email.'

'On Monday, when your photo ... came on the news, Spenser recognised you. I told him to ... call the police, but he didn't. He said ... there'd be no point, that the rules for famous people ... weren't the same for everybody else, and going to the police ... wouldn't do squat. That's when he decided to contact Lockwood, and then ... Lockwood told the world. Lockwood is always sending out newsletters and alerts. The usual stuff, like the ... government is ... poisoning the water, or vaccines ... give you cancer. He sent out an email saying you and your ... wife were going to try ... and flee before an arrest could be made, and people needed to show up. I asked him not to go. I wish he had listened to me.'

'I wish he had listened too.'

'I want you to burn it.'

'What?'

'We made a lot ... of good memories here, but Spenser ... is only going to remember the bad ones. Burn it, and maybe ... he can start fresh.'

'Are you sure?'

'I'm sure.'

I wait for her to change her mind. She doesn't.

I set a box of matches on fire. It lights up like a flare. I toss it through the front door and the effect is immediate – flames race along the trails of petrol and climb the walls.

We watch the house get brighter. Windows pop from the heat,

and flames spill out and lick at the roof. Sparks catch onto the flag, and then that burns too.

'Does it feel good?' she asks.

'No.'

'That's a pity.'

I get it then. Why she told me to burn it. 'You were lying about burning the house to make a fresh start.'

'Of course,' she says. 'You need to see ... how this feels bad when you thought ... it would feel good. This is how ... you will feel if you carry on down this ... path and hurt Spenser. Burning ... my home to the ... ground to show you that is worth it.'

I am in awe of how special this woman is. 'Spenser doesn't deserve you.'

'That's not for you to decide.'

I don't say anything.

'More importantly, you need to see ... how people can make mistakes. If you hadn't ... walked into my ... bedroom you ... could have burned ... down the house with ... me in it. In the morning ... you'd be waking to ... the news ... you were a murderer, and ... you'd be sorry, the same ... way Spenser is sorry.'

It's getting harder for her to talk now, but everything she has said – she's right. She's absolutely right.

'You win,' I tell her. 'I can't ever forgive your husband, but I promise to leave him in peace.'

'Thank you.'

Lights are switched on in the neighbouring houses, and doors are opened and people wander out. No doubt the fire department has been called. The police will be coming too. I leave Ellen on the front lawn in the heat of her burning house and walk back to the car.

Chapter Sixty-Three

Dallas Lockwood is going to die. That's a given. After all, the world is out of whack when a guy like Lockwood can be alive while a boy like Zach can't be. Lockwood made the world think we were guilty. He invited a crowd so large we couldn't be protected from it. Spenser Barkley may have been the one to push me, but Zach's death and Lisa's hurt, that's on Lockwood.

He's going to die. That's settled.

The question is, how?

Before I can answer that, I pull the car over. My body is shaking so much I can't drive straight. Not with anger at Lockwood, but with the shock of what I almost just did. Ellen was right that I could easily have set fire to her. It was only dumb luck that I kept pouring gasoline into rooms when I had already poured enough. The same way it was dumb luck that Spenser pushing me ended with Lisa fighting for her life. If I had five minutes alone with the guy, would I kill him? Forgive him? I suspect the answer is somewhere in between.

Fire trucks race past me, and I can see the glow from the fire in the sky. When I've stopped shaking, I pull back out from the kerb.

It's a ten-minute drive to Lucas Pittman's house. There is one patrol car parked outside and no media. The story isn't here. It was earlier in the day when the police were searching the house, but not now. I drive around the block. I find the house that backs on to his, figuring that climbing fences has been working well for me and will continue to do so.

I park a few houses away. I syphon out more petrol, but I don't fill as many bottles this time. Barkley's house went up in a fireball so easily I figure I don't need as much. I go through the property and lower the bag over the fence, then follow it, the drop not as far because of a raised garden. There's enough moonlight to get an okay look at Pittman's house. The scene doesn't match what happened here. There are no twisted weatherboard walls, no crows perched on the gutters watching me. This house is like any other in this street, this neighbourhood, this city.

I leave the bag and check the windows and back door. They're all locked. I can't get to the front door without being seen from the street. I'm weighing up using the prybar when I hear footsteps coming. I duck behind the garden shed in the corner of the yard as a flashlight comes into view. It's one of the officers. He's doing a check of the perimeter. He sweeps the light over the house, and if that beam goes over the back fence he's going to see the bag. I hold my breath, as if that can make a difference. The light moves over the yard in a way that suggests he's not expecting to find anything, and he doesn't. He reaches the back door and unlocks it. His light moves past the windows inside, and then a light comes on in a smaller window. He's using the bathroom.

I hide the bag behind the shed then go through the back door. I take the opposite direction from the bathroom. I end up in a lounge that faces the street. I lie on the floor behind a couch, worried the officer will hear how loud my heart is beating, or smell the petrol and fire from my clothes.

Only the officer doesn't hear my heart, not over the flushing toilet five minutes later, his footsteps and then the door closing behind him. A few moments later a car door opens then closes. Then there's nothing.

I crawl to the hallway and close the door between me and the lounge. I go out the back door and retrieve the bag. I turn on my small flashlight. I take Willy out of the bag and carry him with me as I go through the back half of the house. Three bedrooms, a bathroom, a laundry. One of the rooms is an office, with a desk and cables hanging out of it that attach to computers that aren't there. There are 12' x 16' photographs of abandoned buildings on the walls, beautifully lit, all artistic, four of them. Kent said some of Pittman's work has become book covers – which these look like they could have been. Is it possible any of our books have had one of his pictures on the front? I need to check, because if they have, then I'll burn our copies and ask my publisher to reprint new ones with new covers.

The room opposite is full of boxes stacked up, spare furniture, old curtains folded into squares. I pull the curtains out and drape them across the floor, knowing they will burn well. The next room is the master bedroom, where everything has been shifted around, the bed against the wall, drawers pulled out and turned over, piles of clothes everywhere.

The next room makes my skin crawl.

It's a bedroom that has been set up as a child's bedroom, posters on the walls, children's books and DVDs filling a bookcase. There is a box of toys on the floor, similar to the one that Zach has, but it looks sturdier, and I wonder, if we'd spent twenty dollars on a stronger box instead of ten, would we be in the situation we're in now?

But it's the sex doll on the bed that cranks the creepiness factor up to the maximum. At first glance it looks real, except for the face, with lifeless blue eyes and a forced-opened mouth that smiles at the edges. It looks like it has a lot of heft to it, a lot of weight. It's wearing a T-shirt that says *It's always Happy Hour here*, and I'm sure it was, but not for the doll.

The things this doll has seen, the things it has had to endure, I doubt it ever wished to grow up to be a real boy. Maybe at first glance it might look like the real thing, and maybe at first glance that was enough for Lucas Pittman, and then one day it wasn't.

I empty the bottles through the house, the carpets and furniture and curtains soaking it up. I pour some over the bed. The doll looks up at me, still smiling. I figure he's suffered enough, and doesn't deserve to be burned alive. I pick him up and drag him out of the bedroom, then tell myself off for being so stupid. If this doll really could wish for anything, it would be to be put out of its misery. I dump him in the hallway.

I leave the bottles behind. I won't need them anymore. What I have in mind for Dallas Lockwood doesn't involve burning his house down.

I ignite a box of matches and toss it into the hallway.

I grab my bag and step up onto the raised garden and climb the fence.

I don't have to figure out where Dallas Lockwood lives after all. He's on the other side of the fence, filming me.

Chapter Sixty-Four

Kent watches as water is pumped into the house while smoke pours out. The roof has collapsed, the left wall is now in the garden, pinning the fence beneath it, and the front wall has fallen inwards. She can see burned-out appliances in a burned-out kitchen and one remaining leg of a table. There are two fire engines, lights flashing, hoses snaking across the wet street, a dozen firefighters hovering on the edges. The neighbours are out watching, and media vans are showing up. There will be no doubt in anybody's mind – as there is none in hers – that Cameron Murdoch did this.

And, the thing is, she doesn't blame him.

Ellen Barkley told neighbours and paramedics that she set the fire. How or why, she wouldn't say. Kent will do her best to make sure the confession holds up and that Cameron Murdoch is left alone. He has been through enough.

She phones Thompson. Even though he has been suspended, she wants to tell him. She's unsure if she wants his career to survive this. He showed poor judgement this afternoon. She has always thought he was a good cop, and now she's thinking he's the kind of cop the country doesn't need. She doesn't doubt people are saying the same about her. He answers after a few rings. He sounds like he's been asleep, which makes sense, since it is now after one in the morning.

'I'm assuming you don't have anything good to tell me,' he says.

'Cameron Murdoch burned down Barkley's house.'

'Jesus, why'd he do that?'

'Why do you think?'

'Yeah. Fair enough. Was a stupid question. Anybody hurt?'

'Nobody. Murdoch did it, but Ellen Barkley is claiming responsibility, probably out of some sense of guilt for her husband's part in all of this. Neighbours found her sitting on the front lawn watching the flames. Apparently she's not long for this world – a few days at the most. Some kind of aggressive cancer.'

'And the son?'

'He was staying with family.'

She wonders what that will mean for the son, both parents taken away from him within days of each other, one to jail, potentially for years, and the other taken away forever. She doesn't know if there's other family to take him in, or if he'll end up in the system.

This case ... everywhere she turns, just misery piled on top of misery, the ripple effects still spreading.

'What's Murdoch saying?' Thompson asks.

'No idea. We don't have him in custody.'

'Where is he?'

'I don't know.'

'You can't check the tracking software?'

'We were ordered to disable it. So no, I don't know where—'

'You have to get to Pittman's house.'

'What?'

'If he burned down Spenser Barkley's house, he's probably on his way to Pittman's too,' he says, talking quickly. 'You need to call whoever is watching the house and let them know.'

'I will.'

'Do it now. We need to find him, otherwise all our houses might be next.'

Chapter Sixty-Five

I figure it's fate. Destiny. The universe can't balance the scales, but it's letting me know it's sorry. I see two possibilities. The first is Lockwood has been waiting here for me to show up, figuring I would. The second is he knows my trick of climbing fences and has been following me since I got into my neighbour's car. He's hoped and he's figured I was going to do something stupid, and he's hoped and figured right. He'll have this fire recorded. He'll spin it as me destroying evidence. He'll have recorded the other fire too. He'll spin that as me being vindictive towards a man who had the courage to stand up and say molesting children is bad.

'You want to tell my viewers what it is you're doing here?'

The camera and the light coming from it have paralysed me. Less petrol means it's going to take longer for the house behind me to become an inferno, but even so, it's only a matter of time before the noise wakes people. The neighbour whose yard we're in will be one of the first. I don't want to be standing over Dallas Lockwood's body when he comes outside to investigate.

I brush past and go out to the street, knowing he will follow me, and he does. He asks what was inside the house I didn't want the police seeing.

I look for potential murder weapons as I walk to the car. A rock from the garden. A broken branch. An empty beer bottle in the gutter. I could push his head into the ground. Into a letterbox. Into a fence. I reach the car. I put the bag onto the trunk. It clunks, which reminds me that Willy isn't the only thing in there. Parked opposite is the convertible I saw outside Ellen Barkley's house earlier. It must be Lockwood's.

I unzip the bag. Willy looks up at me. And beneath Willy is the prybar. I practise the move in my head, stepping into Dallas, swinging the prybar from the side. One blow to the head ought to do it. There's going to be blood but hopefully not a lot of noise. I turn to face him. There are no signs of life in the street, and I can't hear the fire, but I can see smoke and a glow coming from a hundred metres away. I reach back into the bag and pull Willy out. I want him to see this too, plus he can help. I switch him into my left hand, then reach back into the bag for the prybar. I keep my hand in there.

Lockwood is asking questions. I could get him now, while he's talking, but I don't. I could get him now, while he turns to see what I'm looking at over his shoulder, but I don't. Or I could wait till he's done with his questions and returns to his car, and get him then. But I won't. Instead I let Willy fall to the ground. I hate doing that to him, but I'm sure he understands. Lockwood looks down, and I tighten my grip on the prybar, and the target is easy, and—

I don't.

I don't, because burning down a house is one thing, and caving in the back of somebody's skull another. I let go of the prybar and take my hand out of the bag. I don't know if I feel more like a coward for wanting to have hit him, or a coward for doing nothing. Lockwood picks Willy up.

I put my hand out. 'That belongs to my son.'

'Your son won't miss him.'

'Let me have him.'

'That just makes me want it even more.'

I should have hit him with the prybar.

You still can.

'I'll tell you what,' says Lockwood. 'I will give you the toy back if you tell me what evidence you came here to hide and why you snuck back into your house on Monday night?'

'What?'

'I know that was you who attacked me. What were you doing there?'

'Haven't you done enough?'

'What's that supposed to mean?'

The glow of the house is bigger, but the street still quiet. The police outside Pittman's house will have noticed. I hope they're not putting themselves at risk by trying to flatten the flames with blankets. I hope they're standing back and waiting for the fire department to arrive.

'You know exactly what I mean, and you know exactly what you did. What happened to us, what happened to Lisa, *you* did that.'

He smiles. 'You're full of shit, Murdoch. You always have been. People might have believed you years ago when you said you didn't steal my book, but now they're seeing what kind of person you really are. They're seeing you're the kind of guy who handed his kid off to a paedophile. You're done, and I'm going to make sure the world sees it.'

'What are you talking about?'

'You gave your son to Pittman so he could have a little fun, and as soon as you're arrested, Pittman takes the boy somewhere to kill him, somewhere he can be found, and the time of death will show you were in custody when it happened, and bang, you're innocent. International publicity. Hell, you'd even get to write a book about it. Only Pittman panics and crashes, and that retard kid of yours dies before Pittman can kill him.'

You can still hit him with the prybar, Mr What If says.

Maybe.

After all, you're still carrying it...

No, I'm not.

You might want to check on that. Don't believe me? Then look down. You took it out of the bag.

I don't look down, but Mr What If is right. I can feel the weight of it. I wasn't aware of picking it up.

Really? Is that what you'll tell the jury?

'Don't call him that.'

'Hey, I'm saying what everybody is thinking. Your kid, he's about as re—'

'You're a real piece of trash, Lockwood. You appeal to people's darkest fears and tell them how the world is out to get them. You'll say anything for the attention. Give me the toy, and you can write whatever it is you want to write. None of it matters now anyway.'

'Okay,' he says. He puts the camera on a nearby letterbox so it can keep filming. Then he hands Willy over, and when I go to grab him, he pulls him back, turns him upside down, puts a leg into each hand, and gets ready to pull.

'Don't,' I say. 'Please—'

He rips Willy in half, stuffing falling out from the two equal-sized bits. He steps forward and pushes them into my chest. I get hold of one but the other one falls to the ground, because only one of my hands is free.

I step towards him.

'Take your best shot, tough guy,' he says, because it's what he wants, it's why the camera is pointing at us. He hasn't seen the prybar because I've kept it behind my thigh, so I take my best shot, and it turns out it's how people say it is in movies and on TV and in real life too: they say you lose control.

That's what I do.

I lose control.

Chapter Sixty-Six

I get him just above his right temple. It's possible he could have blocked it, but I think he wanted the blow. Getting assaulted would make the story better. But by the time he realises it's not my fist coming for him, it's too late.

It's also too late for me to stop. Even if I wanted to.

Which you don't.

Which I don't.

You wanted this from the moment he accused you of stealing his book.

Mr What If is right.

And now you got it.

Lockwood's head tilts to the side, and he opens his mouth to say something, but nothing comes out. One eye blinks rapidly and one hand starts twitching. He takes a step towards me, holds the pose, then his other foot takes a step back, and he looks confused by this turn of events, as if the wiring in his body has gotten mixed up. Then his front foot twitches, and he moves back and he falls, landing on his ass in an upright position. He looks to his side, putting the dent in his skull on display. There's no blood. At least not yet. Then he tips to his side, and his head hits the kerb, this time the other side of his head, this time a smaller thud and smaller twitches and probably a smaller dent too. His eyes blink rapidly.

I stand still, watching him as he convulses, one of his hands slapping against the road, then the slapping stops, and the convulsing stops.

And Dallas Lockwood stops.

I grab his shoulder. I give him a little shake. I was expecting something, but I wasn't—

Expecting this? Sure you were. You can be honest with me, we're all friends here.

'You okay, Lockwood?'

I drop the prybar onto the lawn and check him for a pulse. There's nothing. Lockwood isn't okay.

'Hey, wake up.'

He doesn't wake up. He can't. First of all, he'd need a pulse. Second of all, he'd need that thick dent in his skull popped back out. Which means I'm going to jail. Going to jail for killing the man who was hell-bent on destroying my family. And the thing is, I don't deserve to go to jail for this asshole.

You don't have to.

Go on.

What if Lockwood just disappeared? People might think you killed him, but who would know for sure? He must have a thousand people out there wanting him dead. Come on, Cameron – isn't this the kind of thing you've always thought you could get away with?

Once again, Mr What If is right. This is where the rubber meets the road. The moment where I learn if all the jokes I've made onstage about getting away with murder are actually jokes at all. Getting rid of a body is difficult, and getting rid of a car almost impossible. Even so, I'm going to have to do both. I find Lockwood's key in his hip pocket. I run over to his car and pop the trunk. There's not a lot of room, but he'll fit. Lockwood is a little bigger than me, but when I go to pick him up he feels twice the size. My back aches under the strain, and vertebrae and ribs threaten to pop out of position as I haul him over the road and jam him into the trunk. Only he won't fit. His car is too damn small. Most of him is in there, but his right leg won't go in. I poke at him and wrench him into different positions, but it's no good. It's going to take a saw to get the geometry to work. Which means putting him into the passenger seat. When I go to pull him out, he won't move. He's wedged in there. I put all my weight into it. I can't get him to budge.

Sirens in the distance. It's only a matter of time before fire engines and police cars come screaming past this street, and when that happens people are going to spill out of their doorways. I can't be here when that happens.

I cross the road and put the two halves of Willy into my borrowed car. I pop the trunk to see what my options are. I'm hoping for a blanket or a tarp, but the only thing in there are a couple of bungee cords. The sirens are getting louder.

I grab my bag and zip it up around Lockwood's leg. It's not ideal, but it covers what needs to be covered, even if it does look ridiculous. I hook a bungee cord into the latch of the trunk roof and pull it down tight and hook the other end under the bumper. I lock up my neighbour's car. When I look at it, the car doesn't stand out. It's nothing more than a normal sedan parked in a normal place.

Two fire engines and two patrol cars blast past the intersection ahead of me. I duck down and wait for one of the patrol cars to turn back, but none does. There is something bugging me, that I am leaving something behind, but I can't stay here. I get into the car and start it, then remember. The prybar. I left it on the lawn. I run over the road and scoop it up and run back. If I had remembered it earlier, I might have been able to work Lockwood out of the trunk with it.

I drive for a few blocks with the lights off, then the rest of the way with them on, taking side streets when I can. Remembering the prybar hasn't stopped the feeling that I have missed something.

I drive around the edge of town, past the airport to where small farms grow from the boundaries of the city before bigger farms take over. When I see headlights ahead, or behind, I turn off the road and wait for them to pass. I'm doing exactly what Dallas Lockwood wanted to catch me at. He's finally got the inside scoop.

I can't phone Andre and Rita because I don't have my phone, so I drive unannounced to their house. Andre and Rita are early to bed and early to rise kind of people, but this week I doubt they've been getting much sleep, evidenced by the fact there's a light on in the kitchen window. The gate is locked. It always is at night, a length of chain wrapped through it with a push-button lock. I tap in the combination then open the gate and drive through. I roll up to the front of the house and stop next to Rita's car. Last time I saw it, Lisa had parked it a few blocks away from our house. The front door to the house opens, and Andre steps out. He's wearing pyjamas. Kahn follows him. Andre holds his hand up to shield his eyes from the headlights. I switch them off. I switch the engine off too.

I get out of the car, and he lowers his hands. 'Cam? What are you doing here? It's not even...' he says, then looks at his wrist, only he's not wearing his watch. 'Can't be much later than two in the morning.'

'Where's Rita? She up too?'

He shakes his head. He steps into a pair of gumboots that are outside the door, then steps off the deck and toward the car. 'She's taken some sleeping pills. Whose car is that?'

'You said if I needed anything, you'd be there for me.'

'I did,' he says, after a small hesitation.

'Well, this is me needing something.'

'What's going on here, Cam? Best you right out and tell me.'

'I need to bury this car.'

'What?'

'I need it gone.'

'What have you done?' he asks, and he steps closer, and he notices the trunk is open, with something sticking out from it. 'What is it you have in there?'

'It's not a what,' I tell him.

'Jesus Christ, are you telling me what I think you're telling me?'

'The last thing I wanted was to bring this to you, but I don't have any other options. You either help me, or I go to jail.'

'Who's in the trunk?'

'Dallas Lockwood.'

He takes a step back. 'He's dead?'

'He is.'

'I told you. I damn well told you not to—'

'It's not like you think. He confronted me,' I say, which is mostly true. 'Look, what happened to him was an accident,' I say, which mostly isn't true. 'But with everything he said about me on the news, you think the police are going to believe that?'

He doesn't say anything, but I can see him thinking it through. Kahn moves around to the back of the car and takes a sniff.

'He called Zach a retard. He said we were better off with Zach dead. His next story was going to be about how we paid Lucas Pittman to kill our son. I snapped. I hit him. I didn't mean it to happen like this, but if I call the police I'll end up in jail.'

'He said those things?'

'He did.'

He nods thoughtfully. 'Sounds like he was baiting you. Was he recording you?'

Oh no.

'Cameron?'

The other thing I missed. The camera is still sitting on the letterbox. 'He was.'

'And you fell for it.'

What are the chances of somebody finding that camera? 'Look, I don't have a lot of time. I didn't mean for it to end like this, but it did, and I—'

'You don't seem upset about it.'

'I'm not.'

'I never would have thought it until this week, Cam, but you scare me.'

'I never did anything to Zach.'

'I know that, and I feel nothing but shame for ever thinking you might have. But this...'

'Lockwood is the reason we were arrested. Take him out of the equation and Zach could still be alive. Lisa sure as hell wouldn't have been hurt, because he's the reason behind those crowds being so large. You have a decision to make. You either call the police or you help me.'

'You're asking me to be an accessory.'

'Don't tell me that if you could have gotten your hands on Pittman or Lockwood you wouldn't have beaten the hell out of them.'

'Beaten, yes. Murdered, no.'

'Please, Andre, I'm asking for your help. I'm asking you to help me hang on to what family I have left. It's either that or I end up in jail.'

He chews at the nail on his thumb. 'You want me to bury the car.'

'Yes.'

'With him in it.'

'Yes.'

He keeps chewing at his thumb.

'You can do it, right?' I ask him. 'You can dig a hole big enough?'

'I can dig a hole big enough for the car, but I can't dig one big enough for him,' he says, nodding towards the body.

'I don't understand,' I say. 'We keep him in the car.'

'Think about it,' he says.

'We leave him in there, and—'

'And what? You have me get up every morning and look out over my farm knowing there's a dead guy buried out there? I'm sorry, Cam, I don't want to help you out, but I will, but that help only extends so far.'

'So what would you have me do with him?'

'I don't know. You're the crime writer. You figure it out.'

Chapter Sixty-Seven

The scene is similar to the one Kent just left. Hoses across a wet street, flashing lights, neighbours out watching, only this time she's here early enough to see the flames, to see windows and wood popping, to feel the heat from it. The walls of Pittman's house are still standing, fire lapping over the outsides of them, flaming pieces of curtain dissolving and floating into the sky.

Thompson is leaning against his car, watching the fire. He looks visibly shaken, the guilt from the arrest compounded by one more thing. What's next? Will Cameron try and burn down the police department? There are now officers watching Thompson's house, and some at hers too. Officers have entered Cameron Murdoch's home and found it empty. He must have climbed the back fence to leave, and he's done the same thing here to avoid the police. Half the department is now looking for him.

'This is my fault,' Thompson says when she walks over to him.

'No, it's Cameron Murdoch's fault,' she says. 'It's Lucas Pittman's fault. It's Spenser Barkley's fault. You made a mistake, but it wasn't a deliberate one.'

The right-hand side of the roof dips, slowly at first, and then it crashes into the bedroom, shifting the point of the large A-frame onto a forty-five-degree angle, one end against the ground, the other still high up on the walls. Embers leap from it onto the fence. They are doused before they can take hold.

'I'm going to go,' she says.

'Go where?'

'Dallas Lockwood's house.'

'What?'

'I think it could be Cameron's next target. We know they have a history. Also, we found cameras hidden inside the Murdoch house. We think Lockwood gained entry to the house on Monday night and planted them. I went there a few hours ago to question him about it but he wasn't home. We also know Lockwood sent an email to his followers this morning to wind them up. He asked them to come to the house. It's why there were so many people there.'

'Shit.'

'Was it you?'

'What?

'You heard me. You wanted an audience for the arrest, and you got one. Was it you that's been tipping Lockwood off?'

'Fuck you, Rebecca.'

'I have to ask.'

'No, it wasn't me. I've never even spoken to the guy.'

'Okay. I'm sorry.'

'Whatever.'

'Look, Murdoch is working through a shit list, right? I've already got officers at Lockwood's place, but I'm going to go check it out anyway, and if Cameron shows up I'll deal with him.'

'Fine. You do that.'

'Fine, I will,' she says, because if she went home she wouldn't be able to sleep anyway.

She leaves Thompson to watch the fire as the A-frame roof lets go of the wall and continues to topple over, one side flat against the ground, the other side pointing into the sky.

Chapter Sixty-Eight

We move the car into the barn and cover it with a tarpaulin. Andre says we'll take care of it in the morning, that if we were to fire up digging equipment in the middle of the night we'd be apt to draw attention. Which is fine, because I need to get back to the camera.

Andre takes Kahn inside, gets dressed, grabs his keys and then drives me back to Pittman's house. He drops me off four blocks away. I want to say 'thank you', but before I can, he says, 'Save it. I'll see you soon.'

I make the walk. I don't pass anybody, and there is little traffic, a couple of media vans that I duck into gardens for so they don't see me on the way past. I get to the car and it's how I left it. The camera is on the letterbox. I snatch it up.

Is there anything else? Did you leave your driver's licence behind? Writing about crime isn't so tough when you have all day to think about it, but when the sirens are heading towards you it's not so easy, is it?

The thing is, there is something else, because the feeling I haven't tidied everything away still won't disappear. I walk around the car, looking at the ground, looking for what that might be, but there's nothing here – just paranoia.

I drive back the way I came. Andre is waiting for me next to Lockwood's car. I reverse up next to it and pop the trunk.

'Before you ask,' he says, 'I haven't reconsidered. I'm not having this guy buried on my land.'

'I wasn't going to ask.'

'And before you tell me, I don't want to know what you're doing with him.'

'I wasn't going to tell you, but I am going to need a shovel.'

I unhook the bungee cord and remove my bag and get the trunk open. Andre doesn't shy away from seeing a dead body. He's seen others, and in far worse shape, and he isn't afraid to get his hands dirty. Lockwood's shoulders have gotten wedged between the bottom and the top of the trunk. It takes the two of us working at him to get him free. We switch him into the other trunk, first laying down a picnic blanket. We consider wrapping him up tight in polythene or a tarpaulin, but it'll only make him more difficult to handle at the other end.

'Come by first thing,' Andre says, when Lockwood is squared away and the tarp is back over the convertible. 'The sooner we get the car in the ground the better.'

He stands in the driveway and watches me leave. In the glow of the brake lights he looks like he's been soaked in blood.

The car is heavy in the back, and I feel Lockwood's body shift when I take corners. I stick to side streets and I drive through suburbs. Nice houses. Not so nice houses. Big parks and big malls, and small parks and small malls. Big churches and small churches and ugly churches and simple churches. I choose the hundred-year-old church where my dad had his funeral, in a part of the city where the newest house is fifty years old. The gate that leads into the graveyard next to the church is closed, but it's not locked. I get out and open it and drive through, the church becoming hidden by large poplar trees to my left, while rows and rows of dead people line the landscape straight ahead. The graves expand outward, mostly old ones near the church, then newer ones as I drive further. I drive slowly with my lights off, enough moonlight to see where I'm going, knowing it's only a matter of time before I find what I'm looking for, thinking it'll be five minutes, but ten minutes go by and then fifteen, and I'm almost at the point of giving up when I find it – a mound of dirt piled up and hidden by a tarpaulin.

I come to a stop and walk carefully towards it, pointing my flashlight at the ground, not wanting to fall into the open grave that must be nearby. I find it a few metres ahead, a rectangle freshly carved from the earth, waiting to be filled. It's deep. They're always deeper than you think they're going to be.

I put the flashlight on the ground next to it, then go back to the car. I get the trunk open and wrench Lockwood out. I carry him over and drop him next to the grave. I ought to feel guilty but I don't. Either murder is easier than I thought it'd be, or it hasn't sunk in yet.

I grab the shovel. I put it across the width of the grave and swing from it to lower myself in. Then I dig. The ground is hard, and I have to stomp on the shovel and stab it down, but the earth comes away. I dig at one end and pile dirt at the other. When I'm down half a metre, I hook the shovel back over the top of the grave, pull myself up and scramble out.

I roll Lockwood into the grave. He thuds heavily into the bottom. I grab his camera. It's still recording. I hit stop, then scroll through the footage. Like I thought, he started following me from my neighbour's house. He's filmed everything, including his murder. I erase the footage and take out the memory card. I lower myself back down. It's too soon for rigor mortis to have set in, so I'm able to fold Lockwood in half, getting his face close to his feet, then getting him into the hole I've carved out. I scoop the dirt back and level everything off. The ground is higher than what it was, but shouldn't be noticeable.

I drive back out the way I came in, tossing the prybar and the now broken-in-half memory card and camera into the small lake along the way, along with the blanket. I drive past the church, thinking I'll be coming back here next week for Zach's funeral.

It's four in the morning when I get back to the motel. I take a long shower. The bandage is covered in dirt. I take it off and dump it into a bin. I turn on my phone and see I've missed a bunch of phone calls from Kent, the first one coming in at one a.m., the last one coming in twenty minutes ago. No doubt she's calling about the fires. She hasn't left any messages.

I don't call her back.

I turn my phone back off and I go to bed.

I think about Dallas Lockwood, the look on his face when he tore Willy in half, the look on his face when he realised it was more than my fist swinging at him, the look on his face when I rolled him into the ground.

There's something else too. Even though I got the prybar and the camera, I know somewhere over the last few hours, when the rubber was meeting the road, there's been a slip. Those two things briefly separated, and in that moment I've overlooked something. If Lisa were here, she'd spot it. It's what makes us a great team.

Only Lisa isn't here.

And nor is Zach.

Chapter Sixty-Nine

Cameron Murdoch is having an out-of-body experience. When he wakes up to daylight – he's surprised he even slept – he takes another shower. This is the first morning in the rest of his life when his son is no longer in it, but it's also the first morning in the rest of his life when he's a killer. He's numb. He feels old now, older than he's ever been, older than he ever thought he would feel.

I watch Cameron Murdoch dry himself then get dressed in the same dirty clothes from last night. His knuckles have torn skin and spots of blood. It's not a traditional out-of-body experience, because I'm not watching myself from outside, but rather from within. I'm a passenger, going along for the ride.

Cameron checks out of the motel.

'How was your stay?' the motel clerk, a woman who is as tall as she is wide, asks him.

I don't say anything, but I hear Cameron say, 'Good, thank you.'

'You look familiar,' the woman says. 'You on TV or something?'

'I have that kind of face.'

Cameron gets into his neighbour's car.

Cameron drives away.

Cameron makes lefts and rights, and he indicates, and by the time he gets to his neighbourhood he has no memory of even driving there, and he thinks, Cameron thinks, did he drive? Or did the Hand of God pick him up from point A, and drop him at point B? He can hear a storm on the horizon. Can't see it, but can hear it.

Cameron parks the car up Mr Crawford's driveway. He gets out, and Mr Crawford comes out of the house, and Mr Crawford says, 'Are you okay, Cameron? You don't look right.'

'I'm good, thank you,' he hears himself saying, and he looks up for the storm. It's getting louder. He can hear the wind. Can't feel it, but can hear it.

Cameron takes the bag out of the car and the two halves of Willy.

Mr Crawford looks him up and down. He takes in the dirty clothes and the soot, and he nods slowly, and he says, 'Gonna be a hot one today. I think I might give the car a good clean. Get it looking like new. You think that's something I ought to get about doing?'

'Yes,' Cameron says.

'I might detail it on the inside too.'

'That's a good idea,' Cameron says, having to talk louder. The storm is here. Can't see it, but he can feel the pressure building in his head.

Cameron climbs the fence.

Cameron drops down into his yard.

The storm catches up. It's loud, a loud rushing sound like he's in a wind tunnel. Cameron collapses onto his knees, and we hold our hands up to our head, and I close my eyes and wait it out. The storm passes, and I am no longer a passenger. But, when I end up in court for killing Lockwood, I'll say that I was.

I get to my feet. I can hear Mr Crawford spraying the hose over his car.

I go inside. The window has been replaced and the broken glass cleaned up. The crowd outside is a fraction of what it was yesterday, but the front lawn has been covered in flower bouquets and teddy bears and cards. I change into fresh clothes and toss the dirty clothes into the washing machine and turn it on.

I go into the lounge and put a rubber band around Willy to

hold him together, then turn on the TV so we can watch the news. There is a woman being interviewed. Her hair is red, and her eyes are red, and her face is red too. She's crying, and mad, and like many of us, broken.

'...fault,' she says. 'Of course it is. Cameron Murdoch killed my boy, the same as if he had taken out a gun and shot him.'

I have no idea what she is talking about.

'Only he didn't shoot him,' the journalist says.

'No, but he may as well have. And before you say my boy shouldn't have been there with all those other people, let me remind you it was his God-given right to go to their house and be angry about it, the same way as all those other folks.'

'The Murdochs had nothing to do with what happened to their son,' the reporter says, and it could be Rolled Sleeves, I don't know, it doesn't cut to him. The camera stays on the face of the woman in pain.

'I don't know how Cameron Murdoch did it, but he did it. We all know he did it. You ever read his books? A man like that, a man who can write twisted things like he writes, well, he has to be wrong in the head, doesn't he? And it's like that man said on the news a few nights ago, if anybody can get away with a crime like that, it's a crime writer. I know what people are going to say. I know they think my son got drunk with his friends, and they were acting the fool dressed up like nuns and priests, and that it was an accident he fell from the top of that pyramid, and they'd be right to say that. But the bottom line is if Cameron Murdoch weren't a killer, then my boy would still be alive.'

Chapter Seventy

We all know he did it.

The woman's words hang in the air long after I've turned off the TV. I stare at them, I watch them hang, I watch them shift on the breeze, these words, these six words that will always be with me. It doesn't matter what I say, or what the police say, we all know I did it.

What if there's some way of proving…

'Yes?'

Well, what if…

'Yes?'

I'm sorry. I got nothing.

I remember the young men dressed as nuns and priests. I remember somebody screaming for help during the arrest. I feel bad for the woman who has lost her son, I truly do, and for the boy too, but I refuse to let myself feel any sense of guilt. I don't have any left to spare.

I carry Willy down to Zach's bedroom and rest him on the bed. Soon I will tidy the bedroom up, and it will stay tidy until the day I die. There is a commotion outside. I get to the door before the bell rings. It's Kent. She's always here. I ought to turn my office into a guest room for her.

She squeezes past me without an invite. 'How's Lisa doing?'

'I haven't called the hospital yet. Why are you here?'

'I wanted to come by and check in on you, and give you some updates.'

It's bullshit. She wanted to come by to see if I smell like smoke. Or maybe they've found Lockwood already. 'I don't want you here without my lawyer.'

She sighs, and she slumps, and she relaxes, and she asks, 'Do you have coffee?'

'What?'

'Do you have coffee?'

'Yes.'

'Good. Because you look like you could do with it, and I sure as hell could. Please, Cameron, I'm not here as a police officer.'

'What are you here as? My friend?'

'Why don't you freshen up, and I'll make us some coffee, and then we can talk.'

I thought I was fresh. But then I realise my hair is sticking up, and I haven't shaved in days, and even though I showered at the motel, there wasn't any soap. I go into the bathroom and spray around some deodorant, and I wash my face and I do my hair, and I look at the man in the mirror, and I don't recognise him, but he looks better than the one who walked in here. I put fresh bandaging around my hand. I call the hospital.

Back in the kitchen Kent has made two cups of coffee. She's started on her one. She's made mine strong. Kent was right – I did need it. It's the only thing she's been right about all week.

'I rang the hospital.'

'And?'

'And there's no change. The doctors say there's no chance Lisa can go to Zach's funeral, but every chance she will be in hospital for some time, potentially months.'

'I'm sorry,' she says.

'Yeah, there seems to be a lot of that going around. Look, I have things to do. So ... again, why are you here?'

She seems to be struggling with whatever it is she wants to say, and in the end she says, 'Let's go for a drive.'

'To the station?'

'No. Please, I know you hate me, and you hate all of us, and I don't blame you for that. I really don't. And I have no right to ask you for anything right now, but I would like you to come with me. Like I said, I'm not here as a police officer.'

'Fine. But let's make this quick.'

Chapter Seventy-One

Neither of them finish their coffee. They go outside. The media is back in force, but the good folks of Christchurch who came for the show over the last few days have stayed away. When questions are asked, Kent takes a moment to tell them the Murdoch family has suffered a great loss, and that the police are looking to learn more about Lucas Pittman. She thanks them for their time, ignores their questions and promises to give them more information at a twelve o'clock press conference, which she has every intention of handing off to somebody else so she can go home and sleep. She's beat. She didn't get home till four in the morning, after spending almost two hours sitting in a quiet street, watching a quiet house not being set on fire. She'd be at home right now if it weren't for the fact officers saw Cameron Murdoch arriving at his house earlier and called her. Given it seemed Murdoch climbed over his fence last night to leave, it made sense he'd come back the same way.

'The story will fade,' Kent says, when they get into her car. 'They always do, and you'll get your privacy back.'

'Do you think that woman in the news was speaking for everybody when she said "we all know he did it"?' Cameron asks.

'What woman?'

'The one whose son died outside our house.'

'That wasn't your fault,' she says. 'And no, she's not speaking for everybody at all. There was a vigil outside your house last night, did you know that?'

'No.'

'There were hundreds of people here. They lit candles, and they held hands, and they cried and they prayed for you.'

'They're just trying to make themselves feel better for what they did.'

They drive in silence for a while. From the direction they're going, she's sure Murdoch has figured out where she's taking him.

'Where's Thompson?' he asks.

'He's been put on leave.'

'Will he lose his job?'

'There'll be a review into what happened. He made a bad call.'

'That's how the police sum up what happened to Lisa? As a bad call?'

'No,' she says. 'Of course not.'

'He's a bad cop,' he says. 'He let his anger cloud his judgement. From day one he thought we were guilty.'

'We were all wrong,' she says. 'Not just Thompson.'

'Yeah, but Lisa was the one who got hurt, not you, and not Thompson.'

They pull up at an intersection next to a car with a stereo so loud Kent's car vibrates from the bass.

'I've been thinking about something since yesterday,' he says. 'As soon as you knew Zach hadn't run away, you must have looked for people in the area with a record for sexual offences involving children. How come Pittman wasn't interviewed?'

Kent was hoping he wasn't going to ask her this. She looks ahead, and she flexes her grip on the wheel. She exhales loudly, then she says, 'He was.'

'What?'

'Detectives spoke to him at his house.'

The car with the loud music pulls away. She stays sitting at the intersection even though it's clear. She keeps staring straight ahead. She can feel Cameron's eyes burning into the side of her face.

'They went there, and they went inside and they looked around. Pittman didn't raise any red flags.'

'Which detectives?'

'I can't tell you that right now,' she says, but it was Vega and Travers, two good detectives, and she likes to think if there had been anything there to see they would have seen it – only they must have missed something.

'You are kidding me. Tell me you're kidding me.'

'I'm sorry, Cameron. We—'

'It's Mr Murdoch from now on.'

'I'm sorry. But they spoke to Pittman, and—'

'And you people went there with your minds made up. You went there thinking I was guilty and couldn't see anything else.'

A car pulls up behind them and toots. She carries on driving.

'You could have saved Zach.'

She says nothing.

'When were you going to tell me this?'

'I'm telling you now.'

'You should have told me yesterday. You ... you could have prevented this.'

'I know how this must sound to you, but—'

'I don't think you do know,' he says, 'because if you did, I don't think you'd be in this car with me alone right now.'

She ignores the threat. 'I spoke with the detectives who interviewed him. They questioned him and searched his house. They said he said nothing, and they saw nothing to indicate he knew anything about Zach. Obviously they were wrong, and obviously there will be some type of review.'

'You said Zach's bag was found under the bed. How did they miss that?'

'One of the detectives looked. She said it wasn't there.'

'Bullshit. She didn't look. If she had, she would have found it. Zach was probably in the house somewhere and—'

'He wasn't there,' she says. 'If he had been they would have found him. They checked under beds, and in wardrobes, and his car and the garage – they checked everywhere.'

'And they didn't find anything in the house disturbing enough to warrant further investigation?'

She knows what he really wants to ask, only he can't ask it. He wants to ask about the room set up as a child's bedroom and the doll. Asking would be admitting he was there.

'There were things that were disturbing, but nothing illegal, and like I said, nothing to suggest Zach had ever been there.'

'They probably barely looked. Why would they? You already had your suspects, didn't you?'

'That's not how it works, Mr Murdoch. The parents are always considered suspects, yes, but that doesn't mean we stop looking elsewhere. The thing with Lockwood, all the things he said on TV, we already knew that. Of course we did. We started putting that together from the moment we knew your son was missing, so of course we were—'

'Oh, so it's our fault for saying those things onstage and in interviews.'

'I'm not saying that.'

'It sounds like you are.'

'You can't blame us, Mr Murdoch, for thinking the very things you've said for years you were capable of doing.'

He doesn't have an answer for that, and she hates herself for having said it.

'I'm sorry,' she says. 'I wish things had gone different.'

'I honestly don't know what to say. All of this could have been avoided. Zach would still be alive. Even if Zach wasn't being kept there, Pittman was keeping him somewhere. If your guys had figured that out, he would still be alive.'

She doesn't answer.

'You said Pittman's neighbour said he was agitated. That was probably because you guys spooked him. You know, I can't help but think of what we spoke about yesterday, about bad cops keeping their jobs. Tell me, how is it possible you guys can interview Pittman and not see that he had our son, and interview us and not see that we were innocent?'

'Don't you think I've been asking myself that?'

'Why should anybody ever trust you again? Huh? I'm serious. Why should you wake up tomorrow and still be a police officer, when you've proven you're bad at it?'

'You know, Mr Murdoch, you're probably right. And there's every chance tomorrow I'll wake up and decide not to be.'

That quietens him, and she's grateful. When they're nearly at Pittman's house, she says, 'Ellen Barkley died this morning.'

'Who?'

She ignores the question. 'She had cancer. She died a few hours ago in hospital. She was hanging on for months, but went down-hill quickly over the last few days. You want to know what the last thing she did in this world was?'

'I don't even know who she is.'

'Cancer-ridden and bedridden, she dragged herself through her house, pouring petrol everywhere, then set it on fire. She made her way out to the front yard to watch it burn.'

'Why are you telling me this?'

'She didn't say why she did it, just that she did.'

They pull into Pittman's street, where there are media vans, and police cars and spectators. The fire has brought the story back. A barrier is lifted aside so they can drive through. They stop in front of a house that is no longer a house. There are walls, but they're charred, and there are wooden beams, but they're bent and warped, and others have turned to ash. A sidewall is down, making the house-no-longer-a-house look like a diorama, with a view of furniture that is no longer furniture, but slabs of twisted metal, and melted polyester and toasted wood. The roof has pancaked the bedrooms beneath it. Metal poles and timber joists are being used to brace the remaining walls. There are holes where there used to be windows. There are blackened stumps in the garden. The garage is a pile of roof tiles topping off a pile of rubble. There's a fire engine parked out front in case the whole thing flares back up.

'This is Barkley's house?'

She stares at him then she says, 'No. This is Lucas Pittman's house. Or was. He grew up here.'

'Wait. I don't follow. Why—?'

'Save it,' she says. 'Everything you said earlier, you're right. I made mistakes, and I have to live with them. But right now I'm not being a cop, so just listen, would you?'

'Fine. I'm listening.'

'I know you did this. I know—'

'I didn't—'

She puts her hand up. 'Let me say what I brought us here to say. Okay? Can you at least hear me out before you deny you were here, then remind me I'm the worst cop in the world? Can you do that for me, Cameron?' she asks, feeling tired, feeling exhausted, feeling the pain of the week burning inside her. 'Can you do me that one small thing?' she asks, and it's stupid, but she feels like crying. He's got every right to be mad at her, but she gets it. She fucking gets it.

'Okay,' he says, and he hears her out.

Chapter Seventy-Two

'The first thing I thought of when I heard Spenser Barkley's house was on fire was, I hope that makes Cameron feel better. Twenty minutes later, when I saw Pittman's house burning down, I thought, I hope that makes Cameron feel better too, because no doubt he deserves to feel something other than heartache and pain. I know you did this, Cameron. I know and I don't care, and if you promise that this is it, that you're done, then I'm going to do everything I can to help you.'

'It wasn't me.'

'You weren't home last night. Where were you?'

'I stayed at a motel. I couldn't be at home, not after ... with ... you know, and with all those people out there.'

'You climbed your fence when you left your house?'

'I couldn't exactly go out the front.'

'Because of the media.'

'Yes.'

'And you didn't want them following you. You drove?'

'I walked.'

'You walked.'

'That's what I said.'

'I tried calling you several times during the night,' she says.

'I had my phone turned...' *Fuck.*

'Cameron?'

You are fucked.

'What's wrong?'

What's wrong is I know what happened in that moment where the rubber slipped away from the road. The thing I couldn't see in the small hours of the morning. I didn't turn Dallas Lockwood's phone off. It's still in his pocket, transmitting from the bottom of his grave.

What if somebody rings it as mourners are standing around, burying a family member?

Maybe Lockwood turned it off himself, or perhaps the battery went flat, or maybe he didn't bring it with him.

And maybe none of that happened, and the police can track him.

'Cameron?'

'Huh? Oh, I was saying I had my phone turned off.'

'Are you okay?'

'Look, is this going to be a thing? Every time something bad happens in this city, you're going to show up on my doorstep? I thought you didn't bring me here as a cop.'

'No. This is me giving you a pass. I know you were here, we all do, and I know you didn't walk last night because you were seen driving home this morning in your neighbour's car. Before you tell me I'm wrong, let me tell you that I'm going to do my best to make sure we can let this slide. But this is also me giving you a warning. What's done is done, and nothing you can do can change that, and those responsible for it have been punished.'

Not all of them.

'I wasn't here last night.'

'You're a bad liar.'

'Uh-huh. And if you had figured that out from the beginning Zach would still be alive.'

She doesn't have an answer for that.

We pull away from the kerb. The barriers get moved, and the crowd parts.

Back home the street is empty except for two patrol cars parked out front. The media have gone to the police station to prepare for the press conference. I hadn't noticed it before, but there are dozens of burned-down candles in the gutters. Kent walks me to the doorstep. She asks about Zach's funeral, and she says she'd like to come along if that's okay.

'I don't want you there. Honestly, Detective, I can't stand the sight of you. In fact, I never want to have to see you again.'

She nods and says nothing, and goes back to her car.

I go inside. All the evidence the police took away on Monday is back. Computers and tablets and files and folders, clothes, shoes, everything, all of it stacked on the dining table.

I have the urge to set fire to this place too.

Three houses in one day.

Could be some kind of record.

Chapter Seventy-Three

I don't burn my house down. Instead, I call Andre and ask him to come and pick me up. Even though my car is back, I don't want to use it. I have the bad feeling Kent might have put a tracker on it to see what, or who, I'm going to burn next. It takes fifteen minutes for Andre to arrive, and he parks out front, the street still empty. For now. I head for the door.

Take a jacket with you.

It's hot outside, but Mr What If makes a good point, so I grab a leather jacket. Outside, a few neighbours are floating around, and some wave, and some nod, and all of them look sheepish. The guy charging money for his bathroom is wheeling his barbecue off his front yard. He sees me and offers a *what are you gonna do?* shrug.

I get into Andre's car. Rita is with him. Which is fine, because we need to go back to their house before going to the cemetery anyway. I rest my hand on Zach's car seat. They tell me they've just been to see Lisa.

'How are you holding up?' Andre asks, staring at me in the mirror, his question having a deeper meaning than Rita knows.

'I'm doing the best I can,' I say, because it's honest, and because I can't tell them I'm working on my grief by taking it out on others.

Rita does most of the talking on the way to the farm. She says Lisa is stable and doing better, and the reason the doctors can't make any assurances that she's going to be okay is 'you know what people are like these days, always covering their own asses'.

We get to the farm and go inside. Photo albums have been spread over the dining table. Kahn comes padding from the other end of the house and growls at me. Andre tells him to go into the lounge. Which he does, going in there and jumping onto the couch where he's been told a thousand times not to jump, only this time nobody says anything.

'I want Zach to be buried out where my dad is,' I tell them.

'Whatever you want,' Andre says.

'It's beautiful out there,' Rita says.

I look at Andre. 'I'm wondering if you can come with me out there to take a look around. I can't do it by myself.'

'I can do that,' he says.

'You should have said something when we picked you up,' Rita says. 'We could have gone straight there.'

No, we couldn't have, because she wouldn't like what was going to happen there, and anyway, there'd be no point in doing any of it if it turned out Lockwood has left his phone in the car. 'Just Andre,' I say. 'If that's okay. Just for now.'

'Whatever you want,' Rita says, but it's obvious she's hurt.

'Rita, I'm wondering if you can visit my mum. She ... she's struggling, and ... well ... I'm thinking it would be really good for her if you were there. Maybe you could drive her to the hospital to see Lisa?'

'Of course.'

'Before you do, can you call the church and make the arrangements, and get somebody to meet us there?'

'Of course.'

Rita heads for the phone, and Andre follows me outside. I walk over to the barn.

'We can't bury the car until Rita is gone,' he says.

'We're not burying it yet,' I say, and I go inside and pull away the tarpaulin. I climb into the car and go through the glove box, and I look under the seats and in all the possible places there might be a phone. There isn't one. Of course there isn't. Why would things be easy?

'What are you looking for?'

'Nothing. Come on, let's go.'

'Jesus, Cameron, we need to get that car into the ground. Let's wait till Rita has gone and we'll take care of it.'

'We will, as soon as we get back,' I say, and I put the tarp back over the car.

We get into Andre's car. He drives. We don't say much. We can't keep asking each other how we're doing, or telling each other that things will get better.

We get to the church. It's grey stone with dark, flaking mortar, sprinkled with moss where the sun doesn't hit. There's a spire at the front with stained-glass windows up high, different versions of Jesus going about his life: walking on water and feeding the poor; and going about his death: dragging a crucifix then hanging from it. There's a large set of oak doors in the centre, large enough to drive a bus through. Ferns line the bottom of the building along the side where it's shady, and flax bushes line the front where it's not. Andre parks in the parking lot, and I grab my jacket.

'You're not going to need it,' Andre says.

I take it anyway.

A man steps out from between the oak doors and approaches us. Father Jacob. He's late sixties. He has warm eyes and shaver burn, and grey hair that is swept to the side. His pants have sharp creases, and his tie is a darker shade of black than his shirt. He doesn't look anything like the priests who were drinking beer outside my house. He presided over my dad's funeral, and he seems to recognise us from then, because he immediately says he's sorry for our loss and shakes our hands. Or he recognises me from the news. After all, Dad's funeral has been one of many over the years.

'Are there any burials happening today?' I ask.

'A couple,' he says. 'We had one this morning, and there's another one early this afternoon.'

That leaves me with a fifty-fifty chance. 'Can I see where?'

'Excuse me?'

'I'd like to see where. To see if that area is the right area for Zach.'

It must be an unusual request, but rather than query it, he says, 'We have a few sections within the grounds we can—'

'Let's start with where the next one is happening.'

He nods, and he tells us it's a ten-minute walk, and we say that's fine, and he leads the way. Nothing looks the same as it did last night. I recognise the church and the poplar trees, but that's it. Graves roll into the distance in a sea of neatly kept lawn, all of it looking the same. Father Jacob knows exactly where he's going. He doesn't act as a tour guide, figuring we're not in the mood for it, but he does say it's a beautiful day and a beautiful time of the year, and that their caretaker works out here six days a week, keeping the grounds in shape.

He's right about the walk being ten minutes. I'm sweating by the time we get there. The day is heating up. The two funerals today are fifty metres apart. The one this morning is all closed up, the people gone, a flat piece of ground with a rectangular patch of dirt. That's not where Lockwood is. He's at the bottom of the open hole in the shade of a nearby pair of evergreen conifers. The conifers – these ones rimu trees – are twenty or so metres tall, meaning it's only a matter of time before they're culled and turned into a pile of coffee tables. Not far away is the small lake I tossed the prybar and memory card into. There are oak trees growing around the side of it that last night I hadn't noticed. In fact I hadn't noticed much of this at all last night. Looking out over the cemetery, there are so many different types of trees it's as though each person going into the ground had a last request, and that request was for a rimu, or an oak, or a pine, or a fir or a kauri, or any one of the dozens of different species dotted everywhere. It's beautiful. Too beautiful for Lockwood, but it's not as if I can move him.

'Zach would like it here,' I say.

'It's one of the cemetery's most beautiful spots,' Father Jacob says.

'Do you mind if we have some time alone?' I ask.

'That's no problem.'

'We can find our own way back,' I say.

'I'm happy to wait.'

'I know you have another funeral to prepare for, and we might be a while. I promise we'll come in and see you before we leave.'

He gets the message. He smiles, and he nods, then he turns around and walks back the way he came.

When he's gone, Andre asks, 'Want to tell me what in the hell that was all about?'

I walk over to the empty grave. He follows. I turn a full circle slowly, looking for any signs of life. Nothing. I take my jacket off and hand it to him.

'What in the hell are you doing?'

I sit on the edge of the grave and dangle my legs into it. I figure Lockwood being in the open hole and not the closed one is a nice piece of luck in a very un-nice set of circumstances.

'What the hell, Cam?'

I carefully lower myself down. It was easier when I had a shovel.

'Have you gone mad?'

'Keep an eye out.'

I pull away handfuls of dirt from the middle.

'What the hell is wrong with you?' Andre asks.

'Just keep an eye out.'

I scoop with both hands and uncover Lockwood's waist.

'You brought him here?'

'I had to bring him somewhere.'

'I thought you were going to bury him in the woods.'

'This would be easier if you had let me bury him at your farm.'

'Why are we even back here? What are you doing?'

I find Lockwood's pocket. If I'm lucky, the phone will be on this side. If I'm unlucky, I will have to roll him.

Turns out I'm lucky. The phone is switched off too. Maybe today will be my day. I toss it up to Andre then go about covering Lockwood again.

'You came here to steal the guy's phone?'

I get the dirt flattened down, then I scuff it up to hide the foot-prints. 'Jacket,' I say.

'What?'

'Lower the jacket so you can pull me up.'

He wraps one sleeve around his wrist and lowers the other down to me. I grab it, kick against the side of the grave, and a moment later I'm pulling myself over the top. I get to my feet and brush myself down.

'Honestly, Cameron, I have no idea what to say to you right now.'

'Then don't say anything. Let's go and bury that car.'

Chapter Seventy-Four

Father Jacob is waiting for us outside the church. I keep my jacket over my hands so he doesn't see how dirty they are. I tell him we like the area he showed us, but thinking about it, I'd like Zach buried closer to Dad. I can see him wondering why I even asked to look anywhere else to begin with, but he's polite enough not to question it. After all, grief makes people do strange things. He tells us he'll see what he can do, that he has to look up the records to see where my dad is and what is available around him, and I tell him we have something we need to do that we can't postpone and can we call him later today? He says of course, and reminds us that he is sorry for our loss. He stays outside the doors to the church, watching us walk back to the car.

'You're good at that,' Andre says.

'Good at what?'

'Lying.'

We don't make much in the way of conversation on our way back to the farm. I open the gate, and Andre drives through and doesn't wait for me. I close the gate and walk the hundred metres to the house, where he's parked his car. I toss Lockwood's phone onto the seat, and then I toss mine on top of it. Last thing I need is my one falling out of my pocket and into the grave we're about to dig.

I go to the barn. Andre is propped up in the digger. The digger is taller than it is wide. It looks like a fat phone booth full of levers, with an arm and claw extending from the front. 'I called Rita. She and your mum are going to go to the hospital to see Lisa. That gives us three or four hours.' He tosses me the key to the house. 'Let Kahn out, would you?'

He starts the digger. The engine is loud, and the booth shudders, and then he's rolling out of the barn. He's right – if we had done this in the middle of the night neighbours from miles around would have noticed. Now it's just one more piece of heavy equipment moving across fields in this part of the city.

He hangs a left out of the barn, goes through a gap in the low wire fence then heads north. I open the door to the house. Kahn is waiting there wagging his tail, but then stops wagging it when he sees it's only me. Even so, he follows me out. Up ahead, Andre is moving from one paddock into the next. The digger is slow, but I'm even slower, and he continues to pull further ahead. Kahn takes a long loop around me then leaves me behind. By the time I catch up with Andre a few minutes later, he's already bitten into the earth, and Kahn is sitting next to a growing pile of dirt. We're at the far corner of the farm, twenty metres short of a line of pine trees that stand between us and a creek that is dry this time of the year and a neighbouring paddock, which is part of a farm that's for sale. There's nobody else to be seen. The cabin swings back and forth, biting, emptying, biting, emptying. There's nothing I can do but stand and watch. Kahn chases a bird for a while, then comes back, sits down for a few minutes then moves further away where it's not as loud. He lies on his front, puts his chin on his paws and closes his eyes.

The hole gets steeper, and the mound of dirt gets bigger. The sun arcs higher up into the sky, then slowly arcs back down. It's taking longer than I thought, but eventually Andre has carved a hole into the earth big enough for a car, deeper at one end, like a swimming pool.

When he's done, he gets out of the digger and inspects his work. Kahn comes over and inspects it too. The deep end is around two metres, the hole not a lot wider than the car and more than twice as long, with a ramp cutting down the middle. The car being a convertible makes things easier. It means the hole doesn't have to be as deep.

'This ought to do it,' he says.

I go and get the car. It bounces and bangs against the earth where tractor tyres have dug long, patterned trenches. My lower back is sore from standing for the last few hours, watching Andre do his thing. I have to fight with the steering wheel when the car slides into ruts. When I make it out to the corner, Andre is leaning against the digger, smoking. I didn't know he smoked. Kahn is sniffing around the edge of the hole.

'I guess we both have secrets,' Andre says.

I move the car into position. We lower the roof then roll it down the ramp.

Filling the hole is a lot quicker than emptying it. When he's done, Andre returns the digger, comes back with the plough and disperses the rest of the dirt through the field, then scuffs up the whole area to even it out. Then he turns on the irrigation and tells me the water will make the dirt sink a little, but he'll go over it again tomorrow.

We sit out on the deck in the sun. It's the middle of the afternoon, and we're covered in dust and dirt. I'm sunburned, and Andre is sunburned too. The bandage on my hand is filthy, and there's a lot of play in it, so I peel it off. He opens a couple of beers and hands one to me. Kahn naps on the deck next to Andre's chair, his head on top of his paws again.

'Listen, Cameron, one thing I learned back when I served is there's often not a lot of black and white. Good people do bad things. Bad people do good things. I don't know where you are in that equation. Good, I think. I like to think you're a good person who did a bad thing, but you have the look about you of a man fixing to do a whole lot more.'

I think about Thompson leading us out the front of the house. I think of all the protesters out there. People willing for bad things to happen so the show could go on. People who wrote songs. Who held signs. Who threatened to kill us.

People who all contributed to what happened.

'What if I am?'

He looks away from me and stares out over the paddock. 'I almost lost them, you know,' he says. 'Rita and Lisa, back when Lisa wasn't much older than ... than Zach was. I was stupid in the way that husbands can get when they don't appreciate what they have, when they think the answers to their problems can be found in another woman.' He keeps looking out towards the hole as he talks. 'I left them, then six months later came grovelling for them to take me back. I remember what I said to you when you first started dating Lisa, warning I'd hurt you if you ever hurt her. What I was really meant was I would hurt you if you did the same thing I had done to my family. Lisa deserved a better husband than the one I had made. She deserved a better father too.'

'Lisa didn't tell me.'

'No, I don't suppose she would have.'

'Why are you telling me this?'

'Because this, helping you cover up what you did last night, it's not the worst thing I've ever done. The worst thing I've ever done is treat my family poorly, and that includes you. I treated them bad all those years ago, and I treated you bad this week. I've been thinking about what you said in the hospital yesterday, when I told you if I'd been more helpful, maybe things could have ended different, and you said I was right to think that. It hurt hearing that, but the thing is, Cam, you were right. I saw what you said to the media yesterday, about there being blood on all of our hands. It's all over mine, that's for damn sure. I was thinking about it while digging that hole, and I've come to the decision that if Lockwood is ever found, I'll tell the police it was me. I'll tell them I killed him and buried the car out here alone. But that's where it ends. You do anything else, that's on you.'

'I can't let you do that.'

'My mind is made up. But as I say, anything else you do, that's on you.'

We sip at our beers and watch the sun move across the sky. Then I tell him what Kent told me about the detectives having interviewed Pittman at his house.

'That can't be right,' he says.

'That's what happened.'

He shakes his head. 'No. You must have misunderstood her. Otherwise that would mean the police could have saved Zach.'

'It happened.'

His grip is so tight on his beer I'm worried the bottle is going to shatter.

'You know, Cameron, your way of thinking, maybe that's the right way. Maybe we should be digging more holes,' he says, and I don't know if he's joking.

Chapter Seventy-Five

Because of the amount of chemicals in her face, Kent can't tell if Amber, Dallas Lockwood's girlfriend, is happy or sad that he's missing. Sad, she presumes – after all, the woman did call her to say she was worried because Lockwood hadn't come home.

'Has he been out other nights this week?' Kent asks.

They are sitting in the lounge at Lockwood's house. The room is full of straight lines and zero curves, except for the girlfriend – for which she guesses Lockwood made an exception. There are framed newspaper articles on the wall, headlines from stories Lockwood has written. She met Amber last night when she came here to question Lockwood about the cameras. She had left her card and told her to get Lockwood to call when he got back – not that she thought he would.

'Every night,' Amber says.

'Monday night?'

'Yes.'

'What time did he get home on Monday night?'

'I don't know. It was really late, I remember that. What does this have to do with him not coming home last night?'

'Did he tell you where he was going last night?'

'He never tells me anything, but I think he's been following that writer guy, you know, the one that killed his own kid.'

'The Murdochs didn't hurt their son,' Kent says. 'He was—'

'Yeah, I know, he was taken by that Pittman guy. But they gave their son to him. Maybe they paid him too. They wanted that kid gone. Dallas is still figuring it out.'

'Does he have proof of this?'

'Not yet.'

'Amber, does this look familiar to you?' she asks, and she pulls an evidence bag from her pocket with one of the small cameras inside it.

Amber shakes her head. 'No,' she says, and Kent can't tell if she's lying. A Botoxed face is a poker face.

'You've never seen any of these around the house?'

'No.'

'You don't know if Dallas uses them?'

'I don't even know what that is. Some kind of camera?'

'It's exactly that.'

'Where did you find it?'

'I can't say at this stage. Can I look through Dallas's office?'

'He wouldn't like that.'

'Even if it helped us find him? We don't know where Dallas is, and you did say he always comes home.'

'I know. I know I said that, but, given the choice between the police going through his stuff, and him not being found, I think he'd go with not being found.'

Her answer isn't surprising, but even so, Kent is disappointed. 'You're making this very difficult for us to help.'

'Can't you trace his phone or something?'

'It's been switched off.'

'Can't you turn it on remotely? I've seen that in movies.'

'No,' she says. 'What time did he leave here yesterday?'

'In the morning. He wanted to be at the arrest. I spoke to him around lunchtime. He said he had more interviews to do and that I shouldn't wait up.'

She wonders if he figured out Cameron was jumping fences and followed him last night. If so, he would have seen the houses being set on fire. Was there a confrontation between the two men? She can let arson slide, but she can't let killing Lockwood slide – if indeed that's what has happened.

'And Monday night? Do you know where he went?'

'No idea.'

'Okay. We need to officially report Dallas missing, and you need to give us access to his office and his phone records, his bank accounts, everything else.'

'I don't know. Can't you find him anyway without any of that stuff? I mean, he's missing, sure, but he's not *missing* missing, if you know what I mean.'

'I don't.'

'Like, he's been gone a day. Maybe we should give it another day. I'm sure he'll turn up.'

'Okay,' Kent says, and she gets up.

'What, that's it?'

'If you don't want to make this official and give us access to more information, then there's not a lot more I can do.'

Amber doesn't look happy with the decision, but then again, she doesn't look sad either. Kent lets herself out. She walks across the driveway, to the corner of the property where the wheelie bins are kept. She saw them here earlier. She opens the lid just as her phone goes. It's Tracey Walter, the coroner. Zach Murdoch's autopsy was scheduled for this morning, and she must be calling with the results. All things considered, she's hoping the boy was dead or unconscious before the accident.

She looks into the bin. It's empty. It was a long shot at best. Then she remembers what the woman who found the shoes said, about her husband being too lazy to care about recycling. Lockwood is one of those people. She checks the red bin too, and there they are, three cardboard boxes matching the cameras found in the ceiling.

She answers the phone.

Tracey sounds out of breath when she says, 'We were wrong.'

'In what way?'

Tracey tells her, and she's right.

They've been wrong about everything.

Chapter Seventy-Six

I clean up in the bathroom so I don't have to look like a man who buried something big when the reporters film him returning home. Andre finds me some fresh bandaging to put on my hand. Then he walks me to his car. He said earlier I'm welcome to use it. I grab my phone off the passenger seat to call Mum to ask how Lisa is, only to find I've missed six calls from Kent over the last fifteen minutes. She calls again.

I don't answer. Instead I switch off my phone.

I tell Andre.

'She knows,' he says, and to his credit he doesn't complain, he doesn't say, 'I never should have helped you.'

'My guess is they found the body at the grave. She's probably on her way out here.'

'What you said earlier, about you telling the police you killed Lockwood, I can't let you do that.'

'You can, and you will.'

'I won't tell them you helped me,' I say. 'I'll say I killed him, and I buried the car out here by myself.'

'Maybe it won't matter what either of us say. Maybe they'll figure it out, and we'll end up cellmates.'

'I'm sorry,' I tell him.

'I know you are, Cam. I know you are. And the truth is, I don't blame you for what you did. This whole thing, when I look back over the last few days, you're the only one who was behaving rationally.'

Kahn sits next to Andre and avoids eye contact with me. I wish it were later in the day. I wish the sun were setting. When it does, it's beautiful out here. I like the idea of one more sunset before ending up in jail.

'You should go,' he says.

'What?'

'I meant what I said earlier. I'll tell the police it was me, and if you're out here when they arrive, that's not going to help our case.'

'I—'

'I mean it, Cam. I want you to go.'

We stare at each other for a few moments, then I shake his hand, and then he pulls me into a hug.

'I'm sorry,' he says. 'For everything.'

'I'm sorry too.'

'I know.'

Andre stands on the porch and watches me drive away.

Chapter Seventy-Seven

I pull over halfway home. Dallas Lockwood's phone is on the front seat. I'm curious to know if it's off because he turned it off, or if the battery died. I hold down the power button. Rather than throwing it into a passing truck, I think it would be useful to turn it on and off at various locations to suggest he's still alive and following me.

The phone comes to life. The battery is fifteen per cent full. I can't get beyond the lock screen because it asks for a code or a fingerprint.

You should have cut Lockwood's thumb off.

'You never suggested it.'

Would you have, if I had?

I angle the phone so I can get more light on the glass screen. The phone looks brand new, a replacement for the one I took from him the other night. It's full of smudges and smears, and some of those smears line up perfectly with the digital keypad that lights up. Four smears to be exact, starting from the one, going down to the seven, up to the two, and across to the three. I try it. It doesn't work. I reverse the pattern. There's a click and the home screen lights up.

I open Lockwood's messages. I go through them, but focus on one from a person called 'Bent'. Bent has been feeding Lockwood information about the case, and I figure Bent must be a police officer and the name he's stored under is appropriate. I can picture Lockwood laughing to himself when he typed it in. By the time I'm done reading the messages, my skin is burning and my muscles are humming. The person who sent these messages had a hand in what happened.

Then it hits me. In the same way that Elsie is L C which is short for Lisa Cross, Bent is short for Ben T. Ben Thompson. I go through the contacts and find that Lockwood has done all the heavy lifting when it comes to figuring out where Thompson lives – unless Thompson volunteered the address, which I doubt. I find some paper in the glove box so I can write down the address and phone number, then I turn the phone back off.

It's no longer enough to burn down his house.

If I'm going to go to jail for killing one person, I may as well go for killing two.

Chapter Seventy-Eight

Thompson lives fifty metres from the beach in New Brighton, a suburb along the coast of Christchurch where sea salt turns windows opaque and cars lose half their bodyweight to rust. His street runs at a right angle to the road bordering the sand dunes that stop the ocean spilling into people's homes. I park near the dunes and step out of the car, the dunes sheltering me from the wind, but not from the sound of the waves crashing on the other side. Seagulls swirl through the air overhead, chirping as they hunt the landscape for discarded fish and chips. I have always loved the beach. I have always loved coming here with Lisa and Zach, but now I have no desire ever to see it again. I pop the trunk and grab the tyre iron. It's one of those L-shaped ones the length of my forearm.

Thompson's house is single-storey and narrow, meaning it must travel back some. Bay windows overlook the street from the kitchen, all of them fogged with sea spray. The guttering along the base of the roof has been patched up where rust has been cut from it, and is waiting to be painted. The lawns are dry, the dirt contaminated with sand, but they look and smell like they were recently mowed. The garden has been freshly weeded and the shrubs recently trimmed. Maybe Thompson spent the day gardening. Maybe they'll hold his wake here. Mr What If was right earlier when he said I would need a jacket today, because I'm using it again, this time to cover the tyre iron.

I reach the door. There's a Christmas wreath hanging from it. Thompson might not be home, or maybe he's home with half a dozen other people. Even so, I ring the bell. I put one hand on the tyre iron and the other on the jacket, ready to slide the two apart.

I can hear footsteps. They get louder, and then there's a lock disengaging, and then the door swings open. I was right about it being Thompson. He looks many things. He looks dishevelled, like he slept in his clothes. His hair is sticking out at weird angles, and his eyes are bloodshot, and he hasn't shaved. He also looks surprised to see me, and then that surprise turns to worry. He knows I can't be here for a good reason. He smells like sweat, and booze and stale pizza.

I drop the jacket. His eyes follow it. Then they follow the tyre iron as it arcs upward. He tries to block it, tries to turn away, but he's too late. It catches him in the bottom of the chin. His head snaps back. He tips over without any attempt to break his fall.

I step inside, trying to decide if I should beat Thompson to death before burning his house down around him.

Maybe I'm a psychopath now.

At the very least you're a serial killer. How does it feel?

All I feel is loss.

Chapter Seventy-Nine

Detective Thompson told Lockwood about the fair, about the girls bouncing out of the castle, about Zach going missing and the assault. He told him about the missing shoes, then those shoes, along with Zach's clothes, being found. Wednesday morning he sent messages saying an arrest was imminent. The messages said he wanted us arrested in front of a large audience. He said he wanted the world to see us dragged out in handcuffs. It proves what I said to Kent earlier, that the police always saw Lisa and myself as guilty. No wonder they didn't search Pittman's house thoroughly.

This is why Thompson was adamant we go out the front door. It's why he refused to listen to Kent. He got what he wanted. Us on display. Then it all crashed down around him.

I close the door and lock it.

Thompson is out cold. I check the rest of the house for family and bedridden cancer patients, but it's empty. I check Thompson's jaw. It isn't broken, but his bottom teeth have crashed into his upper ones, smacking the top from one and revealing a metal pin from a previous repair. There's some blood in his mouth and a swelling lump on the bottom of his chin that continues to grow right through the process of me dragging him into his dining room and propping him up in a chair. On the dining table are a dozen empty beer bottles and three empty bottles of wine. Scattered among them are balled-up chip and peanut packets. The room smells the way run-down bars in movies look. If I lit a match, people might end up picking pieces of us off the street a kilometre away. I close the blinds to the windows overlooking the street, cut the cords from them, then use those cords to tie him up.

I slap him a few times, and he doesn't twitch. Doesn't stir. Doesn't do much of anything except sit there with his head hanging and drool dangling from his mouth and landing on his pants.

I need to know why he focused on me so quickly. I need to know if he feels bad about it.

Then, Ellen Barkley's voice in my head, saying, *You do realise he genuinely thought you had hurt Zach, right? What he did was unforgivable, but you can see why he did it. What he did to you doesn't hold a candle to what you would have done to Lucas Pittman if you could have gotten your hands on him. It was a mistake, and like we discussed, mistakes happen. Detective Thompson may be a shitty cop, but that doesn't make him a shitty human being. Look at the empty bottles ... Can't you tell he feels terrible about what happened?*

'And Mr What If ? What's your take?'

Let me ask you something instead. How much can you live with?

I go into the kitchen and grab a cold bottle of beer from the fridge. I drag a seat from under the table and sit it opposite Thompson. I shake the beer and open it, spraying it into his face.

His eyes flicker open. He looks up at me. His first attempt to say something fails, and his eyes roll back, and he's gone again for a few moments before coming around. Then he spits out a string of blood that hangs from his chin and reaches his knees before breaking.

'You,' he says, and his eyes lose focus then snap back. 'You know,' he adds. He nods, then winces at the movement. He blinks a few times to sharpen his vision, and then says, 'It wasn't meant to happen this way.'

'I think it's exactly what you intended to happen,' I say. 'I know you were Dallas Lockwood's source. I know you wanted as many people as possible to be outside our house, that you wanted them yelling and screaming at us.' I ask him the same question I asked Kent. 'How can detectives spend time with Pittman and not see how he had my son, and spend time with me and Lisa, and not see we were innocent? How? I don't get it. I really don't, but I need you to explain it to me. I need you to explain how that doesn't make all of you bad cops. I need to know how you let this happen.'

He closes his eyes for a few seconds, then he comes back. 'Don't you think I've asked myself that a thousand times since yesterday? Don't you think that Kent has too? But … you're right. I wanted people there, but I … I didn't know it would get that bad. I thought … I was sure, you have to understand. I was so sure you'd done it. You have to know, there's no way we could have known about the other boy by then. We couldn't have. If we had, then things would have been different. Of course they would have been.'

My skin breaks out in goose bumps. The temperature in the room drops. 'What other boy?'

'You don't know?'

'Don't know what?'

He stares at me, saying nothing.

'What?'

'When was the last time you spoke to Kent?'

'This morning,' I say, and of course there have been all those missed calls.

'Then you need to talk to her.'

'What other boy are you talking about?'

'You really don't know, do you?'

'Spit it out.'

'The coroner. She finished her autopsy. I spoke to Kent a few minutes before you got here. The boy in the morgue ... it isn't your son, Mr Murdoch. As it stands, nobody has any idea where Zach is.'

Chapter Eighty

I put the beer down, only I don't balance it right, and it tips off the table and crashes against the wooden floor. It doesn't break; instead it spins slowly, beer glugging from the neck. I feel giddy. Confused. Overwhelmed by the idea Zach is still alive. I can feel the storm from before coming back. I have the urge to jump out of my seat and hug Thompson, only I can't move. The news is incredible, but there's a tinge of pain that comes with it – Zach surviving has come at the expense of another boy dying. For a moment I wonder whether my desperate wish for him to be alive has cost another child his life.

'Call Detective Kent if you don't believe me. She'll tell you.'

I think of all the missed calls I had earlier. The bottle comes to a stop. It's pointing at Thompson. That means I can either ask him to confess a truth, or perform a dare. I opt for the former.

'Are you lying to me?'

'No.'

'I will kill you if you are.'

'I'm not lying. I also don't know anything else, because I'm off the case. You've come here to avenge a son who might still be alive and a wife who still is.'

He's right.

I have to get home.

I have to talk to Kent.

I stand up. I need to move. Movement means momentum. When I push one foot forward, it doesn't go anywhere. My legs tingle. I sit back down. I'm lost at sea. A warmness spreads through my body. With it, there is calm. Everything is going to be okay. I smile. I can't stop myself. Zach is alive. He's alive, and the man that hurt him is dead, so wherever Zach is, he's safe.

'So where—?'

'I don't know anything else. I really don't. I'm lucky to even know that. Listen to me, Cameron, we made a mistake. *I* made a mistake. And we're paying for it. *I'm* paying for it. But if you do this, if you do what you came here to do, then there's no going back. This ... this right now, it can stay between us. You let me go, and I don't tell anybody. I mean it. It's not like one of those bull-shit offers you see in movies, where people promise they'll keep their mouths shut. I'm serious, and I'm serious because I messed up. I'm serious because I had this coming. In a way, I'm glad you're here. I deserved this. But right now we're even. You walk away, and it stays that way.'

'We're not even,' I tell him. 'Lisa is fighting for her life because of you.'

'Don't you think I know that? You have a get-out-of-jail-free card, Cameron. You won't be any use to your son or your wife if you kill me. Everybody will know it was you. You'll go away for twenty years. We're going to find Zach, and Lisa is going to be fine, and you've done nothing bad here, nothing I didn't have coming. Walk away, Cameron. Go and see Kent, and she'll tell you everything. Maybe she already knows where Zach is.'

I look at the tyre iron. It's on the table where I left it. I look at

Thompson. This man helped ruin my life, but now my life isn't as ruined as I thought.

'And that'll be it? You won't come and arrest me?'

'You have my word.'

I stand up. I pick up the tyre iron. 'I'm leaving you tied up. You'll work your way free over time. But we have a deal.'

'We do. Walk away and we never have to see each other again.'

So that's what I do.

I walk away.

Chapter Eighty-One

I drive calmly because I feel calm. There are reindeer staked into front lawns, and Santas on roofs, and tinsel and lights hanging from windows. None of it has ever looked so good. People are mowing lawns, they're walking dogs, they're holding hands, they're playing neighbourhood cricket in cul-de-sacs and flying kites in parks. They all look happy. Christmas is coming, and like the song says, it's the most wonderful time of the year. Since Monday, all I've wanted is to wake up from this nightmare, and now it's happening. Kent might not know where Zach is, but it's only a matter of time before she figures it out. Lisa will wake up, maybe today, if not, then tomorrow. By then Zach will be home.

I call Kent.

She picks up right away.

'Where are you?' she asks.

'Is it true?'

'Where are you?'

'Is it true? The boy in the back of the car, is it somebody else?'

'It's true.'

'I'm on my way home.'

'I will meet you there in fifteen.'

It's after six in the evening, leaving us with three hours of daylight. It's barbecue weather. A bright-blue sky. Christchurch can have its ups and downs, but this time of the year there isn't anywhere else I'd rather be. We've already done our Christmas shopping for Zach, but I'm going to go out this weekend and buy ten Christmases' worth of gifts for him.

The media have upped their game along my street. There's a barricade at the end of the block. It gets moved aside. People snap photos and shoot video. I park in the driveway, and the questions come loud and fast. There are more flowers and bears in the front yard. I go inside. My arms and face are sore from too much sun, and my hair is windswept, and even though I freshened up back at the farm, I can still feel a thin layer of dirt coating my body. I need to get cleaned up. I don't want Zach seeing me like this.

Kent has gotten here before me and let herself in. She's pacing my living room. She stops pacing. 'Take a seat.'

I sit on the couch in the same place I sat on Monday when Kent first asked her questions, and she's sitting in the same place too. Kent has regained some of the composure she lost yesterday.

'Listen to me, Cameron, things are evolving quickly. We are in a race against time now. Wherever Zach is, it's possible he has no access to food or water. It's imperative you're honest with me. Did you burn down Pittman's house? Keep in mind if it wasn't you, then we—'

'It was me.'

'Why?'

'Why do you think? I didn't want that place standing anymore. A thing of evil happened in there, and the only way to make sure it never happened in there again was to burn it. I'm sure you can understand that, Detective.'

'You burned down Spenser Barkley's house too?'

'Yes.'

'Why did his wife admit doing it?'

'She thought it would be a lesson about revenge not feeling so good.'

'Was she right?'

'I'm still not sure.'

'Is there anything else you're not telling me?'

Well, there's Dallas Lockwood, buried deep in the ground. There's Detective Thompson, tied up in his living room. 'Nothing.'

'How did you know your son wasn't the boy in the morgue?'

'Excuse me?'

'When you rang before, you asked if it were true. How did you know?'

Shit. That was a mistake.

'Cameron?'

'Dallas Lockwood told me,' I say, then immediately regret it.

You should regret it. The lie will work for now, but will fall apart if Thompson tells Kent you paid him a visit.

'When?'

'Just before I called you. I was at my in-laws'. He was waiting out front, and he was asking me about it. Somebody must have told him.'

'You saw him.'

'Yes.'

'What else did he say?'

'He just said that he knew it was another boy that had died,' I say, but I need to add something to that. Lockwood would always have a shitty angle. 'He asked me if I was happy that another child was dead instead of Zach.'

'Sounds about right. Did you know about the email?'

'The one where he asked his followers to gather at our house? Ellen Barkley told me about it, and to be honest I felt like punching him when I saw him, but at the same time I felt like hugging him because he was telling me Zach might still be alive. Only I couldn't believe it, because I thought maybe he was lying to me, just to upset me. That's why I called you.'

You should be a writer.

'He say where he was going?'

'No, but he followed me for a while. I figured he was coming here, but he turned off a few blocks earlier. Who was the boy who died?'

'His name was Ryan Bates.'

I remember him from the missing-persons website. 'That's the boy who went missing from that park down south last year?'

'That's him,' she says.

'Can you tell me what happened?'

'I can,' she says, and then she does.

Chapter Eighty-Two

She's talking to a very different Cameron Murdoch now, one that is at a midpoint between the version he was yesterday and the version she met five years ago. He has hope. Talking to him now, she doesn't know how she ever could have suspected him of hurting his own son.

She tells him about Ryan Bates. Last summer Ryan had refused to leave the park where he had been playing, and his parents had driven away. He was eight years old. His family moved down from Auckland to Dunedin a month earlier so his dad could take a new job. Ryan didn't like the change. He acted up. He rebelled. The park he disappeared from was in an old neighbourhood, one half bordering a newer one, the other half bordering a forest. The kid ran around, and he played on the equipment, and when it was time to go home he refused. He said he hated their new house and he wanted to go back to his original home, and if he couldn't do that, then he would make a new home in the playground. Both his parents said fine. He could do that. Then they drove away. They parked around the corner, waited two minutes, then returned.

It was the middle of the afternoon, but it was cold, and there hadn't been any other kids out playing. No joggers, no dog walkers, no couples walking hand in hand. Ryan was gone when they got back. They called the police. At first, the police figured Ryan had walked in the other direction. He had set his sights on Auckland and gone for it. It's the sort of thing an eight-year-old kid would think they could do. Walk six hundred kilometres to the top of the South Island, smuggle their way onto the ferry to cross to the North Island, then walk the remaining five hundred kilometres home. They'd get twenty minutes into that journey, thirty at the most, then give up.

Whether he walked one kilometre, or two, or five, or whether Lucas Pittman took him from the park and into the forest that adjoined it, they may never know.

'I read about him a few days ago,' Cameron says, and she can tell there is an internal struggle taking place. His son is alive – at least potentially alive – but at the expense of another. She feels the same way. She wanted nothing more than for Zach to be safe and sound, and now they're some way towards making that happen, while Ryan Bates' parents will have collapsed into heaps, unable to comfort each other.

'All the grief, all the rage, all the heartache I felt yesterday when I thought Zach was dead, that's now with Ryan's parents. Not only that, but they have to deal with the knowledge their boy was with Pittman all that time. I don't ... I don't know how to feel. How is it, in two minutes, a monster can swoop into your life and change everything?'

She thinks about the explosion that scarred her. Sometimes that monster only needs two seconds.

'The parents were suspects, but they were cleared. They made a bad decision – a decision many parents would make to teach their child a lesson,' she says, and she can remember her own parents leaving her and her sister at a mall once when they refused to behave. They were also gone for only two minutes. That's ample swooping time. And is what Cameron said to his son on Sunday night about running away any different? No. She doesn't think it is. 'Their decision is one they will never recover from.'

'Was he alive when the car crashed?'

'He had barbiturates in his system. He would have been unconscious and wouldn't have felt a thing. We think Pittman kept Ryan and Zach sedated so they would be easy to handle. We know from hair found in Pittman's house that Zach was there, and we're now comparing other hairs and DNA found there to Ryan's records, but it will take time. We know he must have been keeping these children somewhere else, but what we don't know is for how long, or how often, he brought them back to his own house, or why. Pittman didn't own a car big enough to transport two children – assuming he had them in the trunk like he did with Ryan Bates. That meant multiple trips if he were to have them at his house at the same time, and multiple trips meant multiple risks – let alone the risk of having them in his house during a routine check.

'We think Pittman had Ryan Bates there yesterday morning when something made him panic, and he was returning him to wherever he was keeping Zach,' she says. But there's another possibility too, one that she doesn't want to discuss with Cameron, because it involves the spade in the back of Pittman's car. The spade suggests a burial, and that means Zach may have been facing the same fate. The question is, who was going to face that fate first?

'It easily could have been Zach in the car,' Cameron says.

'It could have been, but it wasn't. But you need to understand the damage of what you did last night.'

'What damage?'

'Everything we have learned today means Pittman's house would now be looked at through a different lens. We know he was keeping the children somewhere. Your actions destroyed our greatest resource for figuring out where that somewhere is.'

She can tell from his reaction this hadn't occurred to him. He goes pale.

'We collected evidence, and we took several photographs and video, so I'm not saying we have nothing. But you've tied one hand behind our backs.'

'I ... If we don't find him it will be my fault,' he says, and his fingertips go to his lips. He looks like he's going to be sick.

She pulls an evidence bag out of her pocket with one of Lockwood's cameras and puts it on the coffee table. 'We found three of these in the ceilings of your house.'

'What?'

'At first, we thought Pittman had put them there. We thought he'd been using them to keep an eye on your family, and it's how he overheard your conversation with Zach about running away. Now we think Dallas Lockwood put them there on Monday night.'

'Why would he do that?'

'To watch you. My guess is he thought he was going to catch you confessing to killing your son.'

'You'll charge him?'

'We will. But because the cameras don't belong to Pittman, it made us reconsider the idea that Pittman must have been hiding in your ceiling to have overheard your conversation with Zach. After all, it's what Pittman has done in the past. Only there's no evidence he was ever up there. No evidence anybody was.'

'So what are you saying?'

'At this stage, I'm not sure. It's possible Zach really was planning on running away, and he packed his bag, and that same night Pittman made his way into the house. Sometimes you're away for weeks at a time – it's possible Pittman has been here before and was able to make himself a copy of a key. It's also possible he came in here on Sunday afternoon and found somewhere else to hide, and that he still overheard.'

'You don't sound so sure.'

'We'll figure it out.'

She stands up. She walks to the door, and Cameron follows her. 'Listen, Cameron. What you did last night, I get why you did it, but now you can see why you shouldn't have. I don't want you doing anything else. Okay? The news will break soon that Zach hasn't been found and that Ryan Bates has been, and when that happens your street is going to fill back up with media. Why don't you consider going to your mother's?'

'I will,' he says. Then, he adds, 'I know this has been tough on you. But bring Zach back to me, okay? If you can do that, and if Lisa pulls through, then everything can be forgiven.'

Chapter Eighty-Three

Zach. Alive somewhere.

Zach. Alive somewhere that we can't find because I set fire to Pittman's house.

Zach, coming home later today, or tomorrow, at the latest.

Dallas Lockwood missing after bugging my house with cameras. That's why he came here on Monday night. After I left him, he didn't leave. He stayed and did what he came here to do. Without a body, or a car, can the police prove anything?

The update hasn't hit the news yet, and the street outside the house is calm because of that. When it does the crowds will come back. The flowers and teddy bears will be raked underfoot as people return to accuse me of having hurt Zach. Perhaps they will say the same things Lockwood said, that we gave our son to Pittman.

I want to go to my mother's house, but I can't leave here until I've tidied. Zach doesn't like change, and at the moment that's what the house is: change. It's everywhere, from the curtains that were torn on the broken window to the moved furniture and dismantled offices and missing letterbox. Seeing the house like this could trigger a CZM.

I start with the clothes. Rather than hanging them, I load them into the washing machine, first taking out the ones I wore last night and tossing them into the dryer. I throw the sheets into the laundry too. I set the offices up. Zach's tablet has been returned, so I put it on charge so he can watch as many cartoons as he wants. I put things back into the lounge, getting everything to where it ought to be. The toybox hasn't been returned, but I'll go out later and buy another one. Not a stronger one, because I don't want Zach climbing it, but one that is the same. I'll buy some locks for the windows too and some alarms that are activated if windows are opened. I keep monitoring the news, waiting for the breaking report that Zach is still alive.

I get down to the final box. It has smaller items in it, and a checklist of where everything was taken from. It has Lisa's handbag. Spare house and car keys. Our passports. Our backup credit card, our foreign cash. There's a small zip-lock plastic bag with the international SIM cards for our phones. We use them so we don't end up paying exorbitant roaming prices. We have a spare phone too, in case one of us loses ours – which I did, by a tennis court in London a few years ago. Looking through the box, I can see the police haven't returned the phone.

I wonder why they've held on to it.

That wondering gets me checking the list of items they took – only it's not the wondering, it's me wanting to prove Mr What If wrong, because Mr What If has been tiptoeing around something ever since Kent said she doesn't know what happened on Sunday night. She took some guesses that relied on coincidences, all while avoiding one thing that would explain everything.

What if...?

'Don't.'

But Mr What If refuses to be quiet. *What if the phone was never here?*

The only way to keep him quiet is to prove him wrong, because I know what he's thinking. He's thinking that because Pittman wasn't in our ceiling, then he couldn't have overheard my conversation with Zach. He's thinking that the only other person in the house who could have heard that was Lisa. He's thinking that Lockwood's theory that we handed Zach over to a convicted paedophile has some truth to it. But he's wrong. Of course he is.

Well?

I look down the list. Only one SIM card is listed. Which I admit is also odd. I check the bag. I had assumed both SIMs were in there, but there's only one. So, one missing phone, and one missing SIM card, and no big deal. I check the drawer in the bedroom where they came from. The phone isn't there. I check my suitcase on the chance I left it in there from the last time we travelled, and then I check Lisa's. Some universal power adaptors, some cables, but no phone, no SIM.

What if—?

'Shut up.'

Come on, you need to—

'I said shut up. It's a mistake, that's all.'

Then prove it.

I will.

I call Kent. 'The list of things returned to me, how accurate is it?'

She's hesitant, and then, 'Very. Why do you ask?'

'Is there any chance you took something and it wouldn't be listed?'

'None. What aren't you telling me?'

I can't tell her about the missing phone until I know what the missing phone means. Kent might be able to help me figure it out, but she'll push that figuring into the direction of the worst possible scenario, one that would vindicate the grieving mother on TV earlier when she said 'we all know he did it'.

'Nothing. I'm curious, that's all.'

'What's wrong?' she asks.

'I can't find one of my thumb drives. It has photographs of Zach on it; it's always in the top drawer in my office, and it's not here.'

'Okay,' she says. 'I'll look into it.'

'Thanks.'

'Is there anything else?'

'Nothing.'

'You sure?'

'I'm fine,' I say, but I'm not fine. Zach is missing and our travel phone isn't here, which means...

Yes?

Which means Pittman took it.

What? He figured out you have a spare phone, and he took that and one SIM card, and left all that foreign cash?

Exactly.

Or?

There's no reason for Lisa to be using it. The most obvious explanation is we left it in a hotel on the other side of the world. It wouldn't be the first thing we've left behind by accident, and it won't be the last.

'Are you heading to your mother's house?' Kent asks.

'I'm thinking I'll head to my in-laws' instead.'

'I'll have somebody drive you, and I'll come by later to check in on you.'

We hang up.

For argument's sake, let's say you didn't leave it behind. Let's say Pittman didn't take it. You know why people have second phones, don't you?

I do. To hide the fact they're having an affair.

No. Because there's nothing illegal about that. They have them when they're organising the kidnapping of their own son.

What Mr What If is suggesting is impossible. First, there's no way Lisa and Pittman could know each other. What does Mr What If think? That she put an ad online asking to meet a paedophile? Second, Lisa has been an emotional wreck over the last few days. Zach disappearing has been killing her.

Let's come back to the phone not being here.

No.

Why would Lisa hide it somewhere else?

She didn't.

It's not here, because Lisa knew the house was going to be searched. She knew it would be found. She gave the phone to Pittman when he took Zach away.

And what? I slept through it? Mr What If has been listening too much to Dallas Lockwood.

Remember how you felt Monday morning? Like you had a hangover? Maybe she drugged you. Perhaps she's still using the phone. She might have hidden it somewhere else that night and picked it up on Monday night so she could stay in touch with Pittman. Maybe it's out at her parents' right now. Isn't that why you told Kent you were going out there? To look around? Come on, Cameron, how many things are you going to lie to yourself about?

This is crazy. Crazy stupid. These ridiculous thoughts of Mr What If's are giving me a headache. At the very worst it's possible Lisa is having an affair, but most likely the phone is in a lost-property box under a counter in a hotel in Paris.

Yes, but not the SIM card. Those foreign SIM cards stay in your phones until you board the plane to come home. Sure, the backup phone might have fallen out of a suitcase, but that card came home. And if I'm wrong, then prove me wrong. Go to your in-laws' and take a look around. Because ... you know ... what if?

Chapter Eighty-Four

The phone call is odd. She doesn't believe Cameron Murdoch about the missing thumb drive, and she's tempted to meet him at his in-laws' to question him about it. He knows something, but if it were something that could help find his son, wouldn't he say? She thinks he would. Maybe he's found something to do with Dallas Lockwood. When Lockwood left the cameras behind, did he take something too?

At the moment she's standing outside the burned-out shell of Lucas Pittman's house. She wasn't kidding when she told Cameron earlier that he's destroyed their best chance of figuring out where Zach is being kept. Structural engineers are determining how to remove the roof to give them access without the walls caving in. That means they have to brace up as much of the house as they can, and that takes time – time that Zach Murdoch may not have. There are forensic technicians waiting to go back in, though what they can find in a burned-out house she isn't sure.

There are no longer any fire engines in the street. Cordons have been set up keeping the media fifty metres away, not that there's much in the way of media or spectators, though she expects that to change when the news gets out about Ryan Bates.

People move aside as the first of two one-hundred-ton cranes arrives. The cranes are all-in-one, a large arm and a cabin secured onto the back of what looks like a flatbed truck; the thick arms, painted yellow and extendable up to sixty metres, hang out over the front of the cabs. She would have thought one would be enough, but the engineers have told her it will take two to stop the roof sliding and spinning. One crane parks up past the house, and the other one stops short. The drivers wait inside the cabs for instructions.

Next to the house, four people in hard hats and fluorescent orange vests are discussing something. They've managed to thread two heavy strops through the roof and out the other side. One of them signals the drivers over; they step out of their cabs and approach. Now there are six people in hard hats forming a decision, which they do with big gestures and finger-pointing. The drivers climb up into the cabins at the back of the trucks, and the arms tilt upward and turn and begin to extend. When they're in position, hooks are lowered, people on the ground gesture *slowly, slowly, slowly, stop*. Which the drivers do. One of the engineers – the smallest of the group – scrambles onto the roof and connects the hooks.

The cranes groan, and slowly the roof begins to rise.

Chapter Eighty-Five

There is no surging. No screaming. The crowd hasn't grown since I arrived home. Questions come my way as Original Wrestler walks me to his car, and I don't answer them. It's after eight o'clock. We drive through town, passing bars and restaurants lit up with neon. The night clubs look dark and abandoned, but soon teenagers pretending to be adults will be queuing up to get in, along with adults pretending to be teenagers. Garbage trucks are picking up bags of trash and road sweepers sucking up discarded cigarette butts and plastic bottles. We pass a twenty-four-hour gym, the windows lined with people on treadmills staring at their phones. Further west we pass car yards and motels and malls, then we're driving past the airport, where one plane is coming in and another is leaving, one set of folks with the right idea about this city, another with the wrong. Beyond the airport farmers are taking advantage of the long daylight hours, dragging ploughs through fields and loading cows into trucks. My headache, that I thought had left me, has come back.

We get out to the farm. Wrestler parks up, short of a pukeko that has been flattened by a car, its buddy flapping its wings and squawking at a large rat trying to drag the dead bird off the road and into a tussock. We sit and watch it, the rat giving up, but it'll be back.

'I'm sorry about how it all went down with your family,' he says, and it's the first thing he's said since he came to my door. 'And what you did last night, I would have done the same thing. I hope everything works out, I really do,' he says, and we shake hands.

I get out, and he drives away, but whether he keeps going, or turns around and sneaks back to keep an eye on the house from a distance, I can't tell. Rather than unlocking the gate, I climb over it. I walk down the driveway. I called ahead earlier to let Andre and Rita know I would be staying here tonight. Andre gets to the door before I do. He's showered and changed into a pair of pyjama bottoms and a singlet. His skin is still red from his day in the sun. 'Is it true?' he asks. 'They just said on the news it wasn't Zach in the car.'

'It's true.'

'Why didn't you tell us?'

'I only just found out, and I wanted to tell you in person,' I say, and I realise I haven't spoken to my mother yet either. I need to fix that.

'They're saying whoever burned Pittman's house down destroyed the police's best chance of figuring out where Pittman took Zach.'

'I know.'

'Everybody thinks it was you. Was it?'

'It was.'

He nods, and this is going to go either way. 'I can't blame you. You couldn't have known. This ... knowing what you did, knowing it makes finding Zach harder, that must be a hard thing to bear.'

'It is.'

He puts his hand on my shoulder. 'We're going to get him back.'

I tell him I need a few minutes to call my mother. He disappears inside, and I sit down on the edge of the moat and make the call. Mum cries with joy, and she says our prayers were answered, and I guess they were. We talk for five minutes, then I head inside. Rita is on the couch watching the news. I say yes to a hug from her and no to a coffee from Andre. Andre sits down, and I take the couch to their left. The TV has been muted. I tell them everything about Zach that Kent told me, but I don't tell them about Lockwood's hidden cameras. When I'm done with the telling and the non-telling, Rita says I look exhausted and that everything is going to be okay, that they know Zach is alive and it's only a matter of time until he's back with us.

Don't forget why you're here.

I haven't forgotten.

It's a little after nine o'clock. It's still light outside, but the sun has now sunk behind the trees on the edge of the farm, casting the grave of Lockwood's car into shadow, not that we can see that area from here. My headache is getting worse. I ask if they have some aspirin.

'Sure,' Rita says, and she disappears to get some. On the TV a weatherman is telling us tomorrow is going to be another hot one. A perfect day to take Zach back to the fair or to the beach. Rita returns with the aspirin and some water.

'You sure you don't want something stronger?' Andre asks.

'Water is fine,' I say, and I knock back the aspirin.

At ten o'clock I tell them I need to keep my strength up and am going to bed. They agree it's a good idea and they'll do the same. I head down to the guest bedroom where the bed has been made fresh, probably by Lisa before she left here yesterday morning, ahead of coming home to get arrested. There are towels folded on top of it. On the drawers are the clothes Lisa wore to the station on Monday. They've been washed and folded. Next to them is a framed photograph of the three of us, taken during the winter when it snowed. We built snowmen in the paddock, and Zach laughed all day long when he decided he needed two carrots for each snowman; an upstairs carrot and a downstairs carrot.

I go through the drawers, which are mostly full of old clothes of Lisa's, and some of Zach's clothes too for when he, on occasion, spends the night out here. I search over and through and beneath them, and when I don't find the phone I'm relieved, because it means I was right about losing it overseas, or about Pittman taking it.

Would she really hide the phone in such an easy place? What if the police searched? And let's not forget losing the phone overseas doesn't explain the missing SIM card.

I tip the mattress up. I go through the bedding. I go through the wardrobe. I go through the en suite. No phone here, or there, or anywhere. It can't be, because Lisa had nothing to do with Zach disappearing, and she's not having an affair.

It does, however, make me an awful person for ever suspecting anything.

No. It just makes you a good crime writer. Or...

'Or?'

Or it's somewhere else. You don't know the phone isn't wherever Zach is.

No. I'm not doing this anymore. I'm not going to listen to Mr What If.

I put things back into the drawers. I put the clothes Lisa wore on Monday in there too, then pull them back out, knowing she'll want me to take them home. They get messed up in the process, I shake out the blouse to refold it, and there's a smudge of white paint on the bottom of it.

The same way my world shifted when I lost Zach, it shifts again, and when the floor falls out from beneath me, I follow it down, spiralling, spiralling.

Spiralling.

Into a world that's nothing but square pegs and round holes.

Chapter Eighty-Six

The process is measured in centimetres. As the roof lifts, it becomes evident that despite there being two cranes, it's going to spin. Guide ropes are attached to the corners to help. The roof groans at the peak of the A-frame, but they continue to raise it slowly, watching for signs of it splitting apart. It nudges the walls of the house, and the lift is halted so one wall can be braced. She can see inside now, and what she sees makes her think this is all in vain. What the fire hasn't destroyed, the water surely has.

The process carries on. The centimetres become a metre. The A-frame groans and creaks, and everything is paused again as the engineers discuss what will happen next. If the roof falls apart, it could end up knocking down the entire house. But they also can't let this drag out. Zach, if he is still alive, may not survive the night.

Her phone vibrates with a text message from Vicky Curtis, telling her to check her email. Earlier, even though Lockwood's girlfriend wasn't keen to officially report him missing, Kent did. It gave her an opportunity to get information from Lockwood's phone. It may be crossing a line, but somebody in the department has put this investigation at risk, and they need to know who. Even though Lockwood is no longer considered missing – she has Cameron Murdoch's statement to thank for that, along with Lockwood's phone coming to life briefly earlier today – his phone usage over this week has been examined. It is dodgy territory, trying to find out a reporter's source, but they need to be able to stem the leak before it spreads to future investigations.

She reads the email. All the numbers have been tracked down, except for one – a prepay mobile first activated six months ago; a burner. There's a document attached, and she opens it, a single page of phone numbers going back to Monday. The burner phone number has been highlighted. It's been used three times to contact

Lockwood, once on Monday afternoon, again on Tuesday afternoon and the third time on Wednesday morning.

She responds to the email and asks if they can get records for the burner number, to see what other phones it has called. Vicky says they'll need a warrant for that. Getting one could go either way.

The roof has been raised two metres. Three of the original engineers have moved back, but the fourth stays closer, watching, gesturing again with his hands. Despite the guidelines, the roof nudges a wall, which shifts, and even over the engine noise Kent can hear the engineer yelling for the drivers to stop.

The drivers stop, and engines die, and the two drivers step out to join the engineers. There is more gesturing and more pointing, and then one of the women looks into the house, and she frowns and she tilts her head, and then the others stand next to her, and they frown and they tilt their heads too.

They turn to Kent all at the same time and wave hurriedly for her to come over.

Which she does.

At the same time, the roof suspended above begins to groan. She can't be sure, but she thinks the distance between the feet of the A-frame has grown.

'Look,' the engineer says, the one who climbed onto the roof earlier.

'At what?' she asks.

Before she can answer, another engineer yells for them to get back. They move away from the house as the groaning roof gets louder. She was right about one side of the A peeling away from the other. One half falls back into the house, knocking an external wall over in the process. The other half dangles above. From all around the site people are swearing. Dust and ash balloons into the air.

'What did you see?' she asks, turning back to the engineer who pointed inside the house.

The engineer coughs, then wipes dirt away from her face. 'There were floorboards, twisted and broken, pointing downward, but some of them were floating too.'

'Floating?'

'The water was pooling up. I can't be sure, but from what I could see, it looked like there might be a room down there.'

Chapter Eighty-Seven

I stand behind the bedroom door until I can hear Rita and Andre have gone to bed. I give it a few more minutes then sneak into the hallway. All the lights are off. I go to the lounge and through the doors that open onto the deck, taking a flashlight with me. Kahn stirs from his dog bed next to the couch and stares at me for a moment, then goes about getting himself back off to sleep, where he can chase rabbits.

It's dark outside. The barn is thirty metres from the house. I walk them calmly, first keeping the house between me and the road, and then a line of trees, and then the barn, in case Wrestler is out there watching. I step inside. I turn on the flashlight. The tarpaulin that covered Lockwood's car has been folded up and put away. Hay bales stack one wall, and power tools and equipment stack another. There's the digger we used earlier today. There's a tractor, a plough, irrigation equipment, mountain bikes, outdoor furniture, neatly stacked lumber. I go to the wall where power tools hang from pegs. There are shelves along the base stacked with paint containers. Last summer when we painted our house, we had several containers left over that Andre said we could store here. Paint dripped over the lips of the containers when they were used, giving me colour samples of what's inside. I match the smudge from the blouse to our kitchen. The container holds ten litres and has half of them left. I open it and swirl a paint stirrer inside. It hits against something. I angle the container and use the stirrer to drag it upward.

In our next book we have a corrupt cop wrapping a gun inside a plastic bag and hiding it inside a can of paint. It was Lisa's idea. We debated it, about how willing somebody would be to store something in such an awkward place when they needed it again, but we decided being awkward was better than ending up in jail. It wasn't something we had seen done in books or movies. Did she know back then she would be using it in real life?

I get the bag out. The paint stops me from seeing what's inside, but I know what it's going to be. I wipe the plastic bag down with a rag, then get it open. Inside is a second plastic bag. I pull it out. There's less paint, mostly from my fingers now. I clean them, then open the second bag, careful not to spread more paint anywhere. I pull our spare phone out. I switch it on. I have to wait a long ten seconds for it to come to life, ten seconds in which I try to prepare myself for what's to come.

I tap in our code, thinking Lisa may have changed it, but she hasn't.

There are no text messages.

No voice messages.

No contacts.

No email.

The phone is completely blank.

I go through the call logs. They've been deleted.

The phone is useless.

Then the phone gets a signal. It always takes longer with the international SIM.

And then it beeps.

Chapter Eighty-Eight

There is just the one message from a number I don't recognise, sent last night, while Lisa was in hospital.

Hello.

I stare at the word. My chest is pounding, and my vision is blurring at the edges. I consider calling the number it came from, then decide against it. The person who sent this, do they not know Lisa was hurt? Do they know where Zach is? And if so, what would they do once they realise I'm onto them?

I look at the number, focusing on it, thinking that I was wrong about not recognising it. I dig through my pockets for the piece of paper I wrote on earlier when I turned on Lockwood's phone. I find it in my back pocket. The address and phone number for Detective Thompson. I unfold it and hold it next to the phone, and even though the numbers match I check them five times because I'm so sure there must be a mistake – but there's not. Detective Thompson and Lisa, in touch with each other on secret mobiles. There's no reason for Thompson to text Lisa, let alone on this phone, to a SIM number he couldn't possibly know. And yet he has, including a message last night. Is that message for me?

I sink onto the floor and lean against the bench. I stare at the phone, at this evidence that my life is a lie, that my wife is a stranger. I feel numb all over. My fingers are tingling. Even though I have found the very thing I came here to find, I still can't believe it. There has to be another explanation. I search for it. I try to get pieces to fit that don't want to. I think back over the last month, the previous six months, the last year. There were no signs of Lisa having an affair. No signs she was planning anything.

She was going to the gym more.

That's true.

And running more.

She was, but that doesn't mean anything. Running and training ebbs and flows, there are weeks when—

You're missing the point. She wasn't at the gym. She wasn't running. She was with him. With Detective Ben Thompson. Come on, how much more proof do you need?

Proof of an affair, maybe, but proof she was in on Zach being abducted? Why would she do something like that, and even if it were true, what is her connection to Lucas Pittman?

I look at the piece of paper. Something else hits me then. This afternoon, when I was at Thompson's house, the first thing he said when he came to was, 'You know.' He didn't mean that I knew he was the one who had been texting Lockwood. He thought I had figured out he was involved with Lisa.

If Lisa does know what happened to Zach, does that mean she knew about Ryan Bates?

No. Because that would mean...

It would mean all sorts of things, but right now you don't have the luxury to sit here and figure them out. You have to find Zach.

I have to call Kent.

If you do, she's going to ask how you recognise the number as Thompson's. What are you going to tell her? That you saw it in Dallas Lockwood's phone after you killed him? And if you're wrong about any of this, then Lisa is going to become a suspect for nothing. What good have the police been so far? How many times do they have to prove to you that you can't put your faith in them? All they have done is bring grief to your family.

What's the alternative?

You could pay Thompson another visit.

Mr What If is right. About all of it. I can't go to the police. They've made too many bad decisions – or, as Kent would say, bad calls. And in the case of Thompson, purposefully bad calls.

I put the phone in my pocket. I grab one of the mountain bikes.

I can't borrow a car because if Wrestler is out there he will follow. I use zip-ties to hold a similar prybar to the one I used last night to the length of the bike frame, then drop a small pair of side-cutters into my pocket to remove it later. Both tyres are flat – it's been a year since we last used them, maybe two. There are two more bikes – Lisa's one also has flat tyres, and the third one is Zach's, which is too small for me. I look around the barn for the pump. On Monday, each wasted minute felt like one where Zach was only getting further away, whereas now each wasted minute is prolonging me getting him back. I spend five searching for the pump, finding it on the shelf next to the wheelbarrow, presumedly last used to pump the wheel on that. I spend a few more minutes putting air into the tyres, and then I'm pushing the bike slowly over the gravel to the edge of the first paddock. I ride, putting distance between myself and the house. I keep in a straight line for a hundred metres then angle to the right, heading towards the road. I bike across a paddock that a month ago was full of hay. The ground has ridges and dips and the ride is uncomfortable. There are rabbits scooting across the field and there are possums in the trees. A warm breeze is starting up, the result of a nor'west wind that comes out of the Southern Alps a hundred-and-fifty kilometres away and heats up as it races over the Canterbury Plains and into Christchurch. People say nor'westers are like full moons, how they make normal people do crazy things, and crazy people do even worse. I'm not so sure people need excuses.

I head for the boundary. A couple of cars come and a couple of cars go, but with the trees between me and the road I don't have to worry about being seen, and even if I was, so what? I'm not breaking any laws.

At least for the moment.

The angle gets me to the road and the edge of the farm at the same time. Once I'm on the road I'll be able to make better time. On this side of the trees is a metre-high wire fence. I lift the bike over it, then lift myself over, then push through the trees. A single cow is crying loudly from one of the nearby farms, either lost, or hungry or sensing something dangerous has just entered the night.

I sit on my bike on the road going nowhere.

This is stupid.

Yes, the police have made some serious mistakes, but I have to admit that they weren't that far from the truth. They suspected Lisa and myself, and they were half right. And how could they have figured out the whole truth when one of those doing the figuring was covering things up? Finding Zach is too important to do on my own. What if I go to Thompson's house, and he gets the better of me? Or what if I go there and kill him before he tells me where Zach is?

I have to call Kent.

I can't remember her number, so can't use the backup phone, and my phone is back in the house. I look at the text message again. It dawns on me I can get around the fact I can know Thompson's number without having to mention Lockwood's phone. I program him into the phone as a contact.

I ride back along the road. It's quicker and easier, and if Wrestler is out here somewhere then I can ask him to call Kent. But if he is, then he's parked even further away, because I don't see anybody. I climb the fence but leave the bike behind. I jog down the driveway. There are still no lights on inside, which is good, because this isn't a conversation I want to have with Andre and Rita before I call Kent, nor is it one I want to have after. I walk around to the back deck and the open lounge door. There's a cold, dim light coming from the kitchen. Andre or Rita must be rummaging around in the fridge.

I don't want to talk to them.

I just want to get my phone.

I walk quietly inside. As I move through the lounge, more of the kitchen comes into view. The fridge door is open, but there's nobody in front of it. I keep moving. The angle changes. Then changes some more. Andre is face down in a puddle of chocolate milk, one arm pinned beneath him. Kahn is next to him, lapping up the mess.

Chapter Eighty-Nine

The walls have been secured. The half of the roof that didn't fall is resting on the street, but the other half is inside the house, almost flat against the floor, propped up in places where it's landed on rubble. The engineers are calculating the best way to get the strops beneath it – a best way that doesn't include somebody trying to make a path beneath it through the rubble. Kent shines a flashlight through a gap beneath the side of the roof into what used to be the hallway. She can make out what the engineer was talking about earlier – floorboards floating a few metres away. Seeing them makes her feel sick. The second location where Pittman was keeping the kids – has it been here the whole time? The news that Zach Murdoch wasn't in Pittman's car has now been made public. Once news of this room gets out, everybody will be asking the same question: Has Cameron Murdoch burned down this house with his son still inside?

Yesterday, who did Pittman move first? Zach or Ryan?

The gap between the roof and the ground isn't big enough to crawl through, but easily big enough to get a camera in there. The engineer who spotted the room is crouching next to her, tying a bolt onto a long piece of string. She's wearing a facemask that has gone from white to grey because of the ash and dust. Kent guesses hers must look the same. When the string is on tight, the engineer reaches beneath the roof and tosses the bolt into the water. There's a loud *plop*, and the string is quickly pulled through her hands as the weight sinks. When it stops, she figures out how much string is left and makes a quick calculation. 'Whatever is under there, it's two metres deep. More, if the bolt landed on something.'

'We need to get somebody down there,' Kent says.

'And we will, once we can figure out how to move the rest of that roof safely. For now, the best I can offer is we can crank the roof a little higher so we can start on pumping out the water.'

The tubes are on their way, and the water will be pumped into large tanks, where they can be sieved in case any evidence is sucked into them. There is also a diver with scuba gear arriving soon. If they can get the roof off soon, he'll head down there with lights to look around.

'If this is an average-size room, say twelve square metres, then we're looking at twenty-four thousand litres of water. The pump is designed to drain fifteen thousand litres in an hour, so we're—'

'Can we get a second pump to speed it up?'

'I'll get onto it. It must have been well hidden,' the engineer says.

'Sorry?'

'The room. I mean, you guys searched the house, right? And I can tell you, if we are looking at a room around twelve square metres, then we're talking about a whole lot of dirt that had to be excavated. Maybe it was dug out when the house was built forty years ago.'

'It's not on the blueprints.'

'Well, maybe whoever built it spent months, or years, hollowing it out and getting rid of the dirt. Or maybe they paid a few contractors some cash at the time.'

'It's the garden,' Kent says.

'What garden?'

'Out back. There's a raised garden. It's where all the dirt went. For all we know, Pittman took months or years hollowing out that room, then using it to build up the garden out the back.'

She remembers what the report said about Pittman's father

being suspected of the disappearance of a teenage boy thirty years ago. Had the room already been hollowed out back then by the dad? Was that boy down there when the house was searched back then? Have there been others? First father, then son – was there an overlap too? She shudders thinking about it.

Then yesterday something happened, and Lucas Pittman panicked, and the two children had to go. The room had survived previous searches – did he think it wouldn't survive one more?

Things begin to arrive. The pump to extract the water. The diver, with his scuba gear kept in the back of a van and out of sight. And a camera operator carrying an aluminium case. Inside is a video screen, and some cable, and the camera and a telescopic pole. The operator attaches the cable to the camera and flicks on the light, then ties it to the pole, leaving a metre and a half of cable between. He gets it through the gap, then pushes it forward until the camera falls into the water. He keeps the pole flat. They watch the screen. The water is hazy with ash. There are no clear images. She can't make anything out. But then there's a shape, something solid and long.

'What is that?'

'I can't get a clear image,' he says. 'A bed maybe? Water is too damn dirty.'

Now that he's said that, she knows he's right. It is a bed. And next to it a chest of drawers, making her think not only have other children been kept in here over the years, but they were kept for some time. Ryan Bates is an example of that.

'And that?' she asks, as the camera shines at a pile of broken and twisted wood.

'Floorboards from above, I guess,' he says.

'No, not the boards. There,' she says, and she points at the bottom of the boards where she is seeing something she was hoping she wouldn't see. The operator shifts the angle of the pole, and the camera moves, and for a moment what she was looking at disappears. But then the moment ends, and what she saw comes back into focus.

It's not a clear view, but it's clear enough – an answer as to who Pittman moved first.

She has never thrown up on the job before, but she does now. She turns and vomits into the garden.

Chapter Ninety

It could be a heart attack. It's been a stressful few days, and if Andre were going to have one, why not now?

I check for a pulse. He has one.

What if somebody did this to him?

'You're useless,' I whisper to Kahn, who, instead of answering, paws at the dropped milk container so that more sloshes from the opening.

If somebody did this to Andre, then that somebody is Thompson. He's in the house looking for me, with no idea I was outside. I grab a knife from the kitchen then decide a knife is too dangerous. I can't risk killing the one person who might know where Zach is.

There is movement from down the hall.

Rita? To come and check on her husband?

Or Thompson, to come and kill me?

I grab the rolling pin and head into the lounge.

There are footsteps getting louder. I hug the wall and hold my breath.

Thompson appears. There's enough light coming from the kitchen to make him out. His jaw is swollen from this afternoon, and there's a large bruise forming. He has a gun in one hand and a small black case in the other. The gun has a silencer attached.

I swing the rolling pin at him.

He sees the movement, and he turns, but he's too late. The rolling pin hits him in the forearm, and the gun flies out of his hand and slides across the floor. He recoils into the doorway, and I take a second swing, and he ducks it, the rolling pin hitting the doorframe and vibrating painfully through my arm. He takes another step back, and he stumbles, and he lands heavily on his knees. He grabs on to the door handle to keep from tipping over. He looks up at me as I line up the shot with the rolling pin. I *want* to kill him, but I *need* to hurt him.

Before I can swing, Kahn charges from the kitchen. He sails through the air at me. I get my hands out in front, and he latches on to the rolling pin, thirty kilograms of dog shoving me over onto my back, where I land next to Thompson, who is scrambling out of the way. Kahn tugs his head left to right, yanking the rolling pin out of my hand. He lets it go, and I get my bandaged hand into his mouth before he can chomp down on anything else. He tries to pull my hand off while I pat around the floor for the rolling pin. He gives up on the taste of bandage, and latches on to my arm instead. He whips his head side to side, trying to yank my elbow from its socket. I grab him with my other hand and try to pull him away, but he's too powerful. I roll my body and shove him into the wall. His teeth tear deeper into my arm.

'Let go!'

He doesn't let go.

'Let go, goddamn it!'

He still doesn't let go. I swing him into the wall again, and I punch at him, and I try to yank his mouth open, but all that happens is the holes in my arm get bigger, and his resolve grows stronger.

The rolling pin. Where did it go?

I keep my arm extended, trying to keep his mouth away from my face as far as I can. My fingers find the rolling pin. I grab it up and swing it hard into his head.

He lets go, and he yelps, and he runs down the hallway into the master bedroom.

I sit up. My arm is full of holes, and wet with blood, and hurts like hell. It feels like every joint from the tips of my fingers through to my shoulder has been dislocated.

Thompson has regathered his poise, his breath and his gun.

Chapter Ninety-One

Thompson points the gun at me. 'I didn't want this. I didn't want any of this.'

'Rita and Andre? What did you do to them?'

'I sedated them. They'll be out to it for a few hours, and they won't remember anything, so don't worry about them. Now roll over and put your hands behind your back.'

'And if I don't?'

'Then I'll shoot you.'

I do as he asks. He zip-ties my wrists together. My arm is on fire.

'Now get up,' he says.

I roll onto my side, and get onto my knees then onto my feet. We go into the lounge, Thompson shutting the hallway door behind us so there can be no more surprises from Kahn. He retrieves the small black case he dropped. It's half open. There are syringes in there.

'That dog must really hate you,' he says.

'Where is Zach?'

'Come on, let's go.'

'Go where?'

'Outside.'

'Why?'

'Do I really have to spell it out for you?'

I sit on the couch. 'Actually, yes, you do. If you're planning on shooting me, then at the very least you owe me an explanation as to why.'

He takes a few seconds to think about it, then he nods. 'Like in one of your books?'

'Sure, why not? We have time,' I say, hoping that we don't, that Kent will be true to her word and will come out here to check on me.

He sighs, and his body slumps, and he asks, 'Is there anything here to drink? I need a drink.'

I nod towards a cabinet that runs the length of the wall opposite the TV. 'In there.'

He turns on the lounge lights and twists the dimmer so they're on low. He goes to the cabinet and selects a bottle of whisky. It's the same brand I was drinking a few nights ago. Dad died before opening his, but Andre has gotten through a few. He grabs a glass and sits on the couch that's at a right angle to mine. He rests the bottle and the gun on the coffee table, along with the syringes. I look around the room for something I can use to cut the zip-ties and end up focusing on the bottle of whisky.

All you have to do is kick it off the table hard enough for it to break, roll onto the shards of glass, pick one up and start sawing. Easy.

'Where is Zach?'

He pours a drink. He takes a sip and then knocks the rest of it back. I want him to drink as much as he can. I want him to drink so much that he passes out. He puts the glass on the coffee table and sighs heavily, but makes no effort to pour himself a second.

'You found the phone,' he says, running his tongue across his broken tooth from this afternoon.

'What phone?'

'I've been checking over and over, and saw earlier that the message I sent has been received. That means you turned on the phone.'

'I don't know—'

'"Hello". That's what it said. I sent it last night, figuring if you found it, I would need to come out here. I was hoping it wouldn't come to this. I wish you hadn't gone looking. I would have come for it, but I didn't know where Lisa hid it. Where was it?'

'I didn't find it. Maybe the police did.'

'When you came to my house, I thought you had it all figured it out. I thought, well, this is it, and so be it. But you were there for something else entirely. But right now I can tell you're not surprised to see me here. You've put some of it together. Lisa was right about you. You're a smart guy.'

'Not smart enough, apparently. Where is my son?'

'It was the evidence that got returned to your house, wasn't it? You saw the phone wasn't there, and you went looking. It was the only flaw. Am I right?'

'I don't know what you're talking about.'

'If things had gone the way they were meant to, it never would have been an issue. The phone would have gotten put back. I love her, you know. I've never met anybody like her, and I would do anything for her, and now I've done things I never thought I would ever do, but as much as I love her, as much as she's made my life better, right now I wish I had never met her, you know? I wouldn't miss something I had never had, and now – now everything is messed up. Lisa, if I hadn't ... well, things would be different. But hey, it's not like I can put everything on her. We thought we had everything perfect. And it was perfect, right up until the moment it wasn't. We'd never have done any of it if we really thought anybody would be hurt.'

'People always get hurt. Where is Zach?'

'Yeah, I guess they do. When I saw you had read the message, I considered staying at home waiting for you. I thought you'd go there. Would you have?'

'I decided against it.'

'Good thing I came here then, huh?'

'I called the police. They're on their way. Tell me where Zach is, and you can leave before they get here.'

He smiles at me, but there's no humour or warmth. Just sadness. 'I don't believe you. I found your phone.'

'Where is Zach?'

'You need to know, none of this is what we wanted. What happened yesterday with Lisa, that wasn't meant to happen. And Ryan Bates, I had no idea that was going to happen either. It's ... I mean ... it's a mess. A complete mess.'

'Do you know where Zach is?'

'It just got out of control. Isn't that always the way?' He laughs, and he looks at the whisky bottle and thinks on it for a few moments, then pours himself that second drink, this one bigger than the last. He takes a sip but doesn't knock the rest of it back like last time. He sits it on the arm of the couch, his fingers spinning it around on its base. 'I hear it all the time. Things just get out of control. That's what people tell me when I'm arresting them, and now I know exactly what they mean.'

I lean forward. Kahn scratches at the hallway door. 'Please, I'm begging you, tell me where Zach is.'

He finishes his drink and studies the glass, and he says, 'First tell me where Lisa's phone is, and then I'll tell you where Zach is. I promise.'

'It's in my pocket. Right-hand side.'

I lean to my left so he can get to it. Something in my pocket digs into me, and it takes me a few moments to think what it is. The side-cutters. I grabbed them from the barn to cut the prybar free from the mountain bike. He digs the gun into my stomach while he gets the phone. He goes back to his couch and picks up his glass. I shift my body further to the side, forcing my shorts to pull around so the pocket is closer to my hands.

He stares at the glass. 'Your son is dead, Mr Murdoch.'

'You're lying.'

'No, I'm not. And the thing of it is, you're the one who killed him.'

'What the hell are you talking about?'

'He was under the house.'

'What house?'

'Pittman's house. There was a room under there. A secret room.'

'What room?'

'It's where he kept them. It's where Zach was. He was down there in that room under Pittman's house, and then you went there last night and set it on fire. You set Zach on fire.'

'Bullshit.'

'You killed your own son, Murdoch. I was the one who put him down there, and you were the one who killed him. Maybe that means both of us are going to hell.'

I get up and charge him, but he's ready for it. He swings the gun towards me and gets me in the side of the head, and before I can hit the floor it's lights out.

Chapter Ninety-Two

The world is coming in orange. I can't figure out why at first. Something about a fire. It would explain the glow. It doesn't explain the throbbing headache. Or where I am. I squeeze my eyes shut, then take a second attempt at letting in the world. This time I recognise the lounge of my in-laws. I'm propped up on the couch. The TV is going. That's where the orange light is coming from. There's a movie playing ... only not a movie, because there's a ticker crawling along the bottom of the screen, so it's the news. It's a story about a burning house. One of the houses from last night? It could be. Then the fire ends, and there's another shot, this time of a gutted house, walls barely standing and a collapsed roof, some of the framework propped up with braces. I recognise it. Lucas Pittman's house, burned down last night, and tonight it's rubble, and

Zach.

pieces of furniture on display, a crowd of people watching, just like they were watching our house over the last few days. In the background there are people wearing bright vests, and police officers

Zach was inside the house.

moving around. They seem to be looking for something. They're moving rubble about. There's a large section of roof sitting in the street. There's a reporter talking into the camera, my old friend with the rolled sleeves. I can't hear him because of the ringing in my ears, and I think about

Zach was inside the house.

how I got that ringing. I was hit. By? By Thompson. I look to my right, and there he is, on the couch, watching me.

'Welcome back,' he says, though I more lipread him than hear him.

ZACH WAS INSIDE THE HOUSE. THE HOUSE YOU BURNED DOWN.

The storm is coming. I can hear it, the loud rushing as it replaces the ringing, and I can see it, the walls swaying, and I can feel it, the pressure building inside my head. I pull my hands against the zip-ties and feel them dig into my flesh, but there's no give there. The room is spinning. I look back at Thompson. He points at the TV. Over the storm I can hear Rolled Sleeves talking about a secret room found under the house, revealed when the roof crashed through the burned floorboards in the hall. I can feel my heart rate climbing, and the temperature climbing but can't feel the rest of my body. I can hear my pulse in my head, like a drumbeat, gaining speed.

When I try to stand to charge Thompson again, I can't. There's no feeling in my body. The walls stop swaying and the pressure disappears, and the drumbeat fades away. The storm has passed. It's passed, and everything is going to be okay.

It's okay because Zach wasn't in that room.

Zach is alive.

It's impossible I killed him.

Rolled Sleeves says there is still a section of roof blocking access to the room, but they know it's filled with water, with estimates claiming anywhere between one and four hours to pump the water out, depending on who you ask.

But it's okay.

Zach wasn't in there, and everything is going to be okay.

Kent is standing in front of the house. She's wearing a hard hat, and a bright-orange vest, and there's a dirty facemask dangling around her neck. I wonder how many phone calls from her I've missed. Will she still come and see me, to tell me that Zach is okay? Or is she too busy? The entire scene is lit up with floodlights, bleaching the colour from everybody's skin. There are hundreds of people watching, all of them there for nothing. The ticker along the bottom of the screen says 'Body found beneath house of horror', but the ticker is wrong.

'Without the fire,' Rolled Sleeves says, 'the room and Zach may never have been found.'

I shake my head. The TV is lying. Thompson puts it on mute.

'They're saying the police were able to get a camera in there. At this stage the images are poor, but they know there's a body down there. A child. And like I said before, I know he's down there because I put him down there.'

She tried to warn you. Ellen Barkley. You were so close to burning down her house with her in it, and she warned you. She warned you something like this could happen. That you would do something you regretted.

She.

Fucking.

Warned.

You.

And you didn't listen. After almost setting her house on fire with her in it, you thought, hey, why not give it another go? You killed Zach.

I picture the charred hand of Ryan Bates that I saw at the morgue yesterday. That is Zach now – or at least it would be if he had been in the house. Which he wasn't. Rolled Sleeves, the ticker, Thompson and now Mr What If ... all of them are trying to convince me of such a horrible lie, and I don't understand why.

I turn to Thompson. 'Zach isn't down there.'

'He is. I wish he weren't, but he is.'

I shake my head. It hurts. My arm is throbbing, and my back is sore, but arms and backs heal, and tomorrow I'll be able to toss Zach into the air and catch him, and have him laugh the way he laughs.

On TV, the house, from an angle that looks into the hallway, an angle made possible due to a wall missing. People are crouching around the remaining section of roof, trying to figure something out.

'Pittman never took your son,' Thompson says.

Now they're showing a picture of a fibre-optic camera. They're probably explaining how they work, how they can get it into the tightest of spaces.

I keep pulling at the cuffs. I can feel blood running down my arm. I need to get free. I need to find Zach.

The side-cutters. Remember?

I slide to pull the side-cutters closer to my hands. 'Zach is alive. Pittman moved him in the morning. Or the night before. Kent said so. Everything is going to be okay.'

'No. It isn't,' he says. He pours himself another drink.

'I just want my son back.'

'I know you do, Murdoch. I know you do. Only it's not going to happen.'

'Stop saying that.'

'You want to hear this or not?'

'Not if you're going to keep lying to me.'

'I'm not lying to you.'

'See? There you go again.'

'I'm not lying to you. You said you wanted to hear this. If you don't want to, we can end it right now.'

'End it?'

'Come on. You know where this is going. What's it to be?'

'I want to know.'

'I figured you would. Let me start at the beginning.'

Chapter Ninety-Three

'The first thing you need to know is your wife doesn't hate you, but she doesn't love you either. She said your marriage died years ago, for the most part because of Zach. She loves him, but she said he stripped the joy away from her life.'

'Lisa would never say that.'

'I met her six months ago at a bookstore. She was browsing the paperbacks, and I was doing the same. Lisa ... she's somebody you notice, though later, I mean, much later, she would tell me she couldn't remember the last time you had noticed her, not in that way. I guess ... I guess that's common, huh? My wife, I mean ... my ex-wife, she used to say the same damn thing.'

My arm is aching, and I can feel the holes from the dog bite widening as I stretch for the side-cutters. On TV, a muted Rolled Sleeves talks from in front of Pittman's house, lying, no doubt, about Zach still being in there – lying because it makes good ratings. Then the camera pans to the side, where Kent is climbing into her car. Is she coming here so she can lie to me too?

'She was standing beside me reading the back cover of a book, and I was standing beside her pretending to do the same, but really all I was doing was looking at her.' He picks up his drink. 'I asked her if she had any recommendations, and she asked if crime was my thing, and I said to her, "Wow, is it that obvious I'm a cop?" I don't know, I figured she'd think that was cool. She said no, and then pointed out the fact I was holding a crime novel. I laughed, and she laughed.'

I can reach the tip of the side-cutters. Feeling is returning to my body. Kahn keeps scratching at the door, wanting to come through to finish what he started. 'Sounds like a great time,' I say.

'I asked if she'd read it, and she said yes, and I asked if she thought I'd like it, and she said, "I hope so – after all, I wrote it with my husband." I was disappointed she was married, but you know, I liked her, and I'd never met an author before, so I said, if she ever needed help researching any police stuff, I'd be happy to help her out. She said that would be great, and that she actually had some questions, and if I had time ... Well, you know how it goes, right? One day you're having coffee with somebody, and the next you're hearing how unhappy they are with their lives, and not long after that you end up in bed together, and not long after that they're telling you how they're going to leave their husband.'

The handles of the side-cutters are caught in a fold of my shorts. I shift position and work them past.

'Your career was dwindling. She said it was the curse of the mid-list author, that publishers were never going to put money into promoting you. She said you could write the greatest book that year and it wouldn't matter, that there would be no publicity behind it. What your career needed was publicity. Something massive.'

'A kidnapped child,' I say.

'It took some time to get there, but yeah, that's what she said. She knew parents are always the first suspects. She knew we could make it look like somebody had been in your house, that we could stage it so first impressions were Zach was taken, but then second impressions would show something different. The shoes were her idea, so was the toybox. I gotta say, that was clever, and it took her a while to find the perfect one. Zach's clothes, your shoes – putting them into the bin was my idea. I knew there was a street where they get tipped over, and that if I tipped them all over then people would just think it was kids again. It would look like their discovery came down to a piece of luck. It's why I contacted Dallas Lockwood about them. I had to. Because we had tracking software on your phone, and Kent figured if you had dumped the clothes you would go back for them. I had to stop that from happening.'

Kahn bangs against the hallway door, making us both jump. I realise how lucky I am I left my phone at the motel last night. If I hadn't, they would know I went to the cemetery in the middle of the night. They would find Lockwood. I would go to jail, and would have to watch my son growing up from behind bars.

'There was blood on his clothes.'

'Not a lot. I dropped Zach getting him out of my car. It was an accident, and he wasn't hurt, but he cut his knee. I used his T-shirt to clean it up. I knew it would look worse than it was.'

'You hurt him.'

'I didn't mean to. He had been drugged and was asleep, so didn't feel a thing.' He takes another drink and stares at the glass. 'I also knew the glasses would confuse everybody. The night he told you he was going to run away, he told Lisa the same thing. So she packed his bag, put some food in it, then that way you would tell the police what Zach had said. It was a better story than telling the police you had found a footprint in your garden and you thought your son had been abducted. It would make you look like you were lying.'

'You guys really thought of everything.'

'Then there's Jonas Jones.'

'He was part of it too?'

'Not knowingly. We were always going to use him without him knowing. Lisa said she'd give it twenty-four hours before approaching him, but he ended up approaching you first. She knew how that would play out, how the media would see it, and it played out exactly like she said. It was perfect.'

He works away at his drink, and I work away at my pocket, and Kahn works away at the door.

'Lisa knew the public would turn against both of you. They would hate you. She said the more guilty you looked, the greater the anger would be towards you, but also the greater the redemption story when you were proven innocent. She wanted the arrest to take place at your house. She wanted both of you paraded out front. I warned her that could backfire on us, but she insisted it would be worth it. Your books would fly off the shelves. She said printing presses wouldn't be able to keep up with the demand. She was going to leave you and branch out on her own, and with all the money being raked in she would be able to afford full-time help with Zach. She thought that would be the best thing for him.'

'You expect me to believe any of this?'

'When she was out jogging or at the gym, she would be with me,' he says, confirming what I thought earlier. 'We would practise over and over the things she needed to say. The way she had to behave. At first, she was useless. I mean, she wasn't an actor, and if she couldn't pull it off, then the plan would fail. It was our biggest concern. But we had time. Whether we did it this month, or next month, or in six months or in twelve, the plan would be the same. If Pittman was in jail for something else, then we would find another Pittman. Lisa, she improved quickly. Much quicker than I would have thought. In fact, truth be told, I didn't think she would get there, not in the beginning. I have to hand it to her – when she puts her mind to something, there's no stopping her. That was what we had to wait for – for her to get good.'

'And then she did.'

'And then she did. Better than good, but she had to be. After all, she was selling raw pain. She was going to have a breakdown over her missing child, and it had to look authentic.'

I'm close to reaching the side-cutters. I need to keep him talking. 'Then she deserves an Oscar. Tell me about Sunday night.'

'Sunday night,' he says, and he slowly shakes his head. 'You were in the shower when Lisa checked on Zach. He was still awake. He told her all those things about running away. Things weren't planned for that night, but what had happened to you at the fair and Zach saying he was going to run away, it was the perfect opportunity. Lisa spiked your drink and you passed out. But there was a problem. Her second phone, the one she hid from you that she had bought not long after we met, was in my car. We had been together that afternoon, and it must have fallen out of her pocket. She knew she couldn't use her usual phone, because it would be checked, so she called me on your travel phone. It was risky, but I felt the police wouldn't know it was missing if they weren't looking for it, and we were going to return it to the drawer when everything was over. We couldn't return it right away, because it would be checked by the police. So we had to take it away. I took it, and I left it hidden at the end of the driveway out here so Lisa could get it on Monday night. I didn't think we would need to stay in touch, but I wanted the option.'

'And Zach?'

'She spiked his water and made him drink some. I carried him out the back door. After all, it was the middle of the night. I kept him drugged at my house until two nights ago. Then I took him to Pittman's. The plan was to drug Pittman and have him arrested in the morning with Zach in his house. I injected him as he was pulling stuff out of his closet. The drug is fast-acting, knocks people out in seconds. I was getting ready to leave him there when I noticed he wasn't just pulling stuff out of the closet, but he was pulling out the baseboards and the carpet too. There was a door hidden there. I lifted it up.'

'And Ryan Bates was in there.'

'That was a genuine surprise, but a great one, because not only was our plan going to work, I was going to save this kid who had gone missing a year ago. It was clear Pittman had been keeping the kid drugged. I went home, and I returned with Zach. I took him into the room, and sat him on the bed next to Ryan. Nobody was supposed to die. The drugs were only going to keep Pittman asleep for six hours, so I had to wait there and top him up again at four in the morning, and I topped the kids up too, and then I left them. Pittman would sleep until around ten. By then the police would be at his door. Even if he did have time to close the room up, I had put Zach's bag under one of the beds, and I knew that would be found. Nobody was ever going to believe he didn't take Zach. I made an anonymous call to the station after the arrest. Only ... the arrest went badly, and things took longer, and Pittman woke up early. I didn't get the dose right. He must have found Zach right away, and I guess he panicked. He couldn't fit both kids into his car, so he grabbed one and ran. He would have known something was happening, but not what. I guess ... I guess he thought he had time. He must have closed up that room before leaving. The accident was ... well, a tragic accident.'

'You could have saved that boy.'

'I know that. Of course I know that. Like I said, it wasn't meant to go this way.'

'You still knew there was a chance one of those boys was still in the house.'

'The plan was I would search the house and find the room, and find the boys alive. I would have been a hero. But I couldn't go back in because I got suspended. Look, I couldn't have known you were going to burn the place down. I couldn't have. I know you think that's my fault, and Ryan Bates is my fault too, but think about it. If I hadn't been in the house with Zach, Ryan would still be down in that room. Could be he never would have been found.

I'm not the one who kidnapped Ryan. I'm not the one who set fire to the house.'

'You must sleep like a baby.'

'I'm not saying that. Look, getting suspended wasn't part of the plan, but I was going to make an anonymous call ... only you went and burned down the house.'

'Zach wasn't in there. Pittman woke up earlier than you thought, and he moved Zach first.'

'If Lisa hadn't been pushed over, if the arrest hadn't gone bad, if things hadn't taken longer, I would have found those kids yesterday.'

'Ryan is dead because of you, and Zach isn't in that room. Unless there's a third kid we don't know about, that room under the house is empty.'

'There was nobody else.'

'Then it's something else.'

'You sound like you really believe it.'

'Of course I believe it. I don't know what the camera saw, but it sure as hell wasn't my son.'

'Okay, Cameron, okay.' He finishes his drink.

I've got the side-cutters in my hand now. I turn them so the tips are upward. It's a difficult angle, but I get the blades over the zipties. The problem is they're going to click loudly when I cut through.

'I know you're lying about at least some of it,' I say. 'There's no way Lisa would allow Zach to be anywhere near a paedophile, let alone be left in the same house as one. No mother would ever do anything like that.'

'Mothers do bad things all the time. Sometimes they drown their kids. Sometimes they turn a blind eye when new boyfriends molest them. Sometimes—'

'Lisa's not like that.'

'You're right, she's not. Zach was only ever meant to be with

Pittman for a few hours, and Pittman was never meant to be conscious. Zach was never meant to be harmed. Right now you should have both been at home with Zach, getting apologies from the public and offers from publishers.'

'I don't believe Lisa would have agreed to any of it.'

'Not only did she agree to it, it was her idea. All of it. I assure you, Murdoch, it went the way I said it went.'

'Whatever it is you're about to do,' I tell him, 'you don't need to. We can find Zach. You can turn yourself in. It's like you said: what happened to Ryan wasn't your fault.'

He picks up the gun. Kahn's barking gets louder. Maybe he can sense what's about to happen and doesn't want to miss it.

'I don't want to shoot you, Cameron, believe me, but I can't go to jail. Do you have any idea what they'd do to me in there?'

'You could always shoot yourself.'

'I considered it. I really did. I've been considering it since the moment you burned Pittman's house down. But I didn't kill Zach, and I didn't kill Ryan, and now that you know what you did, I figure I'm doing you a favour.'

'This isn't going to work. The police will figure out somebody was here. They'll—'

'Don't you worry about any of that. Now get up. We're going to go for a walk.'

I stand up. 'We can—'

'Now you know everything. I'm sorry, it wasn't meant to go this way. I'm really sorry. Lisa getting pushed over like that, maybe that was karma, huh?'

'And me? Shooting me? What's that?'

'Bad luck.'

Chapter Ninety-Four

Kent isn't breaking any speed limits to get out to the farm to give Cameron Murdoch the news. She doesn't want to be the one who has to tell him what they found, and the fact he hasn't tried calling her makes her think he doesn't know. If he does, she'll be walking into a house so full of grief the air will taste of it.

They will cling to the glimmer of hope. Of course they will. And who could blame them? After all, she was wrong about the body in the car, so there's every chance she's wrong about the body in the house too. It could belong to some other boy who has disappeared over the years. Until the body is identified, they can't know anything for sure. That will change soon, as the first pump was set up before she left, with a second on its way. All going well, the room could be anywhere between a quarter and a third drained by now, and she knows the engineers were making significant headway on removing the rest of the ceiling.

She reaches the farm. She parks outside the main gate. It's locked. Leaning against it is a mountain bike. She kills the engine, pockets her keys and climbs the fence. She lands on the other side as her phone rings.

'We were able to get a warrant for the burner phone activated six months ago,' Vicky says, 'and here's the thing – aside from Lockwood's number, that phone has only ever called and received calls from two other numbers. The first is also a prepay, activated the same day, to which there have been dozens of calls. Then on Sunday night the phone received one call from a different number, and sent one text to that same number last night.'

She is getting closer to the house. There is light coming from the right-hand side – from the kitchen and whatever lies beyond it. The gravel crunches under her feet. She can hear a dog barking.

'This second number is an international SIM, the kind you get so you don't have to pay expensive roaming charges in other countries.' Kent stops walking. Vicky carries on. 'I'm thinking, the Murdochs, they travel a lot, don't they?'

'They do,' she says, and she moves off the crunching gravel and onto the grass. She isn't sure why. An instinct, maybe. An instinct that something isn't right, because nothing has been right from day one.

Vicky carries on. 'I went through the evidence list from the Murdoch house. There were no other mobiles taken, but there was an international SIM listed. It's the same brand as the one being called, but a different number. Two people travelling, you'd think they'd have a SIM card each, right? Makes sense they would, makes sense they would buy them together, and makes sense they would be the same brand.'

She thinks about the call from Cameron Murdoch earlier. About the evidence lists. Did he notice that SIM card missing? Whenever she travels, she keeps a spare credit card hidden in her suitcase in case she loses her purse. Is it possible the Murdochs do the same thing with a phone, and that phone is missing? The front door of the house is in darkness, except for the small circle of light from the doorbell. She figures if people knew she was here, they would have switched on the outside lights or opened the door.

'Detective?'

'Thanks, Vicky.'

They hang up. She doesn't know what to think. Cameron – she can't see him being a part of this. Pittman definitely had his son. It's not like he handed Zach over to a paedophile.

But what about Lisa?

The dog is still barking. Instead of going to the door, she heads right. From here she can see into the kitchen window, but she can't see anything useful. She goes around the corner and down the side, staying off the deck and looking through the large floor-to-ceiling windows. There's a set of open French doors further down, leading into a lounge. She keeps moving, slowly now, and then she sees the last person she would have expected to see – Ben Thompson.

She breathes a sigh of relief.

She isn't out here alone.

Yesterday's events have messed Thompson up, and she wonders if he's out here to apologise for his role. She can't imagine Cameron Murdoch taking that very well. It was probably a mistake for him to come here, but she can't say she isn't relieved to see him.

She goes inside.

Chapter Ninety-Five

As Kahn barks and bangs at the door, I plan out two things. The first is I will nod towards the TV, and I will say, *If everything you said was true, then how do you explain that?* Thompson will turn towards it, and when he does, I will cut the zip-ties, then launch myself at him with the side-cutters.

What are you waiting for?

'If everything you said was true, then how—'

Kent walks into the room. We never heard her pull up, because the gate is locked, which means she's walked.

'What's—?' she says, and that's all she gets to say before she notices that Thompson is holding a gun, and a moment later he's turning it towards her. He takes a shot, out of instinct or malice, it's impossible to tell, just as I can't tell if she's been hit when she drops to the floor.

I cut through the zip-ties and charge him. He spins towards me, but I'm already on him. I catch his hands and wrench his wrist upward until the barrel is under his chin. His eyes go wide, and in that moment I don't doubt he's regretting every waking moment since walking into that bookstore where he met Lisa.

I tighten my grip on his hand, which puts pressure on his trigger finger, and a moment later all those regrets, and the fleshy, gooey bits of Detective Inspector Thompson where those regrets are stored, hit the ceiling.

The Red Mist – not mine, but Thompson's – slowly settles over the furniture. I step back. At the same time, he slumps deeper into the couch, his head going back. His hands fall to his sides, and the gun hits the couch and bounces onto the floor. He rolls to the side and comes to a stop face down in the cushion, and wedges against the remote control, his nose taking the TV off mute. The hole in the top of his head is bigger than the one in the bottom.

I swipe the small case from the coffee table and tuck it into my pocket. Kent makes her way to her knees and peers up over the couch.

'Stay back,' she says.

I take a few steps back. I hold my hands up so she can see my palms. I can feel the blood and meat on my face and in my hair from Thompson. 'I—'

'Shut up,' she says. She gets to her feet. Her face has gone white, and her eyes are big, and she looks like a thousand volts have been pumped into her. She looks around the room, and she takes it all in, but she doesn't know exactly what *it* is.

'Thompson was—'

'I said shut up.'

'Are you shot? Are you okay?'

'I...' she says, then she pats herself down, examines her hands and pats herself down again. 'No. No, I don't think so. You ... you killed him.'

'I didn't have a choice. He tried to shoot you, and he kidnapped Zach.'

She doesn't say anything. She moves around the couch to get a better look at her partner. I take a few more steps back. 'Don't move,' she says.

I don't move.

'He tried to shoot me,' she says.

'He did.'

'You killed him.'

'I had to. Do you know where Zach is?'

'What?'

'Zach. Where is he?'

She looks from Thompson, to me, then to the news on the screen, where it says a body has been found in a secret basement in Pittman's house.

'They're wrong,' I say. 'Zach isn't in there.'

'Then where is he?'

'That's what I'm asking you.'

'Do you have a backup phone for when you travel?'

'Yes.'

'And international SIM cards?'

'Yes.'

'Is that why you called me earlier? Because you couldn't find them?'

'Yes,' I say. 'Lisa was using it. I didn't know.'

'Didn't know what?'

'About any of it. I promise. It was her and Thompson. The phone is how they stayed in touch. They had planned the whole thing. Thompson didn't know about the other boy. Neither of them did, but he found him when he was leaving Zach there.'

She still looks confused. 'You're not making any sense.'

'I know, but it's true. They were seeing each other. Lisa wanted the publicity, so Thompson took Zach and put him in Pittman's house.'

'You need to go back to the beginning.'

I go back to the beginning, giving her the same rundown that Thompson gave me.

She shakes her head slowly, like she's watching a tennis match. At one point she eyes up the couch where I was sitting earlier as if taking the weight off her feet will help her to understand. But the furniture is part of a crime scene, and the crime scene has blood all over it, so she stays where she is, biting her bottom lip and looking at me as if I've taken all my experience from years of telling stories to tell her my most outlandish one yet. When I'm done telling her, she stares at me without any emotion, and I have no idea how much – if any—she believes. What she can't deny is that Thompson tried to shoot her.

Finally, she says, 'You're saying Lisa did this. Lisa and Detective Thompson.'

I am somewhat frustrated that she doesn't sound convinced by anything I've said. But that's okay – she doesn't need to be for what comes next. 'We have to help Andre.'

'What?'

'There,' I say, and I point towards Andre, and she sees him for the first time. 'We have to help him.'

'Is he alive?'

'I don't know,' I say, even though I do – he had a pulse when I checked him earlier. I turn around and head over to my father-in-law without her telling me to stop. I crouch next to him, and like I knew she would, Kent comes over and does the same. 'He doesn't have a pulse,' I say, even though he does.

'I need to call ... everybody,' she says, and she gets her phone out of her pocket, and at the same time she puts two fingers on Andre's neck. 'He's—' she says, and then she doesn't get to say anything else because I bury the needle of Thompson's final syringe into her neck.

Chapter Ninety-Six

Kent jumps up before I can push the plunger all the way down. She moves back, the motion so sudden the needle snaps in her neck.

She hits the couch I was sitting in earlier, then sinks to the floor against it. She pulls out the broken needle. I look at the syringe still in my hand. I got some of the fluid into her, but not a lot.

Her arms fall to the floor, and she stares at me, only she can't move. I lie her on her side into a more comfortable position, and prop her head onto a cushion. She says 'whhm', but nothing else. A drop of blood rolls down the side of her neck. Her eyes close.

I go into the kitchen and wash the holes in my arm. In the window I can see my reflection. My face has a fine spray of blood over it, and there are small chunks of Thompson in my hair and on my shoulders. I peel off my shirt, then rinse my head under the tap and wrap a tea towel around my arm. Between my bandaged hand and the tea towel, my right arm is covered from the elbow down. I drag Andre out of the puddle of milk, into the lounge and put him into the recovery position. I can't check on Rita without opening the door and having Kahn kill me. As much as the damn dog annoys me, I'm not prepared to shoot him.

The news is back on. There is footage of a flatbed truck, and on the back of it are six water tanks, each capable of holding four to five hundred litres. At the moment, two of the tanks have large flexible pipes leading into them from the house.

I find Kent's phone in her pocket, and switch it off and drop it into a bag, along with her keys. I grab Andre's phone, which is on the kitchen bench, and I unplug the home phone, and I toss those into the bag as well. I add our backup travel phone, then search Thompson for a phone and find one in his pocket. It's already switched off. I add it to the bag. I find his keys and pocket them. There is a phone in the bedroom, and Rita has her mobile too, and if Kent wants to roll the dice with Kahn and make a play for them, then good luck to her. I add Rita's keys and Andre's too.

I grab the gun, and I grab a knife from the kitchen, and I go outside and get into the car. I unlock the gate at the end of the driveway, then have to get into Kent's car to move it aside so I can drive past. I drive through, and I turn right, in the opposite direction from which I came in case Wrestler is out there somewhere. I figure Thompson would have arrived from the same direction for the same reason, and I've figured right, finding his car half a kilometre further along. I pass it, hang a left, and then another left a few minutes later and make my way out to the main road.

Chapter Ninety-Seven

Kent can hear voices. In the distance. Miles away. Then not miles away. Much closer. In the same room now. Coming from the TV.

Her arms are heavy. When she tries to move them, she can't. When she goes to stand, she falls onto her side. Her lips are numb, and her tongue feels fat. She can remember everything, but she has no idea how long ago everything was.

Feeling slowly returns. She rolls onto her front and digs her hands into the floor, and pushes herself upward. She gets her knees under her and sits that way for a few moments, not having the strength to push any further. Andre Cross has been dragged into the lounge next to her. His T-shirt has been pulled off. She reaches out to check his pulse. Her arm doesn't move. She tries again, and this time it does. Andre's pulse is strong, and she shakes him a little, and slaps him a little, but he's out of it.

The TV is going, and they're showing a photograph of her taken earlier, where she's still wearing the mask, making her look like she's in the middle of a pandemic. She looks at Thompson, dead on the couch, holes in his head and blood everywhere. She doesn't know what to believe, if any of what Cameron Murdoch told her is true, but the one thing she does know is that Thompson took a shot at her. She also knows before stepping in here, her suspicion of Lisa Murdoch was growing. On the floor in front of the couch is a cut pair of zip-tie cuffs and nearby a pair of side-cutters.

She reaches for her phone, but it's gone. So are her keys. She gets to her feet, wobbling as she does. The dog has stopped barking. On the TV, she can see there is activity at the house. Something is happening, and the reporter doesn't know what, and he sounds like not knowing is driving him mad.

'Welcome to the club,' she says.

She checks Thompson for his phone. It's gone. She can't find a landline either. If Murdoch hasn't stolen her car, she will be okay. She has a spare key hidden under the bumper, a habit an early partner of hers got her into after they couldn't make a callout because he had locked the keys in the car. She makes her way outside, having to grab on to the furniture, and the walls and the door, and when she steps off the deck she wobbles to the side, tries to correct herself, sways and falls. She gets up and carries on. She makes it to the driveway, staying on the lawn rather than the gravel. She is feeling better by the second, and has almost made it to the gate when her ankle rolls sharply under her. She clutches it for a few moments, then tries to get to her feet, but it won't hold her weight. She drags herself the rest of the way, then pulls herself over the fence. Her car has been moved back a few metres. It's listing to the side. At first, she thinks it might have been driven into a pothole, but then she sees there's a kitchen knife sticking out from the back wheel. She pulls it out.

'That's the third,' she says, then finds the spare key.

She gets into the car. Murdoch has put the knife through the police radio too.

The back tyre flops and wobbles and slaps against the road as she turns the car around. It doesn't have to last long, just long enough to get out to the main road where there will be traffic. A couple of minutes at the most. The car slips and slides at the back, and she drives slow to accommodate for it. Her ankle hurts bad, but otherwise she's feeling almost back to normal.

Before she can reach the main road, a car comes towards her.

She turns her car to block both lanes, opens the door, and waves the other car down.

Chapter Ninety-Eight

This time of night, the parking lot behind the hospital is empty. I take the closest spot and I leave the keys in the ignition. I tuck the gun in the waistband of my pants and find the emergency-room entrance, knowing the way I look I wouldn't make it into any other entrance without being stopped. I'm wearing Andre's T-shirt, which is wet with chocolate milk, but a better option than my shirt, which is wet with Detective Thompson. The tea towel around my arm and the blood on my face makes me fit in. Because the wound looks bad, and because it's a slow night, a nurse rushes me deeper into the hospital as soon as I've filled out a form. If she knows who I am, she doesn't say. She sits me on a bed and closes a curtain around me, and tells me to wait. I don't wait, and I slip out past the curtain once she's gone. A doctor asks me where I'm going, so I ask him which way to the bathroom, and he points back towards the corridor I was brought into and tells me to turn right. I go down there and turn left.

I go through a set of doors, and I walk like a man who knows where he's going, which I do. I reach the staircase, and I go up to the fourth floor. When the corridor is clear, I make my way to Lisa's room. The lights are off, but not the lights in the corridor, so I can still see clearly. I sit in the same chair I sat in yesterday, and I take hold of Lisa's hand. So much has changed since I was last here. I think about what Andre said earlier letting his family fall apart before putting it back together. If I had known, if I had suspected, I could have fixed things with Lisa. I'm sure I could have.

'Everything is going to be okay now,' I tell her. 'Zach, he's going to be fine. Think of all the things we're going to do together when you wake up. I want you to imagine us camping, sleeping out under the stars. We'll go fishing, and hiking and mountain biking. We'll spend days at the beach swimming and building sandcastles. Next year we'll take Zach to Disneyland. It will be an amazing year, and the books are going to sell well, and we'll go on tour.'

I let go of her hand, and I take out the pillow from beneath her head.

'Can you see it? Can you see those stars, and those beaches and those roller-coaster rides? And Zach, smiling and laughing the whole time. He's going to grow up to be a great man. You're going to ... you would have been so proud of him. I love you, Elsie. I always have, and I always will, and Zach ... he loves you too. I know you didn't mean for any of this to happen, but everything is going to be okay now.'

I unplug the machine monitoring her vitals.

Then I put the pillow over her face.

Chapter Ninety-Nine

Kent is in the back seat of a patrol car, sirens blaring as they hurtle towards the hospital. She doesn't know for a fact that Cameron has gone there – or even if he's going to hurt his wife if he has – but what she does know is that he's killed Detective Thompson and that he blames Thompson and Lisa for the death of his son.

Earlier, when she waved down the car, she was able to borrow a phone. She called the station and updated them. The nearest patrol car was diverted to pick her up. Others are on their way to the hospital, and a crime-scene unit and an ambulance are on the way to the farm, along with animal control.

They are two minutes from the hospital when the police radio comes to life. There is a hostage situation – Cameron Murdoch is holed up in his wife's room with a gun. Officers are in the corridor trying to keep him calm, and an armed unit is on the way. The machine monitoring Lisa Murdoch's vitals has been unplugged, and nobody knows if she is dead or alive.

She picks up the radio and identifies herself. 'Tell him I'm on my way. Tell him to wait for me.'

The patrol car lurches forward as the officer driving puts his foot down.

A minute later they're pulling up outside the main doors. The armed response team is still two minutes out. The pain has eased in her ankle but flares up when she gets out of the car. She can't walk on it.

'Somebody get me some crutches,' she says.

'How about that?' one of the officers says, nodding towards an abandoned wheelchair by the door.

She doesn't like the idea of it, but it's the only thing readily available. They get her into it then wheel her inside. The hospital is a maze of corridors with different entrances and exits, but she knows how to navigate them. One of the officers' phones rings. He answers it, then hands it to Kent.

'It's Vicky,' the woman on the other end says. 'I'm at Pittman's house.'

They reach the elevators, and the officer who handed her his phone taps at the button over and over.

'You got into the basement?'

'No, but we got enough water drained to see clearly down there.'

'And?'

'And it's crazy,' she says. 'So crazy you're not going to believe it.'

Chapter One Hundred

Kent rolls to the edge of the doorway. She's in a wheelchair, and I don't know why. Maybe something to do with the dose I gave her. The officers who have been hanging around the edges of the doorway have been trying to talk me into handing over the gun, but without any success. I still need it.

'Are you sure you want to take the risk of exposing yourself like this?' I ask her.

'Are you going to shoot me?'

'No.'

'That's what I figured. If you were going to do that, you would have done it at the farm. Is Lisa alive?'

I look at Lisa. The pillow is no longer over her face. Earlier I couldn't even hold it there for five seconds before pulling it away. I couldn't go through with it. Again I am learning what kind of man I am. One who can't protect his family, and one who can't punish those who hurt it. A nurse came in when I was putting the pillow aside, saw the gun then ran back out. I barely had time to consider whether I should stay or go before the police showed up.

'She is. I want her to recover, so she can live with what she did, or decide not to. It's her choice. The same way I have the choice not to live with what I did.' I am holding the gun against my body, the barrel buried into my chin. 'When they said you were on your way, I waited. I wanted to tell you that I don't blame you. How could I? Every step of the way you—'

'Zach wasn't in the house,' she says.

'What?'

'You were right. He wasn't in there.'

'I appreciate what you're trying to do, but you can't talk me out of it. What the hell do I have left?'

'I'm not lying to you. The—'

'I want to believe you. I really do, but—'

'Did you move a doll out of the bedroom in Pittman's house?'

'What?'

'A doll the same size and weight as a child. A sex doll. Did you move it from the bedroom?'

A glimmer of hope. I relax the pressure against the gun.

'I did.'

'And you left it in the hallway?'

'I did. Why?'

'When the roof fell, it punched a whole section of the hallway floor into that basement, and the doll went with it. That's what the camera picked up down there. We didn't know the doll was missing from the bedroom because the bedroom had collapsed and was covered. But it's the doll. We retrieved it. There's nobody else down there. We've—'

'Zach wasn't in there?'

'That's what I'm saying. The basement has been cleared. Zach isn't in there.'

'He really isn't?'

'He really isn't. Cameron, please, I need you to put the gun down. I need you to step away from it so the doctors can check on Lisa.'

'Do you believe me about what I told you earlier? About Thompson and Lisa?'

'I don't know. I think so. But we can go over it all again once you put the gun down.'

'Where is Zach?'

'The basement wasn't affected as much by the fire, but there has been a lot of water damage. However, there's a lot in there to look at. This is the best lead we've had,' she says. 'In a way, if you had never burned down the house, we wouldn't know that room was there.'

'Yeah, we would have. Thompson said he was going to find it. He said it would have made him a hero. Then he got suspended, so he was going to make an anonymous call, but then I burned down the house.'

'Put the gun down, Cameron.'

'Promise me you're not lying to me. Promise me that Zach wasn't in that house.'

'I promise you,' she says.

I put the gun down, and I stand up and step away from it.

Two seconds later my face is being pressed into the floor, there's a knee on my back, and the officers who were guarding the door cuff me.

Chapter One Hundred and One

Instead of dragging me out of the hospital, Kent lets me stand in the corridor as the doctors check on Lisa. The two police officers who tackled me, along with two more, are keeping an eye on me. Further along, Kent is talking on her phone. She looks exhausted. There are smears of soot and ash in her clothes, and some on her face. There is a thin line of dried blood on the side of her neck. She has switched the wheelchair out for a pair of crutches and looks uncomfortable on them.

Inside the hospital room, the doctors are hustling and bustling around Lisa. I can't see what's going on, but there are no alarms going off and no crash-carts being wheeled into the room. The machine is plugged back in and doesn't seem to be panicking.

Kent gets off the phone and hobbles over.

'We've found something,' she says.

'Zach?'

'No. But we found something in the basement. Something that might lead to a location. You have two choices. I either have you sent back to the station where you can wait in a small room for your lawyer to arrive, or you promise me you're not going to pull any more shit and you come with me. What's it to be?'

'I'll behave. I promise.'

'Turn around,' she says.

I turn around, and she cuts away the cuffs and drops them into her pocket.

I turn back.

'I don't know how this is going to play out,' she says, 'but you put one foot out of line and you'll be back in cuffs and on your way to the station. Okay?'

'Okay.'

All six of us walk down the corridor to the elevator, and all six of us get on, and then all six of us head outside and split up into two cars. I sit in the back of the lead car and Kent sits in the passenger seat and one of the officers who tackled me drives.

'Where are we going?'

'Did you look around much when you were inside Pittman's house?'

'Not much.'

'You go into his office?'

'I did.'

'What do you remember seeing?'

'I don't know. Office stuff. A desk. I don't think his computers were there. Maybe some office drawers. Why? What was in there?'

'There were framed photographs on the walls.'

'I remember. They were of abandoned buildings,' I say, and I remember thinking how they were similar to some of our book covers, and being concerned my publishers might have used other images of his over the years.

'That's what we thought. Four photos, four different buildings with nothing to identify them by. But we think they're all of the same building – just different angles and different sides – of an abandoned slaughterhouse outside the city. Nobody made the connection, because there was no connection to be made. But in the basement there's a framed photo four times the size of the ones in the office, and in it you can see the name 'North City Slaughterhouse'. Ring a bell?'

It does. From the news. 'That's the one people call The Laughterhouse, right? Because somebody spray-painted out the 'S'? Didn't a child die out there a few years ago?'

'That's right. And another one a long time ago. Nothing to do with Pittman, so why the photographs? Kind of a weird thing to have on display, right? And why would the one that identifies the building be the one hidden in the basement where nobody could see it? There's more too. In the basement there was a scrapbook. It has articles inside it about Ryan Bates, but also about Dwayne and Xavier Kerr, a father and son who went camping on the West Coast two years ago and vanished.'

I remember reading about them when I read about Ryan Bates on the missing-persons website. 'You think Zach's at the slaughterhouse? You think that's where he takes them all?'

'I don't know. I really don't. But it is north of the city, in the direction Pittman was heading when he crashed. It's definitely worth checking.'

'You think those photographs are monuments, don't you? I mean, it's not like he can hang photographs of his secret graves in his office. You think this is the next best thing, right?'

'Yes,' she says, 'that's exactly what I think.'

Chapter One Hundred and Two

The sirens have been switched on. We go hurtling down the motorway to the north. Outside the windows, the night flashes blue and red, and straight ahead the headlights burn arcs into the night.

Kent tells me that officers and an ambulance are out at the farm, and that Andre and Rita are okay. She tells me officers and an ambulance are out at the slaughterhouse too, that a search of the building is taking place. She says there are acres and acres of forestry surrounding it and that all of it will be searched.

'Search dogs are on their way,' she says. 'If Zach is out there, we'll find him. You want to tell me why you moved the doll from the bedroom into the hallway?'

'I know it's crazy, but ... but I figured that thing had suffered enough. It looked so real, and in that moment I empathised with it. I wanted to help it. I dragged it out of the bedroom before realising I was being stupid.'

It takes twenty minutes to get to the slaughterhouse. The parking lot is lit up like a spaceship. It's obvious the police have invested deeply in the theory Zach could be out here, which gives me hope, until I remember they also invested deeply in the theory that I was responsible.

There are half a dozen patrol cars and half a dozen four-wheel drives. A dozen spotlights have been set up. There's a truss table with laptops, and maps and blueprints spread over it, people studying them. Flashlights are moving past the broken windows inside the slaughterhouse. One of the large double doors in the centre of the building has been busted down, and I can see inside, sixty years of abandoned equipment rusted into the scene out of a horror movie.

'Is there any water nearby?'

'You want a drink?'

'No. I mean, like a river or a lake.'

'Why?'

'I was thinking about what Jonas Jones said about Zach being near water.'

'Everywhere is near water in this city,' she says. 'There are rivers out here, and we'll check, I promise.'

'Where do you want me?' I ask. 'Searching the building or the forest?'

'Exactly where you are,' she says.

'Please,' I say. 'Don't make me sit this one out like you did on Monday.'

She thinks on it for a few seconds, then shakes her head. 'I want to. The more eyes the better, but I can't trust you.'

'You can trust me.'

'I can't have you running around out there. I'm sorry. Either you wait in the car, or you sit down over there,' she says, pointing to the edge of the building. 'Maybe I shouldn't have brought you out here.'

'Please. I can—' I say, and then I look at the way she's looking at me, and I change my mind. 'I'll wait by the building.'

I lean against the wall then lower myself to the ground. The concrete is cold. I pull my knees up and rest my arms on them. There's a loud whirring as a drone goes up into the air. Then another, and another.

'Thermal cameras,' Kent says, then hobbles to the table where all the action is unfolding.

People move in and out of the slaughterhouse. More cars show up, and more lights are set up. After ten minutes a van arrives with police dogs. German shepherds. They disappear into the trees. Then a few minutes later another van turns up, this one with the same bloodhound from Monday. It couldn't find Zach then, but that's because Zach wasn't around to be found. It's going to be different this time. I can feel it.

Can you?

Yes.

A plastic bag comes out. Zach's Superman T-shirt is inside it. The dog takes a sniff then leads its handler to the edge of the forest and starts sniffing around before disappearing into the trees like the other ones. Two minutes later a radio unit squawks from the table, and a big guy with grey hair and a walrus moustache answers it. Then he waves Kent over. I get up, but before I can go anywhere Kent tells me to sit back down.

'They've found something, haven't they?'

'Just wait here.'

I sit back down. The cold ebbs back in. Kent has a conversation then comes back.

'Officers think they've found potential signs of graves.'

'Think?'

'Areas of depressed earth with multiple fungi that can indicate the presence of a body.'

'Zach?'

'Nothing fresh, but Zach's trail carries on.'

'By itself?'

'I don't know.'

'Pittman must have drugged him like he did the other boy. He would have left him out here, expecting to return before Zach woke up. When he didn't, Zach came to, and wandered off looking for help.'

'Which gives him thirty-six hours on us. We won't leave here until we find him.'

'You promise?'

It's obvious that she doesn't want to say yes, but then she nods. 'I promise.'

'Can I help look?'

'No.'

People leave the building and disappear into the trees as the search shifts in that direction. No doubt calculations are being done. How far can a seven-year-old boy walk in thirty-six hours? Adults walk around five kilometres an hour. Zach's speed has to be less than that, and of course he wouldn't have been walking all that time. He would have slept for a lot of it. And he would have been hungry and thirsty, and the terrain isn't smooth, so that would have slowed him down. Plus it's difficult not to walk in circles when you're lost in the wilderness. And, like most kids Zach's age, he can barely walk a kilometre or two without needing a break. How far could he have gone in a day and a half? Five kilometres? Surely more. Fifty? Impossible. But maybe ten, or fifteen. It could take the dogs all night to find him.

Half an hour into that all night, I push myself up and move over to the table. I'm shivering, and my arm is throbbing. There are only a few people in the parking lot now, most having entered the forest. A crime scene van shows up. People grab equipment from the back and then follow somebody into the woods, most likely to figure out if the graves found earlier are actually graves.

'Want some coffee?' Kent asks.

'Please.'

There are several thermoses that were brought out here earlier. Kent pours me a cup. I'm expecting it to taste bad, and it does. Then again, everything does these days. At least it warms me up.

'They should have found him by now,' I say. 'There's something wrong.'

'Let them do their jobs.'

I drink my coffee and I pace the parking lot. I recognise one of the angles of the building from the photographs in Pittman's office. I can't remember any of the details of what happened here a few years ago, but looking at the building I can't imagine anywhere worse to have your life taken from you, or anybody worse than Pittman to have taken it. I finish the coffee and get a refill. Kent has her back to me as she talks on the phone. Even if I could slip into the forest without anybody seeing me, where would I go? All the lights I saw filtering through there earlier are gone, having made their way deeper in. I think back to last night. It wasn't cold, but it's cold out here. Zach's clothes were found in the bin – does that mean he's naked? I realise I can no longer hear the drones, but couldn't say since when. I finish the coffee and go back for a third. Kent is still up on her crutches. They have to be killing her.

Ninety minutes into the search, things happen. A radio starts squawking, and the man with the walrus moustache answers it. Those of us left in the parking lot go quiet and watch him. I can't hear what he's saying, but he turns towards me and watches me as he talks. I move closer to him. Before I can reach him, he nods towards me, and a moment later he smiles, and a moment after that he gives me the thumbs-up.

Chapter One Hundred and Three

They have to hold me back. Zach is okay. He's exhausted, and dehydrated and naked, but he's okay. He's deep inside the woods, and they are bringing him back to me, but I can't wait. I have to know it's true, because everything over the last few days has been a lie – what if this is another one? What if they're bringing back some other kid who has gone missing?

I run to the edge of the forest where everybody entered earlier, and the spotlights light up the first few metres but nothing beyond. I don't know what direction to go, and I need a light of my own. I turn back to get one.

'They'll be here in a few minutes,' Walrus says.

'I have to go in there.'

He puts his hand on my shoulder. 'They're on their way.'

'You don't understand. I need to know it's Zach. I need to know he's okay.'

'It's definitely your son, Mr Murdoch,' he says, 'and he's going to be fine.'

'I still need to know for sure.'

'And you will, in a few minutes. Last thing Zach needs is you getting lost out there.'

I pace the parking lot. I'm no longer holding my coffee and have no memory of putting it down. I think about Dallas Lockwood. I still haven't felt much guilt over what happened, if any, but now that Zach has been found that may change. Twelve hours ago I was living in a world that was falling apart and one I didn't see myself surviving if I lost Lisa too. Now I am going to have to find some way to come to terms with what I've done. I have to, for Zach. Tomorrow, I will tell Kent that Thompson told me Lockwood had figured everything out. That Lockwood approached Thompson, and Thompson killed him. It won't alleviate any of my guilt, but it will stop me from going to prison.

I hear the drones in the distance, and then they're louder, and then they start landing in the parking lot. It's been a few minutes already, and Zach still isn't here. Then there is rustling, and people come out of the trees. But the wrong people. These are search-and-rescue people who didn't find Zach. Then the German shepherds come out, and a few minutes later the bloodhound. Are they doing this on purpose? Making me wait till the last possible moment?

More rustling, more people pushing their way out from the forest, no Zach. Every time, no Zach.

Then ... Zach.

He's being carried. There is a blanket wrapped around him. It covers his body and goes up over his head like a hood, so all I can see is his face as it rests against the shoulder of a burly-looking guy who looks more suited to swinging axes and making log cabins than he does finding lost children. Zach twists to see what's going on. His face is wet with tears, but when he sees me he smiles.

'Dad!'

I rush over to him. We reach for each other, and the burly guy lifts Zach into my arms. I hug him tight, his face burying into my neck. When he says something, I can't hear it until I loosen my hold.

'Am I in trouble?' he asks, leaning back so he can look at me, his voice now dropping to a whisper.

'No, not at all,' I say. 'I missed you, buddy. So much.'

He looks around. 'Am I in trouble with Mum?'

'No. You're not in trouble with anybody.'

'Then why isn't she here?'

'She ... she's in hospital,' I say. 'She was so worried about you and missed you so much it made her sick.'

My legs feel numb as I carry him to the ambulance. When I get there, the paramedics want to take him, but I can't let him go.

'I just need a minute,' I tell them, but that's not right. I need an hour. Or a day. But I'm kidding myself, because really I don't ever want to let go of him again.

'I didn't mean to make Mum sick,' he says. 'And I didn't mean to get lost.'

'It's okay, Zach. Everything is going to be okay.'

'So I'm not in trouble?'

'No.'

'So I can have ice cream?'

'As much as you want.'

I don't want to, but I have to let him go. He needs some gentle encouragement to do the same as he's locked his hands around my neck. He gets loaded into the back of the ambulance, and the paramedics remove the blanket and lay him down. He's so pale and thin. His feet are covered in pine needles, and dirt, and scratches and thin lines of blood. There are scratches on his hands and knees, and his usually floppy hair is full of twigs. I feel ill seeing him like this and have to hold on to the side of the ambulance for support. The paramedics examine him and ask him questions. There is no sense of urgency, nothing to suggest there is anything wrong.

I become aware that Kent is now standing next to me. 'He's going to be fine,' she says, and a moment later the paramedic examining Zach agrees.

The blanket goes back over him. I don't know why I do it, but I turn to Kent and I put my arms around her, and I say, 'Thank you,' and we both start to cry. We hold on tight, and then we let go. I climb into the back of the ambulance, and I hold Zach's hand as we drive away.

SATURDAY

Bodies unearthed from Christchurch mass grave.

CHRISTCHURCH, New Zealand – Police have confirmed on Friday five bodies have now been recovered near an abandoned slaughterhouse after Zach Murdoch, the missing Christchurch boy, was found alive in the surrounding woods the previous night – in a case that has exasperated the local police force and drawn worldwide attention.

The seven-year-old's disappearance from his Christchurch home on Sunday night spiralled into 'One of the most perplexing incidents in the history of the city', eventually leading the police to the grim discovery of human remains – some of which may date back thirty years – police said. 'An investigation will now be launched to identify the deceased and to find out how they died.'

Lucas Pittman, the man at the centre of Zach Murdoch's disappearance, died in a car accident on Wednesday afternoon while fleeing police. It is believed Pittman is connected to the graves, along with his father, Harold Pittman, who passed away from natural causes twenty-five years ago. Lucas Pittman's role in Zach's abduction remains unclear. His death, along with that of another kidnapped child, who was in the trunk of the crashed car, has left behind a torrent of unanswered questions.

The police had arrested Zach's parents, Lisa and Cameron Murdoch – the famous crime-author couple – as initial evidence in the high-profile investigation suggested either or both parents' involvement. Cameron has since been cleared of suspicions, while the police are preparing to bring charges against Lisa for kidnapping. The author, who has published eleven bestselling titles with her husband, is currently in hospital after being treated for a near-fatal head wound she suffered during an arrest attempt on Wednesday.

The Murdochs' son, Zach, was found abandoned and in an apparent state of 'shock and disorientation' on Thursday evening in the woods near the deserted North City Slaughterhouse, Christchurch police told media. The young boy was briefly hospitalised for dehydration and later reunited with his father.

'This family has just been through hell,' Detective Inspector Rebecca Kent, who has been leading the efforts to find Zach, said at a press conference after Zach's rescue. Shortly after the Murdochs reported Zach missing on Monday, a horde of news vans – as well as hundreds of spectators – started gathering in front of the couple's house to livestream developments to an enthralled nation. 'I would ask that the media and public respect the family's privacy, and give them time to come to terms with what has happened.'

The case of the missing Murdoch boy has taken another bizarre twist as local journalist Dallas Lockwood, the man who allegedly orchestrated the mass gatherings outside the Murdoch house, appears to 'have fallen off the grid', police said, without elaborating. A detective with direct knowledge of the case, who wished to go unnamed, told local media 'foul play' was feared in Lockwood's disappearance, and that the case was being investigated in connection to local Detective Inspector Ben Thompson, who was killed Thursday night in what police are calling an altercation involving Cameron Murdoch. Thompson was one of the detectives spearheading the investigation into Zach's disappearance.

At this stage it remains unclear what led the police to search the slaughterhouse premises for the missing boy, and to unearth the mass graves – a discovery that has sent shockwaves through the peaceful island nation with a population of just over five million.

Presales of Cameron and Lisa Murdoch's new book, due to come out in June next year, have already topped one million, and publishers are saying they have struggled to keep up with demand for their previous titles.

ACKNOWLEDGMENTS

This is my second book about a writer, and, like the last one, the murdering aside, I share a lot of traits with my crime-writing protagonists. Cameron's weed-smoking story in this book is one of mine – I was in Canada the day it was legalised and having never smoked before, I gave it the old college try – which led me to taking very small footsteps back to my hotel room and enabled me to 'write what I know'. Another one in this story that happened to me is the guy screaming 'homo' at me from his car window as he drove past me in town. These things go into the books – but, of course, there are things I sometimes have to do research on – which brings me to the sex dolls. I had to Google weight and material, and get an idea of how they were made – which has led to my social-media feed filling up with adverts for things I wouldn't know how to describe, as well as things I can describe that I simply don't want to.

Like always, there are a bunch of folks I want to thank for helping get this book together. The first is the detective inspector who I had lunch with, who helped me map out a timeline of events that would happen in the first few days of a child going missing. I learned a lot. So, thanks Mr Detective for the advice – without it, I would have been lost at sea. It may look like now I wasn't listening, but I was – it's just that sometimes you can't let the truth get in the way of a story...

I owe a debt of gratitude to Karen Sullivan at Orenda Books – if you know Karen, then you know I'm not exaggerating when I say she's one of the nicest people in publishing – and in no way did she threaten to cut my thumbs off if I didn't say that. And also thanks to her team – West Camel for his copy edits, and Cole Sullivan and Sophie Goodfellow and Mark Swan for everything else.

Thanks to Bill Massey, my primary editor on this book, for poking and prodding me into different directions. Thanks to Melanie Roberts, for listening to my plots as they are slowly cooked by Mr What If. Ceren Kumova, who read multiple drafts, and who would debate my reasoning with me. Thanks to Lisa Schwärzer, for letting me bounce ideas off her. And thanks to a bunch of friends who read earlier drafts – Gül Erkal, Fran Schulze, Sahar Ben Hazem, Stephanie Hassall, David Batterbury, my lovely cousin Katrina Cox, and of course Jabyn Butler – without a doubt the nicest Jabyn I've ever met; and if you ever need anybody to bring sizzlers to a BBQ, he's your man. Also, thanks to Sonja BenBehi, for some medical advice that didn't end up in the book because I changed the ending, and thanks to Steve Brownie, for non-medical advice about construction that did. And also thanks to Kevin Chapman and the team at Upstart Press in New Zealand for giving my books a home.

And, like I have in the past, let me sign off once again by thanking you – the reader. You guys have been great and have given me the opportunity to keep doing what I love to do – and that's make bad things happen...

Paul Cleave
Christchurch
June 2021